Mercury with Style

Steve Rzasa

Books

The Interstice Universe
The Echo Watch
Airfoil: Origins
Airfoil: Drake City
Mercury On Guard
Mercury for Hire
Mercury at Risk
Mercury is Hot
Mercury out Cold
Mercury off Course
Mercury with Style

Space Opera
The Word Reclaimed: The Face of the Deep 1.0
The Word Unleashed: The Face of the Deep 2.0
Broken Sight: The Face of the Deep 2.5
The Word Endangered: The Face of the Deep 3.0
Severed Signals
Cryptic Commands
Failed Frequencies
Mixed Messages
Empire's Rift: A Takamo Universe Novel
Strife's Cost: A Takamo Universe Novel

Science-Fiction
Man Behind the Wheel
Multiverse
For Us Humans

Fantasy
The Bloodheart
The Lightningfall
Just Dumb Enough (contributor & editor)

Steampunk
Crosswind: The First Sark Brothers Tale
Sandstorm: The Second Sark Brothers Tale

CHAPTER ONE

June

I was lounging on the deck, licking pineapple ice cream from a spoon as the sun rose on the Pacific Coast, when the astral fiend smashed through the sliding glass door.

Good thing I never vacation unarmed.

The pulsar stave rested on the table next to my chair, its foot-long metal surface gleaming as the early morning rays soaked everything gold. Twisting inscriptions seemed to come alive as I dropped the bowl of ice cream and swept it into my grasp. I willed it to life, sending a surge of yellow-white energies rippling from end to end. The stave sprang into equal-sized segments, each one tethered to its neighbor by writhing sparks.

All in all, an amazing weapon of tremendous power.

Which I had a half second to admire before the fiend's tentacles flipped my chair, sending me face first into the sand.

Ever stick your face into sand after you've eaten ice cream? Probably not. My advice? Avoid it unless you want a beard of sand.

The tentacles slithered toward me in a blink, furrowing the sand and gouging the smooth terrain with the jagged claws punctuating their length. Nope, nope, nope. Wasn't about to let those things touch me, even if it was clothing they intersected. If the astral fiend got a good grip on my, he'd bear-hug every last ounce of energy from my body, leaving me a desiccated corpse version of my otherwise handsome self.

And nobody wanted to see Mercury Hale, Dead Guy.

I rolled from the danger zone and slashed the stave at the nearest tentacle. What I wanted was that oh-so-satisfying sizzle and *snikt* that happened when the stave's energies cut through astral fiend flesh, leaving behind a smoldering stump and viscous, dark blue ooze. Disabling the fiend's primary mode of attack left it vulnerable to me going on the offensive until I could dig into its core and trigger an epic—and literal—meltdown.

Instead, the stave rebounded off the black and violet hide, leaving a blistering scorch mark.

Wait, what?

That's not how it's supposed to work!

Unfortunately, the monster slavering after me wasn't gonna sit back, crack open a beer, and relax on the beach while I puzzled over the latest snafu. He tore after me, obscuring my vision in a spray of eye-itching sand.

Good news? It blinded him, too.

Astral fiends. Big on fury, small on brains.

I flipped backward, my athletic skill augmented by the absorption of extradimensional energies into every cell of— You know what? Easier this way: The pulsar stave gave me superpowers.

Plus, I could pool them into the reservoir of my prosthetic leg, courtesy of Procyon Foundation's technical wizards. Of course, I wouldn't have minded owning two real legs, but hey, when you cut one off to escape death, you can't be picky.

Halfway through the flip, time slowed, its headlong rush mired by those same energies—or at least, that's what it looked like. It was really my senses becoming hyperactive, to the point I thought the school was gonna tell me I needed medication before they'd be allowed back in class. I caught a breathtaking view of the deep blue ocean, the snowy foam churning where the beach met the sea. All upside down, of course.

I whipped the pulsar stave around and channeled a truckload of energy through it for a blinding blast that could have been unleashed from the sun.

The impact set off a resounding *BOOM* that echoed along the coastline. The beach house's remaining windows rippled but, thankfully, didn't break. The fiend hurtled ten feet back, crunching onto the deck, mangling my chair.

And shattering my poor, neglected bowl of ice cream.

"Seriously?" I landed, right knee down, left knee up, fist punching into sand. Eat your heart out, Iron Man. "The one morning I *don't* eat something that's good for me!"

The fiend was on its back, if a twelve-foot-wide lump could have a back. Opposite of its gaping maw of glistening fangs, I guess. But it inverted itself in a flicker, compressing until the front and back switched places. Three bulging crimson eyes glared at me and the scream the fiend issued from that aforementioned mouth was so intense, so shrill, I could feel its vibration through the air.

"Yeah, well, I'm pissed, too." I planted my rear foot and separated the stave into two glowing halves with a sharp twist of the center section. "Sounds like everyone's disappointed."

The fiend threw himself toward me, pinwheeling tentacles thrashing at the ground at the sky. Embedded claws chewed up the decking. I winced. Loredana's face? Yeah, I imagined what it would look like as soon as she realized things were getting broken that we'd have to pay for.

At least it wasn't our house.

I flung myself horizontal, twisting as the tentacles brushed by my bare toes. Even that brief contact was enough to send an icy shock up my nerves, like I'd gotten when I'd tipped my toes in the ocean first thing in the morning every day for the past week.

A couple blasts from the stave halves blistered the monster's backside. Still didn't pierce the hide, which, I might have mentioned, was not how things were supposed to work.

I landed in dune grass. The blades scratched my arms and face the same as if I'd stuck my nose in a pile of pine needles. I spat green from between my teeth.

A tentacle whipped out and snagged my leg.

Good news—it was the fake leg.

I let the fiend drag me closer to his mouth, squinting through the murky, rancid breath. If I could line up a shot—which would be easier if he'd pull me straight in rather than bouncing me like a yo-yo—I could maybe gouge a hole clear to his core.

Maybe.

Halfway there, the fiend froze. His eyes flickered, like lightbulbs getting ready to burn out.

I grit my teeth. And tasted pineapple-flavored grit. Which reminded me of the ice cream and only ticked me off all over again. "Come on, come on. Breakfast is served …"

No luck blasting him. His tentacles lashed back and forth in front of his face, even as he didn't bother trying to make me his next meal.

Nope. Instead two more tentacles thundered down at me, including the one that had a scar from where I'd slapped it with the pulsar stave.

"Fine, be that way," I muttered, and swung with both halves at the wound.

Sparks exploded between us. There was a sharp sizzle and an acrid stench, something I'd never smelled from a fiend before. And instead of blue goo, I got violet-streaked cerulean … grease, I guess. Too liquid to be goo.

The fiend howled at the sky, sending a flock of seagulls who'd strayed too near squawking in the opposite direction.

I grinned, the kind of grin you use when, yeah, you're happy, but you've also got a bit of frustration to work out and you've found a decent target to absorb it. The guy had ruined my morning. My *vacation* morning. With my wife.

The fiend's severed tentacle flopped onto the sand. It wriggled like a worm that knew the fishing hook was coming, spewing the colorful grease from its ragged end.

I let the pulsar stave's energies surge out of the prosthetic leg, glowing across its surface, until the tentacle latched onto it baked from the inside, shriveling to a blackened husk.

That made the fiend scream even louder. Go figure.

He was down two of his eight appendages and—

Hold up.

Sparks were *still* falling from both ruined tentacles. They weren't leftovers from the pulsar stave, either. And what were those patterns? Strange, geometric lines where usually I'd be staring at the striations of, well, fiend meat.

The fiend glowered at me. Okay, it's hard to say how I knew he glowered, because no eyebrows. But then he summoned two of his unhurt tentacles, and with cold precision reserved for a landscaping pro, pruned his damaged appendages, leaving the six healthy ones.

"Crap," I blurted.

He shot at me. I mean, shot, like he'd been launched from a cannon. No time for me to leap or somersault or do something else impressively gymnastic. All I could do was brace myself as he slammed into me, mouth first.

My worry that I'd somehow wound up with the world's smartest astral fiend was alleviated when he didn't eat me, because the bozo had all his tentacles clustered in front of his face. See? Bad guy dumb.

Small comfort when we exploded through the oceanside wall of the beach house.

I bounced off the remnants of couch stuffing, green striped upholstery shredded like confetti. Even as my brain absorbed blows the human body complained about, all I could think was, *Of course he spawned in the living room, through the most comfortable piece of furniture in the house.*

"Darling?"

Loredana's voice trickled out of the bathroom, nearly lost behind a spray of water and a soaring anthem. Sounded like Beethoven. Just as easily could have been Coldplay.

I grunted as the fiend stabbed at the floor, spikes shattering tile and puncturing the wood underneath. Missed my own vital appendages by a couple inches. "Yeah?" I shouted.

"Everything all right?"

The astral fiend shrieked at me, fangs gnashing a foot from my face. I planted the stave on his forehead, pressing him back. "Not really! I could use an assist!"

"One moment!"

"Hey, honey?" I cried. "Step on it!"

Nothing but musical notes from an awful, off-key symphony. Great. Probably she was singing in there again.

No problem. I had it handled.

That's what I told myself as the fiend wrapped its tentacles around my arms.

An intense cold like nothing I'd ever experienced lanced through my skin, into my muscles, turning the bones beneath to icicles—at least, that's what it felt like. I swore that when I gasped, my breath came out as frosty feathers.

Look, I'd had an astral fiend try to feed off me before. I knew I'd been dying then. I knew if he'd stayed attached, all Loredana would have to look forward to after she exited the showed was a mummified husband. To have and told hold, in sickness and in health, was about to be a really short-term agreement.

But the monster stayed latched on for what seemed like an eternity. Cold as it was, I didn't think I was gonna die. I was just—frozen.

Help.

Yeah, that's exactly what I thought, because I couldn't say the words. I even prayed, because in as dire a situation as I was in—

Help.

Hang on a second.

That wasn't me.

I wasn't saying the word. It rebounded in my brain, a marble of a plea plinking inside a metal pipe, echoing across my thoughts.

No matter how I struggled, I couldn't get free of it. The word pounded against my consciousness, wrapping tendrils around every effort I made to think of something else, anything else. Come on, man! It wasn't killing me, but I could feel myself sinking away from the world. The ocean roar faded. Fiend's shrieks got muffled.

Fine! I'll help! Whatever it took to shut the dumb thing up.

Which it did. Like a snap of the fingers. Sounds and motion whipped into normal speed, so fast I thought my neck would break. At the very least I was gonna have to pay a trip to the chiropractor. Good thing Procyon had one on staff.

The tentacles whipped out from me, slashing at the walls. Soothing seaside paintings tore from their frames. A cabinet exploded, raining plates across the ruined living room. A dining room chair next door was smashed to splinters.

Enough of that.

I corkscrewed through the air, arms and legs tucked in tight, passing over the astral fiend's head like a ballistic missile. The stave sliced across its hide, digging gouges deep enough to fit my fist inside.

The fiend rolled the injuries away, flailing at my torso. Trying for a second meal, I guessed, but if that was the case, why hadn't it sealed the deal? I should have been a freeze-dried version of myself.

I tumbled and landed feet first against the wall—one of the few on that side of the house still standing—and let off a blast of the stave's energies. Bullseye. The yellow-white beam cut into the wounds I'd just inflicted.

But he wasn't backing down. No way. He inverted again, bringing his fangs my way.

That's when the bathroom door open.

Steam licked at the walls. Loredana strode out, like she was ready for a peaceful stroll along sandy shores, except her long red hair was still sopping wet and she clutched a towel around her, bunched up across her chest and under her armpits. Sapphire colored eyes seemed to glitter, like they always did when she was fresh out of the shower. The freckles on her nose and cheeks had multiplied this week, as did the ones on her shoulders.

All in all, a gorgeous picture, Mrs. Lark-Hale.

The hand not holding onto the towel swept up an MP5 and opened fire.

The submachine gun chattered, breaking whatever tranquility was left—and man, between me and the astral fiend, there hadn't been much to begin with. Bullets chewed into the fiend's wounds, drawing out more screams and way too much of the grease.

But her expert marksmanship did open up a hole to a shining blue mass.

The fiend's core.

I launched myself at him, ignoring the barbs that tore up my shirt, and fixed the stave back together as I dove toward the wound. He hooked me again, but I was moving so fast I shredded the tentacle that tried to wrap itself around the pulsar stave. It was close enough that the hide brushed my skin.

Tenebrae.

The word sliced through my mind as sharply as a shout, like he'd bellowed it in my ear.

The pulsar stave stabbed deep into the cut, energies flaring as it touched the core.

Contact.

I willed the stave to unleash everything it could, every spark it could draw out of itself and me. My prosthetic leg felt like a stick of lead.

Golden light burst ahead of me. It was like staring into the sun. Bad idea, right?

The fiend collapsed in on itself, and then burst. Popped. That good old great blue flash, followed by *snap-BOOM*—and bam, one less monster in the world. Well, in this world.

I lay on the floor, panting.

"You seem to have overexerted yourself." Loredana's bare legs were inches from my face.

"Yeah—so—I'll skip our walk." I wiped gray chunks of greasy fiend hide from my face. Nasty. "Guess it's my turn for a shower."

She propped one hand on her hip, and leaned the MP5 on her

shoulder. A thin smile perked the corner of her mouth. "And here it was I thought we'd be celebrating the anniversary of one month without a sighting. Alas. I'll owe Elizabeth."

"Hope you didn't bet our rental fees." I sat up. My back rested against the largest remaining segment of the couch. "Want me to call Garvey?"

"Indeed. We shall need a considerable cleanup crew."

"No kidding. The room is trashed."

"To whom were you speaking? I heard you say something."

I frowned. Who had I been talking to? Someone controlling the fiend? Like Whisperer, or one of my archnemeses who'd been grafted into his ethereal persona? Or the fiend itself? "Don't know. It was tougher than usual. Not bigger. And when I finally cut it …"

I prodded a piece of fiend hide with the pulsar stave, which had reverted to its dormant state of metal rod. There were those weird patterns again. "See?"

Loredana squinted. "Remarkable. All the more reason for us to contact Procyon immediately."

I was about to ask why when I realized what she had, only a second or two later. The astral fiend had popped, sure, but then it was supposed to sublimate—as in, melt away until nothing remained. Evaporate into thin air.

The pieces of this one stayed put.

"Right." I hauled myself to my feet. "My phone's on the counter. I'll call it in."

Loredana kissed me on the cheek. "Then, Mister Hale, you did mention you needed a shower."

"Yeah. Yeah, I did." I grinned. Man, I loved her.

She walked lazily back toward the bathroom, humming a tune.

I dialed and held the phone to my ear, but before it could pick up, a stray thought appeared in my brain. I called after her, "Since when did you need your machine gun in the shower?"

Loredana shut the door.

CHAPTER TWO

W e got ourselves packed up and ready to move out of the beachfront vacation home right before Procyon's cleanup crew pulled up.

For all anyone knew, it was literally that—two white Mercedes vans, those narrow, vaguely futuristic models, parked nose to tail on the street. A silver SUV pulled up behind it. Six men and women in gray T-shirts and cargo pants disembarked from the vans, donning protective masks and gloves and a bunch of gear that made them look like they were stepping into a hazardous waste dump site.

Which, I figured, was a reasonable assumption. This wasn't the standard aftermath of a tussle with an astral fiend.

Usually, I got wind of a rip between this world and the Interstice, that gloomy, storm-riddled dark dimension that straddled portals between various other interesting places. I waited for an astral fiend to pop through, then I killed it. The thing melted away into vapor. Then it was all over but for the insurance adjustors.

"So, when was the last time Procyon had to deal with debris?" I licked the last of the pineapple ice cream off my spoon. Forget breaking another bowl—the carton was almost empty, anyway.

"Before my time," Loredana said. "And my predecessor's.

Suffice it to say the protocols had to be quite literally dusted off."

"Ah. Something that didn't go missing when the Historic Vault got raided."

Loredana folded her arms and stood aside as the Procyon techs hustled inside. She'd gotten dressed in Capris and a coral-hued blouse. Her hair was dry, but still smelled of the flowery shampoo she favored.

I sniffed. Then again, so did I.

"Mrs. Lark-Hale." Garvey, the head of Procyon's security division in San Camillo, nodded to us as he led a team of four men out of the SUV. I wanted to tell him to crouch so he quit blocking the sun. Worse than an eclipse, that guy, and probably as big as a small moon. Black sunglasses hid his eyes. He'd trimmed back his beard so the brown hair was a sharper, fuzzier outline of a jaw that could have cut through our front door unaided. "Mr. Hale. We'll secure the perimeter."

"Little late." I scraped the bottom of the ice cream carton. "It's in pieces."

"He means for additional threats." Loredana smiled at Garvey. "Very well. What alerts from local law enforcement?"

"The manager's already been on the phone. They know to stand down. Utilities problem."

I snorted. "Gas leak again?"

"Those old pipes, can't trust 'em." Garvey's face was solemn.

Sure. But whether or not the neighbors would buy the official explanation was something else entirely. A handful of people had gathered across the street, couples conversing by their respective mailboxes. A balding, overweight guy in tank top and way-too-short shorts hugged his tiny terrier like he was the only thing standing between the yipping mutt's frenzied destruction of us, the interlopers.

Could've been worse. The houses on either block spaced by petering dunes and lopsided fences. Distant neighbors. No eyewitnesses.

But, you know, gunfire. Monster screams. Those tended to

catch people's interest.

"Make sure the samples are shielded from view when they're brought out," Loredana said. "This is hardly the manner of incident over which I wish to face questions at the next chamber of commerce luncheon."

"Understood." Garvey issued orders to his security crew, who wore the same black polo shirts and black pants as he did. The Procyon logo—a four-pointed silver star overlaid on twin black parallelograms—perched on the left breast of each shirt.

As soon as they'd scattered to go do security stuff, I plunked the spoon into the empty container. "So. Pieces."

"Indeed."

"And I gotta say, while it's nice it wasn't my apartment being wrecked this time—"

"I don't know how I shall explain this wreckage to Cordelia," Loredana murmured.

"—Still begs the question, how'd an astral fiend find me? Or us? Or both? I thought Liz said tachyon spikes were on the decline. I haven't gotten a call-out for weeks. Hence the vacation, right?"

"Clearly the Whisperer is endeavoring to gain our attention. One wonders if he has any originality left."

I shivered, not from the copious amounts of frozen dairy I'd gulped, but from the mention of the name. Yeah, I know, I'd just thought of him myself, but Loredana rarely said the name aloud, and I, for one, wasn't keen on thinking that our primary adversary was suddenly upping his game after staying quiet for a month or so. "Let's not dwell on that, okay? I'm more interested in the part where an astral fiend starts keeping odd hours."

Loredana shielded her eyes as she examined the morning sky. I counted five clouds on a sheet of the brightest blue. "No, this does not fall within the norm."

"Seems to be our normal these days. The not normal."

"Quite. Mercury, when I mentioned hearing you speak during the commotion ..."

"Ah. Right." I scratched the back of my neck. "It happened

when the fiend tried to drain my life. It was freezing cold, but I didn't feel lethargic like I was on my way out of this mortal plane. The deeper I got into whatever hold he had on me, the more I could hear a voice. Nothing fancy. Not a whisper, either. It was everywhere. It filled every crack in my brain. I couldn't focus on anything but the word."

"What word?"

"Help."

She arched an eyebrow. That was her equivalent of a torrent of profanity. "The astral fiend requested your assistance?"

"Wasn't a request. It was—like a holy order. Should've had trumpets and fanfare and the whole marching band. That's what it felt like. I couldn't have broken loose."

"Yet, you did."

"Only by agreeing."

There went the other eyebrow. "You agreed to help a monster?"

I waggled the spoon. "I said whatever was gonna keep me from being turned into a Mercury-sicle. I'd have promised to take it out for pizza at Carlito's if that's what it wanted to hear. Anyway, after that, it was all over but the slicing and dicing."

"Though it seemed a tougher specimen, judging by the wounds I saw and the blistering on the hide fragments."

"Yeah. Got any insight on that?"

"Again, we shall have to consult our archives, but to my knowledge the pulsar stave has never failed to penetrate a fiend's skin. One would surmise our most valuable source of intelligence in this matter should be able to shed considerable light."

I bet she meant Wilhelmina. Previously known as Sherry Jean Crown, but you try calling that to her face. I'll eat popcorn while she lays you out flat. She'd been Procyon's operative in the 1980s and 1990s, I think, but had given it up when a horrific encounter with multiple astral fiends had cost her the lives of her husband and daughter.

It was the same battle that had left me an orphan.

If she and my parents hadn't stopped the fiend when they did, things would have been a lot worse for San Camillo back then. I got that. Didn't make it any easier to grow up with jerks for so-called "parents" until I hit adulthood. Procyon snapped me up not long after community college turned out to not be my thing.

Yeah, Wilhelmina would know an awful lot about being the operative and any funny tricks astral fiends might like to pull. But then I did some math. It took me a while.

"Curious." Loredana was watching a couple of techs approach with a white container, unmarked except for a silver stripe etched with black letters—*Biohazard, Samples, Case 4061022.*

"Kinda what I was thinking."

"You were wondering about the strange composition of the fiend's body?"

"Hmm?" I shook my head. "No. I mean, I noticed, but I filed that away as something Liz would figure out for us. Hey, so, when I came on board—when Procyon brought me in to be the operative—Wilhelmina had been out of the picture for a while."

"She had."

"And …" I made a rolling motion with my hand.

"And, what, pray tell?"

"You're cute when you're coy."

"Almost as adorable as you when you've become vexed."

I rolled my eyes but couldn't suppress a grin. "Seriously, Loredana. Who was the operative before me?"

Her jaw tightened. She wasn't mad, I didn't think. Trust me, I'd gotten that one figured out pretty well. We'd only been married a year and a half, but we'd worked together for a while before the big date, and it wasn't like she had an explosive temper.

The techs excused themselves as they carried the container through the door and toward the waiting open side of the second van.

"Because there was one, right?" I spread my arms. "It's not like there was zero astral fiend activity for, what, a twenty-year span?"

"You've never asked me that before."

"Never really cared." I stage-whispered. "There's rumor I can be sorta self-centered."

Loredana pressed a hand to her chest, but even with the playful gesture, I could tell by the way her face had locked up I'd asked a question to which she hadn't prepared an answer.

"Don't tell me *you* don't know," I murmured.

She opened her mouth but instead of answering, smiled as the last of the techs approached. "All finished, are we?"

"We retrieved everything we could, ma'am." This from a Latina technician whose brown eyes flicked across her phone as she scrolled through a list on her phone. "I'd recommend it get sprayed down to neutralize any flecks we might have missed. We don't want to risk contamination."

"Very good. We'll leave you to it." She crooked a finger at me.

I dug it when she got all James Bond.

We grabbed our bags from the bedroom and left through the side exit. My Subaru, a blue sporty ride with a spoiler, a vent hood, and bronze-colored wheel covers, crouched in the carport, ready to rip down the streets. I mean, I wasn't gonna speed that much. Loredana had wisely noted the more I did to avoid the attention of law enforcement in everyday life, the less likely I was to get my face plastered around town. I agreed.

See? Maturing.

As soon as I started the engine, though, I pounded a drumroll on the steering wheel with my fingers and at the crescendo, blurted, "Spill."

Loredana rolled her eyes. "There was a span of years prior to your arrival at Procyon during which we did not have an operative. One does not pick the next person suited for the role off the streets, Mercury. Files have to be consulted. Intelligence is contacted for their input. That is part of their job, after all—maintaining watch on individuals who might share the same genetic markers."

"Meaning, the markers I carry, from Meda. You need someone

descended from the people who live in that dimension."

"Of whom there are no doubt many, but not all have the correct markers to allow them to use the weapon."

"Okay. You had a gap after Wilhelmina was told to take a hike."

"After her resignation."

"Whichever. And other gaps?"

Loredana shook her head. "I don't know their names. But they were the operatives prior to your arrival. I believe the gap was four years on either end. Three or four."

Yikes. I couldn't imagine going that long without someone watching out for rips between the Interstice and Earth, leaving ordinary people defenseless against the occasional rampaging monster. "What was the backup plan? For those gaps, I mean."

"I am not certain, because I could not find recorded proof, only log entries for 'Contingency.'" She smirked. "Dated as far back as 2006. Though my theory is that we have already met her, and not long ago, brought her into the San Camillo fold."

I puzzled that one until the woman's face appeared in my mind's eye surrounded by flashing lights, like I'd hit the Daily Double and Alex Trebek—may he rest in peace—was expecting an answer. "Edie."

"I think so."

Wow. Edith Pathkiller—our current Forecaster, the person who could dream about when and where the next astral fiend would appear. Successor to Marigold Yen, who'd run that department my whole tenure at Procyon Foundation, up until Marigold revealed herself to be part of a long line of very bad women who were keen on ushering a literal hell on Earth. She was absorbed into the Whisperer in the first major battle that had spilled into this world in a long time.

But Edie, she was descended from one of Procyon's founders. And I'd seen her handle a bow that had some kind of extradimensional power, if the runes carved into its body and the glowing arrows it launched weren't a big enough clue. "She could have filled in before I got there, but not in the early nineties. Maybe a family member? Her line …

I let that thought trail away as I pulled out into the street. Loredana waved at Garvey as we headed out of the neighborhood. But my brain had rewound to a couple statements ago. "Hold up. You said *they*. As in, more than one. There were multiple successors after Wilhelmina?"

"Two, I presume." Loredana exhaled. "Because I was told of the twins when I inquired, years ago. And then I was strongly asked to never again inquire, by Manager Jackson himself."

My head spun. "Two operatives. One right after the other."

"No. They served simultaneously. And they were neither dismissed nor allowed to resign. They vanished."

Disappearing operatives. An astral fiend asking for help. Blanks in Procyon's extensive record.

"This day just gets better and better," I said.

CHAPTER THREE

O ur cottage was in a neighborhood off the 311 South, outside Huntersville. The former farming community turned bedroom suburb of San Camillo had looked west for its new fortunes. Not that the beaches were crowded. Locals didn't advertise it much. Most of the vacationers tended to be on a weekend from the city.

No way we wanted to start getting day trippers from Los Angeles, or worse: tourists from New York.

Coming up through the south side of the city gave us a gorgeous view of San Camillo—the single homes and brownstones increasingly wedged together, with gleaming skyscrapers standing guard downtown. San Camillo Bay was a broad curve of sand and sea to the west, with piers jutting out here and there. The old monastery hunkered on the hills to the north, and the eastern suburbs did their best to crawl up the emerald slopes of the Arbor Valley ridges where the 311 wound deeper into northern California.

I could care less about the renovations underway where Court Street met DeLeon, because seriously, who was gonna move into brand spanking new business blocks in the most drug-infested, rundown sector of the city unless some major social services remedies got into play? Man, listen to me—spouting from the

Procyon Foundation community assistance playbook.

No, I had eyes only for home.

Our new headquarters had the polish of squeaky-clean glass. It wasn't a tall structure. Each of three cylindrical towers topped out at seven stories. But the new glass of the windows that covered every curve except where three strips of white concrete slashed down each tower, reflected sparkling waves in bold azure shades. You could even make out the triangular flecks of reds, yellows, and greens from the sailboats plying the bay. Like it was dropped there right off a brochure.

Headquarters sat on the same footprint as its predecessor, the one that a powerful entity called the Hedron of Orbits had mashed into rubble with a focused, localized earthquake. That's what you get for messing with a sentient relic. But I'd destroyed it with the help of my superhero pals, Airfoil—aka Drake City librarian Brandon Tusk—and Gemini—or as he preferred, Dominic Zein, an architect from Rampart, Colorado, who was on Procyon's payroll as a different kind of operative.

It was also where I nearly died.

I shuddered as the memory of dark, churning waters rose up. I swore it tunneled my vision. *Not gonna happen. Not again. Help me out here.*

"Is everything all right?" Loredana glanced up from the messages on her phone.

Breathe, Mercury. You're here. With her. Not under the bay. I reached down and rapped my knuckles on the prosthetic leg's polymer shell. Yep, still there. I mean, not the real one, but I spent a long time coming to terms with its supercharged bionic replacement. "Yeah. Just a flashback. The watery kind."

"I see. You haven't had one of those since our jaunt to the south Atlantic last year."

"Don't worry. Not a full-blown panic." I grinned. "See?"

Loredana chuckled. "By all means, if you are the resident expert on you, I shall bow to your wisdom."

It felt good to be able to joke about the sensation that had nearly paralyzed me with fear not too long ago. No way I wanted to be in that spot again. So, I ran over and over in my head what Ramos told me about fear. Then again, he meant it was something he didn't need to have since he was on God's team.

But if Ramos figured I could quietly appeal for a little help from that side, I wasn't about to argue.

We flashed our Procyon IDs at the cinderblock gatehouse, where a woman with a security ballcap pulled so low over her eyes I swore she didn't have any nodded us through. It didn't look like the foundation was less vulnerable than it had been to the attack that had led to its destruction, but, well, they wouldn't be top secret defenses if I blabbed about them, right? Let's just say that the black metal fence surrounding the parking lot and the immaculate lawn was the most visible aspect, besides a handful of security folks scattered around the property.

IDs got checked again as we entered Tower Three, but it was the receptionist who handled public appointments, so it was just a matter of showing off that lovely stripe on our clearance cards. If any of those public were present, they'd have seen Loredana Lark-Hale, newly married head of Procyon's Operations, a familiar face at community fund-raisers and charitable organization boards. With her, her husband Mark, a technician of sorts. Lots of behind-the-scenes-work.

If you asked the rest of the crew, they'd joke that he was a custodian.

I snickered to myself. They weren't wrong.

The seventh floor was home to Tracking, Forecasting, and the manager's office, set at equal distances around the circular floor plan. The hall leading in was white tile with a black diamond set every so often.

"Do be easy on her." Loredana pressed her right palm to the silver panel set on the right of double wooden doors. "Elizabeth has been spinning her wheels, so to say, with the data we acquired on your favorite creature."

"Cyber-spider news?" I rubbed my palms together. "We've

been waiting forever. Sweet."

Loredana put her finger to her lips. The doors slid open.

"No, no, no, no!" The voice burst out into the hallway like a police siren. And trust me, I've heard plenty of those echoing down the street while I hurried away from the scene of a monster slaying. "Come on, Cyril, this isn't fair!"

Oh, great. She was complaining to the computer again.

Tracking was dimmer than the bright hallway outside. Not hard to see, just fewer and softer lights throughout the curved space. That way the dozens of screens throughout stood out even better. Six people worked at various monitors, perusing streams of data I couldn't make heads or tails out of. The center monitor was as big as a banquet hall table, portraying a map of San Camillo and the surrounding counties.

The desks were laid out like we were standing on the bridge of the starship *Enterprise*, with a broad semicircle of consoles at the center. Elizabeth Stojan was spinning slowly in a chair of black metal and mesh, using a yellow Converse sneaker to push off when she ran out of momentum.

"Hey, Liz." I tapped the bulky hard drives perched under her desk, my shoe thumping against the casing. "You, ah, got tech issues?"

Liz crossed her arms. Her spiky pink hair soaked up the glow from her desktop, which was really a giant tablet. She scowled at the graphics flickering on there. "Maybe. Yes. I don't know."

She huffed her cheeks. Seemed like a balloon about to burst.

"It's okay." I patted her shoulder. "Let it out."

"Oh, dear." Loredana pulled up a chair, sat, and crossed her legs.

Liz's face, those Arabic featured kinda serene right then, scrunched up. "I've been working on the composition of those stupid cyber-spider carcasses for months and no matter how many simulations I have Cyril run he can't figure out how something as tiny as the symmachites were able to mutate and grow into those creatures because there's nothing in Procyon's records I can use as a baseline and I'm just so *sick* of not having any answers that I, I, I could kick my chair!"

Which she did. Clear over to Tracking's doors. The chair rebounded with a firm *crack*.

Heads turned. Murmurs bubbled up but no one seemed upset. Or even startled. The techs had the same reaction as someone who saw an interesting bird fly by. Hey, look at that. And then, back to work.

Not the first tantrum they'd seen.

"I get it, Liz." I sat on the edge of her desk. The flat panel part, not the screen. I wasn't about to butt dial something that could open a portal, or worse. "It's been pretty quiet. I'm not surprised you're not getting enough data."

"It isn't fair," she muttered. "Then you guys call with an astral fiend attack and we didn't even catch it!"

"Rips can be missed," Loredana said. "Though I am surprised Forecasting didn't give you any warning. Or us for that matter."

"Weren't even tachyon spikes." Liz dragged her chair back. She took a long, loud slurp of pop from a giant cup. Then she tapped commands on the tablet screen. "See? Past two weeks."

She wasn't wrong. the jagged purple line racing across the line had a few tiny rises, but nothing like the big leap you'd see if a rip formed, and an astral fiend came screaming out. I frowned. That begged an important question. "Are you telling me this thing didn't show up?"

Liz nodded.

"Yeah, no. It was an actual fiend, Liz. I didn't imagine it. Because I sure didn't imagine losing a perfectly good bowl of ice cream."

"At least it wasn't a pizza."

"Been there, done that." I ran a hand through my hair and got a whiff of pineapple. "Okay, what about a diagnostic test?"

Liz made a face like she'd stepped in astral fiend muck.

"You know—"

"Careful," Loredana murmured.

"In case the equipment was miscalibrated." I didn't catch the whisper from her until I'd blurted the whole sentence, and even after the last word popped out of my mouth, I realized my mistake. Heat raced up my cheeks. "That's, ah, assuming there was a glitch. Which there wasn't. Probably. Because you and your team keep the detection equipment in top shape. All the time. Right?"

Loredana chuckled.

Leave it to her to find humor in my misfortune. Liz really didn't. She glared at me like she was ready to get out into the field and tussle with monsters. "The equipment is working. The drones are working. What isn't working is Cyril's stupid brain because he can't get a baseline for comparison to analyze those cyber-spiders!"

Another image appeared on the screen. I recognized those guys. Big as a dinner plate, spindly legs, sharp pincers, not unlike the facehuggers from *Alien*. We'd tangled with their teeny-tiny cousins, nanites called symmachites, right before my wedding, when an ancient urn unleashed them into the command of another baddie who had a black sword that let them boss around whoever the nanites possessed.

Which turned out to be nearly all our superhero team, with the exception of yours truly.

"I get that, Liz, but check this out." I held up my phone and showed off the screen in classic gameshow host style. "Courtesy of your friendly neighborhood crime scene creator."

Liz's eyes widened. She took a long, slow, draw on the pop. "Is that—is that a cross section of the fiend you killed?"

"Yep."

"That's similar to cyber-spider composition."

"Also, yep."

"But when the cyber-spiders teleported themselves, we could track them. They utilized miniature breaches through the Interstice connecting two points in our world. Like the fiend-hound."

Yikes. Didn't want to think about that bad boy. "So, these guys could be related, right? My fake fiend and the spiders."

"Maybe." Liz smiled. "Oh! And Garvey said you were bringing samples, didn't he! I'd almost forgotten."

"You were a tad distracted." Loredana pointed at the computer hardware under her desk.

"What? Oh." Liz blushed. "Sorry about all that. Cyril's been working so hard, and it isn't really his fault considering how much of the Historic Vault was ransacked but when you're trying to put together the pieces of the puzzle without the picture from the front of the box—"

I cleared my throat.

"Right. Samples." Liz hopped up from her chair, bouncing on tiptoes. "I'd better prep the lab, so the guys down there know what to expect. But before I go—you get the problem, right?"

I held up my right hand and counted off. "Astral fiend showed up in daylight. It didn't vaporize when I killed it. And its arrival didn't show up on your scanners that detect rips."

"And ..."

"Forecasting offered us no warning of its impending incursion," Loredana said.

Liz waggled four fingers. "Yep! That's what we have to unravel. If I can compare the cellular composition of your fiend with the spiders, maybe we can get lucky and find a point or two of similarity. As for the rip ... I mean *no* rip ..."

She didn't finish the sentence. I didn't like it when she didn't finish sentences. "How's that even possible?" I asked. "No way a fiend could make it from the Interstice to here without using some kind of portal, and those portals generate tachyon bursts. We've got the hardware to detect those."

"Yeah, unless there was a glitch." Liz stuck out her tongue with me.

"Never gonna live that one down," I muttered.

"There is another possibility," Loredana said. "One which we haven't discussed."

I nodded. So did Liz. We both saw it, I think, but I had to be the one to voice it. Because, really, when have I missed a chance to shoot off my mouth? "You're thinking it didn't come from the Interstice."

Loredana raised her hands, as if to ponder the question.

I didn't want to ponder. I wanted to be pointed at the new threat so that if any more showed up, I was there to stop them— and preferably not when I was in the middle of relaxing. Which was a lot. Those things had better start respecting my personal life, know what I mean?

"I suggest we check in on Ms. Pathfinder," Loredana said. "Elizabeth, do be so kind as to contact us with updates once you've had a chance to analyze the samples."

"You bet!" She clapped her hands. "This is gonna be great! Almost as great as you borrowing my sword to fight zombies!"

She hurried from Tracking. I chuckled, both at her abrupt shift from sour to exuberant, and the way the rest of Tracking kept on monitoring tachyon fluctuations without her. "Okay, let's be fair, I didn't do any slaying with the sword."

"No. That was the older version of our wizard from yet another dimension."

I led the way past Tracking's double doors. "I think Bowen's actually a summoner."

Loredana's eyebrow raised.

"Yeah, never mind." I smirked. "Is this the part where you get to chastise Edie for falling asleep on the job? Even though being asleep helps her do her job?"

"Certainly not. I have the utmost respect for Edith and value her role both as a tremendous source of prognostication and her family's heritage as Procyon's quiet but firm backbone." She let herself have a tiny smile. "That does not mean, however, that I will not be equally firm."

"Awesome. You being firm equals somebody else being nervous. Always fun to watch."

"Do you honestly think Edith will be scared of me?"

Ah. Never mind. I don't think I'd ever seen Edith Pathkiller scared of *anything*, let alone a regular person like Loredana—even though she was a regular person with phenomenal aim and a demonstrated skill with firearms. "Nah. But it's fun to imagine."

"Perhaps you should concentrate your imagination on the conundrum we face."

"Yeah. I'm not looking forward to cleaning up more of these kinds of astral fiends if we can't see them coming. The sooner Liz can figure out how to track it, the better. And if Edie can see it coming before that, jackpot."

The door to Forecasting was framed in black tile, in a hallway of soft carpet and soothing yellow lights that set pale walls aglow. It was also locked.

Loredana had put her phone away, only for its notification chime to sound. Whoever it was, the new message made her frown. "Bother."

"What?"

"We're requested. In the manager's office. He has questions for us."

Oh, great. Because after having a vacation ruined, visiting Alvarez would be like having teeth pulled. By a Klingon. Not big fans of painkillers, based on my copious *Star Trek* knowledge. "Let me guess. It's about the morning fun."

Loredana sighed. She replaced her phone and smoothed her skirt. "In part. It has more to do with our newfound fame—or should I say, our notoriety."

Oops. That. "Well, tell Mr. Manager I'll be there as soon as I get whatever good's Edie's got."

"Don't tarry." She was already on her way down the hall. "We all know patience isn't his virtue."

"He's not alone," I murmured.

CHAPTER FOUR

Three seconds later, I tapped the door panel with my ID card. It blinked green. The latch clinked.

"Come in," a voice called.

Shudders. It wasn't Marigold's voice. Not that same, soothing, sing-song tone. But it filtered through the door in the same way, like we hadn't rebuilt the place after an angry artifact had ripped it down.

I eased into the room. Leave it to Dominic Zein—Procyon's architect on call had done a great job of getting the details of the previous Forecasting office recreated. Soft, pale-yellow lighting turned a cushy carpet into a sea of butter. He'd even put the righthand side door with the silver lettering "Forecasting Supervisor" emblazoned on frosted glass. It glowed amber. Talk about expensive tastes. There were two chairs, one wooden antique with a caned bottom, and the other a thick, plush model upholstered with maroon velvet. A long couch of gold fabric was the most comfortable of the bunch.

Edith Pathkiller sat cross-legged in the middle of the floor. All that furniture? It had been lined up neatly against the far walls, except for the antique. She could have been enjoying an early morning meditation after a quiet night's camping, judging by the way she was dressed in a flannel shirt with cutoff sleeves and blue jeans that had long lost their knees. She was also barefoot. Never could figure out, when she was holed up in the makeshift Forecasting office at our interim silo base, where she kept her shoes.

Her hair, long and black was braided over the shoulder that sported a maroon pawprint tattoo. A tiny gold wolf piercing shone on her nose. I never asked her if the adornments had anything to do with her being a member of the Cherokee nation, which she was, or whether they were symbols passed down through her family, which had helped start up Procyon in the 1840s when Marigold Yen's ancestors had tried to unleash hell on Earth. But Dominic and I had found her secreted away in rural Nevada, supposedly guarding a top-secret sensing array used to determine when and where astral fiends would appear.

Turned out, there was no array. It was all her.

"Hey." I sat in the chair nearest the door. Would have been better off lounging on the couch, but I doubted Forecasting wanted smelly operatives sprawled there. "Got a question for you."

"And I have one for you." An eye opened—dark brown, like farm soil, or coffee. A perfect match with her copper skin.

"You heard about our fun new visitor this morning? The one that ruined a perfectly good bowl of ice cream in the middle of my vacation?"

She nodded.

Okay. "Any insight as to how nobody saw it coming? Including you?"

"You must think I've been sitting here like this for the past hour because it promotes healthy posture."

I opened my mouth, lost the quip I had prepared, then ran with, "Uh. No."

Edie smirked. "My question. What do you want from me?"

"Oh." I scratched the back of my neck. A chime jingled on the other side of the closed door. I'd come in ready to do some interrogating, but I should have known better. Every trip to Forecasting was like going to the dentist, with less tooth pain and more introspection. "Answers, I guess."

"You guess?"

"Answers. Like, why we got no warning of this one, and why Liz still can't pick up a trace of how it got here."

"That presumes there's only one way to this world from the others, through the Interstice."

"Okay." I held up my hand and ticked off fingers to catalog the possibilities. "Rips linking the Interstice to Earth, here in and around San Camillo. Smaller versions that astral fiends and other nasty critters use to travel distances in this world, mini rips that don't spend a lot of time in the Interstice. Then there's the Transect. Dominic says it's like a subway tube linking his living room to the same space in an alternate version of this Earth, passing through the Interstice but not accessible in there. Unless you fall out. Which he has. Plus, you know, Dominic yeets himself back and forth from his apartment like a yo-yo what I guess is a different version of the mini rips."

"Is that all?"

"All Procyon knows of."

"All you know of."

I sighed. "Look, really not in the mood for vague mentions of possible conspiracies this morning. Are there or aren't there? And did this fiend come through them?"

"I never said I had answers, Mercury. I have as many questions as you."

"Well, that's super." I rolled my eyes. "Because what I really wanted to do this morning, besides surf, was have a conversation that sounds like, 'Do you know?' 'I dunno. Do you know?' 'I dunno.'"

"My role here isn't to see all. It's to judge where time is leading, and where it's been. What you saw, what we felt, it's happened before, and time is approaching when it has to happen again."

Hello. "What *we* felt?"

"The creature's presence." Her gaze pinned me to the chair same as if she'd used knives. "It cut into my dreams. Brought itself into my mind, and we spoke."

"You talked to it?" I grunted. "Better than me. All I did was try to shove him back out because he wouldn't shut up."

"And what did you learn from him?"

I shrugged. "He—it—kept asking for help."

"Did you?"

"What?"

"Help."

Awkward. "Only if you consider blowing it to pieces help."

She shook her head. "Then your mission's unfulfilled."

"Whoa, hey, wait a minute." I pushed out of the chair. Not sure where I'd planned to go, but I wound up pacing the perimeter of the office. "Last I checked that's not in my job description. 'Killing astral fiends.' It's literally at the top of the list—if there was a physical list."

"And what when they're not astral fiends? What becomes your mission then?"

"To save people from threats and destroy them. The threats, I mean. Not the people." I blew out a breath. "You know what I'm saying."

"I do. Do you?"

I threw my hands up. "Okay, sure, I get it. Tell me how to stop these things and I will! That's my deal."

Edie snapped her fingers at me. The sound could have been a gunshot. I froze, not sure why it had made me stop pacing. "Sit. Here."

I folded my legs beneath me, taking up a position that mirrored hers. "Shoes on or off?"

She stared at me.

"No harm asking, Edie."

"Edith. Give me your hand." She held hers out, palm up.

I scooted backward, on my butt. "No way. Last time you offered, I took a vision trip to the future. In Oklahoma."

"You don't have to be afraid of the future, any more than you fear the past, which is long gone."

"My past sucked. The present's way better. And the future can stay where it is, thanks very much, until I'm ready to deal with it. Tell you what—instead of being vague, tell me what you felt when that fiend voice mentioned its buddy Tenebrae."

Edie's hand snapped out, a snake striking at its prey. Her grasp around my wrist was like a handcuff. "You—heard that name? When?"

"At the end of the fight. When I finally agreed to help the stupid thing." I wrenched free. "Hands off the merchandise, got it?"

She reached for me again, both arms, but I was ready. I caught her in the chest with my knee, pushing her up and over, so that she landed against the door with a *whump*. Meanwhile, I'd rolled into a crouch, hand on the pulsar stave, ready to bring it to life for a good old-fashioned Tasering. Yeah, I'd used it before to knock people senseless.

Edie flipped over, more acrobat than counselor. Her braid smacked against her shoulders, and she stared at me, eyes glowing like LED bulbs. "Tenebrae calls. You will answer."

Definitely stave time. I aimed it like a wand, yellow-white sparks coruscating in the air around the weapon. "Hey. Okay. Nobody's going to answer anything, except maybe you, when you snap out of it and tell me what's going on!"

The eye glow faded, but only enough to reveal her pupils. "Tenebrae balances. The twilight walls collapse."

Sounded like nonsense, but familiar nonsense—like what crazy talk came out of Marigold's and Arkwright's mouths when they'd sipped too much of the Interstice Kool-Aid. Walls collapsing. As in, the barriers between dimensions?

She eased out of her crouch, movements liquid, like a mountain lion uncoiling to pounce. Which can turn out bad for the pouncee, if that was a word. Probably not. Her eyes flickered again. "You don't stand in my way?"

"I stand in the way of anybody who's got plans to blow up my city, my state, my country, and the world, in that order. But I don't think that's something Edie would ask me, is it, Whisperer?"

The light blazed back. Edie shot forward, in perfect imitation of my speed run that I use when I've sponged up a crazy amount of tachyon particles via the pulsar stave. That was the bad news. Good news? My reaction time was up to—wait for it—speed.

But I wasn't going for a kill shot. Whatever was happening to Edie was outside of her control. I hoped.

I pivoted and swept the stave up under the blur that I was pretty sure was her leg. It was enough to send her tumbling across the room, where she slammed into the couch, knocking it over. Then I hurtled in her wake, driving my knees into her back. "Stay down! Sound good."

She flipped me off with enough force that I slammed into the ceiling. I wound up on my face, nose buried in carpet, as she leapt atop me.

And grabbed the pulsar stave.

Bad move. Her attempted seizure set off a literal power struggle in the weapon, as energy surged through our arms. There was a terrible whine, underlying a growl that rose like a hungry car engine. My teeth buzzed in sympathy. Worse than any dentist visit.

But no way was I gonna let whatever was pushing her around take the stave away. Not this time.

I forced my will through the weapon, demanding it to listen. Hey, after all, I was its boss, right? No idea if that was the best tactic. Eventually, Edie's hands slipped. I shoved up off the carpet, pinning her against the wall, with the stave held under her face.

"Talk," I growled.

"Help," she murmured.

The light fled from her eyes. Back to the normal human version. She sagged to the floor, sweat dripping from her face, when there hadn't been a drop before.

I wasn't smelling like lilacs, either. Had I even gotten a chance to shower after the morning's fight? "Edie? You okay?"

"Edith." She shook her head like she was trying to empty out her brain. "Did it leave?"

"Ah, well, I guess so, because you're not trying to steal the pulsar stave and also, you don't have evil eyes." I gave her a thumbs up.

She rubbed her face. The sigh she made was ragged, like she'd had the worst night's sleep. "This isn't right. I knew it would happen again, and here I am, powerless."

"What happened again? That possession deal?" I glared. "It would figure the Whisperer would try—"

"No. Not him. I'd push him back." Edie scowled. "This is the work of another entity. One that should be banished."

"Okay." Definitely not what I'd bargained for when I'd walked into the office. "Are we talking the same as the voice I heard from the new fiend? Because you just asked me for help just now and that seems to be the request of the day."

"I can't answer."

I rolled my eyes. "And that's not going to work for me. This thing. You said it happened before. Was it back when you were the contingency for Procyon?"

Her head snapped up. Never knew you could see fatigue slough off a person, revealing the energized version beneath, but that's what I seemed like. "Contingency."

"Yeah. Educated guess. I must have hit paydirt because you're not happy about it." Nothing like stating the obvious, right? I'm a pro.

"Contingency was a long time ago. That isn't me. Not anymore." She brushed past me. "I have to go."

"What? Now? Look, we've got a fairly malicious new threat, Edie, and I'm gonna need a lot more than mysterious mutterings and you trying to casually murder me for my weapon." I grabbed her shoulder. "Give me five more minutes."

"Get your hand off me, and I'll give you the rest of your natural life, which you'd lose otherwise." She glared at me over the pawprint tattoo.

Fair trade, I'd say. My fingers eased back.

"Contingency was my role for a few years. It was what it

sounds like—me, as the person Procyon would call in when there was no operative at San Camillo and when the rips became more active. I was too young to handle it. My decisions never worked out for the best."

"Couldn't have been too bad. You're descended from a Procyon founder. Both Alvarez and Tyrone Thomas out in Drake City were ready to hand you a crown and a scepter. Full royal treatment."

"If you think that, you'd better re-examine why I was running a secret office disguised as an antiques store."

"It was for your protection." I blinked. "Oh. So, that cover story was a cover story."

She didn't answer. Instead, she opened the frosted glass door.

Didn't know what I was expecting. A weapons locker? A mediation space? A salad bar? Nope, just an office, with desk of black and silver metal, a computer, and a pair of chairs. No paintings. No photos. No decoration of any kind. And way too thick a layer of dust over everything to have gotten much use.

Plus, shoes. A pair of silver sneakers. I knew they had to be around somewhere.

Edie retrieved a leather bag, slung it over her shoulder, and snatched a battered phone from a chair. The bag's contents rattled as she left the office. You know, like it might be full of arrows and a bow that could channel the powers of the Interstice, not unlike the pulsar stave or the Echo Watch or any number of artifacts that hailed from my home city of Meda. She slipped her feet into the silver kicks and was headed to the exit.

"Hey." I blocked her way out of Forecasting. "What the heck am I supposed to do in the meantime? If you remember this thing—"

"My memories are suspect. The past ..." She shook her head. "When it comes to this threat, Mercury, you're better off leaving it alone until I can get some solid answers."

"Is that where you're going? This isn't just an armed run to Starbucks?"

She pushed me aside—gently, but firmly, like a principal redirecting her wayward pupil back to class. "I can see where this is going, and when it's going to end. Let me redirect the present so the future isn't a disaster."

I watched her go, my arms folded, as the door to the hallway swung shut.

Had to say. Least boring visit to Forecasting ever.

CHAPTER FIVE

ector Alvarez was murdering his keyboard when I arrived in his office.

Okay, so you can't kill a keyboard. No soul, no sentience, blah blah. But, man, if you could, I would have called the cops and asked Ramos to slap our manager in cuffs.

"About time you showed up." Alvarez was a short barrel of a guy, sporting a neatly trimmed goatee and moustache combination. He must have gotten a haircut recently, because his thick, wavy 'do was less like a nineties Pierce Brosnan than I remembered. He was dressed in his favorite outfit—black shirt and silver tie. His jacket, of the same pewter shade, clung to the back of his chair. "Give me one second.

"One," I whispered to Loredana. Then I plunked myself down in the sleek chrome chair with black cushions and inhaled deeply of heavenly aroma permeating the manager's office—coffee. Talk about lineup. Twenty bags packed the minibar. Nothing else was allowed near the giant oak desk, except for a tablet glowing onto Alvarez's face.

Loredana waited a few feet from the desk, hands clasped behind her back.

Alvarez sent his email with a click of the mouse. Then he leaned his elbows on the desk. "Do you know who that was? To whom I had to send a lengthy and fabricated explanation of this morning's events at a certain beach near Huntersville?"

I raised my hand.

"Stop it, Mr. Hale." Alvarez glared at me. "I'm not in a mood for your games."

"Hey, I figured you didn't want me blurting out an answer. Since you don't like anything I say." I shrugged. "Next time I'll text you."

"Whatever fallout there has been from this morning's altercation with the astral fiend," Loredana said, "I can assure you it has been contained."

"Contained?" Alvarez shook his head. He spun his monitor so we could see the screen, then queued up a video.

I winced. Grainy, yeah, and of dubious origin, but you could see a small outline of yours truly tangling with a twisting, writhing creature, right before we smashed our way from the deck into the house. Looked like someone took the shot on a phone, from a couple homes over. "Not my favorite part."

"This isn't like your previous fights that have gone public," Alvarez said. "Those are at night. More easily deniable."

"News flash, boss—the battle at Rosa Roja Park with Alexander Arkwright last year wasn't exactly dimly lit. You know, the one where he tried to earthquake us and the SCPD to death?" I slapped my hand down on my leg for what I thought was terrific visual effect. "What's the big deal? This is fifteen seconds of blurry video game stuff compared to that."

"The big deal is that now, everyone's watching." Alvarez turned the screen back far enough so he could see what he was clicking on. "Local TV news is running the clips. MSNBC is linking it. So is Fox News. CNN. Even Newsmax, so help us all, Joe Rogan. The near destruction of San Camillo on a semi-regular basis last year has clued people to something strange happening in their city. Half the people think it's a hoax. The other half think it's a cover-up for terrorism."

"Doubtless they're drawing links to these events and Procyon."

Loredana could have been a marble statue. Her gaze flicked to the screen and back to Alvarez. "One can only assume having our headquarters destroyed at the scene of the last of these major calamities only served to solidify that connection."

"Never mind that San Camillo Bay was orbiting our property." Alvarez sagged into his chair. "I was emailing Homeland Security. Again."

"Agent Bowe?"

He nodded.

Great. I wrinkled my nose. Hudson Bowe had been on our heels and in our way ever since his boss and partner, Serena Cyr, had gone to the dark side—figuratively at the Procyon battle, then literally when Loredana shot her, and she fell into the Interstice. "I get it's a pain. But what am I supposed to do? Ask the monsters to quit breaking their rules and stick to showing up at conveniently abandoned structures in the middle of a pitch-black night? Unless you think Liz can rig up a way to forward that message, we're out of luck. Our best bet is whatever she can find connecting our attacker to those cyber-spiders and symmachites that are new on the scene."

"Hardly new," Loredana said.

"New-ish." I spread my hands. "I feel your pain, Alvarez."

"I really don't think you do." He reached for a steaming red mug on the corner of the desk and sipped his coffee. Dude. Without even offering any to us? "Loredana, I appreciate your proximity to this incident but I'm moving you off it. There's urgent matters that need your attention."

She cocked an eyebrow. I was about ready to do the same. We were always Mister and Misses with Alvarez. Using her first name was like giving her a promotion. Trust me, I noticed I didn't get the same treatment. "I fail to see, sir, given the dearth of Interstice activity these recent months, what could be of greater import."

Alvarez took another long sip. "The board is sending a representative here."

"Bloody hell." Loredana sank into the chair next to me.

I glanced between them. They'd mentioned the board before, but it was in passing, hushed tones, like they didn't want to invoke its appearance. All I knew was, when I stopped Marigold and her husband, Winston Yen, from establishing a permanent breach between Earth and the Interstice, they'd sent members to San Camillo to make sure I wasn't thrown to the law enforcement wolves. And again, when the disaster at Cavill Cemetery had barely been enough to turn back a zombie horde—and the feds came for my head a second time—they'd pretended they had no idea where I'd gone.

"I'll need you to make sure the board rep is brought up to speed on our current operations." Alvarez looked at me, like a cat examining a clueless robin in the front yard. "And I'll need you, Mr. Hale, to be nowhere near said rep."

"Check. You want her to run interference while I figure out the new monster problem."

"That, and I could do without a rant from the board when they find out you're in trouble again. I don't have to remind you how many times they've stuck out their collective necks when you've been a nuisance."

"Don't worry." I tapped the side of my head. "Just cataloged them."

"Which rep are they sending?"

"No idea. Though—" Alvarez checked his watch. "He'll be landing in two hours. Round up whatever resources you need to allay his concerns. I'm not asking you to pull the proverbial wool over his eyes, but …"

"You'd rather if he were given an overview of our current situation, with assurances all is well in hand." Loredana nodded. "I understand. I shall coordinate with Mr. Garvey and Ms. Stojan to compile all the relevant data."

Alvarez nodded. Always a welcome sign. But he didn't provide any more info, so, bad sign.

Loredana touched the crook of my elbow with her index finger. The gesture was, *Time for us to go.* "All right. Guess that's what we get for now."

"Thank you, sir." Loredana ushered me from the office.

Before I could get fully ushered, I leaned around her and asked, "How's about letting me poke around the Historic Vaults while Loredana's got our board visitor distracted? Because I'm feeling the need to delve into some local tales and see if anything like this has happened before."

Alvarez winced. "I don't think so. Not yet. Give me time to make sure he's clear of the facility. Plus, I'm not entirely sure he doesn't have ears inside our walls."

Informants? Political maneuvering? Yippee. "Pretty please?"

"Just go."

"Okay." I smirked. "But remember last time, telling me to keep out of the vault didn't work so hot. As in, I snooped anyway."

Alvarez glared at me.

"I'm sure allowances can be made." Loredana's tone was firm. Not sure whether that sternness was directed at me or Alvarez, but I don't think either was willing to argue. "Good day."

"Mr. Hale?" Alvarez stood and reached for his jacket. "Homeland's around town. They're already sniffing at the rental house, though our people have long since cleared the site. I'd be a happy man if you avoided any interaction with them."

I saluted him with a sloppy three fingers to the forehead. "You and me both, Mr. Manager Sir."

Loredana shook her head as we got to the elevator. "Must you needle him so?"

"He hasn't fired me yet."

"I imagine that has more to do with your skill and your abilities with the pulsar stave than your charm."

I gasped and brushed my forehead. "Such words."

"Do behave. How was your visit with Edith?"

"She freaked out at my questions, got possessed by an unknown entity, then tried to take the stave." I shrugged. "Typical."

Loredana frowned. "This is disturbing."

"You think? Try finding out you put a me-sized imprint on Forecasting's ceiling. Anyway, she's run off to go find us some answers. I think." I shook my head. "Not a team player, that lady."

"You will convince her to toe the line." She kissed my cheek. "I'll likely have to skip lunch. I'm sure part of my task will be to dine with the board representative, in hopes he's as taken with the local cuisine as he is with my beauty and my talent for data collation."

"That's why I married you." I sighed. "Big on collation."

She winked as the doors shut. I blew out a breath and craned my neck until the stiffness popped.

Edie being weirder than usual. Board member snooping around. An antsy public.

"Not a fan of long lists," I muttered, and headed for the stairs to the sixth floor.

The lab didn't have any signs denoting its purpose. Heck, nothing above the fifth floor of Tower Three did. The regular employees of Procyon, those guys and gals who thought they were serving their community by providing a public benefit —which they were, God's honest truth—weren't even allowed to the top three floors. Made it all the easier for the techies and the people like me to fiddle with objects and elements that weren't the kind of thing you wanted to carry on a crosstown bus.

I don't think San Camillo Bay Transit Authority gave discounts for extradimensional refuse in your carry-on.

A pair of security guys stood guard outside frosted glass doors. Silhouettes drifted behind them. All it took was a flick of my ID and they nodded in perfect unison as the doors slid open, admitting me into a sterile, medicine-smelling version of a high-end boutique.

The walls and floors were white, edged with chrome. The far

wall was tinted glass, allowing copious sunlight in and a beautiful view of the bay without allowing someone with binoculars—or even a close-up drone—to peek inside. Chunks of moldering astral fiend were spread across six metal tables.

I leaned over the nearest one, taking care not to interrupt whatever beams were trickling out of what I guessed were scanning devices affixed to either end of the table. They looked like the old *Star Trek* phasers. You know, from *The Next Generation*?

"Please stand clear." A young Indian guy with glasses and a brusque tone, Narang, appeared opposite me. He didn't bother meeting my gaze. Whatever was on his tablet was way too important. "The cellular analysis is a delicate process."

"No harm, no foul," I said. "Not planning to poke my nose in front of those phasers."

He looked up, a frown creasing his face and making him seem about thirty years older. "TNG? The ones that resembled Dustbusters."

I snapped my fingers and grinned. "That's my guy."

"I'm glad you made it down." Liz approached, holding a pair of tongs like she was searching for the barbecue grille. Problem was, nobody was gonna sample the steak in its grip, because it was a rare cut of astral fiend. "I wanted you to get a closer look at this. Weird, huh?"

I shied away, trying not to gag. The chunk of hide reeked of old sewer and moldy bread, with a subtle hint of vomit. "That's, ah, interesting. Doesn't need to be contained?"

"Oh, it's inert. There's nothing about its composition that could infect you or vice versa. Okay? The astral fiends aren't of this dimension. Their bodies don't play by the same rules as ours and usually, when they die, they're just gone."

"But not this one."

"No, and that's what's so cool!" She let the chunk drop onto the table. "Narang's the one who found the first point of convergence."

"Bravo." I bowed.

"It's what Liz expected." Narang turned his tablet so I could see the graphics. Two microscopic images had been enlarged and contrasted, by hundreds of times, according to the tiny magnification readouts in the corners. "But yes, I confirmed it. The sample on the left is from the cyber-spiders you recovered at the closed sushi restaurant on the Promenade during the first encounter. The sample on the right, from the fragments retrieved from your rental at the beach."

"Our *destroyed* rental," I muttered. "Did I forget to mention that I'm still technically on vacation?"

"We haven't finished the full scans yet," Narang continued, clearly not bothered by my predicament, "But the similarities are more than obvious. I suspect the scans will further confirm genetic similitude."

"They're the same," I said.

"Not exactly." Liz prodded the chunk with her tongs. "You can't tell, not by looking with just your eyes, but these leftovers are disintegrating. Slowly. I mean, they'll probably be gone tomorrow afternoon. What's important is—"

"These aren't regular astral fiends," I interjected. "Someone's modified them."

Liz chewed her lip. "No, that's not it."

"So, what?"

"The thing you fought wasn't an astral fiend at all, Mercury. It was a copy. A really close one, yeah, but once you get beneath its hide, the similarities fall apart."

I stared at the remnants. It had fought me like a fiend. Used a lot of the same tactics. But it hadn't killed me, even when I was trapped in its grasp. Should've drained me dry.

Then there was the talking in my head bit. Which was the whole reason Edie was off to wherever she'd gone. If anyone was gonna extrapolate from that weirdness, it would be the lady who could dream about a monster's arrival.

"Is that why you couldn't track it?" I asked. "Because it wasn't a real fiend?"

"I don't know. Not yet." Liz spun the tongs on her finger. Narang took two steps away and went back to managing the scanners. "It would explain the lack of a tachyon spike. But we've got to consider whether or not it came from the Interstice. Confirming it's not a fiend—not a real one—lends to that theory."

"Theory of …"

"This creature is something else. Something new!" Liz's grin faltered. Probably because I was glowering. "Okay, it's not cool that it attacked you, but it's a novel life form! Who knows where it came from? Maybe it was pulled here from another dimension."

"That would mean wherever it came from is the same place that spawned the symmachites," I murmured. "And their big brothers."

"They definitely got around using the Interstice." Liz frowned. "The cyber-spiders did, I mean. The symmachites—we never tested their transit abilities. There's not a lot to go on."

"Well, you guys had better get cracking, because if this thing has pals, I don't want them showing up unannounced."

"It'd be really, really nice if I had more variables for Cyril to chew." Liz's eyes widened. "Do you think we could snoop around the Historic Vault?"

"It's still a mess. And Alvarez told me to stay away, until after—" Hmm. He probably didn't want us broadcasting the board visit. "Further investigation. I'll let you know."

"Okay. I'm worried, Mercury. No one's ever mentioned a fiend or something like one coming into our world without accessing the Interstice."

I glanced at the table again. Not a thrilling thought, especially given how much of Procyon's resources were focused on minimizing threats from that dimension and the ones linked to it. The Interstice was the hub for all that wacky activity. "Then we'd better find out where this guy located a back door," I said, "So we can slam it shut."

CHAPTER SIX

Thing is, I had a hunch that door had been opened before. Call it intuition.

Also call it, secret files given to me by Loredana's best gal pal.

I sprawled on the couch in our Tabb Terrace condo. The sounds of the city filtered in through the open window—the rumble of cars and busses, the clatter of shoes on sidewalks, the warble of nearby pigeons. Smells I could have done without. Nobody wants to sniff the aroma of hot garbage. But I couldn't deal with being closed off all the time in the air conditioning. I needed to feel the city around me.

Don't ask me why. It helped to have that feel when it came down to tussling with astral fiends. One more familiar variable.

I frowned at the image on my tablet. Speaking of familiar ...

It was a scan of an old photograph, labeled "1903." The young guy in it wore an old-fashioned pair of sunglasses—well, probably height of fashion for him. He held a weathered piece of tree bark, one that had the smoothed edges of something found underwater. An enterprising artist had carved a giant cyber-spider into the surface. And I do mean giant. The thing easily towered over the warriors in it, the guys with bows and arrows.

Oh, and also the Spanish conquistadors in their signature

armor.

Cordelia Keyes, Procyon Intelligence, had given me a tiny flash drive loaded with all sorts of secret files last year, when Loredana and I had taken a field trip to Miami. Seemed she was privy to a bunch of things that we weren't. Hence me chomping at the bit to get into the Historic Vaults again. I had a hard time believing Cordelia was the only one with access to this information.

Didn't help that the more I dug into the files, the more questions I had.

Most of them were images. Some photos, some scanned documents. There were letters dated from the late-20th Century clear back to the Gold Rush era, which was no surprise, given Procyon was founded after one particularly epic battle in 1848.

Problem was, I couldn't read any of them.

I'd spent a year trying to find a match online, coming up blank. They kind of looked like a mix of Greek and Latin alphabets. Whatever. Constant scrolling made my eyes dry, my head ache, and my stomach gurgle.

Fortunately, there was leftover Carlito's in the fridge.

I snagged a slice of pepperoni pizza, slapped it on a glass plate I was pretty sure was reserved for a holiday dinner, and kicked back on the couch again. Whoever had kept these records off Procyon's radar was keen on secrecy, going so far as to employ their coded alphabet. But I could garner enough info from the pictures to figure out what had happened.

Cyber-spiders, in giant form, had existed somewhere on Earth a few hundred years ago. Florida, I was guessing, based on the swampy background in all the photos and the prevalence of Spanish armor in the old carvings. My archaeologist buddy in each of the pics—a Black guy I nicknamed Young Indy—wasn't just the one digging up artifacts. He could be seen pointing at crates, standing toe to toe with bigger guys in khaki uniforms.

I blew out a breath and closed the latest image. "You know, Googling 'Secret Alphabet in Hidden Monster Records' would be really helpful about now," I muttered aloud to the empty living room.

Even if Loredana had been there and not out schmoozing with the board member, she wouldn't have much more for me than a sly smile and a kiss for encouragement. She'd left this as my side project, busy as she was getting Procyon's public side back on its feet. There were chamber of commerce meetings, city council meetings, meetings, meetings … You get the picture. I was thankful that she'd never dragged me to any of that stuff. She didn't talk about it much, either.

Bet she liked fighting her way through the belly of a shipwreck or shooting at a fiery astral fiend from the trees way better.

I grinned and opened the next folder on the tablet. Huh. There was one I'd missed. Young Indy, from a distance, with crates stacked beside a horse-drawn wagon and a spindly old motorcar. He was deep in conversation with two other men—an elderly fellow with a cane, face half hidden by a snowy beard, and a mustachioed guy with a rifle slung on a strap over his shoulder. Rifle guy had the sleeves of his white shirt rolled up, suspenders stark lines against the stained outfit. The older one wore a vest, sleeves rolled up in the same manner.

Both their faces bore more than a passing resemblance to the kid's.

"Family reunion?" I muttered. "In the middle of the Florida swamps. What was this, the great cyber-spider hunt of Aught Eight?"

True, I hadn't seen any evidence of the actual monsters, big or small. But those guys had been on the lookout for something.

Worst part was, they all seemed familiar. I couldn't shake the sensation I'd spotted one face or another. Probably in the Historic Vault, last year, when I'd rifled through their files without, um, proper authorization.

The contents had been on lockdown at the abandoned missile silo north of the city, where Procyon had made a secret base of operations in the months after the Hedron of Orbits had wrecked headquarters. I could get why Alvarez was antsy about letting me near those files. They'd only just gotten moved into the new building's expanded vault. Security was tight. Access was limited.

No one wanted a repeat of the contents falling into the wrong hands. Namely, Serena Cyr's.

I rolled my eyes—at her? At myself? At the situation? Take your pick—and set the tablet aside. What a pain. What a mess. I needed to empty out my brain.

I reached under the couch for my sketchpad. It was a battered collection of drawings, mostly things I'd dreamed or envisioned or made up. I flipped past Loredana's face, a gleaming dark sword, and astral fiend after astral fiend. Not a lot of happy little trees for this guy. Didn't matter. I found a pencil in the couch cushion and opened to a blank sheet.

The image that formed from the graphite was a looming shipwreck, floating on top the waves like shipwrecks generally don't. I lost track of time. Lines blurred, smudges formed, and the side of my palm went dark from rubbing against the image as I shaded and shaded.

Onto the next page. A long, slender sword, blade so black I wore the pencil's tip down to a stub. The light dimmed. Thunder rumbled in the distance as clouds rolled in.

Then a forest. A massive astral fiend, wearing flames like I would a T-shirt.

I rubbed my eyes with the back of my hand. It was past five. No wonder my back was stiff. I hadn't moved from the couch in hours. Which my bladder reminded my about two seconds after I stood up and stretched.

My phone had a message on it when I returned from answering the call of duty. Loredana.

<Sorry I've been out of contact. Our gentleman from the board insisted on room-by-room tours of our facilities—both of them. Be home around 7:30. Word from Liz?>

<Nope. Zero.> I tapped the side of my phone. Not to distract her too much but … <Got new pix from the Cordelia files. Maybe you know the faces?>

<I shall look.> Then she sent a kissy-face emoji.

<Love you too, babe.>

I went to the open window, where the curtains blew in earnest. A cold front battered the city, dumping buckets of rain as lighting slashed across the sky. I leaned against the frame, soaking up the cool moisture and the fresh breeze. Perfect rainy evening for hanging out

My phone buzzed. I glanced at the caller ID.

Ramos.

"Nope." I tucked it back in my pocket.

Fun fact! Ignoring your phone does not make it stop vibrating. Especially when the caller rings a second time.

Great. Didn't he know I was out of the crimefighting game? Even the news had gotten the hint.

But it was Ramos. Nothing short of dropping a tactical nuke into his lap would get him to stop bugging me. And I bet even then he'd find a way to pester from Heaven.

I took the call. "Yo."

"A whole syllable. I'm honored." Ramos' speech was precise, and I know people use that expression a lot, but seriously, the guy used his words like people had hoarded them instead of toilet paper and he'd managed to find a stash at a Wal-Mart thirty miles outside city limits. "Were you planning to ignore me all evening?"

"That depends. You planning to call me every fifteen seconds?"

"Until you answered? Yes."

I sighed. "Nice to hear from you to"

"*De nada*. Get down to Court, *pronto*."

He and I did enough business I knew he didn't mean the place where judges hung out. "Any good reason I'd want to leave my comfy living room in the middle of a thunderstorm to hoof it downtown to the worst neighborhood in San Camillo?"

"The Mercurians are at it again. And Wilhelmina's mixed up in their nonsense."

"Crap." *Those* guys? And I'd told her she should steer clear. I mean, it probably had about as much effect as sternly warning the sun not to rise. "Okay, hold the fort. I'm on my way."

"Better suit up. These kids respond better when you look the part."

Which meant I wasn't driving. He wanted me to make a grand entrance, like Spider-man, sans web. Which meant I was getting wet.

I hung up and eyed the pulsar stave. It sat on the kitchen counter, propped against the open pizza box.

"Super," I said.

Ah, Court Street. Poster child for urban blight. If you wanted crumbling brick rowhomes or asphalt so riddled with potholes, you'd swear it belonged on a bombing range, it was your kind of neighborhood.

To be fair, not everyone who lived there was a criminal. Which was one of the many reasons Wilhelmina was fond of it. She'd amassed a following of young men and families doing their best to delay the decay.

When I'd had to moonlight as a superhero to cover the bills, I'd kept it on my radar as best I could. There's only so much one guy can do for a city that experiences hundreds of crimes every night. After the Hedron of Orbits, and the uptick in extradimensional craziness, I'd let the patrols slip. Things had bumped back up for a while.

Until the Mercurians stepped in.

Or maybe I should say, stepped in it.

I leapt across the last alleyway before hitting the intersection of Court Street and DeLeon, landing atop the apartment building with a splash. A literal splash. The puddle was full of pigeons a split second before touchdown. I grimaced as their crap sizzled where it came into contact with the golden energies coursing through my suit, tracing wild patterns across the black and gray fabric.

"Yikes," I said. "They're multiplying."

Last time I'd paid attention to the headlines, a handful of young men had donned golden shirts and black track pants so they could put the smack on crime. They'd put strips of black electrical tape around their arms, until they resembled bumblebees. Seemed ridiculous, right?

Until they'd started whaling on criminals with sections of steel pipe.

And their fan club grew into an outright gang.

Thirteen people—including two guys with gray in their hair and four women—were spread out along one of the side blocks beneath the bridge, pursuing a group of ... Hoodlums? Miscreants? Whatever. Bad guys with guns. Punk kids, mostly, probably extorting money from innocent victims nearby. Or trying to, because six of them were on the ground, clutching arms or ankles. I saw one of them aim a gun, only for a pipe to smash against his wrist as two Mercurians put him on the sidewalk.

All that fun ground to a halt when SCPD squad cars rolled onto the scene.

That was my cue. I flipped off the roof, somersaulting five stories, and slammed into the center of the street hard enough to crumple pavement. Relax—I picked a spot that was already ruined.

Everyone in the running fight froze in place, weapons raised, and stared at me—the gang members with their tattoos and gaudy clothes and designer sneakers, and the Mercurians with their gold face coverings that obscured everything from their noses down.

"Okay, boys and girls." I spun the pulsar stave, letting it trade power with the suit until it was a blur of sparks. "Bedtime. Everybody clear out."

A few of the gang members dropped their weapons and ran for the cops. I'd never seen anybody look so happy to get nabbed by police officers and body checked against a Dodge Charger.

"Mercury!" A young woman hurried up to me. I assumed young, from the voice and what I could see of her face. And the eyebrow piercing. Not a lot of Boomers going for a tiny silver ring like that. She was Latina, with long, dark hair secured in a ponytail. "You're here! Finally. We've been waiting for you to take out this trash."

Discordant cheers went up from the rest of the group.

I shook my head. "Yeah, sure, if I see them committing a crime, I'll lend a hand. Or a stave. But it looks to me like they're running."

Someone worked a gun's slide. Behind me, forty feet away. Left shoulder.

I spun, crouching, and loosed a blast of the stave's energy.

It caught a young guy with spiky red hair in the stomach, smashing him chest-first to the street. He moaned and clutched his stomach, the gun discarded.

"And I'd do it with way fewer risks." I blew on the end of the stave. Steam mimicked smoke. Not too shabby.

"But we wouldn't have to be out here like this if you were doing your job!" The young woman glared at me. Even with the mask, she looked pissed. "This is your city. You have to defend it! We can only do so much."

"Wrong." I pointed over her shoulder. "You call those guys."

Lieutenant Gabriel Ramos led a squad of uniformed officers into the block, shouting commands in English and Spanish as policemen peeled off in two-person units. They jogged toward the dispersing clusters of quarreling criminals and vigilantes— except most of the Mercurians had gone. Straight up vanished. I blinked. No superpowers, sure, but those guys sure knew how to skedaddle.

As did my debate partner. She was sprinting down an alley by the time I turned around. "Hey!"

"So close." Ramos swiped rain off the end of his nose. He had a navy-blue jacket with "SCPD" emblazoned in yellow on the left chest. Water dribbled off the matching ballcap. His gray notebook was tucked into the pocket of a pale-lemon shirt, and the silver clip on his bold green tie glittered under the streetlamps that flicked on during the storm. A subtle cologne interrupted the relentless stench of Court's, um, local aroma. "What's the matter? Did she use big words that disabled your superpowers?"

"You're a comedian." I scratched the back of my neck with the pulsar stave. "Again with these yahoos? Why haven't you arrested them all?"

"We've set a precedent of being lenient with vigilantes." Ramos scowled. "Hadn't you noticed by the way you're not currently serving jail time?"

My skin warmed. "Well, sure. Thanks for that, by the way. Not everybody gets to work with their very own alphabet soup special squad."

"The task force follows up on your activities and we consult with you, not the other way around. You're still not getting into the budget."

I snapped my fingers. "Darn. Missed a government paycheck by this much."

Ramos shook his head. "If you're not too busy basking in your fan club, you might help my officers round up your wayward friend."

"My what?" I glanced over his shoulder.

Wilhelmina, all five-foot-three of her grandmotherly form, was surrounded by four cops, tall kids fresh from the Academy, paired with Detective Stan Bradley, a burly Black man who could have easily bench pressed me.

Except he was shying away from Wilhelmina's whirling dagger.

"Try to take me and you'll bleed!" she snarled.

Just like Edie.

So much for grandmotherly.

CHAPTER SEVEN

approached the cops slowly, hands raised, and grinning—except my mask was pulled down to obscure my whole face. A couple of gun barrels tracked my path as I strolled into their midst. "Hey, hey, let's not get all trigger-happy or commence with stabbing."

Stan Bradley was one of them. He growled. Like, a dog's growl. "L.T., is it still my birthday? Do I get to slap the cuffs on this punk?"

"We already had cake this morning, Stan, and I got half the precinct to sign that card. So, no, no cuffs on Mercury." Ramos waited at the edge of the circle, hand on his weapon. "Disperse and help out clearing the rest of the street."

"You got it." Bradley whistled and twirled his finger. "Everybody heard the lieutenant! Fan out in a two-block radius! You see anybody with a mask and a stupid glowstick, put 'em on the pavement and read 'em their rights."

The cops moved off, whispering as they watched me. A couple snuck phone photos. I pantomimed shooting.

Bradley shouldered me on the way by. "Get your grandma off the street, kid."

"Sorry I didn't get you a present, Bradley. Happy birthday. I'd blow out candles but …" I indicated the mask.

He muttered a phrase that would have gotten him kicked out of Sunday school and shuffled off toward his squad car.

Alrighty. Cops were gone. Just me, Ramos …

And Wilhelmina, still primed to strike.

"Hey." I waved in her face. "It's me, Wilhelmina. Mercury. You okay?"

"Y'all need to stay. Back. Hear?" Wilhelmina's voice was raspy, like she'd gone through a pack of smokes in a single afternoon. I was used to the deep sound, but this was worse off, leftover from illness or fatigue. She glared at me, dilated pupils rimmed in sienna brown.

They had purple flickers around the edges.

I held the pulsar stave tight. If her mind was messed up … All I could think of was how my pals Dominic and Brandon had reacted under the influence of symmachites at my bachelor party. What can I say? It was a heck of a night. Anyway, they hadn't done much talking under the sway of Crux's black-bladed sword. Was this the same deal?

Wasn't eager to pick a fight with my mentor to find out.

"How's about you give me the dagger?" I held out a hand.

She slashed the blade. I yanked my fingers back. No blood. No missing digits.

Ramos had his gun drawn, but not aimed. "*Fix this*, Mercury."

"Easy. Hold up."

"That's what you should be telling her. We need to get this off the streets."

"Look, why don't you go see if your boys and girls in blue rounded up any more usual suspects of trouble for this neighborhood? I can handle one old lady."

Wilhelmina rocked on the balls of her feet. Okay, she was definitely readying to strike. So, why hadn't she launched an attack?

She squeezed her eyes shut. "I … can't see him. Can't sense Tenebrae."

The word stopped me from moving. I let my boots get cold

and soaked in a puddle. Same thing the strange astral fiend's voice—if that's really where the voice came from—had stuck into my head. "Tenebrae," I murmured. "Yeah. I know, Wilhelmina. Don't worry about it."

Ramos looked puzzled. "What did you say?"

"Gimme a second." I held out the stave to Ramos. "Hold this."

"I … No." He gestured to the ground. "Put it there."

I rolled my eyes. Fine. I didn't have time for him to suddenly be squeamish. I never let my gaze break with Wilhelmina's as I crouched, slowly, and lay the stave next to the puddle.

She shook her head. "Unarmed."

Yeah, probably didn't want her to get any fun ideas about who had a weapon still. I lunged for her, catching her wrist between my hands. The dagger fell with a clink and a splash.

Wilhelmina cried out. She blinked, focusing my face. "Mercury? Sakes, child, what're you doing out here in the rain?"

Thunder rumbled between the apartment buildings. Lightning high above illuminated the clouds, creating wild shapes, strange, grasping apparitions.

"Getting soaked. With you and Ramos."

She squinted at him, then again at me. "Why in the world are we doing that?"

"Good question." I picked up the stave and bowed. "Your chariot awaits."

Ramos was kind enough to let us sit in the backseat of his Dodge Charger, while he radioed Bradley for an update. I didn't catch all the details, but it sounded like the Mercurians had vanished among the alleys and into the buildings of people who didn't mind helping them hide. They wound up with eight gang members, all facing weapons and drug possession charges.

"Dang fool kids thought they could do this on their own." Wilhelmina shook her head and sighed. She'd reclaimed her knitting bag. Even thought it was sopping wet—and the kitten knitted into its side looked beyond bedraggled—she'd stowed the dagger between us in the seat and dove back into her newest project. Yellow socks, with black stripes. Her fingers flew as she talked, drops of rainwater plopping onto her sweats. "Lord knows they have heart, but ain't hardly a lick of sense among them. So, I wanted to give them words to abide, make them see some of that sense."

"How'd that go?" I jerked my thumb at the car window, fogged as it was from our conversation. Raindrops slipped down in swerving channels.

"I don't know. Can't recall. Next thing I knew, I was hearing words of my own." She tapped the side of her head. "Wasn't nothing like I'd ever felt."

"But you caught the word. Tenebrae."

She shuddered. "More than a word, Mercury. A presence. Like a body, but no one was around."

I nodded. Felt the same way to me, too, when I was grappling in the beach house. "Did it—I know this is weird—ask for help?"

"No." She squinted again, as if she were searching my face for a bug to swat. "This don't seem all that surprising to you."

"Hey, there's not a lot out there that surprises a guy like me these days."

"That name—"

"Yeah, I heard it. This morning. From an astral fiend that bashed its way through our beach house. Put a pretty sudden stop to vacation."

She put a hand to her mouth. "Loredana? She's okay?"

"Yep, and me, too, thanks for asking."

Wilhelmina snorted. She poked me with a knitting needle. "Figured you were in good shape, since you were bouncing through a rainstorm instead of being prodded by Doc Arne."

Yeesh. Wasn't looking forward to Arne Becker's grumbling review of my injuries. Fortunately, I'd managed to give him the slip back at Procyon. Hooray for minor miracles.

Ramos clicked the car radio off. "Can I give you folks a lift? As in, to the hospital? Or wherever you're staying these days,

Wilhelmina?"

She tapped a needle against the door. "Might be I should avoid this neighborhood for a spell. Some of the boys out there, they don't take kindly to my meddling. My friends can fend for themselves, but I'd rather make myself scarce."

Ramos's gaze pinned me from the rear-view mirror.

I sighed. "You can come to my place. Why not."

"That's kind of you." Ramos started the car. "Then maybe you two can tell me why you're quoting liturgy."

My turn to make a face. "Say what?"

"Tenebrae. I knew I remembered the word from somewhere." Ramos indicated the small laptop computer mounted at his elbow, between the driver's and passenger's seats up front. "It's the term for a service held on Good Friday, meant to symbolize the death of Christ on the cross. Candles are extinguished. A door out of sight is slammed shut. Everyone leaves the church in silence once it's concluded. The service, or variation of it, dates back to at least the 800s."

Doorways closed. Lights put out. My throat was suddenly dry. I could have drained a whole water bottle, even as humid as it was. "What's the word mean?"

Ramos pulled out onto the street, his eyes fixed on the wipers slashing across his windshield. The storm kept dumping on us. No hope of getting back to a bright summer's evening. "Darkness."

I made them tea when we got back to my place. Ramos rightly scowled when I reached for a new pot of coffee. He had a point. I kind of wanted actual sleep tonight. And considering it wasn't going to be at the beach house, I didn't want to stay up grumbling about the fact.

Meanwhile, I got him and Wilhelmina up to speed on the morning's shenanigans.

"Sakes, child." Wilhelmina's hands accelerated as they flew through her stitches, staring at me the whole time. "It spoke?

Can't say I'd ever had the displeasure."

"Yeah. Edie gave me the runaround about Forecasting the arrival. No hints at all about this attack. Zero. Not even a blurp of tachyons."

Ramos smirked. "A blurp. New technical term?"

"Only in my handbook." The kettle's whistle drew me into the kitchen. I blew dust out of a *Dr. Who* mug—relax, I was using that one—and found a couple Procyon ones I liberated from last year's wreckage of Tower One. "But that's why I want to chat with my grizzled old mentor, too."

Something whistled by my ear. I thought a bird had gotten in through the open window—but that was dumb, because there was still a screen in place. Then my eyes registered the knitting needle, quivering against the cabinet where it had embedded itself between two doors.

I turned my head slowly. You know, no sudden moves.

Wilhelmina's glare could have blasted an astral fiend straight back to the Interstice.

"This is much better than streaming a reality show." Ramos loosened his tie and reached for his notebook.

"Er, no offense, wise mentor." I made a show of bowing as I offered her the tea.

"If I'd been mad, Mercury, that needle wouldn't be stabbed into a cabinet." She smiled. "Be a lamb and go get it."

As I did—because I dislike bleeding—I asked, "What about it? You ever tackle a fiend that was impenetrable? Or at least, super hard to stab?"

"No, I sliced them all easily enough. Only times that part of the job was a challenge was when they ganged up on a body." Her smile broadened into a toothy, dangerous grin, kinda like the ones I made when I was in the middle of a monster fight. "But they all fell, mark my words."

"I believe it." I flipped the needle into the living room. She caught it, hooked into her yarn, and resumed her pattern. "But you heard a voice, back at Court."

She frowned. "Can't reckon it makes sense. There weren't no fiends around.

I shook my head. "Nothing from Tracking. I texted Liz on the way over. Sensors were clean. She's got a couple drones scanning in more detail now, but there aren't tachyon bursts like we're used to. It's something else."

"Then I can't figure where the voices came from."

"Okay. So, who else can we ask? What about the twins?"

Wilhelmina's hands froze. She gazed at me, her expression suddenly impassive, like we'd never been friends, and never would be again. "What'd you hear about them?"

I glanced at Ramos. He'd shifted his position on the nearby chair, resting his elbows on his knees, pen poised on his notebook. I guessed it was the same posture he assumed when a suspect was about to get to the juicy part of a confession. "They bridged the gap between you and me," I said. "They disappeared. Loredana didn't know much, because when she arrived—couple years before me, I think—it was already a mystery."

Wilhelmina snorted. "If that's what you call a cover-up, then sure, it's a big ol' mystery."

"Who covered up what?" Ramos asked. "How many people were involved?"

"Easy, Columbo." I sat opposite him. "But, yeah, Wilhelmina, what he said."

She sagged a bit against the couch, her face still locked in stone mode. "Can't say I know it all. Got mostly murmurs at the time. Weren't a soul in Procyon who came to lend me a hand when I left, busy as I was raging against the world and God and everything else would listen. Mind, that didn't mean Procyon left me unchaperoned. They had their folks watch me. Tried to hide it. Like a big ol' shiny Buick hanging around the slums wasn't a giveaway."

My stomach churned at the imagined sight of a 40-something Sherry Jean Crown, living on the streets, slowly wasting away. I'd lost my parents the same day she'd lost her husband and daughter, but I'd still been in diapers. No traumatic memories there. I thought of my grandfather Naos, dead in Procyon's infirmary from a horrific infection brought on by the corpse-fiends that attacked Meda. That hollow ache might not come close to the pain she hid.

"Wasn't much news for me until the young man tailing me stood in the way of some fools thought they could shake me down for money to buy crack." She chuckled. "Took a shine to that boy. He kept me in the loop while surveilling me to Procyon, until he got himself promoted upstairs."

"How far upstairs?" I ignored the hot ceramic of the mug. I felt like I was standing on the edge of a building, right before I'd jump off into San Camillo's streets.

Know that expression when someone gets a twinkle in her eye? Yeah. Wilhelmina's could have been seen from space. "Tippy-top. Of Tower Three."

"Jack Jackson."

She nodded.

"Wow." I slugged tea, ignoring the scalded tongue. "You had a direct connection to Procyon's manager. But he sure played dumb about you when push came to shove."

She shrugged. "Time changes a person. He wasn't the same brash Intelligence kid who watched my back. Lord knows he had enough on his plate. Probably thought I was too far off the deep end to be rescued. Something I'd considered my very self."

"Sorry you didn't get to see him again. He'd have been impressed."

"Hurt like hell when I saw his body on the ground, after that brat Calvin murdered him." Wilhelmina sighed. "But you learn, in this destiny, what we want and what we receive are hardly ever the same. The plan ain't ours."

Ramos nodded. I'd almost forgotten he was there. He'd been another piece of furniture, as quiet as he'd stayed and as focused on his notetaking as he'd been. "But these twins …"

"Those two? Didn't come on the scene until three years after I'd ushered myself offstage. Sherry Jean Crown was dead to the world. Procyon needed a new operative. In that case, they rely on the resources of Intelligence hooked up with Forecasting's insight. Get themselves someone new to wield the stave."

"Staves." I snapped my fingers. Sputtered tea over my knees—and onto the chair, which was upholstered in cream. Whoops. Guess who was scrubbing that night. "Because there were two—yours, and the one my mom brought to Earth."

"Which I wasn't supposed to retrieve."

Ramos frowned. "Since when?"

"She got both halves to the lab, and when Procyon set them near each other, they joined. Permanently." I made a face. "Except I can separate them. Is that why they went with twins? Two operatives were better than one?"

"Wasn't privy to that, child. But it was a good thing they did—at first. I seen them in action a few times. Those boys made you seem like a slouch for a good decade."

Ramos whistled.

Yeah. No kidding. "Ten years," I murmured. "Twin brothers. And you say their disappearance was covered up?"

"I say it, because I saw the aftermath." Wilhelmina seemed exhausted. "Fight got out of hand. They killed a pair of fiends, sure, but when those were dead, they clashed with each other. Don't ask me why—rage, jealousy, drugs. Rumor was, there was a woman. Almost always is. Then—explosions. Whole buildings collapsed."

I was way too aware of my heart pounding against my ribcage.

"All I knew after that was the explosion leveled two blocks," Wilhelmina continued, "And weren't nothing left of the Reverdins except ash and teeth."

There was a lot of tea sipping and note scratching after that. The rain's hills filtered through the open window. I flinched at the curtains when they blew, like I was expecting an attack—because, hey, why not? Another living space destroyed should have been just about due. "So ... Edith Pathkiller."

Wilhelmina snorted. "Contingency. Y'all should've called her

Rookie. Scared of her shadow, that one, but then again, made a perfectly good soldier when it came to following orders. She got chased off by the Reverdins pretty quick when she was called in."

Sure didn't sound like the intimidating Edie I'd seen. "Why'd they call her in?"

"Can't say. I suppose they thought her family name would help the Reverdins stand down when they went haywire. Didn't. Left them to annihilate themselves."

"Well, I—"

My phone buzzed. Liz calling. Hold that thought, I guess. "Hey."

"Mercury, hey! Okay, I know this is a lot of information but bear with me because I've been with Procyon for maybe four years, and I've never seen anything so crazy but then again who would ever think that something as common but weird as an astral fiend—"

"Breathe."

She did. Like she was deep-sea diving. "Okay. So! The astral fiend's remains finally broke down."

"Sublimated? That's what they're supposed to do." I put Liz on speaker and set the phone on the arm of the chair.

"No. Disintegrated. As in, they left tiny little pieces. Microscopic fragments."

"Now that ain't worrying," Wilhelmina whispered.

I shushed her. "Liz, is this just different composition than what we're used to seeing? Maybe something we can use to figure out how to kill it faster?"

"I hope so, because when it broke down, I had thousands of inert symmachites in a container."

Ramos made the sign of the cross.

Kinda what I felt. My throat was way too dry for someone who'd drained half a mug of tea. Super. Now we had dead bodies of mind-controlling nanites. "Well, you better get them in stasis. Still got—oh. The stasis gun won't work without the pulsar stave."

"Narang and I rigged up a tachyon enhancer like the one

Wilhelmina has for her dagger. It's fine. And yeah, they're frozen. Sending you a pic!"

She did. I stared at the miniature image.

That—wasn't a symmachite. "You sure about the diagnosis?"

"You mean analysis?"

"Whatever. These look too—pretty."

Ramos cleared his throat. He'd found our TV remote.

"Hang on, Liz." I paired the phone with the TV while Ramos turned it on, and bingo, we had a 42-inch screen version of the most beautiful starfish I'd ever seen. The body rippled with coruscating light, fading to a pale silver. Gold traceries bled into rigid bronze patterns.

"Lordy," Wilhelmina breathed.

"Their composition's mostly the same," Liz said. "Cyril's digging deep into the differences. Let you know when we have more!"

She hung up. Which, honestly, we almost missed, as mesmerized as we were by the screen.

"This is something new?" Ramos asked. He could have been whispering prayers in church.

"Way new." I considered Wilhelmina's stricken expression. "Decades new, at least."

Keys rattled in the door. Loredana stormed through, rain like jewels in her hair, a white jacket clinging to her bare shoulders. The dress underneath was a stunning burgundy, and her heels clicked across the linoleum like bullet casings falling.

"Just in time!" I grinned. "Want tea? I can get some leftovers if you're—"

"Explain this." She flashed an envelope in my face.

I grimaced at the return address.

Awkward.

Ramos peered over my shoulder. "Fan mail? This I can't wait to see."

"No." I scratched the back of my neck. "It's, um, royalties."

CHAPTER
EIGHT

Ramos was the first one to speak into the super awkward silence. Because of course he was.

You know what I mean. That silence where everyone's wanting someone to say something, but nobody wants to be the first one to do it, because whatever's said is going to sound stupid.

"Wait a minute." Ramos shook his head while waving his hands, like opposing pendulums. "You wrote a book?"

"No. No way! I would never."

Rip. Loredana tore the envelope. She glared at the unfolded piece of paper.

"Hey! Federal offense!" I gestured at her, while giving Ramos a plaintive look.

"Not my jurisdiction." He'd already taken up a stance by her left shoulder so he could read the statement.

Yeah, that's what it was. A royalty statement. "It's my cut. This guy contacted me through social media after the Battle of North Beach."

Loredana's blue eyes remind me of—dangerous blue lasers. "When you were on hiatus from Procyon."

"Forced hiatus. You guys—I mean, Procyon's higher ups— kicked me to the curb." *Careful where you lay that blame, Mercury. She's your wife now.* And I liked marital benefits a lot, thank you very much. "I was desperate for cash, so I wrote him back, and he had a plan … I kinda forgot about it once I started doing the whole superhero-for-hire thing. Then he sent me a link to Amazon, and the first check rolled in …"

"*Mercury on Guard*." Ramos gruntled. "Not bad."

"Thanks. His idea."

"Who is this man?"

I waved my hand. "Some dude from New Jersey. Lives out in Wyoming. Librarian, I think. Look, it's really not a big deal. The names were all changed to protect the innocent, like us—"

"'Cept yours." Wilhelmina sounded out of breath. I frowned, worried she might be experiencing an age-related ailment, but I realized she'd dropped her knitting and has one arm wrapped around her middle. The other was pressed to her mouth. Tears beaded at the corners of her eyes but she looked the happiest, I'd seen her.

"He changed mine too!"

"Lordy. Mercury *Hart*? Oh, child. Much as I want to hear the punch line, this old lady could use a ride home. Don't you think so, Lieutenant?"

"Certainly." Though right then, Ramos was the dictionary illustration of *crestfallen*. "As much as I hate missing a good fireworks show."

Wilhelmina hugged Loredana, which helped melt most of the "I'm going to kill Mercury and dump the body in San Camillo Bay" look on her face. "Good night, dear. You be kind to him, now."

"I will endeavor to restrain myself." The sly smile was directed my way. I breathed a bit easier.

Ramos leveled a finger at me as Wilhelmina practically dragged him out of the apartment. "I know you have a copy of that book somewhere in here."

"Okay, wait! What about the twins? Their mysterious deaths? Wilhelmina's hearing the same name I did?" I rolled my hands, hoping for a replay of our recent revelations.

"I'll text you." Ramos' smirk vanished behind the closing door.

Bang. Never knew how long that sound could echo. Turns out? About twenty seconds.

"Very well." Loredana tapped the paper against her hip. The curve of which, I gotta say, was enough to make me forget for a moment how much trouble I was in. "The book."

I sighed. "Hold on."

I lifted the cushion of the chair I'd been sitting it, rummaged in the space underneath the springs, and came up with the offending volume. "Ta-da."

Her expression softened further. "I'd hoped it was an elaborate hoax."

"You really think I'd go that far to get a laugh?" I snorted. "It'd be easier to shoot milk out of my nose."

She chuckled, then sat on the couch. She patted the cushion.

Awesome. Meant my impending demise was postponed. I flopped down next to her and grinned at the cover. "Don't I look vigilant? I think I look vigilant."

"You certainly look on guard." Loredana's arms crossed. "He doesn't bear the faintest resemblance to you."

"What?" I frowned at the mini-me on the cover, shrouded in shadow, facing astral fiend tentacles. Dude was the spitting image. "He's pretty close."

"Far too handsome," she said, punctuating with a smirk.

"Ha, ha." Sure he was. Wait. Did I suck in my gut? What gut? Did the cover model have better abs? I have abs! I touched my stomach. Loredana's resulting giggle didn't reassure me. "Hey, look, so what? Guy doesn't even know how to wield the pulsar stave. He looks like he's holding a broom handle. Zero wielding skills."

"Don't be offended." Loredana draped her arms around my neck. "Even if the world doesn't know who the true hero is, I am well aware."

Wow. I kissed her. She held me close and brushed her lips

against my ear. Chills.

"It's Ramos," she whispered.

I groaned and gave her a playful shove. She'd earned both. Loredana laughed, and in a flash, she snagged the book. "Hold up. I thought you figured this for a 'juvenile exercise.'"

"It is." She fanned the pages. "But I'm intrigued."

"Right. You just want to see if you're mentioned."

"And what you think of me."

Oh, no. No way. I grabbed the book back. "Then buy your own copy!"

Loredana shook her head. "So, tell me about the grand news."

I winced. Not really grand. "Wilhelmina knew about the twin operatives. Noah and Troy Reverdin. Got themselves killed ten years ago—by who, nobody knows. Sounds like they both went off the deep and blew themselves up."

Her eyebrow arched. "My word. No wonder, then, that I was not informed of their service. At least, not the specifics."

"Yeah. No kidding. Get this, though—Jack Jackson was on the one who kept Wilhelmina in the loop, even while he was supposed to be keeping tabs on her."

"Curious."

"Not half as curious as our wacky new symmachites." I woke up my phone.

"No need." Loredana waved her hand. "Elizabeth texted me a photo. With, unfortunately, her complete explanation."

"Yow. Email or text?"

"Text."

I chuckled. Must have been twenty separate messages, knowing how chatty Liz was. "Here's hoping she can track the things better now that she's got a clearer idea of what they are."

"Indeed. She mentioned something to me about neutrinos and a possible role they could play in early detection. Which would certainly explain why we were unable to detect this fiend's arrival using our typical tachyon monitoring networks."

"Sure." I drummed the book against my leg. She hadn't

mentioned anything about what she'd been up to all day, which, I guessed, wasn't nearly as exciting as dealing with a crazed Wilhelmina and digging up Procyon secrets. "So … How was the guy from the board?"

"Ah. Javon." Her cheeks pinked. "Quiet charming. We toured headquarters, and the silo, once he requested an inspection. He brought me up to speed on the goings-on at the national level."

"Just you. Not Alvarez?"

"He's meeting with the manager tomorrow morning. There wasn't time for dinner."

"Right."

Some of the pink faded from her face. "And what does that mean?"

"What? Nothing. I was acknowledging. Active listener." I tapped my earlobe. "That's me."

Loredana sighed. "I suspected as much. It was not a date, Mercury, nor was it a social call. This was a business matter."

"Between you and a good-looking guy. All day."

"Don't start. Jealousy is unbecoming."

I smirked. "Yeah? Like how well you handled Sirena Cyr?"

She lifted her chin. "That was different."

"How?"

"She was—evil."

I laughed. "Which you only found out later, after you thought I had the hots for her."

"Mercury …"

"Tell me more about Javon."

"Javon Kimball's family has been on the board since the beginning of Procyon. He is concerned about the spate of recent attacks, beginning last spring, and wants to take a more active role in dealing with such threats than the board."

Eyeroll time. "Like we need a suit telling us how to fight the monsters. What, is he going to charge consulting fees? Or just spend his time taking pretty Operations supervisors out to dinner?"

Loredana's eyes narrowed. "I don't like what you're insinuating."

"Hey, not talking about you. I'm talking about him. He could be a sleaze." I gestured with the book. "How am I supposed to react if he's putting the moves on you?"

"Perhaps by trusting that I will not immediately become weak-kneed and fall under his sway." Her voice was as dry as Death Valley. "Yes, of course he's handsome and charming. The latter is the nature of his role, and it befits him to try his best to make those who would swoon in his presence do so. Rest assured that, if I need rescuing from his predations, yours will be the first number I call."

Hmm. I wasn't a rocket scientist, but I could do the math. One jealous husband plus one ticked-off wife equaled two surly people who were gonna have one lousy night. I held up my hands and smiled. "Look, I'm sorry. Yeah, I had a jealous spike. Won't happen again."

"I very much doubt that."

"Okay, I'll work on being less obnoxious about it when it happens. Truce?"

Loredana smiled back and kicked off her shoes. Then she draped her legs across my lap and leaned on the couch. "As long as this still applies."

She pressed a tiny metal token into my hand. It was a miniature slice of pepperoni pizza, with the words "I love you more than pizza" engraved on the back. I'd given it to her by way of apology a year and change ago. Who knew she still had it in her purse?"

"You know it does." I touched her cheek. "I'll always love you. Because you're a total babe."

She snorted a laugh and slapped my shoulder. "Loveable twit. Entertain me with your story of this evening's antics, complete with Wilhelmina and your very own troop of vigilantes, and I shall consider the matter forgiven."

I pushed her legs off and hustled to the kitchen.

"What on earth are you doing?" she balked.

"Hey, I'm no dummy." I retrieved an almost-empty bottle of red wine from the rack, then snagged a pair of long-stemmed glasses. I divvied up the remnants. "Here you are, milady."

"How very chivalrous." She took a slow sip, gesturing with her other hand.

"Okey-doke." I flopped onto the couch, so she could reposition her legs. "Remember how much a pain the Mercurians are, trying to copy me, except minus superpowers? They've officially reached new heights of annoying ..."

"Stop." Loredana set her glass aside and pulled me into an embrace. "I have a better idea."

Yes, ma'am.

The pulsar stave swings down at my face.

Scalding heat singes my eyebrows.

I slash back, blocking the blow—with my half of the stave. Where'd my opponent get his own?

No time to wonder. The attacks keep coming, one after the other, an onslaught driven by furious cries.

I'm on the lip of a rooftop. San Camillo's amber and gold lights sparkle below. Way below.

We're atop Saito-on-Sky.

Who's trying to kill me?

No matter how much I lean into my powers, no matter how much I call out for help, I move slower with each blow. I can't win the fight.

The stave hammers me to my knees. A final strike knocks my half of the weapon from my fingers. I scramble as it rolls to the edge.

A boot heel crushes my wrist.

I scream. There's no agony to match it.

"There was no way you were gonna beat me." The voice is muffled. The figure looms over me, clad entirely in a swirling, featureless gray, like he's wearing storm clouds for his jumpsuit.

"Your time's up."

He has the staves. Joins them together, sending off a blast of crackling energy that turns the night into day.

He peels back his mask.

Me.

"Wait," I gasp.

"Too weak," he mutters. "And too late."

He steps aside.

Edith Pathkiller strolls up.

"Oh, man." I sag with relief. "You're here."

No smiles. No acknowledgement. Nothing but that stern look, coupled with purple sparks skittering around the edges of her eyes.

She lifts her bow from six feet away and lets an arrow fly straight at my forehead.

No!

I tore the sheet aside. I was sweating like I'd run across the city. And there was a lump between my eyes. Probably because I'd rolled clean out of bed and whacked the table.

"Mercury?" Loredana's voice was sleep slurred. "All right?"

"Yeah. Okay." I squinted at my phone. One thirty. My heart thumped along without any hope of getting back so sleep, even if I'd wanted to. The dream had been too intense. I couldn't clear my head.

"Mm-okay. G'back to sleep." Loredana rolled over. Soft snoring followed in seconds.

"Sorry. Not gonna happen yet." I leaned back across the bed and kissed her.

Then I pulled the supersuit out of the closet.

Three minutes later, I sprinted across rooftops, heading deeper into the city.

Took bigger leaps as the apartment blocks and business towers grew, but hey, it was a great workout. The pulsar stave's energies buzzed through my body, letting me sprint faster than a bicycle messenger. Every time I needed a bounce, I pushed off with the prosthetic leg, channeling the tachyon bursts into its reservoir.

Wow.

Talk about flying.

I grinned beneath the mask. Too bad nobody was watching—but even if they were, all they'd see was a smudge against the smog. The suit was in full-on camouflage mode, the gray and black dazzle pattern having refracted to match the background.

Eat your heart out, Predator.

Ack. On second thought, he'd be the one to take that seriously.

I followed DeLeon to Fourteenth and then hung a right down that street until I'd gotten to the Brewery District. Still way too many boarded up storefronts in the neighborhood. A handful of the craft beer hotspots that had popped up in the past decade were winding down for the night, with music drifting up from open windows. Clusters of men, women, and mixed bunches wove their ways along the sidewalks. Nobody walked solo. The renaissance hadn't totally cleaned away the grime from the previous half century.

Lots of cheap rentals, though.

One set of apartments was on the corner of Fourteenth and Juarez, a five-story brick and stone complex of windows so close together you could pass your neighbor the Grey Poupon.

I needed Three Oh Seven.

Okay, I'll admit, it wasn't the subtlest visit, and I should have called, but after the weird day and the dark dream, only one person was gonna be able to make sense of it.

Edith Pathkiller.

Because she'd shown me stuff before—waking dreams that had come true. Like when Loredana and I had gone after the original cyber-spiders in Oklahoma back in the spring. She'd dragged me smack into the middle of what I'd assumed was her vision—and that very scene had played out not a couple days later.

But I didn't have her phone number. And nobody was going to let a semi-invisible vigilante into their apartment building at a quarter to two in the morning.

Instead, I jumped across the street at treetop height and clung to her windowsill like an invisible arachnid. Knocked on the glass.

No answer.

"There's a shocker," I said.

Good news? A light was on. And the window was open a smidge.

"Okay, Edie?" I pitched my voice loud enough—I hoped—so she could hear, and I wouldn't wake the neighbors. "I got a problem. Got time for a counseling session?"

I peered through the glass into the studio space.

Bed was made. Kitchen was clean. Couch was free of mess. Bathroom door was wide open, the space dark and empty. The light I'd seen was from a small lamp on a timer, illuminating a photo of a tiny girl laughing, trying to squirm out of a hug from a grandparent who looked super ancient.

But no Edie.

"Well, crap," I muttered. "Now what?"

So, I broke into her apartment.

CHAPTER NINE

D on't tell Ramos.

I swiped Edie's laptop.

Look, it's not like I had much of a choice. We needed info on where she'd gone, and it's not as if I could Facebook stalk her.

If it makes you feel any better, I slept terribly after I slid back into bed in the middle of the night. Loredana must have been exhausted, because she didn't do much else but murmur, "Jolly good, yes, I'll file that spreadsheet analysis after I shoot him," with her eyes closed.

My dreams? No shooting. Just a spectral Edith Pathkiller glaring at me from a storm cloud, while lightning bolts leapt between skyscraper-sized pulsar staves. Didn't help that they split open the ground, tremors tearing those staves down as a pair of shadows stepped out of the fissures. Their moves mimicked each other perfectly.

And each had a pulsar stave in his right hand.

They came after me, in flashing speed that I recognized, because it was a move I'd practiced. Three times. Kicked my butt, every single time.

I couldn't drag myself out of bed until eight.

Loredana was gone. She'd left a note on an empty pizza box

by the trash can. *Breakfast with Kimball. Too many meetings to count. Doubtless I'll be late. Terribly sorry. Call me, we can get lunch. Love you!*

I half-smiled because I had that stupid laptop tucked under my arm. Didn't get the chance to tell her. Didn't really want to, but those are the kind of things you share when you're married, especially to someone who's technically your boss at a super-secret foundation that handles cross-dimensional incursions.

My next thought? Yeah, not Ramos, like I already said, though there wasn't anyone I trusted more, besides Loredana. He was a cop. A stern one. I'm pretty sure I'd earn some major wrath if I asked his help digging through stolen property. Plus, his knowledge of computers and all things related was limited to how to text and call on his phone, I was pretty sure.

Which left one person. A tech wizard who adored me.

Liz slurped a bright blue frozen drink through her straw. I swore it was glowing, but given the lights of Tracking, that wasn't really a surprise. "Really?"

"Yes, really, Liz." I glanced around Tracking for what felt like the ninetieth time. Only two other techs were on duty, glued to their display screens, like zombies when someone rang the dinner bell for brains. They wore headphones that could have been used by those guys on the airport tarmacs who waved planes in and out. I figured they were noise cancelling but kept my voice pitched low just in case. "Hack into Edie's laptop."

She giggled, choked on frozen drink, then grimaced. She slapped a palm to her forehead. "Ow, ow, ow!" Liz hissed. "Brain freeze."

"You're welcome."

"Mercury, nobody calls it hacking. We don't even need to."

"Look, Liz, if it makes you uncomfortable, I'll find another way, but I really need—"

"Uncomfortable?" She snorted. "It's a Procyon-issue laptop

so we're not talking about private property and besides, if Ms. Pathkiller was worried about someone reading personal information, she'd be kinda silly to keep it on a device I have the passwords to."

I blinked. "You …? Oh."

"Yep." She popped open the laptop lid and, eyeing me with sudden and apparent suspicion, swiveled it around so her eyes were visible over the top edge. "No peeking."

I covered my eyes with my hand but pried my fingers apart wide enough to wink at her through the gap.

"You're a goof." Liz rattled the keyboard, then stopped in mid-strike. She leaned back, searching the ceiling with such intensity I thought she was waiting for the sprinklers to go off. Then she snapped her fingers and tapped on a few more keys. "There! We're in."

"That's it?" I scratched the back of my neck.

"So not dramatic, right? Sorry, Mercury."

"There goes my fantasy of watching an epic hacker at work." I gestured to the space next to her chair. "Can I …?"

"Sure." Her eyes flicked from spot to spot in the screen, following the mouse as she tapped on the trackpad. The desktop of Edie's computer didn't look any different from most others, including my tablet—a few icons for Internet navigation, shortcuts labeled with generic names like, "Recycling," and, "My Documents." Nothing marked "Top Secret Plans I'm Keeping Quiet About" or anything else sinister. "Can you give me an idea of what we're looking for?"

"Not a clue. But she got wigged out during my talk with her yesterday. Something came over her—as in, an external and not so good influence."

"I heard! We ran a boatload of scans once she reported the aberrant activity, without any success, so I forwarded the report to Alvarez and boy did he get down here fast! I though he must have run in, his face was so sweaty—and no deodorant! You could smell him from—"

"Okay, enough, and also, gross." I waved my hand. Way too easy to imagine the stink. "Focus."

"I *am*." Liz rolled her eyes. "So, it was bothering me, because I couldn't bring up any indication of tachyon infiltration—you know, something that might tell us the Whisperer was up to something bad. But then I remembered the neutrinos."

"Right." I nodded. "You had a lead on our wacky new astral fiend."

"Yeah! It was a teeny-tiny surge, but I should be able to track it again. And there were definitely trace amounts of neutrinos in a similar configuration leftover in Forecasting."

"But what's the deal with those and the weird symmachites the fiend broke apart into?"

Liz shrugged. "All I know is, Cyril thinks we'd have a better shot of figuring out where they come from if we watched for neutrino surges instead of our usual tachyon spikes."

"Sounds good." I tapped the laptop shell. "So, can Cyril tell us what Edie's been up to?"

Liz slapped my hand.

"Hey!"

She wagged a finger. "Procyon property, remember?"

"Yeah, and I'm Procyon, plus I already stole it," I muttered.

"Oh. Sure. Well ..." Liz's cheeks darkened. "It doesn't matter much, I'll get Cyril to dig through the hard drive, but Ms. Pathkiller already left us notes."

She clicked on a minimized Web browser. A window opened onto a map of California's border with Oregon. I peered at the tiny location featured in the center.

"Shotgun," Liz said. "It's a small town three hours north on the One Oh One."

Shotgun? Seriously? Not a whole lot up there. "Get me whatever you can out of the hard drive, okay? She might have notes or something else. Anything that'll tell us why she wigged out and went on a road trip."

"You got it." She cracked her knuckles. "Oh, and Ms. Lark-

Hale said she couldn't do lunch. Or maybe dinner. Or both. She's out with Mr. Kimball again."

"Out?" I tried raising my eyebrow in Loredana-esque fashion. I was going for imperious.

Liz giggled. "You know. Procyon tours. Visits with business leaders. Stuff for the community relations side of the foundation. And then they get to spend the afternoon reviewing quarterly performance evaluations of oper—. Oh. Um ..."

"Let me guess. A noun, but not, 'Operations.' More like 'Operatives.'"

Liz shrugged. She became suddenly intent on her monitor, on Edie's laptop, anything but my face.

I felt the urge to plant the pulsar stave through this Kimball guy's face.

Instead, I opted for training.

Hours of sparring with a mechanical set of arms in the Procyon gym did nothing but make me tired. Lunch was leftovers while I read ignored texts from Ramos.

<Mercurians spotted at a protest. Put themselves between police and agitators. No injuries.>

<More Mercurians. Three broke up a drug deal out in Wells Heights. High school kids. Broken windshield of a BMW.>

<Two more Mercurian sightings ...>

I rolled my eyes and tossed the phone away. Seriously, what good was a fan club if all they did was give you headaches?

Speaking of headaches, Liz came up empty, because Edie had used her laptop for the location search and little else. Her emails to an unmarked recipient, lukekay6418, proved even harder to track. Didn't understand all the tech talk, but the email address was proving near impossible to trace. I said *near* because no one should ever count Liz out, but by the time evening rolled around and I glanced at her last text before she went out for Chinese food, she sent nothing but sad face emojis.

That left me with the rest of the night to polish off a plate of tacos, snag a beer from the fridge, and sit out on the steps, enjoying a tantalizing breeze creeping through the stifling air. I rubbed the ice-cold bottle against my forehead. What was the deal with these symmachites? Why was Tenebrae—whatever *that* was—keen on my help, even though it threw a fake astral fiend in my face? And how come Edie took off running?

When was Loredana gonna ditch this punk kid Kimball and spend more time with me?

I winced at the last thought. Super mature.

But I was in a holding pattern. That was the worst part of the job. The calling. The destiny. Whatever. Lots of other people had their parts to play. Me? I was the trigger man. The one who put the monsters down once they reared their heads.

I could have been out fighting crime. Those text messages from Ramos worsened the guilt. Average people, dressing up like me, risking their necks while they chased criminals—that was dangerous stuff. I was better equipped to drop the crime rates, but then again, I was only one guy. If I ran ragged across San Camillo, how was I gonna be any good when the real terrors, the ones no one wanted to admit existed, showed up?

"Don't know how Airfoil does it," I murmured, and sipped on the beer.

The sky had gone dark blue, and the streetlamps flickered on when my phone buzzed. Liz. "Good news?"

"Not on the Edie front. Sorry. But I've got something to take your mind off that—tachyon spike, in the industrial district. The old cat food factory."

I grimaced, then drained more of the beer. "That's gonna smell fantastic. How's it looking?"

"Nine point two on the one to ten quality scale. Particle density's right where it should be for a decent rip. So, you know, it means the fiend coming through's probably a baddie."

"Yeah, they all are these days." I stood and worked a kink out of my neck. Should've stretched more after the workout. "Cat food factory, huh? Send me the address. How much time do I have?"

"It's in your phone, and twenty-seven minutes."

Plenty of time for stroll.

Twenty-three minutes later, I was kicked back on a crumpled crate, head nestled against a moldy bag of Tufty Purr Cat Chow. I know, terrible name. The puke yellow packaging didn't help sell it, nor did the smell, which was just as vomit-inducing. But I let the music from my earbuds jazz me up, a mishmash of Green Day hits, until I didn't care about the rusty warehouse disintegrating around me. All that mattered was the bare patch of floor spreading into the shadows, big enough to house a 747.

"Arrival point is looking good, Mercury." Liz's voice interrupted the tunes, dropping the music volume down a few notches. "We've got Drones Eight and Nine a few yards back from the warehouse, gathering data. Now, that's more like it! Those are the kind of tachyons you'd expect from an Interstice rip."

I could feel a change in atmospheric pressure, like if I were standing on the bay watching a storm scoot up the coast. Something went *clink*. Rats, probably. Knocking over discarded cans. "Funny when the bizarre gets to be so normal you're relieved when it comes back after something stranger, right?"

"Um, I guess so." Her voice trembled a bit. "Still glad I'm in here, behind our new defensive perimeter, and you're out there with the monster but not because I want you to get hurt, it's just, you know, you're the operative and you're really good at it …"

Beeping in the background interrupted her. Even without the sound, I knew what was going on, because the rivulets between the cracked concrete froze over, the ice spreading from a swirling, miniature cyclone building in the center of the open floor. Purple lightning raced up girders. The rip was moments away.

I sat up and drew the stave. Didn't want to light up the place like stadium floodlamps, but I urged the stave to life, until my super suit pulsed with the yellow outlines of accumulated energy. The glow was a nice change from the pitch black all around me.

Until it lit up four sets of eyes. And they weren't the beady pairs belonging to rats.

"It's him! It's really him!" The short, slender woman whooped.

"I *told* you this was the kind of place he was at! This is where the monsters show up!" A gangly Black teen slapped her on the back.

They were grinning, I figured, because of the way the skin crinkled around their eyes, but they had black face masks added to their costumes of yellow striped shirts and black pants. Mercurians. I glared at them, then remembered they couldn't see my eyes or my mouth, until I lifted the lower half of the mask so I could mimic Loredana's trademark scowl of disapproval. Be politic. Be polite. "Are you guys insane?"

A cell phone's flash blinded me. "No way! We're gonna catch the action."

Purple lightning raced together with a roar of air. The rip coalesced with the suddenness of a bomb exploding, showering us with sparks. The breach between our world and the Interstice was a jagged line three feet off the floor, peeling back reality. The space between rippling violet waves was as black as midnight, devoid of all light.

"Wow. Look at that." The woman's tones approached reverence. The rip's purple sheen reflected in wide eyes. Her teeth chattered. "So beautiful."

My earbud crackled. "Fiend incoming, Mercury! Tachyon flux is—um, sideways? The rip doesn't show any signs of abating."

I rubbed at the sweat under the mask. Man. I hadn't done anything more strenuous than yell at idiots, yet. "Look. You two had better run, because what's coming out of that portal doesn't care how much you want to help your community."

"What?"

"Nothing." I twirled the pulsar stave and propped my weight on the prosthetic, ready to pounce. "What've we got?"

"Too much interference to get a clear read but it's way bigger and … hold on. What do you …?" Murmurs in the background filtered across the earbud. "Yeah, I know, but it can't! Let me see that!"

The rip was undulating like a snake coming at me from across a street. I didn't like it when it did that. And worse, the gap between me and the rupture was slowly closing. "Ah, hey, Liz? Want to get a move on, data-wise? 'Cause this thing's trying to come up and shake my hand."

"The fiend?"

"The portal!" I snapped. "Seriously, what's going on in Tracking?"

"We're getting funny readings!"

Tentacles lashed out from either side of the rip, like the creature inside was getting a firm grip before pulling itself out. All the better to kill me with. I scooted backward, shoes dragging on concrete. "Liz?"

"Oh! Okay! I've got it. Telemetry is clearing." She made a small, soft grunt of surprise. "That's kinda cool."

I didn't have a chance to ask what was cool because the fiend stomped out of the rip, putting a school-bus-sized dent in the floor. No, don't ask me how a monster with no feet stomped, because all I know is, he did.

The part that really threw me was his rider.

Yeah. Rider. A figure straddling a narrow portion of the fiend's body, about six feet back from its eyes. Like a knight on horseback, except this one was wearing armor that would have made King Arthur's skin crawl—literally. Overlapping scales shuddered and squirmed, repositioning themselves as the rider clung to the fiend's hide. They were an iridescent, flat black, mottled with gray, each one lined in shimmering violet. The scaly helmet peeled back, revealing a seductive smile and blond hair.

Serena Cyr.

"Hey, Mercury." She raised her right arm. Something I could only describe as a cannon six inches wide and as long as a baseball bat was welded from her wrist past the elbow. "Miss me?"

She fired.

The Mercurian woman screamed. Her younger companion shouted words that would make a *Downton Abbey* character faint.

And things got worse from there.

CHAPTER TEN

Serena's arm cannon let loose a ball of purple-pink lighting, like a birds nest trying to put itself back together, that corkscrewed through the air with the speed of a cannonball. Which was still super-fast.

I was faster.

Energies pent up in my supersuit, channeled there by the pulsar stave, let me hurtle aside. I slammed into the Mercurians, reducing us to a tangle of twelve limbs and three bodies battered by a stack of half-full cardboard boxes. Boxes that felt like they were loaded with rocks.

Bags of cat litter? Seriously?

"Aw!" The Black kid rubbed furiously at his eyes. "That *stinks!*"

"Not as bad as babysitting!" I shoved him down. The next blast from Serena's arm cannon scorched the top of a box inches from his hair.

If that wasn't bad enough, fiend tentacles slashed through the same box, tearing apart our barricade and forcing us to run. Which I'd suggested they do, right away, but since they were semi-paralyzed by what I assumed was abject terror, I did what any self-respecting superhero would do when faced with the need to protect the innocent.

I turned the pulsar stave around and blasted them twenty feet into a giant pile of torn-open litter bags.

Looked like the landing was soft enough. Considering the amount of whining they did after they hit the pile with hefty slaps, they stayed conscious, which was great, because then they could hear my latest advice: "Run!"

The guy grabbed the woman's arm and hauled them toward a section of rusty wall that had peeled back like a tuna fish can.

I spun out of reach of the tentacles, following my own directive, and sprinted toward the wall at a ninety-degree angle from the goofball Mercurians. Even with the astral fiend's shrieks, and the high-pitched cries of Serena's tricked-out cannon, my concentration forced all sounds into a muddled background until all I focused on was my own breathing and footfall.

That didn't mean I was situationally unaware. When the fiend caught up with me, I leapt for the wall.

My boots slammed into the metal. It buckled under the weight, and when I pushed off, it snapped back with the force of a rubber band, catapulting me skyward.

Serena's blasts scorched the air around me. They closed in, until I could feel the heat even through the supersuit's fabric. I gave the pulsar stave a quick twist and separated it into its component halves, which let me cut through an encroaching tentacle and deflect an incoming blast. Two for two.

The astral fiend screamed in response. It landed heavily, the hide bashing the wall. Tremors rattled the beams holding the warehouse up.

I landed in a crouch, high in a set of rafters. "Let's do us both a favor, Serena, and avoid property damage, okay?"

"Are you going to sit there and tell me that now is when you're worried about the fallout from your fights?" Serena shook her head. "With your unpowered groupies mimicking your moves and following you into dangerous situations? But you're upset we might knock down this old building? Misplaced priorities."

"Like yours are any better." Where had the Mercurians gotten to? No sign of them—wait, someone yelled a warning. There: the woman was hunkered by the ripped open swathe of corrugated metal wall. The glow from her cell phone cast her face in pale blue as she held up the dark rectangle. "Whatever happened to a cushy federal salary and benefits?"

Serena laughed. She gazed right at me, but her cannon arm lifted ever so slowly—until it was pointed right at the gawking Mercurian. "I've found something more satisfying. Power. Not the cheap, human power. The real deal."

The moment faltered, like a clock that needed winding, as my brain sped up in vain attempt to figure if I could beat an energy blast in a race toward its intended victim. I repositioned my prosthetic leg, ready for the launch.

"You see it?" Serena smiled. "It took me a while but—"

I hurtled from the rafter, a streak of golden sparks cutting the shadows apart. Serena's words turned to molasses, and her cannon's purple glow incrementally built. I could make it. I had to.

The woman saw me coming and screamed, eyes wide as she scrambled in excruciating slow-motion through the gap.

I was almost there. Could almost get her free. I expected the energy blast to tear me apart—or at least burn like crazy—right before I got there.

Instead, intense cold shot through my body as a tentacle looped my ankle and flung me aside.

Time returned to its normal flow, which stunk for me, because the next few seconds were a disorienting tumble of shattering boxes, tearing cardboard, and exploding bags of cat litter. I wound up on my right side, cradling my rib cage, which felt like Serena had skipped the theatrics and gone right to kicking me forty-seven times with steel toed boots.

"Cute. I like the way you rush to the rescue of any living person who happens into your path." Serena stood atop the astral fiend's tentacle as the beast lowered her with almost regal precision. A choked cry dragged my attention from the strangely calm scenario—to the other tentacle coiled around the Mercurian woman.

Her mask had fallen away. Woman? She was a kid with braces. Late teens.

"Let her go!" The Black guy was back at the gap in the wall. He flung a stubby section of rebar at Serena. Not bad aim.

Serena caught it, crushed the rebar with her gauntlet, and fired the cannon. Metal cascaded down in jagged sheets, pushing her attacker back as he cried out in pain.

Go!

I had pushed up into a starting position, like a runner waiting for the gun, and sprinted for the girl as soon as Serena's attention was elsewhere. Tentacles slapped around me, breaking everything in sight, but other than the spikes of cold reaching for the suit, I didn't feel a thing—not the stabbing pain in my ribcage, not the bruising on my arms. Oh, I'd feel it later. But that didn't matter in the moment. I stepped off a box, flung sideways, then planted both feet so I was horizontal to a support column. Concrete pulverized a second after I left it when the fiend slapped out. Missed, sucker!

The girl was only twenty feet away, near enough I could see the tears glistening on her cheeks—frozen tears on a pale complexion growing ever more ghostly. Her skin wrinkled. But it was a slow drain. Like the fiend was playing with its food.

News flash. That just pissed me off more.

I touched down behind the astral fiend's lump of slime-covered eyes, pivoted, and drove the staves into one each. Blue ichor spurted around me. The swarm of tentacles went limp as a shriek rattled the entire building.

The girl fell from its grip.

I slid down the fiend's backside, boots slipping on the ooze left in the wake of my counterattack, arms outstretched. Almost had her …

Pink and purple light exploded around me.

I lay on my face. Couldn't catch my breath. Pain laced my spine, like Medan daggers plunged into it over and over again at a dozen different wounds. I reached, frantic to slap out what I assumed was a fire. Nothing. The suit was intact. But I might as well have been wearing a wet tissue for protection.

The girl lay on her side, six feet away, shivering. Her eyes were unfocused, the browns of her irises having faded. *Come on. Get up. Get out of here. You can do it.*

No idea whether I said that to me or her.

A jagged metal boot crushed my left wrist with enough pressure that I was gonna be cradling it tomorrow while my Mcdan physiology struggled to heal fast enough. Serena gazed down at me, but her gorgeous face was gone, replace by what I assumed was the armor's mask—a solid gray plate, riven with twin lines cut down either cheek, underneath a glowing purple eye slit. At least, I assumed its where she could see out of. All I could make out was a narrow window that let me see the Interstice itself roiling, a chaotic terrain filled with rough peaks, plunging valleys, and purple lighting that tore the skies apart.

"I wanted you dead," Serena said. "I still do. But we don't always get what we want. Not right away. There's still a part of me that's a rule-follower. The good agent. Except I'm not serving a corrupt homeland. I'm serving the one true power."

I grunted. "Pretty sure ... The Big Guy Upstairs would disagree."

Serena's gauntlet, the one from which the cannon projected, grew until it and the cannon were inches from my arm. I swore the energy crackling at its aperture were enough to give me sunburn. "Just because I'm supposed to bring you in alive, doesn't mean I have to bring you in undamaged. How about you give me a hand?"

Not a bad joke. A groaner, sure. And I'd probably regret chuckling in five seconds when she blasted my hand off. I squirmed under her boot, but the astral fiend slithered across me, lending its ponderous, energy-sapping weight.

Lousy way to go. I wished Ramos would show up, guns blazing. Or Wilhelmina would somersault through a broken window, dagger slicing. Or that I could at least say good-bye to

Loredana.

Heck, I'd even take a torrent of advice from Liz.

The static in my earbud cleared. "Hey! Hey! You've got to get up. The rip isn't closing. It's getting worse, okay? There's a neutrino pulse unlike anything I've ever seen before and I've dispatched Garvey with Wilhelmina so they can close it but I don't even know if the portal device will work on something like—"

Serena kicked the side of my head. The earbud crunched, Liz's rambling lost in the final squeal.

"There we go," she murmured. "Just us."

The rip moaned.

Not even kidding. Just like a ghost.

And then it froze, for a good couple of seconds, and went completely silent. The absence of sound was so jarring all of us—me, Serena, even the fiend, lost interest in each other.

The dark as midnight core of the rip flickered like a TV set losing signal, then exploded with light.

It was like someone had opened a portal onto the surface of the sun and forgot to hand out shades. The light was the most beautiful, piercing sight, consuming my vision without hurting my eyes. Rainbow colors coruscated around its fringes as the spreading illumination ate up and replaced the rip's dark malevolence.

The effects were immediate.

The fiend went into a frenzy, tentacles whipping at everything inside. Me? I had the advantage of being squashed to the concrete. Serena, standing there in all her supervillain posturing, got flicked like a fly at the dinner table.

I thought the fiend was gonna make a run for it, but it charged the new portal, bellowing in anticipation of a better meal, I guessed.

Which made it all the more satisfying when another, *bigger*, fiend poured out of the rip and ripped the wounded astral fiend apart.

The new attacker took its time, plucking tentacles off almost one by one, and with identical shrieks—although, the more I concentrated, the more the new guy's voice sounded like it had a synthesized edge to it. Very eighties electronic. Its hide was shimmery, too, a silvery-copper mix instead of the ichor-slathered violet and obsidian of the real fiend.

I noted "real" because when the dying fiend managed to inflict a wound on its attacker, the new guy didn't bleed. He lost chunks, but he was definitely more resistant.

Okay. Focus, Mercury. Those beasts were occupied with each other. Check on the people.

I scrambled to the wounded Mercurian. Checked her pulse. Still there. The color seeped back into her eyes. "Can you hear me?" I asked.

Her teeth chattered, but she nodded. She cradled herself in vain attempt to stop the shaking.

"Okay. Hang on." I picked her up, straightened, and grimaced as all the injuries I'd accumulated accounted their presence simultaneously.

Thankfully, a clatter of metal let me know that the Black guy had survived the wall's collapse. Bloodied, bruised, outfit torn, but mostly, he just looked pissed off. "Clara!"

"She's alive. Get her to a hospital. Don't be surprised if you get a visit from my friends. Let them do their thing." I waited until he had her in a firm grasp, then pulled him close, nearly strangling him with his collar, and growled, "And don't ever, ever follow me again."

The kid nodded so hard I thought he'd lose his eyeballs. He snuck Clara out through the wall into the night.

"Mercury!" Serena tore a pair of boxes apart. She would have looked way more intimidating in her Interstice armor if cat litter hadn't been clinking off the shoulders. "Call that thing off!"

"Not on my payroll, sorry." I cracked my neck. "Let's let them have their playtime. You ready for Round Two?"

She snarled and came at me.

So, Round Two.

Turned out that nifty gauntlet of hers could double as a blade if she shaped the metal sharp enough. Which she did. I parried incoming blows, but one slid along the pulsar stave, cutting across my arm. Ripped a clean line up the suit, where it was supposed to be tear resistant.

A squeal cut across my concentration even more deeply—the death song of an astral fiend. Serena's ride had just been skewered by the new guy. The light emanating from the portal intensified as the new guy—shiny fiend? I was slow on nicknames, as bad as my head was spinning—pulled the astral fiend's core apart, spraying their end of the warehouse in blue ooze. The corpse began sublimating almost immediately, so, definitely a regular one.

Serena struck a blow that sent me spinning. I stopped the spiral with my back foot, a tremor rising into the stump where my real leg should have been, seizing the leg. That kept me on my knee when I should have been leaping back at her.

"Tell me where it came from!" she snapped. "Who brought that fiend after me? What do you know about it?"

"Nothing I'd tell you." I used the stave as a cane. I really didn't know. But I had a hunch.

That hunch materialized as a new, blazing light flooded the entire warehouse, bleeding into every corner. The pulsar stave sang with energy, and I mean that literally. Like a full brass orchestra was blaring between my fingers.

Serena screamed, because her armor was sizzling.

A faint shape stepped through the light—a human shape, with no features. But it spoke, as clearly as if it'd been standing behind me.

Tenebrae.

Help.

Banish.

Finish.

The new fiend disintegrated into a cloud, the miniscule flecks dragged back into the fading light. Darkness spread from the rip, returning it to the normal black and purple, as the figure dissipated like a dream. In its place, a new shape barreled out, a shadow that took form and, more importantly, took Serena by surprise when it struck her with a shining, tri-bladed axe.

The shockwave threw her at the nearest wall. Serena punched through, armor melting away, revealing her lithe body in a form-fitting gray shirt and pants. Purple lightning encircled her limbs.

Before I could get a fix on her, or stop her from regaining her footing, she melted through a miniature version of a rip.

The big rip—the one that had spawned the whole mess—snapped shut. I was left crouched on the floor, panting for breath, the only other sound the scratch of leather boots through kitty litter spread on the floor.

"Mercury." My brother, Teget, knelt beside me, with his axe held at the ready. It hummed with the energies of the Interstice, like a tuning fork in harmony with the pulsar stave. "What madness has brought me here?"

"I was hoping …" I held back the bile rising in my throat. "You could tell me. Before I throw up."

Serena disappeared. Yeah, I know, everybody had that part figured out. Couldn't find a trace of her on the scans. Drones Eight and Nine circled the industrial blocks for hours, staying above the clouds, where SCPD couldn't see them. Ramos and his Extraordinary Crimes Task Force—SCPDECTF—cordoned the area so the damaged building could be cleaned up. Didn't envy whoever it was they dragged in from public works to sweep all the cat litter.

Didn't matter. Zilch. Not so much as a blip, in terms of clues as to her next whereabouts.

But we got plenty of footage.

"Freeze frame!" Liz slapped her touchscreen tablet-console. Drone Nine had captured a blurred image of Serena during the battle. "So that's the armor you were talking about? Cool."

"Super cool." I shifted the ice pack on my wrist, which dulled the pain from a fierce stab to a throbbing ache. "Wasn't as cool to battle as you'd think. Can you get us any info on its composition?"

Liz resumed the video. "Depends on how accurate a scan the drones could get me through the interference from the rip ... Hey, where'd it go?"

"The armor? Run it back in slow motion. You'll see." I'd only noticed because my powers had slowed things around my—or at least, upped my perception so that everything *seemed* slow. I'd never actually timed it. Didn't get that many chances to check my watch in the middle of a life-or-death struggle.

But when Liz replayed the footage, she saw plainly as I had the way the armor melted off Serena.

Hang on. Not off. Into.

"She has absorbed the shell." Teget sat in a nearby chair, spinning the axe's silver and brass handle between his fingers. As familiar as his face had become at Procyon—with his head shaved bald, dark moustache and goatee combo neatly trimmed—he still stood out because of his style of dress. Nobody else went for loose-fitting linen tunics under a leather vest, over gray trousers tucked into boots that had a decidedly hand-tooled appearance, right down to the brass rivets,

I think Liz was jealous, by the way she kept eyeing those boots. They weren't Chucks like she preferred, but hey, what was? "That's, um, new. Look, she's limping away? How badly did you injure her?"

I squinted at the screen and Serena's miniature form until she vanished through the smaller rip. "Not enough to make her stagger like that."

"Same side where she was shot," Liz murmured.

"Say what?" Thankfully, my brain put the pieces together just a few seconds after rearranging them. She was right. Serena had infiltrated Procyon's temporary base out in the old missile silo north of town a while back and had opened rips right smack in that facility's version of Tracking. Loredana's timely arrival had introduced Serena's abdomen to bullets.

"You know, it's really not fair that she didn't die." Liz scowled as she closed the drone's video file and dumped into a case folder with the day's date and tagged it "Active."

"On that point, none of us would disagree." Teget slapped my shoulder. "It is for the best, then, that I was able to aid you in your moment of need."

"Hey." I rolled the tightness out of my shoulder. "Not a lot of 'need,' thanks very much. If those Mercurians hadn't been stuck underfoot, it would have been a whole lot easier."

Teget grinned. "Of course. The armored warrioress was of no concern, was she?"

Liz giggled.

I glared at both of them. "Look, if I froze up and got my butt handed to me by every new thing we saw roll out of an Interstice rip, I'd have been dead a long time ago. So, move past the 'Ha, ha, I rescued Mercury,' to the obvious—what were you doing there? And why was a fiend playing a horror version of *Monty Python and the Holy Grail*?"

"Oh! The Black Knight!" Liz cried. "'Tis only a flesh wound!'"

"I have never met this Mr. Python …" Teget stroked his beard. "But if the legends of the Grail are true, and he has found it—"

I shook my head, which was a mistake, because the contents of my skull rattled like marbles. Ow. "Never mind, Teget. Spill the details."

"I have been on several forays through the Interstice through the waypoint outside Meda, in our most ancient forest. We have not suffered any incursions, for which we are most grateful, but word of sightings elsewhere in our lands had disturbed the city fathers. Word of the Kutsatuta returning."

Great. Kutsatuta. Roughly translated as unclean. They were Medans banished from the city for high crimes and misdemeanors, especially during the reign of my grandfather, Naos. Bad move on his part, because they joined up with Alexander Arkwright and were instrumental in stealing the Hedron of Orbits, which in turn betrayed Arkwright and nearly destroyed San Camillo. "She was with them?"

"It seemed as much. It was on one of my forays I witness her don the shell."

"The shell of what?"

Teget shrugged. "For that, I do not have a name. It is a fabled armor that has its provenance deep within the Interstice, at the darkest core of the realm in which the Whisperer resides."

I grimaced. Didn't help my headache. Or my wrist pain. "Hold up. You're telling me, the powerful artifacts you've been protecting—the ones guarded in Meda's temple—they're not the only ones? There's some that exist outside it?"

"More than exist. This shell was created during the height of our conflict millennia ago, during the civil disarray that nearly destroyed our realm and led to the collection of many relics in the Atrium of the temple."

"Meda's schism," I murmured. "This armor suit dates from that time, but was built by the bad guys? And no one's seen it since?"

"Not until I glimpsed the treasonous woman wear it," Teget growled. "Bestowed upon her by the Whisperer himself, it would seem."

"Too much seem, not enough certain." I leaned back in the chair, cradling my injured arm. "Okay. Look. Serena said she didn't want me dead. Who knows what the Whisperer would want with me alive—but whatever it is, it's probably bad."

"Duh." Liz was deep in the case file, perusing screen after screen of data in the form of text, charts, and images.

"Thanks for the analysis. I'm serious. Her showing up right after Edie's got spooked and gone AWOL? Bad timing. And then there's the whole other fiend showing up—"

"Oh!" Liz kicked the underside of her desk. Teget leapt to his feet, axe brandished, and I was pretty sure he would have slit her console in two if she hadn't been beaming like she'd won tickets to the next five Comic-Cons. "Sorry. Buy yay! Because Drone Eight picked up way more data on that other fiend's arrival than we'd been able to get before! I can tell you right away that it didn't come from the Interstice."

I made a face. "But I saw it come out of the rip. The drones did, too. Didn't they?"

"Sure, with the naked eye. Or naked lens. Lenses. Whatever." She blew out a breath and her pink spiky hair swayed. "Look!"

Liz produced a graphic on her screen and swiped it up. The

huge monitor at the front of Tracking blazed with the graphic. It was easy to understand, and there was no way I was gonna admit my relief aloud. The Interstice was a big purple oval. A thin black line lanced left, terminating in a jagged purple slash—the rip.

A yellow line lanced up out of a cloud of sparkles, intersecting the rip. The sparkles were labeled with a huge red question mark.

"This is—strange," Teget said slowly.

"Not really. It explains the neutrinos I've been reading. Told you I'd be able to get some more data once I knew what to look for! Okay, so stay with me—" She leaned closer, elbows balanced on her knees, and whispered, "I think there's another Interstice."

Teget and I stared at her, then glanced at each other. "That's … Not a thing. Right?" I gestured to Teget like he should chime in, because it was really bothering me that he wasn't.

"I do not know," he said.

"See? No such thing."

"Mercury." He frowned. "There are mysteries of the universe that only its creator knows for certain, and He has not chosen to reveal all to us. Time will tell."

"Super." I pinched the bridge of my nose, forgetting all about the ice pack, which dripped condensation into my eye. "Because one evil dimension wasn't enough."

"But this is good news!" Liz said. "We know whatever's using the rips is hijacking them, kind of interfering with their formation and—I'm pretty sure—even taking over the astral fiends as they're in transit. That's why the chunk of the one that attacked you was infested with symmachites."

"Wait wait wait. The symmachites are from the Interstice, though. You tracked their tachyon signatures this spring. When Loredana and I hopped across the country to track the bigger brothers down."

"I know, but those were mutated. Specifically engineered to breach into the Interstice. These, the real deal, they're not—and they latched onto the astral fiends, rebuilding them."

"So, the one that attacked me while I was on vacation …"

"It was in the middle of being, I guess, reprogrammed."

Teget paced a tight path in front of Liz's console. "I do not comprehend all of what you speak, but if I can discern but a fraction, then I understand that someone or something is attempting to come into this world by, as you would say, hitching a ride along the portals from the Interstice."

Liz clapped her hands and blew Teget a kiss with both sets of fingers. "Hot and a genius!"

"Well." If Teget blushed any harder, he'd stay Bob the Tomato for the rest of his life. "I thought my transit was out of the ordinary. It was a long moment that passed."

"You're kidding. What about the guy?"

"Which guy?" Liz frowned.

"The glowing figure. You're telling me it's not on the drone footage?"

"Just the light changes," she said. "There wasn't a discernable figure."

"Sure there wasn't," I muttered. "Come on, guys, how many more times do I have to hear Tenebrae before somebody other than crazy Edie takes me seriously?"

Teget's boots squeaked on the floor. He tightened his grip on the axe. "Tenebrae."

"Yeah. That's the name."

"How do you know it? Tell me."

"Hey, relax." I stood. If Teget was gonna spaz out, better we took the discussion into the hallway. All the high-tech gear in Tracking reacted badly to superpowered weapons—and probably the tachyons emanating from them when their owners got worked up. "I just said—"

"Tell me!"

Teget's voice rebounded off the ceiling, a metallic thunder to the two words.

"Hey." I swept the pulsar stave up under his nose, and let it sit there, inches away, hoping it would sizzle his nostril hairs. Must've got his attention because his posture slackened. "Chill.

Out. It's a name. Whoever's pulling these extradimensional strings has that name and has asked me for help."

"Did you answer?"

"Why does everybody—! Yeah, I said yes. To get him to shut up."

Teget groaned and sank into his chair.

"Who is this guy?" I kicked his boot. Because, I figured, that's what brothers do. "Who's Tenebrae? And what's his game?"

"I do not know his aims, nor how he has survived." Teget's voice trembled. As panicked as he looked, I thought he was gonna ask for a comfort blankie. "But it was he who ended the schism between the two factions of Meda. It was he who single-handedly ended the death and destruction that could have ripped worlds apart."

"How?" Great, even my tone went *sotto voce*.

"By obliterating five thousand warriors from both sides with an unyielding light, so bright that another thousand were blinded and when the deed was done, clouds shrouded our land for days." Teget shivered. "And that, brother, is why he is Darkness."

"Darkness." What Ramos had called him. Said it was a Latin phrase. "But he's Light. And from a—what, an alternate Interstice?"

"We can find out." Liz's hands flew across her board. "Suzi? Re-task Drones Ten through Twelve. Get their sensors tuned in for neutrinos but concentrate their search areas on any known rip manifestations in the past, um, eighteen months, for now."

"On it!"

The tech spoke? I grunted. Something about the line of inquiry spurred my memory of black and white photos, plus their accompanying coded documents. "So, what're the odds we've got records of this? Like, a previous phenomenon?"

"No way. Cyril just ran about twenty searches. Twenty-two. No mention that fits what we're looking for."

"Hang on." I know, I know. Cordelia Keyes told me to keep it secret. But since neither Loredana nor I were getting access to the Historic Vaults any time soon … I opened a saved file on my phone. "Here."

"That's—they're—" Liz fumbled for the phone. Her hands trembled. "I've never seen anything like it. How old is the photo?"

"A hundred plus. They were here, whatever the cyber-spiders or the symmachites or their assorted relatives are really called. And my source was, ah, pretty sure Procyon didn't want anyone to know about it."

"If this is a path that leads to Tenebrae, I would not walk it, Mercury," Teget said. "No matter what these images reveal."

"We all know that's not gonna happen." I rolled my eyes. Seriously. How many times had I been blessed with an abundance of caution? "Liz, I'm gonna send you a file. See if you can translate it."

"Right. Got it." She wrinkled her nose when she downloaded the encoded document from her email. "Ew. That's a nasty code. Give Cyril a few days. Maybe less, if he's not cranky."

Wasn't about to ask how a hot rod computer could be cranky. Probably was worse than the blue screen of death. "Speaking of Cyril, what'd he crack from Edie's computer? Anything about Shotgun? The town, that is."

"Um, just that she was really interested in their bars. She'd hit every website and Facebook page. Even trolled Instagram. Really focused on photos."

I nodded. "Gotcha. She was looking for a familiar face."

"Yeah, like his." Liz shook her head, gaze still fixed on my phone.

"Who?" I craned my neck. Oh. She'd moved to the next photo in line, the one of trio of related guys in the middle of a Florida swamp. "The geezer? I don't know. Not my idea of great way to spend retirement."

Liz stared up at me. "Don't you recognize him? I mean, okay, he's not as old in the official record but he's still *hot*, like Idris Elba hot—"

"Liz. Name?"

She let her fingers do the talking. Or tapping. Whatever. Point was, a new window brushed aside her assorted data, including the encoded letter. A dossier appeared, with the same Procyon letterhead and insignia that anyone who worked for the foundation's supernatural side of things had in our databases. This one, though, was edged in twin gold lines over a sepia background.

The guy's face smiling out of the left corner, in a sepia photograph, did indeed belong to the same old dude in my secret stash of cyber-spider data. Except he only looked to be in his forties. And the image was cracked. Like, on a glass plate? Plus, the edges were tattered.

"Lucas Kimball," Liz breathed, with the same tone she reserved for uttering the name "Jason Momoa."

Kimball. "As in, the young board member guy? The one Loredana's been palling around with?"

"As in, one of the two founders of Procyon, and a good-looking ancestor, have to say."

I did my best to not jump. Teget, of course, brandished the axe again, because apparently all this talk of weird Interstices and Tenebrae upped his brandishing game. I managed a slow turn and a quizzical glance, instead of yelping.

Loredana had entered Tracking, unobserved by us three goobers, and stood just inside the door, accompanied by two guys from security. She wore a curvy black dress, which ended abruptly at the shoulders and knees, with a gleaming silver necklace. Had those sapphire earrings, too, the very same I'd used to hunt for her location when she'd been cast into enemy hands through a portal.

Didn't like it that the guy next to her was admiring them just as much as I was.

It was his voice, deep and mellow, that had spoken. Handsome kid. And I could say kid because he barely looked out of college. A few inches shorter than me, but if he had been a student, he didn't spend all his time behind a computer screen. His body was compact and tense, ready for a tussle, even though he was sporting navy-blue jacket and slacks, both pinstriped. He smoothed the pale-gold tie, showing off a pair of gold rings on his right hand. Warm golden-brown complexion, with waves in his hair so perfect I kinda wanted to check my 'do and make sure it was combed. Which it wasn't guaranteed matted from the supersuit.

"This is him." The kid grinned and held out his hand for me to shake. "The main man."

I used the pulsar stave to slowly nudge the offered shake aside. Sue me. I didn't feel like cozying up to the guy who appeared to be on a date with my wife. So, I sidled up to her, looped an arm around her waist, and kissed her on the cheek. "Hey, babe."

"Good evening." She touched my face, gently turning me toward the kid. "So glad we were able to get away from our endless meetings, only for you to present a cold shoulder to our guest."

Ah. "The board guy." I grinned back at him. "You bored yet?"

"Not anymore." He hadn't moved his hand. "Javon Kimball. Procyon Foundation board of directors, which makes me your boss's boss's boss. So, shake the hand that pays you, all right? Then tell me what's up with my granddaddy's greatest-grandpa."

CHAPTER TWELVE

O kay. I was being petty. Could you blame me? The Javon kid had spent way more time with Loredana over the past couple of days than I had.

Plus, he was rich. Double-bad bingo.

Loredana's hand slipped down to my side and interlaced her fingers with mine. I caught a sly wink from her and those gestures, those simple moves, reminded me to A.) not be a jerk and B.) that she loved me.

If the new guy—excuse me, the board member—noticed, he didn't let on. He had his hand deployed like a cruise missile ready to launch.

"Nice to meet you." We shook. And yeah, we did the grip test thing. His was unsurprisingly strong.

"Same." Kimball nodded.

Should've been just a couple seconds but Loredana sighed and said, "If you're both quite through crushing each other's phalanges and metacarpals, I suggest a release of pressure, since both of you own sets of hands invaluable in their own ways."

We broke free, Kimball chuckling after her speech. "When she's right, she's right. Tell me, Loredana, any comments on the value of my hands?"

Her smile was dazzling, but you couldn't miss the firm threat behind her expression. "Vital to sign those very same paychecks, as you so drolly put it."

"Man." Kimball mock punched my shoulder. "She's feisty. I like that."

"Me too." I tapped the stave against my leg. "What's up?"

"What's up, Mercury, is I'm taking stock. Of Procyon in general, you bet, but of this branch—the real deal—in specific. Things have gone crazy. There's been too much of Procyon in the public eye, and an alarming number of messes around here. Wanna guess what the common denominator is?"

"Don't you mean, who?" I stuck a thumb to my chest. "Word of advice: Don't try subtle. You're not good at it."

"Yeah, you're probably right. I tend to get things done out in the open. End zone. In plain view of the crowd." He leaned back against the wall next to the door, arms folded. "You get that, right?"

"I do. So ..." I gestured to the room. The room in which no one else was speaking, I realized. If Liz buried her face any more in her screen, she'd be among the circuits. Teget had retaken his chair, but he slapped the axe against his palm in deliberate, measured motions. His gaze never left Kimball. "What's your point?"

"Mr. Kimball's directive is to present the board a thorough review of our facilities in and around San Camillo," Loredana said. "It's what has made the past few days such an utter whirlwind."

"Sorry about that, man," Kimball added. "Didn't mean to keep her all to myself."

Loredana's smile never wavered, but I suspect if it had been anyone other than a board member being smart, she'd have verbally eviscerated him. Or maybe literally, if I was lucky. "So, Mercury, please don't mind our intrusion. I'm sure you can bring your operations supervisor up to speed on our current status at a later time. I shall be home this evening with plenty of time to spare."

My watch—and myriad display screens throughout Tracking—told me it was well past 11. "Sounds like a plan."

"Then you can stop staring at Mr. Kimball in such a fashion. You and your brother." She glanced at Teget and raised an eyebrow.

He suddenly discovered intriguing runes carved on the axe handle and ignored all of us. Even started whistling.

"What fashion?" I grinned. "Just checking up on the visitor. Tough guy. Looks like he played football."

"Really?" Kimball snorted. "Why, 'cause I'm Black?"

I froze. Great. Way to back myself into *that* corner, with a board member, no less.

He must have sensed my distress, because his dour expression gave way to a grin once more. "I'm just playin' with you. UDC. Center."

University of Drake City. Offense. I took note. "Look, it's been great locking horns with you, but we've got to get back to business."

"Like I heard—something to do with my ancestor." He rolled his hands. "Go on."

Um … A rapid-fire slideshow of everything we'd learned so far and how it linked together flashed through my brain. Tenebrae's appearance, plus the constant pleas for help. The hijacked astral fiends. Possible "good" symmachites. Edie's freak-out. Her connection to the Reverdin twins, who were operatives before I showed up. And now Serena was clad in Interstice armor, that might have been worn by Tenebrae when he—or it, I guess—singlehandedly ended a civil war among the Medans.

It was a big, tangled knot of threads. And it felt like no matter which one I tugged on, the stupid ball got tighter.

One thing I knew: I didn't need micromanaging. "We'll get back to you when we've got more. C'mon, Teget."

We brushed between Loredana and Kimball, though I made sure to land her a kiss on the cheek as I pivoted past.

"I think we got off on the wrong foot, Mercury." Hold up. Kimball had stuck himself in my way, with Teget coming up short in the hallway beyond. Kimball's jovial grin smiled, his eyes narrowing enough that I knew he wasn't finding anything about me amusing. Which was a bummer. "I'm not some lackey sent here on a hunting expedition by the board. I *am* the board."

I rolled my eyes. "Okay, Dredd, if you say so. I'm sure all the college grads who still have their diplomas and mortarboards stuffed in their back pockets get to randomly show up at HQ and boss the operative around. Step aside so I can get back to work."

"Or what? You're gonna sick your guard dog on me?"

Teget snarled. Didn't sound canine, but it conveyed his meaning well enough.

Kimball, to his credit didn't flinch—which meant he was either brave, or stupid. Funny, I had trouble telling the difference between the two sometimes. I know, right? "Call him off and read me in on the mission."

"Gentlemen." Loredana stepped between us, and I internally chuckled at this human chess match we were all playing, until she planted a hand on each chest and shoved us both. Neither being prepared, both Kimball and I stumbled a step. "That is *enough*."

"You're crazy." Kimball smoothed his tie, glowering at her. "Been smiling and chaperoning me all around town for forty-eight hours, now suddenly you're acting like my ma?"

"When your behavior lapses to that of a kindergartener, that is apparently the remedy needed," she snapped. "I won't tolerate any further headbutting. You're not rams, though I have no doubt your skulls are as thick. Mr. Kimball, the nature of Mercury's work, which I oversee as head of operations for headquarters, is too sensitive to be bandied about to anyone with a visitor's badge who happens through the door, no matter his clearance level— or heritage with Procyon. And Mercury? Show respect to that heritage. When the time is right, and we have more solid leads, you *will* read Mr. Kimball into this case. Am I clear to both of you?"

"Absolutely." Her tirade didn't dampen my mood. Hey, I was used to them, long before we got married. Wouldn't be a week at work without them. Kimball, though ... Poor guy couldn't seem to decide if he wanted to go for suave again or try the bluster.

He settled for cold indifference. "I'm heading back to my hotel. Better to call Alvarez and issue my complaint that way. Here's hoping I can bother him at home. Loredana, I'll see you tomorrow at ten for the advisory meeting. And there'd better be a page-long summary of this so-called 'case' ready for my ears."

"Understood."

Kimball turned and found himself toe to toe with Teget. "Problem, Paul Bunyan?"

"Your disrespectful ways would lead to your end were you in my lands," Teget growled.

Kimball smirked. "Best you remember what dimension you're in, baldy."

He left us in a triangle of simmering anger and resentful silence. I blew out my breath and ran a hand through my hair. "So ... That was fun."

"Is that all you have to say?" Loredana folded her arms.

I kissed her again. "Hi, honey! How was your day? Mine was great! Killer armored Serena and all!"

She giggled, then put her hand to her mouth in what I guessed was desperation to not snort along with it. "Ahem. I imagine it was. But you're unhurt. Battered, I see."

I shrugged. "No worse than usual."

She hugged me. "I'm sorry I couldn't be here to quarterback the call for you."

"Quarterback?" I mimicked her famed raised eyebrow. "Football follower, now, are we?"

She elbowed my ribcage. "Quiet, you. Mr. Kimball is quite convinced of his sports prowess. I hadn't the heart to tell him I'm a devotee of the truly named sport."

"Seems like a great guy. Charming. Flashy. Has a face I want to beat in."

"Be nice. He really is well-connected." Loredana indicated Teget, who was preoccupied with the elevator into which Kimball had disappeared. The security boys had snuck into the elevator with him. Must sting to need an escort throughout an organization you're supposed to be in charge of. "Hence his knowledge of our brother's provenance."

Well. That was different. Not a ton of people knew who Teget was, and where he was from. We tried not to advertise dimensional crossovers on the foundation's website. "Fair, but do I really have to bring him into our newest mess?"

"Minimally. Give him enough information to show him we have leads, and their being pursued." She patted my cheek. "Surely you and Elizabeth can compile a succinct summary."

"You bet!" Liz spun in her chair, kicking with her Chucks to accelerate. "We can put together a full report with as many details you need because Cyril has everything already stored under the case notes even though they're not really organized when I first start out because my system's more freeform than what was—"

Loredana held up a hand, her expression pained. Liz pinched her lips together, eyes wide. I hoped Loredana didn't make her wait long. Jokes aside about me being the janitor, I didn't want to mop up brains if her head exploded. "Give me what you can, please, but redact liberally. The less of a trail into our operations Mr. Kimball can follow, the simpler all our jobs will remain."

"That's why I married you." I pressed my hands to my heart. "Because you're stubborn like me."

"And because I am a paragon of beauty."

I blinked. Teget burst out laughing. He held onto his stomach as the chuckles subsided, and even rubbed tears from the corners of his eyes.

"You're not wrong," I said.

"Come." She looped her arm through mine. "Dinner awaits."

"I already ate but you know me. What's an extra meal?" I jerked a thumb at my brother. "Mind if we set another plate?"

"Not at all." Loredana smiled. "Though should I ask if he's experienced the equivalent of jet lag between Earth and Meda?"

"Worry not about my need for rest, Lady Lark." Teget looped his arm through Loredana's other and deftly tugged her from my side. "I shall remain fine company no matter in which realm I reside."

He swept her out the door, winking at me, as Liz dissolved into laughter.

Spoiler: Nobody wanted to cook that late at night. Thankfully, Carlito's was doing takeout. They'd been shut down with a bunch of other eateries, victims of the governor's health orders dealing with the coronavirus pandemic. Then they opened, a brief shining glorious few months of eating outside, only to get shuttered again. How they were still in business was anybody's guess; federal loans probably helped. But the delivery kid kept his mask on at the front door and I did likewise to accept our order of calzones. And no, I didn't have on the supersuit's mask. I'd had one printed up of the cover art. From my book.

Loredana did not, in fact, murder me when she saw it.

"I won't even ask from where you ordered that monstrosity." She poured glasses of root beer for all of us.

Teget sniffed at his, then sneezed when the bubbles hit his nostrils. "Peculiar concoction."

"Needs ice." I dumped in cubes and watched it fizz. But after a bite of calzone, I waited until everyone was chewing in silence before asking, "So, I'm going after Edie, right?"

"Of course." Loredana glanced at Teget. "Would you mind terribly accompanying your brother?"

"Not at all. Someone must make sure he treads with care."

"Says the guy who hitchhikes his way out of the Interstice through astral fiend portals," I muttered. "But still awesome. And I'll take one more guess, hoping I'm on a roll—we're not telling this Kimball guy about this plan, right? Or at least, not inviting him along."

"Correct on both accounts. I will, unfortunately, have to remain here, as he's in town for at least a few more days. Though he has not given us a departure date."

"I should hope it is near to the horizon, rather than far from sight," Teget murmured.

"You liked the guy about as well as I did?" I snorted. "How'd I ever guess? You were super polite."

"I did not like him. His manner struck me as arrogant. And there was something about his presence that alerted me to a potential threat."

"If you mean redirection funding, that very well be." Loredana sighed. She kicked off her shoes. "Let me handle Mr. Kimball. I suspect he is flexing his muscles, as an heir to our founders is wont to do. Save your inquisition for finding Edith Pathkiller."

"Yeah. It'd be a lot easier if we knew what she was looking for before we went looking for her." I wiped sauce from the corner of my mouth with a Carlito's napkin. See? Manners. "But this Tenebrae thing has her on edge—and acting slightly, temporarily possessed. Which is bad. So, as long as Liz can keep an eye on these new astral fiends and watch how the symmachites are jumping from wherever this new dimension is into ours, sent for who knows what reason, we should get some answers. I hope."

"And then there is Serena Cyr."

"Your favorite person." I grinned at her.

Loredana arched an eyebrow, which was code for "Watch your mouth." "Yes, so you've mentioned. Any thoughts to her motives?"

"Not killing me. She wanted me alive. Which is worse, I'm gonna bet. That means Tracking has their hands full watching for two kinds of incursions. You might want to dial up Gemini and keep him on standby."

"Already done."

I nodded. Dominic Zein's specialty was transportation, by means of wristbands. Interdimensional wristbands. Don't look at me like that. Also, he chased down evil twins from an alternate Earth, so he had a busy schedule. "Good deal. He'll be handy if we need extraction."

"I've made arrangements. Though I must say, it does not inspire confidence when you suggest such a contingency."

"Hey. Don't worry about us." I backhanded Teget in the chest. "He'll be more fun than dragging Ramos along. Epic bros."

"Thank you." Teget dissected his calzone with a knife, as if he were filleting a salmon.

"And what of Wilhelmina?"

I winced. Forgot.

"You'd better call her." Loredana took a long sip. "Lest her wrath exceed an astral fiend's."

Boy, when she was right, she was right.

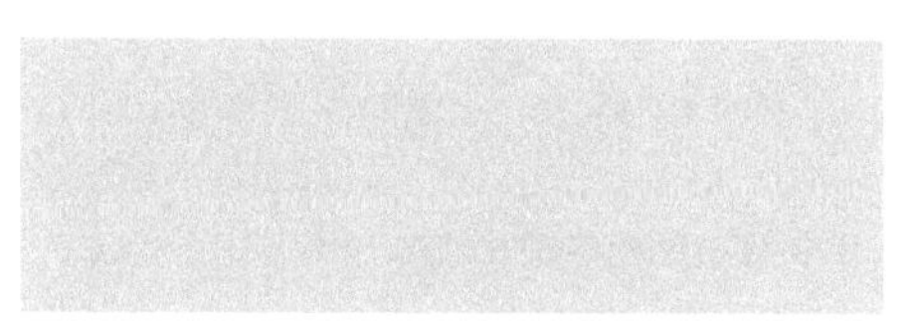

CHAPTER
THIRTEEN

Wilhelmina was a no show.

"Sorry, child." She coughed, a rattling sound, then blew her nose so loudly I thought she'd shatter my phone. "Whatever this bug is, it hit me hard last night. Ain't had more than a few hours of sleep."

"Great. Then you won't miss out on the road trip."

"I'll stay on the phone to Garvey in case we get astral fiends wanting a tussle while you're gone after Edith. Be mindful of your backside, you understand?"

"That's what Teget's for."

"Mm-hmm. I'll keep you in my prayers."

"Thanks." I shifted in my seat. "And if you get any worse—"

"There's no fever, and I can breathe just fine, 'cept through my plugged-up nose. Don't you worry. I'll go get tested as soon as I think it's something else."

I didn't want to imagine how that "something else" might put my mentor—the lady who steered me toward the truth of my very existence—on a ventilator in an emergency room stressed out with super-sick patients. Head colds are bad. Nobody wants to be the one to catch the big coronavirus on top of it. But she'd had her vaccination, so I could put most of the worry behind. "Okay. I'll hold you to that. Just wanted to make sure you were good before we left town. See you."

"That's awfully sweet. Don't get yourselves stomped by whoever you might run into." She chuckled, the sound devolving into a cough, then hung up.

"Stomped." I snorted. "I tell you, where's the confidence in our abilities?"

Teget didn't answer. He was too busy staring out the window at the passing buildings. As often as he'd been to Earth—which was only a handful of times, I had to remind myself—he hadn't gotten used to the technology-heavy society I lived in. Sure, Meda had crazy powerful relics, but those guys were apt to view a microwave as awe-inspiring.

Now, by window, I did mean of window of my Subaru, and yes, I was already driving when I called Wilhelmina. Technically we hadn't "left town," because we were scooting up Bay Avenue toward the One oh One leading out of the city. Still had a few blocks before the multi-story apartment complexes and offices faded into sprawling suburbs that gave way to forested hillsides.

"Shotgun, Oregon." Teget read the words off my phone with care, like was worried about conjuring a new enemy to fight. He pecked at the touchscreen like he'd discovered the Rosetta Stone buried in Egyptian sands. "So many uses for the single word."

"All of them related to the firearm, but we're not here to play *Jeopardy!* while you're riding shotgun. Anything from Ramos?"

Tap. Tap. Tap. Like a leaky faucet. It took every drop of my limited patience to refrain from tearing the phone out of his hand. But I wasn't about to drive and text. It was bad enough monsters kept wrecking my cars.

"The lieutenant is preoccupied with protestors." Teget frowned. "Protestors of what?"

I sighed. "A lot of stuff, right now."

"And as an officer of the law, he hears their requests for justice?"

"Something like that." I tried not to picture Ramos behind a wall of officers in body armor, tear gas canisters and pepper ball rounds flying as bottles and rocks came their way. That was a bad scene for protestors and cops alike. Thankfully, San Camillo had quieted down a lot since the major protests last year. "Tell you what: Read up on it while we drive. We've got three hours and I need to think."

"In that statement resides the opportunity for me to tease you about how deeply you must think, brother." Teget reclined his seat, grinning at me over the phone.

Nice. Guess for all its differences, Meda wasn't without cutting wit.

But his Google searching, interspersed with occasional grunts of surprise, kept him from yapping the entire ride. Gave me plenty of time to focus on the mishmash of the past few days, so I could figure out if Tenebrae was behind this mess or was just an unhappy coincidence. It sure didn't seem like was playing for the enemy team, since he destroyed Serena's astral fiend. Which mean he wasn't necessarily on Syndax's side.

I turned up the volume on the Rolling Stones until I could feel the soundwaves from the speakers against my leg. There were also his repeated requests for help. Which, okay … What was I supposed to do about it? If Tenebrae really was from another dimension, and had put an end to Meda's civil war thousands of years ago, didn't that put him in a heavier weight class? I think that's a boxing metaphor. Whatever. Point was, it made as much sense as Ramos going to his young twin daughters for manpower at a protest turned violent.

No matter how many songs I listened to, or how many times I ran back through the chain of events that lead from my ice cream breakfast getting interrupted to our discovery of Tenebrae's dimension lurking beyond the Interstice, one thing was blindingly obvious …

We were being followed.

No, not in my rip-related missions. Though, that would make a lot of sense. No, I meant, right then, for the last hour leading up to Shotgun's town limits. As in, the black Dodge charger with tinted windows. Never strayed more than a couple car lengths from my bumper, no matter what speed I tried, or if we got passed.

"Great." I nudged Teget. "Hey. Sleeping Beauty."

He'd been snoring softly the last half hour. His snorts sounded like a congested dog's. He tried to discreetly wipe drool from the corner of his mouth. Family trait, I figured. "Yes? Is there danger?"

"Maybe." I tapped the rearview mirror.

Teget frowned at it, then peered at the passenger side's mirror. "You believe it could be the enemy, following our scent."

"If it is, they're not interested in hostilities."

"Well, then." Teget retrieved his axe from the backpack at his feet and wound down his window. A warm breeze, carrying the salt tang of the sea, rushed in, negating the whole point of having the AC cranked up. "Let me pay our unwanted fellow travelers a visit and ask them their purpose."

"Hey! No! Sit!" I grabbed the hem of his shirt. Last thing we needed was for a guy wearing a blue tank top and khaki shorts climbing onto the Subaru's roof and hurtling onto the hood of our chase car. "Not doing the whole fighting on a moving car thing, okay? I've done enough of that to film footage for a Jerry Bruckheimer movie."

Teget glanced at me.

"Lots of explosions. Car crashes." I shook my head. "Never mind. Look, keep the axe out of sight, okay? Let me try something else."

So, I wound down my window and stuck my arm out. I waved, then pointed right, repeatedly jabbing my finger toward the curb. Then I pulled over.

We were coming down a slope toward Shotgun, the town straddling a forested creek that meandered into the Pacific through a broad marsh. The speed limit dropped, and the road got wider, leaving plenty of room for a Subaru to park.

I wasn't so sure about the silver Ford F-350 pickup that passed our tailgating Charger.

It rumbled to a stop three feet from my bumper, so that it loomed over my much tinier ride. The Charger rolled past, then pulled onto the shoulder a hundred feet ahead, brake lights blazing.

I tipped up my sunglasses at the guy who swaggered up from the driver's seat of the pickup. "Lemme guess: I got a taillight out."

"Not my jurisdiction." Hudson Bowe, agent of the Department of Homeland Security and general pain in my rear end, grinned under a pair of aviator shades. Don't know why he needed them. Dude was blocking out the sun, like he could single-handedly kickstart a second ice age. I wanted to know how many cows he ate to get as big as two football players, a younger, blond Santa Claus in white polo shirt, blue jeans, and cowboy boots.

I smiled back, trying to concentrate on his pleasant expression instead of the huge, silver-plated Desert Eagle pistol riding in his holster. "I thought you were busy tracking flying superheroes in Drake City. East Coast isn't any less humid than here, you know. Get yourself demoted to surveillance of everyone's favorite monster slayer?"

"Everyone's favorite? Says who?"

"YouTube. And probably TikTok, but I'm too old for that."

"Yeah, you're a regular old man at twenty-eight." Bowe rapped on the roof. "How's the family?"

"Sleepy."

"Fully prepared to defend his honor, along with his brother's," Teget snarled.

"Whoa, there, down boy." Hudson spread his hands. "I'm just keeping an eye on you fellas. Remember, Mercury? That's what I said I'd be doing."

"Yeeeeaaaahh ..." I dragged the word out. "You were, uh, more abrupt and about ninety percent angrier last time we talked. What's the deal with happy new you?"

"Might ask you the same. Where's Ramos? And Wilhelmina? Not coming on this road trip."

"You know, as much fun as it is not answering each other's smarmy questions, why don't we cut the crap—why'd you follow me all the way up here?"

"Because we got word Syndax has moved people through southern Oregon in the past few weeks—weapons, supplies, too. So, when I see you show up in an area that's got me worried, that doubles my worry."

"Only double? Must be losing my touch."

"You're a hoot, Mercury." He flipped open a pocketknife and worked the tip of the blade under his thumbnail. "Okay, explain your road trip, then."

"Visiting a friend. If I can find her." Look, Bowe had been a jerk from Day One, but he'd been doing his job, so I figured he was owed at least a fraction of the truth. But it also wasn't any of his business. Procyon didn't answer to the feds. Well, maybe the board did. And people like Ramos.

Not me.

"Work friend or personal?"

I shrugged.

Bowe nodded. Couldn't tell if he was still grinning, but his tone got flintier. "Tell you what—stick to our prior agreement. Monsters for you, people for me."

"Where's Serena Cyr fit into that description?"

"Let's let the first person to drag her in call that one."

"Appreciate that."

He leaned in and thumped on the roof. "Take my advice, Mercury—people could give you a hard time. More than usual. Especially here. Steer clear of the hard cases."

He left me to puzzle his cryptic remark. Sure, we were headed into a small town, but it's not like I hadn't been to one and gotten funny looks. Didn't like it but got used to it.

"Was the man of law saying he will ally himself with us?" Teget asked as we drove down the hill.

"Not really. But I don't think he'll mess with us either." Which suited me fine.

Now I just had to find our missing Procyon Forecaster in a tiny seaside town. Piece of cake.

Okay. That piece of cake was moldy and stale. I should have thrown it out.

But seriously! Shotgun, Oregon, had a population of a thousand. That didn't count the extra couple hundred from tourists stopping by, driving up and down the coast. Some of the restaurants among the row of old brick buildings lining the highway where it became Main Street were closed—two of them forever, according to the signs, but there were outdoor dining spots and at least one bar with its front windows rolled up so the tables were open air.

Teget and I flashed Edie's picture at every single one. Not a hit among them.

We even ventured down the side streets, checking at the pair of motels, and stopped at the piers jutting out into the marshes. Deeper channels wound out to the oceans. Between the fishing boats and the kayakers, lots of people were coming and going. Most of them gave us funny looks when I showed them Edie's photo on my phone.

At least Teget kept the ax in his backpack, so the looks weren't even funnier.

What? I wasn't about to have him leave it in the car. Besides, it kept people at further than six feet of social distancing from us, which was fine by me.

A few hours later, my stomach was in full-on revolt, since it was mid-afternoon, and we hadn't eaten lunch. Teget steered us toward Roscoe's Grill, a rundown cement block building with chipped paint that revealed two previous layers beneath but whose open doors tantalized us with the most heavenly beef aroma imaginable. I thought my guts were gonna rip free and feed themselves when I spotted the menu of two dozen different burger combos.

Forty-five minutes later, we had beers, burgers, and fries on the table. Not bad for quarter past four.

"This is getting us nowhere." I belched, then checked my phone's texts. One from Liz—no luck on Edie's whereabouts. She was untraceable by modern electronic means. And I knew if she wanted to avoid us, she could. She had the ability to sense people like me and Teget, those gifted with the ability to operate tachyon-based weapons.

"Then I suggest we savor our repast until we can discern the path forward." Teget was a pro at repasting, all right. He'd demolished all but a mouthful of one burger and was starting on number two. Of *three*. "Furthermore, what better way for you to reclaim your sabbatical which was torn from your grasp."

"Reclaim my ... Ah. Vacation." I smirked and raised a beer bottle aloft. "Wouldn't hurt to relax for an hour or so before we start investigating again."

Teget clinked his bottle against mine. "To future battles and assured victory."

"Right on." I took a swig. Suddenly, everything didn't seem as bleak."

"Hey, China virus."

Ex-squeeze me? Fun as it was traipsing around this Podunk town for a missing Forecaster, my patience was in short supply. Like, toilet paper shortage short supply. I glanced over my shoulder. "You better have a massive, Hulk-sized reason for talking like the biggest, fattest idiot on Earth."

Oops. There were six of them. Burly, four white, two Black. They looked like they came from the docks, overalls and all. The ringleader was a young bald kid with a thick red beard I guessed was covering up two of his three chins. "You heard me. Go back to China and take your plague with you."

I couldn't help chuckling. "Not even close to my home port, buddy. Screw you." I turned back to Teget, winked at him ...

And found myself on the sidewalk, my chair skidding across the concrete. Big fat jerk had kicked it out from under me.

I burst out laughing.

Teget was on his feet. "This is no time for joviality! Let me loose to teach these curs the manners they lack."

"Yeah, I know." I got to my feet, knee aching above the prosthetic leg. I wiped a tear away. "That's why I'm laughing."

"You've been nosing around town, when you should be getting your diseased kind off our shores," Redbeard snarled. "Ain't gonna let you take any more jobs from us."

"Dude, I have no idea what you're talking about, and I'm definitely not from China, but if you want to tango …" I drew the pulsar stave, twisted it until its halves separated, and twirled them like batons. No need to waste powers on these jokers. "I'm all about the dance."

Made it even more impressive when Teget whirled his axe, which he'd removed from his backpack.

Of course, these guys had an assortment of non-gun weapons—two hunting knives, a length of steel pipe, a crowbar, and aluminum baseball bats. On the upside?No guns. They also weren't ravening astral fiends or vengeful warlords from another dimension. Two to six was pretty good odds.

"Charlie! Lay it down."

Great, another bystander? The new guy was just as suntanned as the others, with a five o'clock shadow that clung to sharp cheekbones. Stormy blue eyes struck each of us in turn, like the guy had X-ray vision. The downtown breeze tousled sun-bleached sandy brown hair. He wore blue jeans and a button-down short sleeved shirt, untucked. He smelled of sawdust and varnish.

Of greater interest was the bulge of a gun at his waistband.

"Get lost, Jake." Charlie glowered at him. "You know what I said—"

"And you know I'm a fan of concealed carry, so put your toothpicks away before you contract lead poisoning."

Cheesy, yeah, but there was no mistaking the stern command. Guy had buckets full of authority. Enough that, after thirty seconds of me devising seventeen ways to disarm the six men without putting anyone in the hospital for too long a stretch, grumbles spread among the group.

"You're drunk," Jake said. "Go home, or I call the sheriff and you get taxied in a squad car. Your choice."

The choice meant they swore at him but meandered off. A couple cast glares back my direction. I flipped them off.

Teget growled, his axe shining under the sun.

Jake regarded us with a cool amusement, his thumb hooked near his belt—near his gun. "So, you're the guys asking around about Edie. And judging by the exotic hunting tools, you're Procyon."

"Yes. To the first. Can't confirm or deny the second." I reconnected the pulsar stave and tucked it down by my leg. Didn't like the way he was staring at it, but who could blame him? Then again, I didn't like how he hinted he knew what our real jobs were. "She's a friend of ours. You know her?"

Jake chuckled. "I do, but I bet she'd wished I didn't." He removed his wallet and showed off a credential of him smiling, with a stylized "JD" atop an anchor as his logo. "Jake Drinkwater, private investigator. Edith Pathkiller's ex-husband."

I stared at him. Probably would have given the same look if he'd morphed into a werewolf—and since I'd met a were-*fox*, the expression had gotten used before.

"This," Teget said, "Bears mulling." He reached for the remnant of his burger and scarfed it down.

CHAPTER FOURTEEN

B efore any disgruntled visitors could drop by and accuse me of infecting the entire Western Hemisphere, Jake guided us to the east side of town and up a rutted fire road to his cabin.

"Follow me up," was all the direction he gave as he hopped into a dingy white and brown Ford Bronco. The Subaru was parked a couple blocks away, in plain sight, so catching up was a breeze.

In the meantime, I had Teget text Liz with my words and his glacial typing: <Met Edie's ex! Check Jake Drinkwater. PI?>

His cabin was a sprawling structure of faded wood, with a generous porch and windows under the peaked roof. I couldn't figure out why anybody would brother sitting on their porch so they could stare at trees, until I climbed the steep staircase up to it and turned around. The ocean filled the horizon atop the jagged pines. Now *that* was a view.

Teget took a deep breath and spread his palms along the top of the porch railing.

"Nice, isn't it?" Jake leaned against the jamb. A quiet song drifted through the open door. No, not banjo music. I would have speed run all the way back to San Camillo. "Haven't minded the solitude up here, not by a long shot."

"It conjures the memory of home, and the great forests of my youth," Teget said. "You have been blessed."

"Can't argue that." Jake hooked a thumb. "Interest you guys in a drink?"

"Water's fine." I stifled another burp, courtesy of the beer and burger. At least I'd gotten to finish the meal. "Don't let us keep you from dinner."

"I won't. Meanwhile, you can tell me what Edie's done to get her in trouble."

Huh. Here I thought I was the only one to call her that. Though, if he was her ex … "How much do you know about her work?"

Jake shrugged as we followed him inside. The living room had a couple of sagging couches, both refugees from a thrift shop circa 1972, and a wooden rocking chair that looked hand carved. The kitchen off to the left was a tight space with a slate floor and a narrow island, the top covered with unopened bills, a couple newspapers, and two empty cans of Mountain Dew. Jake swept the whole mess into a trash can. "She was never chatty about the details, but let's just say I'm fully aware Procyon does much more than build affordable housing and improve community green spaces. She had a hand in the fight against the things that go bump, but she didn't tell me what that hand was."

"Close enough." No point in getting into operational secrets with this guy. "We got into a review of her past and she was freaked out by, ah, an old acquaintance."

Teget, who was examining the flintlock rifle hung on display over the fireplace, gave me a look like he'd smelled my last burp but didn't offer a comment.

Jake dug around in the fridge and came up with mustard, mayo, lunch meats and cheeses, and lettuce. Those all got dumped on the island counter. He grabbed a loaf from the breadbox next to the fridge and favored the hunting knife tucked in a sheath on his belt for cutting slices and spreading condiments. "Is she okay?"

"I was kinda hoping you knew. We'd tracked her to here. I mean, it's where she seemed to be going. But she hasn't been in touch, and no one's seen her."

Jake grinned at the sandwich he was carefully stacking, and shook his head slowly, as if savoring not just the smells of his upcoming meal but a favorite memory. "She'd do that. Even when we were married—sometimes before. Wander off to spend time in nature, away from anything manmade, and especially people. Too much interference, she'd say, their personalities and their energies getting in the way of her perceiving."

"Perceiving what?"

"Time. She was big on that. Never used her gift or whatever you'd call it to do things like, I don't know, predict when I was going to leave the toilet seat up ..." He chuckled. "She could tell things were coming, though. Big and small. Like storm clouds building on the horizon. You read about it all the time, people who 'sense,' but she was truly gifted."

"But she hasn't come to you."

"I haven't had a civil conversation with Edie in six years. Maybe longer." Jake cracked open a new can of Mountain Dew and took a long drink. He swirled the contents, seemingly deep in thought.

I tried to imagine being estranged from Loredana for more years than I'd been with Procyon. My stomach turned, and the discomfort had nothing to do with how fast I'd chowed down the super-late lunch. No way I'd be a happy camper when two random—and armed—guys showed up at my front door with bad news that A.) She'd gone missing, and B.) It happened not a mile from said front door.

"We would be grateful for what assistance you could lend us in our search," Teget said. "For she is a formidable warrior, no matter her strange visions and, of late, aberrant behavior."

Jake chewed on a bite of his sandwich. "Warrior, huh? Rumor had it she did consultant work outside Procyon. Security."

"Yeah. It's hush-hush." My phone buzzed. Liz. <Call me.> "Hold up while I take this."

"No problem. Either of you guys hungry?"

I shook my head as I aimed for the door, but heard Teget clear his throat and answer, "What sustenance have you?"

"Guy's gonna empty the fridge before we get back on Edie's trail." I leaned on the porch railing, turned around so I could see Teget chatting with Jake, and dialed Liz. "Hey, it's me."

"Good news! There really is a Jake Drinkwater, private investigator. He's licensed by the State of Oregon. Found him on Facebook. It sounds like he has some happy clients—I mean, happy with him, because this one lady hired him to see if her husband was having an affair, and he was but it wasn't with their babysitter like she thought, it was with the garbageman—"

"Too much. Way too much." I rubbed at the bridge of my nose. "Okay. See what else you can send me about him."

"Well, you can Google, too."

"Wait, are you arguing with me?"

"Duh! I'm up to my earlobes in tachyon feeds and neutrino pulse readouts! Do you have any idea how complex it is to separate out neutrinos from the normal radiation we track?"

"No."

"It's hard! Cyril's actually getting warm, which almost never happens because he's liquid cooled." Liz blew out a breath that reduced the other end of the call to static. "Sorry. We're getting all kinds of weird scanner results from the drones, but nothing's happened yet. No rips, no hijacking like we saw with Tenebrae. Garvey's taken some of the bulkier sensors out on the road, in disguised vehicles. I can't get through to Wilhelmina."

"She's home sick. I'll ask Ramos to check in on her."

"Um, that probably won't happen. There's a bunch of protestors camped out in Rosa Roja Park. SCPD's trying to get them out, a hundred moms are blocking the way in. Guess nobody wants to pepper spray somebody's aunt!"

"Okay. Can Loredana get anyone else to come up here? Generic security toughs, maybe? We could cover a lot more ground searching for Edie with more bodies."

Liz giggled. "She said she has to continue Mr. Kimball's tours because Mr. Alvarez told her, 'Don't let him off our leash.' She did that thing with her eyebrow and stormed out. I thought she was gonna break a high heel!"

I snorted, both at the description and the way Liz's voice dropped into a nasal, whiny imitation of Alvarez's. "So. No Ramos. No Garvey. No Wilhelmina. I don't suppose you heard from Dominic."

"Yep."

"Yep ... And?"

"Oh. He's in Venezuela. I think. Or is it Bolivia? Anyway. He's, um, on assignment for a lookalike."

Ah. The old evil twin hunt. Guess Dominic must have gotten a lead on another infiltrator from the other Earth. "Well, tell him as soon as he wraps up, I could use an assist."

"Already on it."

It's not like Loredana hadn't already made contact but annoying him might better get the point across. Besides, I liked annoying him.

"Need anything else?"

"No. Oh, hey, wait. Did you get that letter decrypted?"

"Still crunching it! That's why Cyril's been working so hard. It'll take a while."

"And Edie's computer?"

"She was definitely looking for your guy. Search results for private investigators in southern Oregon, access to county property tax records, but I didn't find any indication that she found specifically him."

"Got it. He says he hasn't seen her."

"Her ex-husband! Really?"

"Uh, I was hoping you'd tell me."

"Sure. Right! There's no marriage license that I can find, but you know, they might not have it online up there. Or they might not have legally gotten married."

"I'll check into that." I shook my head. Not that Liz could see it. "This is nuts. She's got to be around here somewhere. Maybe we should just wait for her to come back. But as much as she knows about Procyon's past, I can't run the risk she's in danger of losing it."

"Losing what?"

"Her edge. Her cool. Her brain, for all I know. But if we're gonna dig any deeper into Tenebrae's background—if a weird glowing being can *have* a background, we've got to bring her back right now. This isn't a time for losing marbles."

"Of course! We'll find her, Mercury. We're good at that."

"No offense, but what we're good at is slaying monsters and stopping the end of the world."

"Oh. Well ..." Liz cleared her throat. "I'll get back to you!"

I rejoined Jake, who was finishing up the crust of his sandwich as Teget concluded a tale by saying, "... left the riven remains of the *ch'irak'i* staining the grasses of our ancient forest!"

"That's great." Jake drained his can of soda, crumpled it, and tossed it over his shoulder into the waiting trash can. "Your pal here's a heck of a storyteller. Where's he from?"

"Not around here." I glanced at the globe decorating a bookshelf in the far corner. "Cleveland."

"Doesn't sound like he's from Cleveland."

So much for that bluff. But seriously, what's a Cleveland voice sound like? I overrode the itch to Google it.

"I suspect you guys either have a plan of attack and struck out," Jake continued, "Or you're winging it."

Teget and I shared a glance. "We work best when we can apply an existing plan and modify it on the fly if it doesn't work out," I said.

Smooth.

Jack chuckled. "Okay, winging it. And I'm assuming you don't want the local PD involved. Otherwise you wouldn't be wandering the streets without their help."

"Bingo. There's some people involved who might be looking for us, and her."

"Vile fiends and their demonic ilk," Teget muttered.

"Demonic?" Jake asked.

"Figure of speech." I glared at Teget, hoping he could read my unspoken *Do not tell this guy the truth about monsters and evil beings from other dimensions!* At least, not all of it. Not yet. Not until he was vetted.

"Okay. Tell you what: I'll make some phone calls tonight, see if I can lean on a few old friends. If Edie's around, they might have heard whispers. And I know people close to the police—not on the force, so don't worry about anyone blabbing to them. If she's around, though, she'll be keeping quiet." Jake snapped his fingers. "Or camping. Hiding out in the woods. There's a couple roads we can try. What's she driving these days?"

I blinked. Erm. Probably an important detail. "I'll check with the office."

"Good." Jake grabbed his car keys from his pocket. "Hang out here. I'll take a spin up the mountain, see what I can see. Shouldn't be more than an hour."

"Yeah, and we'll help." I jerked a thumb at Teget. "He's all about forests, big or small."

"But he doesn't know his way around this one. I do." Jake shrugged. "I guess if you want to tag alomng, I can bring him."

"Mercury." Teget touched my shoulder. He whispered, "Splitting our forces will not serve us in this situation. Nor will it be to our advantage if we leave this abode with our host, only to find the warrioress has arrived in our absence."

"You want to stay here?" I led him away from Jake, into the living room. "We can't keep an eye on him if we do."

But even as I argued, I realized he had a point. We could use this place as home base, wait for Liz, touch base with Loredana and the rest of the team …

And snoop through Jake's belongings.

Did I say "snoop"? I should have worded it as, "enjoyed his hospitality."

"Yeah, good plan, Jake." I grinned. "Mind sharing your stash of Mountain Dew?"

Thirty minutes and three cans of the Dew later, I was drumming fingers on Jake's desk. Wasn't much to see—utility bills, photos of himself or with friends or with three different ladies, assorted papers from the State of Oregon, news articles on various forest issues affecting the region. "Okay. Okay. Okay. Nothing much. Can't see anything weird. I didn't want to move it. Make a mess. You know? Because he's a private eye. He'd notice. Right? Right? He'd figure it out. Say something. Know we did it."

Teget sighed as heavily as a bear who couldn't find more honey. He set down the globe he'd been examining. "I fear the fizzing potion has driven you to distraction, brother."

I rubbed my face. My heart skipped along. Probably the caffeine more than anything else. But it had been a long day. He wasn't wrong.

"You need rest. These events wear upon you." He settled into the rocking chair and patted the hideous, faded orange couch. "Come."

"We need to—"

"This Jake, the investigator, will return. I will find what we can from him. We cannot discern any more of his nature from these scraps. His willingness to help, and his actions moving forward, those will reveal his true persona."

As bad as the couch looked, it felt amazing, like putting on your favorite pair of sneakers you'd worn for the past three years. I stretched out, head propped up on one arm of the couch, feet kicked over the other.

"Take ease." The rocking chair creaked, back and forth, slow and steady. The rhythm soothed me, like the waves coming ashore outside the beach house.

He was right. I needed sleep.

But the more I drifted off, the deeper I went, the creaks dissolved into rumbles of thunder. Lighting flashed across my vision—for real? Was there a thunderstorm going? Or was it in my head?

Focus on something else. Home. Bed. Loredana.

My eyes flew open. The Interstice spread before me.

Picture the most desolate desert imaginable, with dunes of gray sand broken by jagged cliffs and crumbling mountains. The sky was perpetually shrouded in black clouds. Purple lightning ripped the horizon apart. Stone tumbled down stone.

The screams of astral fiends come from all directions.

Help.

He was there—a glowing outline, surrounded in a blinding aura of golden white light. An arm extended to me. Offering a hand.

Mercury ...

Oh, no ...

You think you can change the outcome? You think you have any power in this place? Without the pulsar stave, you're flesh and blood, as fallible as the rest.

A windstorm whipped grit across my face, stinging my eyes. I spat it from my mouth, but it kept filling the air around me, enveloping me in a personal cloud.

The shadow that stepped from it was a hideous amalgamation of voices—a woman's singsong call of my name, a man's bold proclamations, and a ... thing's whisper.

We're always here, ready for you. Threats don't bother us. Saying you will storm our domain—an empty boast. Even he cannot destroy what the Interstice has brought together.

I forced myself to look. A shadow built from the storm, clad in sleek, scaly armor, reached out for me. Claws as cold as icicles plunged into my arms.

I screamed but couldn't pull back. The scales slithered down into my exposed skin, covering every inch, digging beneath the surface. I could feel myself freezing. My blood crystalized.

Help.

Tenebrae appeared between us. Light exploded with rainbow tinge, the shimmer piercing my eyes, washing the Interstice in sharp color.

The Whisperer screamed in a mash of Marigold Yen's and

Alexander Arkwright's voice, capped by a booming, mechanical tone—the Hedron of Orbits. I hadn't seen nor heard from it since Dominic, the superhero named Airfoil, and I obliterated it at the fight for San Camillo Bay, but there it was, melded with the rest of my enemies into a being that was infecting me with death.

Until Tenebrae entered the struggle.

Help, *he said.*

I shouted, my fear subsiding in the wake of furious defiance, and ripped my arms free. Tenebrae's light soothed the wounds, set my hands aglow ...

And I plunged them into the Whisperer's chest.

Everything exploded in an agonized shout.

"Mercury! Awake!"

I was staring up at Teget, and the couch. Because I'd apparently rolled onto the floor. Early morning colors seeped between the window blinds. Jake Drinkwater was a small figure at the end of the room, steam rising from two mugs of coffee.

"Be at ease. You are safe." Sure, Teget said that, but he also had the axe lowered over my face, like he was ready to cut off my head if I started biting.

I grimaced and rubbed the bad of my head. Which made it hurt more. "What's up?"

"You, after screaming," Jake said. "And a lead on Edie. I think I found her."

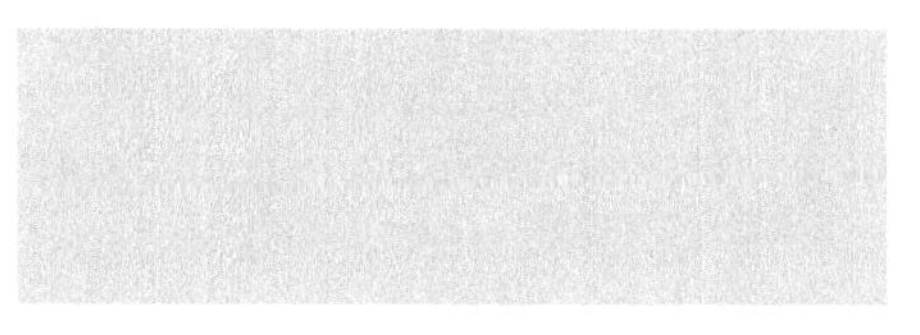

CHAPTER FIFTEEN

If Jake noticed we'd been through his belongings, he didn't say anything. Which made me feel worse, because we'd snooped through the house of a guy who'd had our backs.

Plus, he brought us breakfast burritos.

Now, I'm all about getting down to work, but I appreciate priorities, especially from someone who might be headed into danger but was still willing to sate his appetite with sausage, egg, peppers, and cheese.

I wiped the last crumb from the corner of my mouth as Jake's Bronco eased to a stop behind a stand of pines, tires crunching on gravel. "I'm assuming we've got to hoof it to wherever Edie's at, because I've got nothing but forest in a full circle."

"It's a warehouse on the other side of the clearing." Jake got out of the truck. He clipped a pair of binoculars to his belt, then checked the Ruger semi-automatic pistol riding in its holster. "Two hundred yards."

"Of course it's a warehouse," I muttered. "Even a mile off a countryside road, in broad daylight, the bad guys are hanging out in a warehouse."

"If it makes you feel any better, it's a landscaping company's storage facility."

Well, at least it might smell better.

Jake led Teget and me through the woods, which reeked of damp pine needles and rotting leaves. Couldn't tell if it had rained last night or if the climate kept it that saturated. But it was dark enough under the canopy I had to squint so my vision could adjust.

Teget crept between the trees like a man born in the wilderness—which, I guessed, was close to the truth. We'd battled enough astral fiends in the thousand-year-old forest outside Meda that I half-expected him to jump to the nearest branch and start swinging along, Tarzan-style.

Up ahead, the tree line thinned. Jake held up his hand, then crouched behind a fallen trunk. I did the same. Teget took up a position behind a huge, hollowed stump.

The warehouse was a long, single-story shed that had at least ten garage doors on the side facing us. Black vehicles clustered at three of the entrances. Jake peered through his binoculars. "Yeah, that's the place. Look like the guys you were warned about?"

I took the binocs from him. Boy. When Syndax got serious, they got *serious*. Three SUVs, five guys standing guard. Two more were lugging containers on dollies into the fourth bay door, which stood open. All wore a mix of plain T-shirts, white and tan, with fatigue pants in an assortment of camouflage. And they were armed. MP5 submachine guns.

"Where's Edie?" I whispered. Don't know why. They probably couldn't hear us.

"Not sure," Jake murmured. "But there's another set of guards inside the garage. See them? Three more men."

Eight. Not too many, for me and Teget. Even better odds if Jake helped us in a fight. I frowned. What the heck was Syndax doing out in the middle of nowhere? Had they lured Edie out here? Made a good place to trap someone, I supposed. Put them far from backup if they needed it. Of course, the woods could have been crawling with Syndax soldiers, for all I know.

Right. Soldiers. Like I'd said, fighting them wouldn't be too much of a problem, unless …

One of the bigger guys turned to his short comrade. His eyes caught the morning sun's reflection and glinted purple.

"Super," I muttered.

"What is it?" Teget asked.

"They're jacked up on Syndax's tachyon formula. Which makes them just as tough as us."

"Good." Teget bared his teeth. "I would hate for the battle to be ended too soon."

Jake made a face. "They're jacked on *what*?"

"Steroids, only way worse." I slipped the pulsar stave from its holster and willed it to life.

Jake whistled low. "That's, ah, impressive."

"They don't give them out at Procyon company picnics." I sidled over to Teget, keeping low. "Okay. There's about a hundred feet from the edge of the woods to the trucks. I'm thinking we need a distraction."

Teget nodded. "A swift raid? The destruction of their carriages?"

"Not bad. I was hoping for an explosion."

"Ah. I was thinking we strike a carriage with such thunder it rolls with the same ferocity as a boulder in an avalanche."

"Both sound impressive to me," Jake commented. "But I recommend scoping the place out more before rushing in."

"He doesn't know me very well, right?" I stage whispered to Teget.

Teget chuckled, then covered his mouth.

"I'm serious." Jake's tone firmed up, like we'd insulted his profession. Which we probably had. "We have no idea where in that building Edie is. Running right into their guns will get you killed, and if by some miracle you survive, she could die, too."

Okay, so he was right. "Fine. Go around that way —" I pointed north and see what you can see. Teget, you don't need binoculars, so scout south. I'll phone home to Procyon and let them know what we're up against."

"I shall." Teget gripped the axe. "And the Homeland sentries?"

"Bowe's probably got this place under surveillance anyway.

That's his problem. You guys get going."

To their credit, they moved without further instruction, disappearing among the scattered rocks and rotting stumps. I hunkered against the tree, pulsar stave in one hand, cell phone in the other. Jake's warnings aside, I knew I had to strike, because whatever reason Syndax had Edie in there for—if she was even still a prisoner—was no good.

And yeah, it could be a trap. For me. Serena made it clear she wanted me captured.

I pressed the phone against my forehead and closed my eyes. Let the pulsar stave's energies seep through my body, into the prosthetic leg. I was gonna need a big reservoir of it if I was gonna speed-run into the midst of these guys and not get killed. I knew Teget would back me up. Jake probably would, too, but I wouldn't blame him for bailing. We hadn't even paid him for investigative services yet.

Whatever. Procyon had to have a line item in its budget for Extra Help from Random Samaritans Who Used to Be Married to Forecasters, right?

I texted Loredana. <In Shotgun. Found Edie. Syndax is here. Backup would be nice. Love you.>

Sent it. Then I pulled up the files I'd gotten from her pal Cordelia. As many as I could cram onto the expanded memory, which, thanks to Liz, was considerable. Old documents. Procyon files. There had to be something in there that would get me answers about Tenebrae. Unfortunately, none of the searches I'd done on my laptop had turned anything up.

I wanted to throw the phone against a boulder. Why couldn't the stupid being just send me a message in neon lights? Not crazy dreams—assuming they weren't prompted by too much Dew.

I tapped on yet another folder labeled with random numbers. No sign of Jake yet … But I spotted Teget slinking back toward me. Time enough to check.

Operatives. It was a dossier stretching back decades. And the page was open to Sherry Jean Crown.

I'd never seen Wilhelmina at age 35, not a ton older than me. She stood taller, was leaner, with a body like an athlete's. Big hair, big smile. She could had so much energy in that Polaroid that had been scanned into digital format I swore she'd break through the screen.

"Mercury."

I dropped the phone and swung the stave around. Jake stared, wide-eyed, his hand on his gun. I'd positioned the stave inches from his face. Hoped he wasn't gonna miss it, because if I released my breath, I'd melt it off his skull. *Sorry, man. That was sloppy.* But what I said was, "Got a report, guys?"

"There's windows on the far end," Jake whispered. "Definitely have someone standing inside. A couple of them."

"Many more on the opposite end," Teget added. "I counted seven, standing in a cluster."

"Just standing there?"

He nodded.

"Mine, too," Jake said.

I glanced back at the Syndax crew. They were packing up. We couldn't wait. I had to take the chance.

My phone buzzed. Loredana. <Stand by. DHS notified. Support on its way.>

Stand by? Sorry, babe. No time to wait.

"If you can't keep up," I said to Jake, "Stay hidden. If you can help, do me a favor—don't shoot me in the back."

"Don't worry." Jake hoisted his pistol and grinned. "I'm a terrible shot."

Nice. I locked eyes with Teget. He crouched in a running stance. The axe shimmered with its own subtle light.

I breathed deep. Felt the energies coursing through me in waves. Everything slowed—Jake's blinking, birds chirping. Dust motes froze as golden specks.

Go.

I hurtled across the open ground, running at top speed, which to me felt like I was in a sprint, but to everyone else, must have looked like a streak of light. Teget was beside me. Made the charge feel less crazy that it actually was.

A Syndax soldier turned my way at thirty feet. His blackened eyes, shining purple, widened.

Hey, pal.

I let the end of the pulsar stave brush his gun arm, just the tip, but at the speed I was going—which was really freaking fast per hour—the impact sent him spinning head over boots into the metal shed wall. Left a man-shaped imprint.

Then I slashed the stave along the nearest SUV's gas tank.

It was the truck furthest from the open garage door, and the second I saw the spray of sparks, I veered to one side. Could feel my speed dropping off, meaning I'd burned through the pent-up energies. Which also meant I was gonna stumble to a stop and possibly catch on fire if I didn't wind things down soon.

Did I mention fire? Right. That's because the back end of the SUV exploded, sending a bright but brief fireball into the air and a column of black smoke skyward as the truck bounced up and onto its left side.

I skidded out, kicking up a spray of rocks and dirt taller than me. Panting. Didn't realize how fast I was running until I stopped, because it felt like I'd spent all day in a marathon.

The Syndax soldiers reacted true to form—shouting and shooting. They rushed around the flaming wreckage and directed their gunfire at yours truly.

Which gave Teget the opportunity to literally sweep them of their feet.

He bore in from their right, shouting one of those crazy war cries of his. Sure, it was bad tactics to announce his charge, but I wasn't gonna critique. He was having too much fun.

Meanwhile, I met two Syndax henchmen head-on.

Their gunfire had gone wide—and I managed to block incoming bullets with the stave. Eat that, Luke Skywalker! Did I mention I've been practicing the move? But I digress. We closed our distance enough that one of them threw down his gun and slashed at me with a machete, while the other one opted for swinging his MP5 like a club.

Two for two, then.

I had already separated the stave, so the left hand blocked the incoming machete, setting off sizzling sparks. I twisted sidelong so the MP5 swung through empty air, then cut down at it with the other blazing halves. One second, an automatic weapon. The next, melted metal and plastic. Oh, and harsh burns through the guy's gloves.

His screams distracted his buddy, leaving an opening in which I could plant my elbow in the guy's face. Set him flat on the ground, which was awesome. Burned hand produced two combat knives—because why not?—and came at me, blades flashing.

Gunshots echoed over my shoulder, and he flopped into the dirt, writhing.

Jake advanced, his pistol ready. Guy moved like he had military training. He nodded. "Clear a path so we can get Edie out."

"You got it." I stepped hard on the first soldier's knee, because he was trying to get back into the fight. Nope. Time out. He hollered as his kneecap crunched.

It wasn't personal. I was just tired of those guys trying to kill people and summon hellish monsters instead of getting real jobs.

Teget had torn his way through the other three guys, their bodies sprawled in the dust. Not dead, if their groaning and whining was any indicator. But one of the two who'd been moving boxes on the dollies made the mistake of coming at Teget with a combat knife. The blade cut through Teget's sleeve and sent a spray of blood through the air like someone had set up a garden hose.

Teget roared and whirled, planting the axe squarely in his chest.

The guy grasped the axe handle, mouthing words soundlessly, and crumpled as his legs lost strength.

"Fiends." Teget pushed him off. Blood coated his arm.

I caught up to him, glancing cautiously inside the open door. No gunfire. No movement. "You gonna be okay? Is it bad, or do I need to make a crack about flesh wounds?"

Jake snorted. Teget regarded me with his dwindling supply of patience, while he ripped his other sleeve free and fashioned a bandage in about fifteen seconds.

More gunshots erupted from inside the garage. The last three guys, I figured. But if there were more people at either end of the building, like Jake and Teget had seen, those weren't attacking.

We hunkered behind an undamaged SUV as bullets cracked against the windows and body. Huh. Armored, apparently.

"What's the play here?" Jake swiped perspiration from his forehead. "I have to say, I tend to do more snooping and self-defense than full frontal assaults. Those days are way behind me."

"Don't sweat it." See what I did there? I grinned at him. "I'll take the roof, Teget, if you want to barrel in—but if you're too hurt, I understand."

He scowled. "If I were too hurt to continue, there would be a dozen more of the enemy slain at my feet."

I slapped his shoulder—on the uninjured arm. "Front door for you it is, then."

"Super fun," Jake muttered, but he angled himself around the SUV's bumper and returned fire.

I hurtled from the ground, clearing the tops of the trucks, and landed on the warehouse roof's slope. The smell of fertilizer was stronger up here. So was the cedar aroma. I cut broad gaps in the metal surface. It bowed beneath me. One more ought to—

The roof gave way.

I crashed into the huge open area below, landing atop a stack of pallets. Not my most graceful entry. But I'd had worse.

Surprising the last of the Syndax henchmen that way offered two advantages—I established a position behind enemy lines.

I saw the warehouse was empty of supplies, yet full of corpse-fiends.

Two dozen of them. They were arranged in lines of eight,

strung out in curves between pallets and drums of fertilizer. In the middle of the room, behind the Syndax trio who were losing their battle with Teget and Jake, was a chair. A black-haired figure was tied up in it.

"Edie!" I pole-vaulted off the stack and landed in front of the chair.

It was a mannequin.

They hadn't even bothered to get one that wasn't white.

Oddly enough, she was wearing clothes—

No. A vest. A vest strewn with wires connected to six blocks of lumpy gray plastic. Red digital numbers spun down.

A bomb.

"Mercury! We got them!" Jake skidded to a halt. His face went pale at the sight of the ragged collection of walking corpses, their bodies and clothing in equal tatters, their mouths elongated wide enough to eat a person's face using the glistening fangs rimming the opening.

I reached out for Teget, who was inside the garage door, and had just thrown the last Syndax soldier into daylight. "Get out! Don't let—!"

The door banged shut. We were plunged into a darkness lit only by pale light filtering through windows covered with plastic, the red glow from the vest bomb, and the unnerving purple eyes of twenty-four zombies powered by the energy of the Interstice.

"They rigged the place to blow?" Jake asked, his voice gone reedy.

"Yep." I sighed. The corpse-fiends were closing fast. I reconnected the pulsar stave and willed it to get ready for zombie slaying. "Do me a favor? Somebody get rid of that bomb, before this whole place leaves a crater that makes San Camillo Bay look like the bottom of a Dixie cup."

CHAPTER SIXTEEN

I decapitated the nearest corpse-fiend. Good way to start the fight.

No way I was touching that bomb. Are you kidding? Sure, I could have thrown it up through the hole in the roof I'd created, but what if it had, I don't know, a tamper switch or something? It could blow up if I messed with it.

Way better to focus on the walking dead who were interested in biting me in hopes I'd turn into one of their shambling crew.

Teget roared his outrage. The axe swept through their ranks, cleaving one of the corpse-fiends in half and tearing the chest of the one next to him. Anywhere the axe's shimmering energies touched, the zombie's rotting flesh turned to ash, then melted into a good-old-fashioned puddle of the same blue ooze astral fiends left behind. Which was easy to remember, because a handful of these monsters had, well, tentacles instead of hands, just like their bigger, uglier buddies. Made for easier cleanup—and less likelihood of us getting ourselves infected and turned into slavering, mindless zombies for Syndax.

Because that's what these guys had been. People. Not anymore. I couldn't think about what had happened to their souls. That was Ramos' influence. I had to hope—to beg—that they'd been long dead and gone before they were sent after us. That these were just shells, meat bags being used as puppets.

Easier to handle them if it wasn't actually killing.

"Hey!" Jake fired a couple of rounds into one that had close within arm's reach. It wasn't stopping. "A little help!"

I flipped backwards, the stave creating a golden white circle as it cut apart another corpse-fiend, which promptly disintegrated. I landed beside him, separated the stave into its component halves, and blew Jake's attacker into blue muck.

"That," he breathed, "Was something else."

"Yeah, okay, focus!" I pointed at the mannequin that was wearing a bomb.

"You know I'm not a demolitions expert, right?" Jake holstered his gun and rubbed at his chin, like he was gonna scrub away his facial hair.

"Seems like you have military experience, by the way you acted out there."

"If I did, it wasn't in bomb-defusing!" he snapped.

I rolled my eyes. "At least take a look at the stupid thing and tell me if there's a wire that will make it explode if we try to move it." I blasted another corpse-fiend that got too close, its hissing moan escalating into a shriek as it vaporized.

Jake shook his head. "Right. Because they'd have labeled it for our convenience." He gingerly probed the tangles of wires leading from the blocks of plastique, fingers deft. I expected them to emerge with a thread so he could unravel the vest.

"Careful." I rose and cut a corpse-fiend in half. I could have been more use in this fight, but Jake needed protecting, and Teget was having what looked like the time of his life as he ripped through the zombies. He hadn't been in San Camillo when they'd rampaged downtown on two occasions more than a year ago, but he'd fought them off during several incursions by Arkwright and his forces into our home dimension of Meda.

A wound from those creeps had killed our grandfather, Naos. Probably that's why Teget yelled in their faces right before he sliced said faces off, spatting blue slime across the concrete floor.

"Okay." Jake wiped his forehead. "Good news."

"Hit me."

"No booby-trap."

I exhaled. "Awesome."

"Bad news?"

"Not interested."

"I have no idea how to shut it down."

"What did I just say?" The corpse-fiends were crowding us, pushing into a circle, and even with only sixteen remaining of the original twenty-four—whoops, fifteen, I meant, because there went the head of another—time kept ticking. "How long?"

"Three minutes."

"Screw it." I shoved him aside and grabbed the vest.

"Be careful!" Jake hollered. "You light that thing in here, I'm not kidding, they'll be picking our scraps up off the ocean floor!"

"Thanks for that statement of the blindingly obvious. Teget!"

He whirled, his face dripping sweat, his eyes wild with fury.

"Get the door!"

Probably we should have done that first. But with a pack of zombies closing in, you don't tend to think of escape plans, not when you're a couple of guys like us who've conditioned ourselves to cut our way out instead of running.

Teget, though, barreled through the closing ranks of the monsters, tossing two so high their sodden bodies *slapped* off the ceiling. He crashed into the closed garage door with a thunderous rattle of metal on metal, and an explosion of sparks that made it seem like he'd lit the world's biggest Roman candle.

Fun fact: Sparks make fires. Tiny ones. But when those spread to wooden pallets and cardboard barrel-shaped containers of fertilizer ...

I squinted at the labels. Not fertilizer. Ammonium nitrate. Same thing? Whatever.

"Teget!" I yelled. Not sure what I expected him to do about it.

A long, jagged section of the garage door crashed down. Daylight flooded inside. I blinked, forcing myself to adjust to the sudden lack of darkness.

A breeze blew in, too, fanning the flames.

"Time to go!" I grabbed Jake's shoulder. "Arms around me."

Jake raised an eyebrow.

I whipped sideways, avoiding a corpse-fiend's tentacle, then kicked him into his buddy. No more energy blasts now. "Hug me or get blown up! Your call."

Jake looped his arm around my neck like we were teammates who'd just won the World Series. Teget must have figured out my plan without me saying anything, because he swooped in and let Jake do likewise to him with the other arm.

The corpse-fiends had backed off. Since when did they assess our tactics and formulate a new plan? Could be they were disturbed we'd cut down half their ranks in a few minutes.

Speaking of which …

The red indicators glowed **1:45**.

"Gotta run," I muttered.

Teget shook his head.

Flames shot abruptly toward the ceiling, catching an entire stack of boxes alight. The corpse-fiends backpedaled even more.

And for a second, we had an opening.

I could feel Teget's first step within a flash of mine. Like we were in near perfect sync. The warehouse interior blurred. Talk about jumping to hyperspace! Okay, so it didn't seem as fast as our attack run before, but it was speedy enough to get us to the tree line before we collapsed in a heap among dew-jeweled ferns. I spat pine needles. Graceful stop, it wasn't.

"This is just …" Jake shook his head. "Zombies? Edie never said anything about zombies."

"Yeah, well, she wasn't in on that particular adventure. Too busy watching desert rats." I sagged against a tree.

The SUVs that hadn't been destroyed were gone, as were the Syndax soldiers, including the dead ones. Which, on the one hand, was good. On the other, Homeland wasn't gonna get their guys anytime soon.

"Mercury," Teget said. "The inferno?"

"I know, I know." I brushed my hair. "We should make sure all the corpse-fiends get torched and then call the fire—"

The explosion was a thunderclap that hurled a pressure wave throughout the clearing, reducing the building to a column of smoke and a ball of fire. A mini-mushroom cloud shot forth.

We hurled ourselves over logs and boulders as the blast hit the forest. It was like a typhoon had blown out of nowhere. Branches shattered. Trees splintered. I hunkered down, arms over my head, gasping for breath.

When we finally looked up, the forest was in ruins, and everything was coated in dust. The clearing was a crater. A huge one.

Jake coughed, creating his personal cloud of dust. He looked twenty years older underneath a fine coat of grit. "I think," he wheezed, "We'd better get out of here."

I stared at the towering cloud that reached so high the wind had already caught it and was blowing its top to feathers. My eyes teared up from the debris we'd created. "Yeah. Pretty sure we're about to get the sirens."

We staggered through Jake's front door and strew ourselves around the room—me on the island, Teget across a couch, and Jake into the sink. Well, just the face and hands of the latter. He ran the faucet full blast on cold, scouring grime off his face.

I slapped the pulsar stave down with a *clank*. "So, that was a disaster. Bonus: No zombie horde to eat its way through the sleepy village of Shotgun."

"A considerable victory." Teget's reply came muffled through the cushion in which his face was buried.

"Not as considerable as the mess we left." Jake sighed. "Count yourselves lucky I know the back roads the sheriff thinks are disused. Otherwise we'd be in the county lockup."

"It'd be worse than that, trust me."

Jake glanced over his shoulder, his beard sopping wet. "Feds?"

"Homeland Security."

"You guys, I'm telling you ..." He dried his face and beard with a towel.

Not surprised he didn't have a better reaction. Nobody wanted to be on the feds' radar. Especially Homeland's. I let the pulsar stave balance against a newspaper so it wouldn't roll off the island and staggered to the counter. Coffee. Needed a second cup.

"I'm gonna move your car around the back of the house. There's some tarps back there. The way I look at it, we don't want them knocking down the door if you two have to figure out your next move." Jake held out his hand.

My keys jingled as I retrieved them, fingers still shaking. Man. The more I pushed myself during a fight and leaned on the tachyon energies to the extreme, the worse of a hangover I experienced afterward. Not that guzzling coffee would ease those jitters. Probably guzzling Mountain Dew made it worse.

"Thanks." Jake paused at the open door, a smirk creasing his face. "Try not to blow up my house, okay?"

I gave him a thumbs up.

As soon as he was gone, I let out a ragged sigh. "She wasn't there."

"Of this I am aware," Teget muttered.

"And I walked right into their trap, like the world's biggest idiot." I wanted to smash the coffee mug on the floor, but since it wasn't mine, I refrained. "Those Syndax guys could have told us everything we'd wanted to know! She could have been in their SUV."

Teget sat up, wincing. There was a string of bruises along his right arm. "I find it unlikely that, having lured you with a false representation of the warrioress, they would have brought her to within close proximity. If she is indeed a lure."

"They might want her for the same reason we do," I said. "Tenebrae."

He shivered. "What we have seen, of the light interfering with the dark, is unprecedented in its boldness. The Whisperer desires above all to expand his domain, to claim this dimension and Meda for his hordes."

"Well, as long as you keep the night's blade safe in Meda's temple, that shouldn't be an issue." The pulsar stave and Teget's axe, partnered up with the blade, form a device that could establish a stable gateway between Earth and the Interstice. A permanent fixture. We'd stopped that once. And apparently, the Whisperer wanted a different way in."

"Perhaps. Or perhaps the Whisperer intends to wage war with Tenebrae himself."

I snapped my fingers. Captain Obvious much? "Wow. Okay, I am an idiot."

"If you are waiting for me to disagree, it may be an eternity," Teget said, his tone sly.

"Ha ha. No, seriously—Tenebrae. Every time I've come into contact with him or one of his hijacked fiends—and even in my uber-realistic dream last night, there was a common theme. Help. I thought he wanted me to keep helping in the fight against the Whisperer. Which, duh. That's my job. But maybe ... Maybe the call for help is more personal."

"I see." Teget scratched at his goatee with one of the axe's razor-sharp edges. I hoped he didn't have a shave in mind. "Beware this is not a ploy to lull you into his service, Mercury. Tenebrae appears as light, but his legend is one of ferocity and destruction."

"I get that." I aimed the mug at him. "Don't forget, though— you said he killed the bad guys, too. Maybe it wasn't personal. Maybe he was all about stopping the Medan civil war."

Teget made a face, but I could tell those rusty wheels in his skull were still clanking along. Plus, it was fun to argue with him. See? Brothers.

My phone buzzed. No text—Liz was ringing me. "Yello."

"Mercury! You're okay! We saw the explosion!"

"Wait—as in, via satellite?"

"YouTube." That was Loredana's voice, which had an extra edge to it, and was hushed. "Please don't waste time with frivolity.

An extraction team is on its way to your location. Be advised, Homeland has cordoned off access into and out of the immediate area."

"Whoa, whoa, hold on. I'm *not* abandoning my car."

"Be quiet!" she snapped. "Elizabeth succeeded in accessing Edith's computer hard drive. She was searching through our databases, Mercury. For information regarding past operatives. Far above our clearance levels."

My guts twisted. Cordelia's files …

"Fifteen minutes. Hold fast. And remember the—"

The phone call cut out. I tried redialing. No service? Since when?

"What is the matter?" Teget was on his feet.

"Don't know. We might have to bail. Gimme a sec." I pulled up the operative files. Scrolled past Wilhelmina's grinning face.

Straight to twin white guys.

They were nineteen, according to the date stamp. Noah and Troy Reverdin. Near identical. Blond. Noah had green eyes. Troy's were stormy blue.

A red "Terminated" was stamped across their portraits.

Boots creaked on wood. A shadow fell through the doorway. "Trouble?"

Metal scraped on the island counter.

Jake held the pulsar stave, which for the average Joe was an inert hunk of metal.

It sprang to life, coruscating with sparks and lightning, its sections held apart by the Interstice energies.

"Nice to know," he growled, "I haven't lost my touch."

He lunged at me, brandishing the stave just like I did.

CHAPTER SEVENTEEN

Not the first time I'd seen my own death coming.

But Teget's reflexes weren't addled by caffeine, exhausted as he was.

The ax flashed across my field of view, colliding with the stave and knocking Jake off course.

Jake?

Troy Reverdin. Apparently, a former Procyon operative. Who wasn't dead.

Wasn't much time to dwell on that, though. Teget vaulted over the couch, slamming it into the floor, and slid across the counter. He snatched up the axe and whirled it at Jake—Troy—whoever.

Jake still blocked the blow inches from his neck. He twisted the halves, separating them as he ducked and spun. Sparks flared as half the stave sliced diagonally through the island and its stone counter. The whole thing cracked, slipping along the long cut. It dumped Teget onto the kitchen floor.

I threw myself at Jake, hoping my prosthetic leg had enough energy to draw on, because I'd drained plenty doing speed runs against Syndax and their zombies. The reserve felt low, the barest tingle through my skin, but it was enough of a rush to get me right up beside Jake.

But he saw it coming, whether because he'd literally just

watched me fight or because of past training. Probably both. What it meant was I got tossed through the living room window.

Glass shards and wood splinters rained around me as I tumbled onto the deck. Try getting stung by forty bees all at once. That's how many cuts I got. Not that I counted them, but you get the point.

I heaved myself upright and leapt through the window, crouched on the floor, waiting for the right moment to get into the fray—which was more complex than I'd realized. Watching Teget duel Jake finally got it into my thick head just how skilled Jake was. He matched every attack. None of Teget's feints fooled him. And he wasn't being stupid. Just kept up a relentless attack that drove my brother across the room, inch by inch, until they were within arm's reach of the fireplace.

The clash of axe versus pulsar stave made me cautious. And that's not a sensation I get often. Unarmed, I'd get slashed pretty badly if I didn't time my—

Teget leaned back from a stave's swing, forcing Jake to turn.

I hurtled into his back, slamming us through the rocking chair. I hoped it wasn't an antique because it transformed into a pile of sticks.

Jake grunted, rolled, and brought his elbow down on my throat.

The pain was worse than almost anything I'd ever experience—and trust me, I'd know, given the state of my leg. I could feel my throat swelling. Breathing rode right past Normal Everyday Thing and straight to No Way I Can Do This Unassisted. I was on my hands and knees, gasping. All I could do was hope my body's naturally faster healing could prevent me from suffocating.

And I didn't have to worry about not being any help in the fight, because Jake ended it. He got Teget far enough away that he kicked him in the chest, and with the even greater added distance, blasted him point blank in the chest with the pulsar stave.

The explosion of light sent Teget against the fireplace. The impact knocked bricks loose, and left Teget slumped in ash, his forehead bleeding, eyes closed.

Jake stood over him, the pulsar staves aglow. His shoulders heaved as his breathing steadied and then slowed. Speaking of which, I could see Teget's chest moving, too.

"That," Jake rasped, "Went way better than I'd hoped."

He bent, retrieved the fallen axe, and slipped it through his belt. Then he reconnected the pulsar staves. "I missed this. Didn't think I would, not after I spent the first year and a half crying into beer bottles. I figured I put it out of my mind, along with everything else about my old life. But as soon as I saw you use it, I knew it belonged to me again."

Oh, great. He wanted to monologue. And he was going to get that in free of charge, because while I was still able to breathe, I wasn't going to be reciting the Gettysburg address—or heck, even the alphabet—any time soon.

"So, this must have been a shocker for you. The great Mercury Hale, operative for Procyon, just another cog in the machine. A cog that got spanked by yours truly, when I haven't even wielded the pulsar stave for a decade." Jake grinned. "I don't blame you. Not at all. She's the problem, a symptom of the problem, I suppose."

He shoved aside the other couch with his boot. There was a hatch inset in the wood floor that creaked just like every door you saw in every horror movie. Didn't anybody use WD40 anymore? Jake grabbed my collar and dragged me over, so I could see down into the basement.

Edie was down there, all right, her arms, wrists, legs, and ankles bound by plastic straps. A gag kept her from speaking. Bruises marred the side of her face I could see. Dried blood encrusted her eye, which was swollen shut.

Anger gave me enough strength to slap Jake's hand from my collar.

"Sucks, doesn't it? Me letting you think we could save Edie, when she'd been trapped right underneath where your lazy carcass had been snoring," he said. "I still needed to see you in action for myself, and it didn't hurt that doing so would drain you a bit. Having to fight a horde of those zombies and some Syndax mercenaries made for a perfect scenario."

I coughed, wheezed, and pushed out a word. "Tttroy …"

He slapped me across the chin with the pulsar stave—which was powered down, thankfully. I rolled with it, letting my limbs go limp as spaghetti. No way I wanted him knowing I was conserving my energy. Not with him carrying all the weapons, when all I had was a battered throat and dozens of tiny bleeding cuts.

"Congratulations. You figured it out. Troy Reverdin." He shook his head. "No idea who managed to get operative dossiers onto your cell phone, but that's one of the gutsiest moves I've heard of. You sure Procyon didn't have them killed? Because that's what they do when you step out of line."

Troy paced around the trapdoor. "You know I gave Procyon thirteen years? That has to mean something, more to you even than me. Half my adult life. Noah …" His voice caught on the name. He had to take a deep breath before he could continue in a halting done. "Noah and I were nineteen. We should have been in jail. We *were* in jail, when Jack Jackson bailed us out, promised us a life of adventure. Of *purpose*."

He held the pulsar stave as if it were made of brittle glass. "Because of this. There'd been only one, we were told, and then after the big blow up in 1994, there were two. Two as one. Perfect for a pair of guys like us. And we never would have amounted to anything if it hadn't been for her."

I glanced at the open hatch. A faint, feeble moan escaped.

"Edie has a talent. You've heard. She can sense people like us, like her—ones gifted with the genetic markers of the people who came from another world to help found Procyon." The pulsar stave ignited. Troy gazed at the carvings blazing along its length. "She led Procyon to us, and we fought for it, keeping astral fiends out of San Camillo for years."

"What'd happened?" I croaked. "Get bored?"

Troy sneered. "What always happens. We realized the people

in charge were corrupt and were plotting our destruction. Once we knew, it was easy enough to figure out how to solve the problem. Or I guess I should say, how to get to the root of the problem—the next rip that opened, we killed the astral fiend that came out and wandered in."

"Bad idea."

"We noticed. It's especially bad when the woman who brought you to your destiny …" He gazed into the basement. "The one you thought you loved … When she tries to kill you. Succeeds in killing half of you."

"Ash and teeth." Okay. It was getting easier to talk. Teget was still breathing, though he hadn't stirred. And I knew our extraction was on its way. No idea how long we had, but there were no sounds from outside beyond birds chirping. "That's what Wilhelmina said you were."

"That's what Noah was!" Troy snapped. "Having an RPG fired into your face will do that to a man! But Noah pushed me back through the rip. All I wanted was for us to find the Icon. To capture it. Destroy it. *Something* to upset the precious balance Procyon was obsessed with keeping. Instead, I lost my only real friend. My other *me*."

"She said … You guys went nuts."

"We found the truth. Because we stopped listening to the so-called friends of ours and started listening to the whispers."

I knew how he felt. I'd wanted to burn Procyon to the ground when they turned on me—when they found out I was from another dimension, and that the Icon was actually my brother. But whatever sympathy I felt for the Reverdins got swept away by the tidal wave of horror that washed over me when he said that last word. "The Whisperer. You could hear him."

"Can hear him." Troy tapped the side of his head, a small smile lurking on his lips. Not creepy at all. "Just like you can. I know. I've seen the files. Serena did a great job squirreling those away for a rainy day. Guess what? It's pouring, Mercury. I know a lot more than I did then. I know about Teget. About Meda. About the Whisperer's acquisition of power, slowly but steadily, now that he's one with Marigold Yen and Alexander Arkwright and the Hedron of Orbits. Every bit he gains opens up new avenues. Once he gets the last piece, absorbs the last being he'll ever need to absorb, you won't be able to stop him. No one will."

Tenebrae.

I wasn't about to shoot my mouth off. Shocking, I know. But it fit everything I knew so far, what with the crazy requests for aid that usually didn't follow an astral fiend attack.

Engines revved outside. Trucks were driving up the dirt road to Jake's—Troy's cabin. Great. The Syndax crew, back for more action, no doubt.

That's when I realized Troy's monologuing served another purpose other than stroking his ego. He was waiting for them. To come get me.

Because he was working with Serena. And she'd made it crystal clear, she wanted me alive.

"Face it, Mercury." Troy leaned over. "You're never going to come out on top. Not anymore. Because I have nothing to lose. And that means I'm willing to do whatever it takes to vanquish you."

"Dude." I bowed my head, the perfect impression of a guy weighed down by shame. "That isn't what I realized. That's not the truth."

"What is the truth?"

I glared up at him. "You talk too much."

I grabbed the pulsar stave and twisted.

He caught on, belatedly, because his reflexes were up to par, but he'd let himself think I was beaten down. Not knowing I could use my prosthetic leg as a reservoir for the same energies that powered the stave was a bummer for him.

I poured everything I could muster into a blast—just one, because I was still too worn down for a full-on brawl. The light left me blinking at sunspots and sent Troy out through that same window. There was a huge, meaty thump when he slapped onto the planks. Served him right. My back still ached in sympathy.

"Now you can hand over my weapon." I staggered to the window. Yeah, I know, not my best superhero run. It was more like a three-legged dog going for his meal.

Troy groaned. He pulled himself up on the railing. The axe was just outside the windowsill and the other half of the stave was another ten feet away, at Troy's feet.

I grabbed the axe, then started climbing out the window.

Car doors slammed. Shouts went up. And eight Syndax mercenaries in black and urban camo raised automatic rifles in my directions.

"Crap." I dropped back into the cabin.

Gunfire exploded. Whatever wood the cabin was made of wasn't the sturdiest stuff in the world because bullets punched through along the entire front. Sunshine lit up the living room, making it gorgeous if I were a real estate agent wanting warm images to post on my website. But the gunfire separated me from the stave, as I scrambled toward the trapdoor.

"Alive!" I heard Troy roar. "Alive, you idiots!"

Didn't have time to worry about whether or not Syndax had a breakdown in team communications. I just rolled Teget on his side. He grumbled. Blinked three times. "M-Mercury? What has happened?"

"You're okay? Thank God." I meant it. More than ever. I wished Ramos was here, to say an official prayer, but *Please help* would have to do. "Brace yourself."

"Brace myaaahhhhhh!" His question echoed as he fell through the trapdoor. Because I shoved him in. He slapped down onto the floor seven or eight feet below.

"Good?" I shouted over the weapons fire.

"Once I disembowel you!" he snapped.

"Yep, you're fine." I rolled over as bullets ripped the couch apart and dropped into the dank, damp space.

WHAM.

Ow. Landing on the dirt floor was not the best feeling. Not

from seven feet up. But at least it wasn't concrete.

Didn't help that Teget kicked me in the leg as he ripped the axe from my hands.

"You're welcome," I muttered.

"Shh." Teget held a finger to his lips. "It sounds as if our adversaries are adding a flying machine to their arsenal."

He wasn't wrong. The rumble of propeller took the place of the gunfire, which had died off. Those bozos must have finally heeded Troy's orders. Good. I had to get back up there and get the other half of the pulsar stave from him. Sure, he couldn't use it to make a portal between here and the Interstice, but it was a powerful weapon in its own right. And it was my responsibility to keep it safe.

Wasn't any room for failure.

The pitch of the propellers changed, and there came more shouts. Scared ones. I heard the distant noise of boots scrabbling on gravel. Then up the front steps. Into the kitchen.

Well. That was terrible. We were in the basement. And they were above us. With guns.

I knelt by Edie. She murmured something, tried to rise. I held her shoulder. "Teget, anyone sticks their faces down here, tear them off."

He snarled up at the rectangle of light. "It will be the greatest pleasure."

The first Syndax man who appeared wore goggles and a face mask. He stared at us a split second before he raised his gun—

And a burst of golden light, accompanied by a high-pitched shriek, flung him out of sight.

More flashes. A strange hissing sound, like sand being poured through a hundred sieves. Then the roar of gunfire. Not the automatic rifles. Nope. The new thunder made me think of the heavier weapons Procyon employed against zombies, the multi-barrel machine guns that could spit out thousands of rounds.

Something exploded.

A fire burned. I could smell the smoke. More shouts. More

shrieks, like an electrical sound, and the continued hissing.

"He's down there!"

The voice was steady, firm. Wind suddenly whipped around us. I covered Edie as a bubble appeared a few feet away, shimmering like soap, with a deep, dark rift at its center. I grinned at the sight of a portal opening—with a shining outline of Troy's kitchen on the other side.

Dominic Zein stepped through. Tall, lean, clad entirely in black, with a mask pulled up from his chin to the bridge of his nose. The only color on him was the Middle Eastern tones of his upper face and his fingers.

He pulled down the mask and smiled. "Somebody called for a ride, I hear?"

I could have hugged him. Instead I punched his shoulder. "About time. You want me to clean up after you?"

"No. Not at all. We've got it covered."

We?

"Hey! Get to teleporting and save the debrief for a cozy office, you guys!"

Javon Kimball peered over the side of the hatch. "Cope's got them on the run, but if they dig heavy artillery out of their rides, we're all gonna have to bail out fast. Get Edith to safety! That's your priority."

Dominic grabbed my arm, but I pulled free. "Take her and go," I said. "I can't leave without the rest of the pulsar stave."

"The *what*?" Dominic stared. "You *lost* it?"

"No! No way. Troy Reverdin took it."

"Troy *Reverdin*? You serious?" Kimball glanced behind him and scowled. "Gemini, transport out of there. Now. I'll mop up."

Then the young, annoying board member who'd treated Loredana like his overpaid tour guide disintegrated in a silvery haze, like sand blown by a breeze.

CHAPTER EIGHTEEN

E die was badly hurt. Teget wasn't uninjured himself, but at least he tottered upright, holding his head in both hands like he needed an entire bottle of painkillers.

"Let's get them outta here." I gave Teget back the ax. "And then I go show the old guy how it's done."

"Yes, I think you've done a fantastic job of that already." If Dominic's tone had gotten any drier, he'd have vomited desert. Nasty, I know, but you try coming up with great descriptions when you've been smacked around by someone who was your equal—and maybe better.

Dominic held up his arms. The Echo Watches were wristbands made out of ancient metal, buffed and corroded like they'd been pulled free from an archaeological dig before being used for accessories. They let off a soft glow as they fragmented, the shards spinning around his arms. Winds lashed the basement, forcing me to hold my hand in front of my eyes as they picked up every bit of dirt and errant pebbles they could find. A portal appeared out of shimmering lights, looking for all the world like a window—a hazy, glowing window into a wood-floored loft.

"Next stop, Rampart, Colorado," I muttered, and helped Teget pull Edie upright.

Gotta say—as a mode of transit, it's fast, but rough on the

old digestive system. My body felt like one of the rookie Starfleet officers was behind the transporter controls and was trying to reassemble my atoms by shaking them up in a sealed Tupperware container. Having yourself dismantled and rebuilt in a fraction of second, yet feeling like you were being smeared across a thousand miles with a peanut butter knife …

I may or may not have thrown up.

"Still?" Dominic sighed. He wiped the top of his left shoe against the edge of his couch. "After all these times? I can't blame this on Sammy."

"Leave your Golden Retriever out of this." I wiped my mouth with the back of my hand. "This place secure?"

"Yes. Procyon's office in town can have medics here in minutes." Dominic tapped a message one handed into his phone. "Put her in my bedroom."

"No way. I'm not moving her again." I helped Teget lay her on a couch. I propped a pillow under her head. She murmured, chapped lips forming words I didn't understand. My heart ached. I mean, I didn't know her well. Edie and I weren't gonna bingeing TV shows together any time soon. But she was one of us. More than that, she'd helped save my neck at least once before.

Nobody deserved the beating she'd taken.

"I will guard her." Teget dropped to his knees, harder than he should have. He swayed.

"Yeah, at least until the medics show up and slap you both on gurneys." I frowned at Dominic. "If they're—"

"They'll be all right. I promise." Dominic checked his phone. "Come on. Syndax is on the move, and so is our ride."

Ugh. Back through the portal. I relaxed my mind—and my stomach as best I could, then grabbed Teget's hand. "Won't be long."

He clasped it in return, the grip crushing my knuckles. "Tear them to pieces."

"I'll miss you, too."

Dominic touched my shoulder, and we stepped through that

rippling doorway back into the cabin.

So, "cabin" didn't apply. Not after Syndax had shot it to pieces. "Cheese grater made out of wood" was more accurate. No way a contractor could patch up the place. My brain was figuring out how to explain the damage in a real estate listing. Termites? Squirrels? Astral fiends merged with rabid squirrels? Squirrel-fiends?

Yeah. That's how rattled my brain was.

Didn't help that as Dominic and I materialized, there were still three Syndax mercs ready to fight.

Correction—ready to fight Kimball, not us, because they had their backs to us when we appeared. Sick as I felt from Transition Number Two and with a throat that had been battered, I brought the pulsar stave down across the nearest soldier's shoulder. He crumpled, gun clattering beside him.

Dominic aimed his wrist at the next guy and let loose a screeching blast from an Echo Watch. Worked like a Taser on steroids, reducing the body-armored mercenary to a quivering mass of uncontrollable muscles.

Which left Number Three, who, I had to say, was fast on the draw. He spun on us, twin compact Uzis aimed. Both had extended magazines, which mean dozens of bullets could perforate our less-than-stealthy selves.

And they would have, if a cloud of dust hadn't sprayed from the refrigerator with the force of a fire hose.

The spray sent the last merc tumbling across the living room. He regained his footing, but lost both guns, and slashed like a madman through the air around him. The concentrated dust—it actually more resembled a fine-grained sand, glittering with pale-purple streaks and a blue shine—dissipated into an even finer mist, then whipped around him, forming …

A fist. No joke. A fist the size of a trash can lid.

One blow cracked the poor henchman's goggles and left him limp on the floor, sprawled halfway out onto the deck. Blood trickled from under his mask.

"As handy as that was," I said, "You got any plans to kill it?"

"Not unless you're searching for a demotion," Dominic murmured.

The mist whirled back into dust, which compressed into the shape of a man, which in turn snapped into focus as an *actual* man, a Black guy wearing a pale-gray compression shirt with pulsing blue-violet lines on the shoulders, chest, and back. He had on navy blue fatigue pants, and the gleam in his eyes—well, it reminded me way too much of the purple glow around midnight that Syndax warriors got when they juiced up on tachyon infusions.

"'Sup, gentlemen." Kimball straightened the tight-fitting cuffs of his shirt. No hiding muscles in that thing. He'd kept in shape, on a daily basis by the looks of it, since his collegiate football days. "This place looks cleaned out. Better get moving if we want to catch up with the remaining jokers."

"That's a good plan. In fact, it's my plan. The operative's plan. To get back the other half of the pulsar stave."

Kimball paused at the door, his shoe propped on the unconscious soldier. He opened his mouth, then frowned, then ignored me in favor of Dominic. "I thought you guys were messing with me. You hit his head on a mountain range on the way back or what?"

"No. He really lost it."

"Yeah, right," Kimball grumbled. "To Reverdin? Can't believe it."

"Well, too bad." I peered out the window. Where were all the SUVs? "He's out there. Somewhere. Did he get past you?"

A fireball lit up the trees. Strike one SUV. That was when I realized two of the other SUVs hadn't left. They were charred hulks among the trees—where they'd landed. Upside down.

Probably because they'd exploded, too.

Courtesy of the machine gun hovering above us.

Check that—the machine gun mounted to the V-22 Osprey perched on twin propellers that churned up a windstorm. It twisted and banked, poised perilously at the edge of the deck. A ramp lowered, banging against a railing.

That's when I spotted the distinctive grill and emblem of a Subaru smirking underneath the ruined heap of Syndax trucks. I may have reacted badly. "Are you freaking kidding me?" I yelled.

"Is Edith okay?" Kimball shouted over the roar of the blades.

"She's being taken care of!" I snapped. "Teget, too. So, maybe skip that question and get to the part about how you turn into a fog-person!"

He laughed as we ran for the ramp. "After we snag our lost fish. Come on!"

We hopped up into the ramp, where I landed without twisting my artificial leg—minor triumph—and was struck with déjà vu. I'd been in the same cargo hold, among the same metal chairs mounted to the interior of the fuselage when I'd lead a strike team into the heart of San Camillo's burning forests, not long after I'd lost the leg. Dominic, Loredana, Wilhelmina, and I had teamed up with two more fighters. Okay, they were an ice wizard and a were-fox from yet another dimension. Together, the six of us had brought down a fiery monster than had spanned two worlds.

And our pilot into that hellstorm ...

"Y'all best find seats, or grab a hold of some strapping, because this infernal machine's not stopping for a gander at the sights!" Copernicus Sark hollered at us from the cockpit, all toothy grin and aviator shades with a Chicago Cubs ballcap. No sooner did he announce his folksy warning than he threw the Osprey up and ahead, the ramp groaning closed behind us.

Which was good because Dominic lost his footing. His slipped backward with a yelp.

I grabbed his shirt and hooked the pulsar stave through loose cargo webbing, holding him long enough to keep him inside until the ramp had sealed shut.

"Thanks," Dominic gasped.

"No problem." I glanced at Kimball. "Okay, Board Member Kimball, point me at the guy who's supposed to be dead, and maybe later we can argue about why he's *not* dead and how you do your disintegrating trick."

"Call me Javon. No need for titles in the thick of it, Mercury. Not when there's this much on the line." Javon cupped his hands. "Yo, Cope! Get us as close as you can!"

"Reckon I might could do just that!"

The Osprey lurched into flight.

I struggled forward, clutching at handholds everywhere I could, until I clung to the back of Cope's seat. "Where's Troy?"

Cope pursed his lips. "Can't say I know the fella's name, but Mr. Kimball there's got his sights set on that aeroplane yonder."

By "yonder," he meant skimming the treetops near Shotgun, banking for the coast. Whoever was flying it was good, and had to be, coming that near to the forest so they could avoid radar detection. It was sleek, pearly white, with black wings edged in red. Typical low-key Syndax, looking like an unmarked Learjet but with turbofans in the wings that helped with vertical takeoff. Which would explain its sudden appearance in an area that lacked runways.

"Target locked." Cope drawled the words with quiet confidence, and as much calm as I'd ask for a slice of pizza from Carlito's.

"Maybe don't shoot them down until after I get my weapon back," I said. "How close can you bring us?"

Cope snorted. "How close you cotton?"

"I cotton to ripping the roof off their ride and plunging in through hole."

"Mighty fine plan. Let's see if we can make it happen, Thel willing."

A second before I could ask about Thel and why he or it was willing anything, the floor dropped out from under me.

Not really. But that's what happens when your pilot dives on his target. No doubt he'd tell me—if I could get a word in edgewise over his whoops of delight—that diving increased our airspeed, and we'd need every mile per hour. The bad guys had a jet. Our prop-powered ride could max out at 350, maybe a bit more. That was about 150 mph too slow.

But since we dove on their jet like a hawk, we could get nearer faster.

"Best if you pop the hatch!" Cope called over the engines' roar. "Dropping the ramp will put too much drag on the old girl, and I'll be burned in Avernus if I let her get her blamed tail ripped off!"

"I'm all for not doing that!" I flung the hatch open. Not easily, mind you, because of the wind rushing by. I hung on, my shoes balanced on the edge. Eat your heart out, Tom Cruise.

"Hey!" Dominic shouted in my ear. He was lucky I had a firm grip with both hands because my instinct was to lash out with the pulsar stave. He about bought himself a beheading. "I would recommend a safer approach, but if you're determined to skydive without a parachute, by all means!"

I blinked tears away from the wind cutting into my eyesight. The Syndax plane grew closer. I could make out ripples from the jet exhaust. "You can nail a teleport target that small?"

"Of course! Yes." Dominic smiled. "I was able to get us onto and off of a flying sailing vessel in another dimension, wasn't I?"

"You sure were." Except it was moving way slower. And was three, four times as big. And had an open deck. And wasn't tube shaped. And … I shook my head to rattle my brain back on track. "Okay. We can do this."

"Gonna stand here giving each other pats on the back until you pull the trigger and do this thing?" Javon was right behind us, a cell phone to his face. "My vote's to shoot it down and pluck the pulsar stave from the wreckage."

"No way!" I pushed past Dominic, away from the hatch. The deck rumbled underfoot, and I swayed liked I'd gone through a six-pack of bottled beer in one night. Which I'd done when I was in a bad place. "I won't let you obliterate our most powerful weapon!"

"Half of it, Mercury. And you got the other half. A blast like that's barely gonna singe the stave." Javon glared at me, all traces of his joviality fleeing. I could see why he'd made his way onto the board, and it didn't have as much to do with family connections as I'd thought. "We're bringing the plane down. Right now. Cope! Bring us about and light up the target!"

"Cope! Don't you dare! Or you're killing two operatives!" My heart thudded, not with fear at what I was about to do, but at losing. Losing what made me special in everyone's eyes—my ability to kill astral fiends and otherwise hold back the forces of darkness. Forces that seemed like they were spreading, one step ahead of anything I could plan.

I wasn't about to let Procyon, or my friends, or Loredana, down.

So, I threw myself out of the plane.

"Operative!" Javon's order snapped after me, the words ripped away by the wind. But forget the word. I thought I'd get my skin torn off, too. Rushing air was the only sound.

I blotted out the forest, the shoreline, the receding town. I stabilized my dive with my arms, rocketing toward the airplane. Couldn't be any more than a few hundred feet away.

Really hoped Dominic had made his move. Or this was gonna hurt.

A cold blast of air spun me off course. Light enveloped me. Arms crushed my ribcage.

And like that, I rebounded off the backside of Dominic's couch. In his loft.

"Mercury!" Teget leapt up. He had bloody washcloths in his hands. A pair of EMTs in dark blue jumpsuits bent over Edie, Procyon logos tiny against their collars. "What happened to—?"

The scene lasted two seconds, tops, before Dominic yanked me back through a portal, and as it reassembled my body in midair, he shouted, "Brace us!"

I stabbed down with the pulsar stave and struck fuselage.

My shoes scrabbled for purchase on the slick, curved top of the airplane as it screamed along. Dominic clung to me, doing the same. Okay. Good. If we could hold on, I could carve my way inside. The stave cut along the fuselage, peeling it back like a can of sardines.

But before I could get us in to safety, the front hatch of the plane blew off, pinwheeling away into its exhaust.

Serena leapt onto the wing, armor glistening in the morning sun. The full helmet obscured her face. No need for taunts or threats. She fired the arm cannon at my head.

I yanked the stave free.

Dominic and I tumbled away as the section of fuselage we'd just abandoned exploded, throwing flames and fragments into our faces. The energy blaze singed my eyebrows.

What the heck? She was destroying her own mode of escape! I panicked at the thought she'd also destroy the other half of the pulsar stave, just so I couldn't get it back.

That was, until Troy leaned out of the same hatch. "Serena!"

She nodded and aimed straight up.

At the descending Osprey.

Its nose erupted in gunfire as the Dillon cannon shredded the Syndax airplane's left wing, but Serena's energy blast was quicker and more devastating. It punched a blistering hole through the Osprey's center, blowing out the top. I saw a propeller blade fling off in a crazy corkscrew.

Which left Serena enough time to jump off the plane, with Troy right behind her, the pulsar stave a lightning bolt in his hands.

Together they spun into a purple-rimmed black rip, the same kind Serena had fled through. A whip-crack of thunder later, they were gone. And I wound up with two airplanes that were falling apart as they plummeted to the ground.

"Hang on!" Dominic's Echo Watches whined above the roaring air. We blinked out. My head hammered like I'd found the world's worst migraine.

Our stopover in his loft this time was so fast, I wasn't even sure we'd fully materialized. I swore I saw an afterimage of Teget hurrying out the door at the same time I saw a repeat of him rising from the couch, bloody washcloths still in hand.

Then we popped back through the portal inside the Osprey's bay. The moment, I saw our surroundings, I lunged for the cockpit. Cope cradled the side of his head, blood dripping between his fingers. I slashed through his straps until I could manhandle him free. "Got him!"

"Javon's here!" Dominic grunted as he helped the board member-slash-disintegrating man sling an arm over his shoulder.

The Osprey bucked, groaned, and tore into two pieces.

The front portion, containing me and Cope, dropped away, a hollow bullet. It happened so quickly we rose—or at least, didn't fall as fast.

Dominic dove out of the aft section, Javon a limp package, as they rushed toward us. No way he could close the gap in time.

I twisted and fired the pulsar stave at the broadside of the Osprey's cockpit.

Metal melted and glass exploded. Cope and I got a push away, not much, but enough.

Dominic's outstretched hand grabbed the pulsar stave as the Echo Watches spun into a frenzy. Above us, the Osprey's fuel tanks exploded, flames racing through the sky.

There was a huge, blinding white flash ...

WHAM.

Dazed, vision blurry, bones aching, muscles burning. I stared at a wooden ceiling, brick walls all around us. The sudden silent hurt my ears. They refused to pop from the abrupt change in air pressure.

A pile of the four of us lay on the floor of Dominic's loft, beaten. Bleeding.

Minus half of the pulsar stave.

We'd lost our chance.

And my car was buried under a pile of crumpled SUVs.

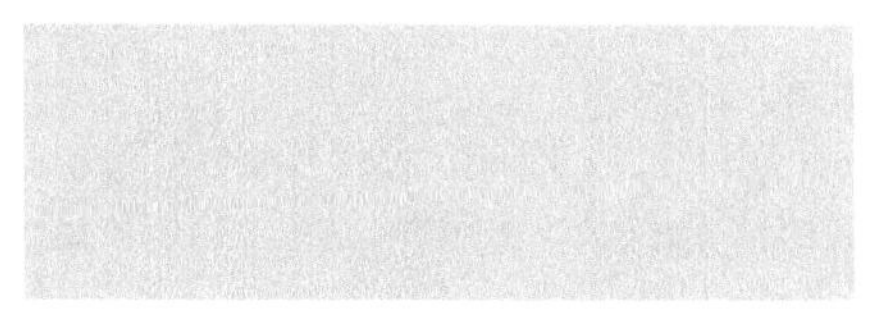# CHAPTER NINETEEN

Hospital time.

I'm kidding. No way the six of us were going to the hospital. That kind of battle injury is not what you want showing up on the bill from your HMO.

Instead, we were packed into Procyon's infirmary on the seventh floor, around the curved hallway from Tracking and Forecasting. Not listed on the official company roster, of course, or even on the building plans. It was painted white and powder blue, with gray tiles, and crammed with exam tables. The place was lit by warm bulbs behind long, transparent strips.

Medics in lab coats attended to each of us. Edie got priority from two people, who hustled her stretcher behind a folded white partition. Teget was next, having gotten the worst of the beating, but he seemed like he was resting okay against his pillow even as a young Black woman probed bruises along his ribcage with gloved fingers. All of them were in surgical masks.

Doctor Millennial was on duty, as always. Shouldn't have called him that, I know. Arne Becker only looked like he should have been either scribbling poetry or serving lattes at a coffee shop, what with the handlebar moustache and thick beard. His hair was equally lavished with care, which I guess was good, because with that much product riding on his face he wasn't about to lose any on his patients. When was the guy ever gonna shave?

Right then, though, his face was covered with a surgical mask from the bridge of his nose to underneath his beard's southern perimeter. Didn't know they came in that size. Doc Arne swiped fog from behind black-rimmed glasses. "I'm managed to keep this place nice and quiet for a long time, Hale. Is that why you felt the need to deliver me a full-blown fiasco?"

I rolled my eyes, then wished I hadn't. Even *that* hurt. "Yeah, Doc. It was top on my list: 'Make sure to annoy our physician when apprehending bad guys.' Even underlined it."

"Apprehending? I didn't hear Security say you'd brought anyone in." He gestured at my shirt. Code: Strip.

I peeled my shirt off, grimacing as I went. The bonus of accelerated healing was offset by the increased pain when things got bad enough. "Hey, I'm not the only one who got stomped. Feel free to share the blame."

"Speak for yourself." Dominic held a cold compress to his forehead. He removed it, peered at his reflection in the infirmary's long windows, and winced. "Well, at least I don't have to hide the injury from Jess."

"Best come up with a cover story with it, for the rest of your crew who don't know." Javon leaned against the door frame. Of all of us, he'd come out the least scathed.

"Yes, I'm familiar with doing so."

I snorted. Always nice to see another operative who didn't like being micromanaged. I thought I had the monopoly. "How's Cope?"

"Bumped and bruised! No broken wings." He was leaned back on a stretcher, fingers laced behind his head, with a bandage over his left eyebrow. Another med tech, this one a six-and-a-half-foot tall bald guy with tattoos up the back of his neck, was wrapping Cope's left ankle. "Ain't but a slight sprain. Can't say I've ever been plucked from a crash by magic before! 'Cept for the time I showed up in this world, of course."

Dominic opened his mouth as if to ask a question, but Doc

Arne's upraised hand acted as a muzzle. "Please don't. No. I do *not* have time to go into who is from what dimension. Bad enough a third of my patients aren't the same kind of *homo sapiens* as need regular medical care. You, for one, Hale, don't look like you've suffered anything more than a regular beating, so I'll leave you to your healing while I check on Ms. Pathkiller. I won't bother telling you to rest up since I know you'll blithely ignore your doctor's orders."

I mock saluted with two fingers. "That's me, all about the blithe."

"When you're done with that attitude, perhaps you'll explain this colossal mess and waste of manpower." Alvarez bulldozed past Javon, leaving two Procyon security beefcakes out in the corridor.

Loredana brushed between them. We met in a hug, which was the best sensation I'd had in a couple days, but also hurt. Because, injuries. "Are you all right?"

"No, he's not all right, because of the massive security breach he let happen," Alvarez snapped. "I'm listing reasons in my head for why I shouldn't have the two gentlemen waiting outside escort him to a holding room."

"What's that fella all tarnal bothered for?" Cope asked.

"The loss of one of the pulsar staves." Teget still had his eyes closed, but his voice was as clear as the proverbial bell. And just as loud. "And the destruction of your winged craft."

"One of those is worse than the other," Dominic muttered.

Cope shrugged. "I reckon so, but if there's another bird for me to fly—"

"The pulsar stave is our greatest asset! No one is going to compare it to a machine we can easily buy again!" Alvarez's neck reddened, and his cheeks flushed. If he gripped his phone any tighter, I was worried he'd crack the screen. Instead he leveled it at my face. "I've tolerated your foul-ups, Mercury, but this time you've brought us a certified catastrophe."

"Hey." I stepped up to him and pushed the phone and its

attendant hand aside. The security boys flanked Alvarez in a second, hands on Tasers. Loredana put her arm across my chest. "I did what I was supposed to. I found Edie and brought her back. The rest of this mess wouldn't have happened if she hadn't run off after a dead operative who she was mixed up with ten years ago, the same guy nobody ever thought to tell me about! Typical Procyon secrets. They cause more danger than they hide."

Alvarez sneered. He looked on the verge of offering a counterpoint, but Loredana cut him off with, "I suggest both of you refrain from further insults and allow us to assess the situation. Yes, Operative Troy Reverdin is alive, however unlikely that fact may seem. He is in possession of one half of the pulsar stave. And he is in league with Serena Cyr."

"Which means, he's taking orders from the Whisperer, too," I added. "Jake—Troy told me as much."

"Indeed. Elizabeth has her team focusing on locating the pulsar stave, based on its unique tachyon signature." Loredana raised an eyebrow, completely nonchalant, like she wasn't holding me back from getting into a brawl with Alvarez and his guards. "Not unlike the method used to track Mercury when he was a fugitive from our cause."

"He what now?" Cope blurted.

Dominic shushed him.

"Our goal now is simple: to find our enemies and prevent whatever scheme they have in mind. One assumes it has something to do with revenge, given than Mr. Reverdin indicated his brother was killed by Procyon."

Alvarez shook his head. "I don't have that information. I'll have to gain access to the files. If Mr. Kimball is willing to grant access at the board level …"

"No problem. I'll see to it." Javon made a face. "All I can tell you is the Reverdin boys were causing trouble back then. But I was just a kid."

"Was?" I dug into my pocket and produce the tiny flash drive. "I'll get this to Liz instead."

"What is it? Hand it over." Alvarez had his palm out.

"Sorry, I don't think you're authorized." I grinned. Sometimes, needling him was worth the consequences. "You'd better save your indignation for Edie. She's the one who's got all the answers. Because, you know, she was the one Procyon sent to kill the twins."

Doc Arne's tablet fell to the floor. Everyone stared at him in the silent moment, his face red, as he stood beside the partition that obscured Edie's bed. No idea what the med techs were doing back there, but several pairs of shoes kept shuffling.

"Your insistence on sharing classified information with the wrong people and keeping other information for yourself is what's the greatest danger right now," Alvarez said. "You will forward the relevant data to me as soon as Tracking has what it needs. And then we'll discuss from where you got the data."

"A reliable source," Loredana said. "One which we shall not reveal. But legitimate, nonetheless."

Alvarez glanced at Javon, his expression somewhere between desperation and constipation. Javon shrugged. "Fine. Report to me at once. I'll be on the phone to Homeland Security, which is still cleaning up your mess. Then I want this whole matter written up. Statements from all of you, so we can get our story straight when the feds come knocking."

He stormed away, the guards lingering for a couple seconds to glare at me. I did the whole "I'm watching you" V-shaped fingers gesture from me to them and back again. Only then did they speed walk to catch up with their boss.

"I suppose that could have gone better." Loredana sighed, then pulled me close for a kiss, her arm block becoming an embrace. "Are you certain you're all right?"

"Yeah, I'm good." Good as I could be. Good as I could feel with half my purpose for being gone, in the enemy's hand.

"You did well, you know, making sure the others got to safety."

"What, no critique about losing the plane?"

She smirked. "Not at all. I full intend to make Ms. Cyr repay us."

Dominic cleared his throat. "Not to cast shade on the hero's spotlight—"

"But he's gonna anyway," I whispered to Loredana.

"—But I think the rest of us did a fair amount of the heavy lifting in this matter." He slapped the side of Teget's bed.

"Yeah, thanks, Gemini. I hadn't noticed my brother's battered state." I rolled my eyes. "Of course we wouldn't have gotten out alive if Dominic hadn't beamed us all out. Repeatedly."

"You're welcome." He sat back in a chair, arms folded. Yeesh. Somebody was testy.

"There a problem you want to share with the class?"

"Now is hardly the time, Mercury," Loredana said. "Let's make our way to Tracking …" She held her hand to her lips. Her expression had gone suddenly pale, so the freckles stood out like fireworks. "Oh, dear."

"What's wrong?" I touched the small of her back.

"The stress of these days … Excuse me. I shall meet you in Tracking in fifteen minutes." She rushed from the infirmary, banking down the corridor at a speed that was just under running and I wasn't sure was possible in heels.

"Your recklessness lost you the pulsar stave," Dominic said.

"Ouch," Javon murmured.

I glared at him. "You're still here?"

"Someone's got to manage when the manager's busy and Operations runs to the can." He smiled. "Let's hear what the man's got to say, right?"

"I thought he and I were on the same page." I glanced at Dominic. "Are we?"

"Of course. I have your back. But I'm worried about everyone else's. You don't take this calling seriously enough."

Okay. No equivocation, was there? "Just because my secret weapons aren't welded to my wrists doesn't mean I don't treat them with caution."

"Then how could you let someone take it?" Dominic pushed from the chair. Its legs squealed on tile. The pair of med techs looked up, caught each other's gazes, and found things to do on the other side of the infirmary.

"Do not question Mercury's devotion to this cause." Teget's eyes cracked a bit, so he could peer at our bruised gang. "He has given more than you can imagine. This is our parents' legacy. Our grandfather's. They have all paid the price for him to fulfill his role."

And I love thinking about all the people who died because of me. The ache behind my heart grew, as did the heat in my face. "Dominic, I'm gonna give you the benefit of the doubt that you're just mad and that's why you're saying stupid stuff."

"It's not stupid. It's an analysis. A needs assessment, like you would do when you have to redesign a building or create a new one from scratch." He pointed at me. "You'd better find a solution, quickly. These devices—these *gifts*—they're not something to be trifled with, and left lying around in a stranger's house for him to pick up."

Wait, what? I stared at Teget, who avoided my gaze. Guilty much? He ratted me out.

Dominic reached beneath his shirt and extracted a set of battered dog tags. I couldn't make out all the text but the name "Marin" jumped out at me. "I won't question your sacrifices, Mercury, but if you can't take it more seriously, you'e putting all of us in danger and making it harder for us to go home to the people we love."

"Okay, everybody shut up. Right now. Here's the deal, boys." Javon leaned on my shoulder. "You three? You stay in here and rest up. Cool down. Me and this guy are gonna take a stroll downstairs. Clear the air, and our heads. Then we check on Edith and get a plan. Want to argue it? Too bad. This is an executive call."

"Like shooting down the airplane?" I muttered. "Missed that in your debrief."

"Oh, Alvarez knows. So does Loredana. I'll man up and take the heat." He jerked a thumb toward the door. "Let's go."

A walk suited me fine. Dominic's abrupt conversion to angry and uptight was stifling, so the fresh breeze off San Camillo Bay was perfect. It was even a cool wind, great for breaking through the summer day's heat.

Javon led us past the gatehouse at the west edge of the parking lot and across the new concrete pathway lining the bay. Onto our new pier. A grandfather and his grandson, both of Japanese descent, were fishing off to our left.

"So, what's your deal?" I gestured at Javon as we walked. "You know. The powers. I've got sticks; Dominic has the Echo Watches. You have an ancient belt buckle that makes you go all dusty?"

Javon grinned. I'd seen the same self-sure expression in the mirror. Cocky? Yeah. But backed up by experience. "No gear. It's all inside me. Passed down from generation to generation, man."

"Like the Medan genes that let people like Wilhelmina and Dominic use the relics."

"Sort of. Mine are more—fluid." He knelt and extended his hand. It dissolved into a cloud, but a cloud with direction. Like a swarm. The particles filtered through the planks, raining into the water, before swirling back up in a loop that reconnected with Javon's wrist. Next thing I knew, he was holding a scallop shell as the last bits reformed his fingers. "They're me. And not me. All the same, you know?"

"They. Creatures?"

"I think you guys been classifying them as symmachites. A different strain, from what I can tell after seeing your guys' files. The ones you found are … Wild, I guess. Controlled only by the black sword's edge. These? They're allies. Longtime. Like old members of our family." Javon tossed the shell, then spun it out into the bay. "I never thought it was real. My daddy's stories, and my granddaddy's. Until the day I got these."

"Is that why you brought me down here?"

"You asked." Javon pointed farther along the dock. "I brought you here to see him."

Ramos. He was leaning on a piling.

"From what Loredana says, that might as well be your family on this Earth. He's the one who'll clear your head." Javon slid on a pair of sunglasses with red-gold lenses. "And when you're clear, that's when you'll be ready to get back in the game. Dominic's wrong. I've seen you. Read the reports. Why'd you think I came out here?"

"Loredana said it was to review Procyon."

"Yeah. And that's you, my man. So, come meet me with Edith. She's got the answers."

I nodded. I got it. Really. But I didn't want to talk to anyone about what I'd just gone through. All I needed was the next mission. Couldn't screw that up, right?

Ramos nodded as I approached. "I heard you've had a rough forty-eight hours."

"You could say that. What's the deal? Here for a pep talk?"

"It's not your fault."

I snorted. "Sure it is. I trusted the wrong guy. He stole my weapon, and then, despite not having fought monsters since I was a high schooler, wiped me and Teget all over the floor."

"So? You can't go blaming yourself for every disaster that happens when the enemy strikes, Mercury. You're not all powerful."

"That's not what you said when zombies showed up downtown. You blamed me." The accusation still stung. Nothing worse than having a father figure disappointed in you. Irritated by me? I could handle that. Anything but disappointment, especially from Ramos.

He grimaced. "I did. I was wrong. It wouldn't be the first time."

That was when I noticed the bags under his eyes, and the

general sag to his expression. "Hey, uh, you look as terrible as I feel."

"Hmm? I should. Endless protests, it feels like." He shook his head. "There's so much fear and hate coursing the city's streets right now. But there's love, too. A man gets shot by police, so angry people burn stores, and neighbors show up to help the business owners get back to their feet, while still others raise signs to call for justice. And my officers—good men and women—try to hold it all together."

"Oh." I scratched the back of my neck. Really didn't feel like grousing about my circumstances. Maybe he was the one who needed to clear his mind. "Where does that leave you?"

Ramos swiped through images on his phone. He held it up. "You haven't been on the *Breeze* much, have you?"

It was a panoramic photo from downtown, about Fifth and DeLeon. The intersection was strewn with CS canisters, paper, and crumpled water bottles. Twenty people were picking up debris alongside city workers. And there was Ramos, on one knee, facing a Black man wearing a gold face covering with a black fist on it. They had their hands on each other's shoulders and heads bowed. A tall, thin white kid with buzz cut hair and an American flag on his T-shirt stood behind Ramos, hand extended to Ramos' other shoulder.

"How?" It was the only word I could find. "This stuff has gone on for a year. How does none of this faze you?"

"It does faze me, all the time. But there comes a point at which all I can do is lean on the promises of God. So, I pray, and wait. Things aren't going to go the way we think they should."

I sat on the pier, letting my feet dangle of the edge. The sight of the sloshing, dark waters made my heart quicken. Not in a good way. I'd almost died here. My prosthetic leg clunked against the wood. Yeah, I'd had to cut it off. But the fear was contained. Not gone. I'd had to work hard over the past year to keep it that way.

Ramos sat beside. "You talk. I'll listen and pray."

CHAPTER TWENTY

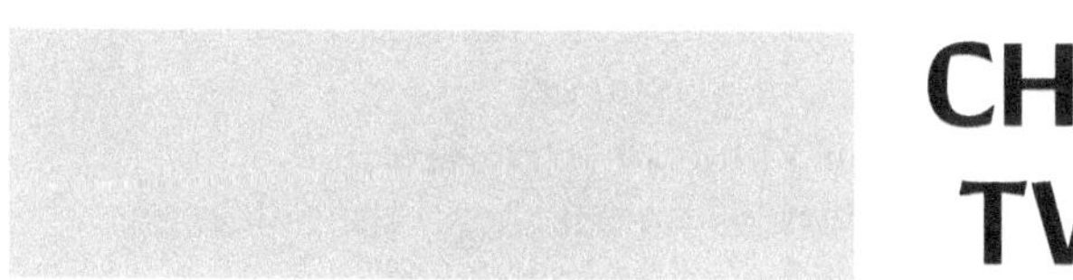

Everybody involved in the Oregon incident was confined to Procyon property. Alvarez didn't want us decamping until he got things straightened out with Homeland and his own higher ups. Which meant he dragged Javon into a bunch of meetings over the next two days. Or maybe Javon did the dragging.

Anyway, the rest of us spent our time between the temporary quarters and the various amenities scattered throughout the three towers. I tried to go for another walk, but Garvey stopped me at the front door.

"Sorry, sir. Media's been pretty hot. I can't let anyone who was a participant outside."

I rolled my eyes. "Come on, Garvey. Dominic's already beamed himself back to Rampart to get new instructions from our office there. And Cope was in the Osprey the whole time! It's not like anyone saw him."

"Mister Sark's already used to keeping a low profile when he's not in a cockpit, sir, since he's—not from around here." With his arms folded, Garvey had the same girth as a statue of a Greek god.

"I was just out there with Ramos—"

"Yesterday. The manager broke the news after he found you went for the stroll."

"It was a mission debrief and counseling, without costing Procyon a dime." I spread my arms. "I saved us money!"

Garvey looked about as convinced as if I told him he'd grown four horns and webbed feet. "Sorry, sir."

"Quit saying that."

"Well, sir, maybe you should quit asking me to break the rules." He smiled, then flicked his fingers.

"Are you dismissing me? I'm not a five-year-old."

"No, but you're stubborn as one of them. I should know."

"Yeah? Got a snot-nosed version at home?"

"Three of them." His phone buzzed, and he excused himself to take a call.

I sighed and headed back upstairs to the seventh floor. I'd already spent three hours in the private gym, getting in a workout and accessing the secret room where I could spar with the animatronic version of an astral fiend. Didn't help the restlessness.

Speaking of Greek, I knew a great restaurant that delivered. I brought up the speed dial menu on my phone. What? If you don't have at least a handful of your favorite eateries ready to call at a moment's notice, you're doing it wrong.

A text popped up from Loredana before I could take the plunge. <Infirmary recovery room, please. Edith is ready to discuss.>

My hunger vanished. Okay, so maybe it just lessened. A little. But I was way more intrigued by what she wanted to spill.

I took the steps two at a time all the way up.

The new version of the recovery room was off to the infirmary's left, but didn't face the corridor, like it did in the previous building. Instead, I had to swipe my access badge across the panel of a locked steel door with a vertical window slit. The room itself was at the end of a short hall that ran the length of the infirmary.

Loredana was seated at Edie's bedside. Javon leaned against the far wall, arms folded, looking bored with his surroundings but with his body tensed for action. I could see it in the way he kept the second door, which lead directly into the infirmary, at his right shoulder.

Edie looked terrible. The swelling on her face had gone down,but had left long dark bruises in its place. She was sitting up in bed. No wires or tubes, other than an IV and a heart rate monitor. Her scowl softened a bit when she saw me. "I didn't get to say it: Thank you."

"No problem. Just part of the job." What else was I gonna say? That I wanted to rattle her into barfing up everything she'd kept quiet?

"Yes, I know. However …" She took a deep breath. "I knew you would come. I saw it. But I couldn't see Troy waiting for me. That's not supposed to happen."

"You'd tracked him to Shotgun, though," I said. "By the way he tapped into the Interstice, like I do."

"Not as clearly. His was a faint echo. But it was familiar." Her eyes glistened. Was she crying? Loredana took her hand. Edie squeezed until Loredana's knuckles were white. "I wanted to be wrong. He was supposed to be eliminated."

"Take it from the top, Edith." Javon was firm but sounded kind.

I expected Edie to glare at him, but instead she nodded in his direction. "When an operative dies, Procyon takes possession of the pulsar stave and finds a replacement. The Pathkillers and the Kimballs have coordinated those efforts since the foundation's first days."

"Edie and her ancestors seek them out," Javon said. "Senses them. The Kimballs have the finances and the connections to get them in the right place at the right time to join Procyon."

"Okay." I glanced between them. "Except Wilhelmina left. Not killed in battle."

"Extenuating circumstances," Edie said. "First, the discovery of a second pulsar stave. There'd only been one for decades, until that attack in 1994 that left your parents dead."

"Whoa, hang on. You know about that?"

Now *there* was a look between her and Javon. "Our families knew. It was kept a top-level secret within the organization for years," she said. "There were some who questioned the wisdom of letting Sherry Jean Crown leave, considering all that she knew."

"Why not off her?" I made a face. "It's not like it'd be a big deal to secure another secret, right?"

"It was unthinkable, and more importantly, the case was made that she should remain at large as a hedge against attacks aimed at you. Which never came. But which were always on Procyon's radar."

"This case that was made." Loredana's interjection was as polite and soft as a governess asking for a second cup of tea. "Might we inquire as to who initiated it?"

I already had a good guess. "Jack Jackson."

"Nailed it," Javon murmured.

"Mr. Jackson—Jack, he was a good man. He bent a lot of rules in those days." Edie smiled, then winced. She held her side, leaning toward the edge of the bed. Javon was there in an instant, bracing her shoulder. She patted his hand. "He was with Intelligence. Did a lot of work digging up Procyon's secrets, while keeping them safe not only from outsiders, but those inside the foundation who couldn't be trusted. Many went missing from the Historic Vault, never to resurface."

"Some of which had to do with my kin." Javon looked at me. "My kin, and expeditions they made to Florida and thereabouts. Coded letters. Those kinds of things."

My heart pounded. Cordelia's files. She'd claimed she'd kept them safe for a reason. Her partner, Randy Kyle, wasn't Procyon, but he was Jack Jackson's estranged son. "That's … pretty interesting."

"The twins, please." Loredana's prompt was a whip in the middle of the awkward silence.

"My mother, Luann Pathkiller, found them. Nineteen-year-olds, high school dropouts, not for lack of brains but for lack of challenge. They were in training for the Marines. Mom approached them, made the sales pitch, and they instantly dropped out."

"Yeah, I bet hearing you get to fight real monsters would top peacetime deployment," I said. "Did she pick them because they were twins, and you had two staves?"

"Partially. Also, because it was what she'd foreseen. That moment, when they accepted—it came to her mind as clearly as the memory of my first day of middle school. I was just 13 then, but I can still remember mom's excitement."

"Troy said it'd been a decade since Noah died."

Edie nodded. "They were operatives for thirteen years."

I whistled. And here I thought the four and change I'd put in had been a long stretch.

"Rips didn't occur as often in those decades," Loredana said. "Historical data indicates tachyon breaches came in waves, with crests increasing slowly over the years, until a single catastrophic event, before declining."

"Like how things picked up a year and a half ago, before I found Teget," I said.

"Precisely so. Which means 1994 was another peak—"

"So was 2010," Javon muttered. "'Cause our families saw it coming. Edith's more than mine. But we knew a storm was gonna break."

"The rips, or the twins?"

"Both." Edie's voice had gone monotone, dull. "They'd dabbled in the Interstice. Become obsessed with the Icon."

"Probably because you guys drill the importance of finding the dumb thing—which turned out to be my brother and who knows who else before that—into every operative's head," I said. "Big surprise the twins were excited about it."

"Excited is the wrong word. They believed the Icon was actually a threat. They thought destroying it—or him—would end the danger of the astral fiends. Which is why they stopped killing them."

"Stopped—killing fiends?" I thought my eyes were going to

pop out of my head. I couldn't imagine. "What the heck did they think they should do, hand out tourist maps?"

"The Kimballs bypassed the board, went right to Jackson, to bring in a Pathkiller to set things straight," Javon said. "With the Reverdins foolin' around with rips, someone had to kill the fiends before they got out of hand. Edie held them off as best she could, but her bow is no pulsar stave. It came to a head when Edie and my granddad, Henry 'Box' Kimball, brought the twins in for a sit down."

"Didn't go well, I'd guess."

"Turned into a smack down." Javon shook his head. "They were outta their minds. Ranting about bringing down the walls between us and the Interstice, so we could find out the truth about the Icon and see that the one who was orchestrating everything in that other dimension wasn't so bad. They tore the place apart, but Granddad, he gave as good as he got. Put one of those punks through a wall. But he got stuck when a rafter fell on Luann."

"It was left to me," Edie said softly. "Jackson gave me direct orders to eliminate the twins. So, that's what I did."

"They ran off after the latest rip to open," Javon said. "Big one. Four fiends came through. Of course, those lunatics didn't care the rip had opened a block away from a residential development that had new families moving in. But the fiends did. They went straight for dinner. The Reverdins took out one fiend in their way. Left the rest for Edie."

"I should have faced them. Fought them hand to hand." Edie's eyes brimmed with tears again. "But I couldn't. I destroyed the fiends. Warred with them until I was spent. When the dust settled, they were gone, but the rip was there. Troy and Noah came back through. Smiling. Giddy."

She gripped the side rail of the bed, pulling herself forward. The plastic cracked under her fingers. "Smiling, when they'd nearly killed my mother and put countless people at risk. I fired both RPG rounds, to be sure."

Loredana nudged me. She'd retrieved her tablet—from her

purse, maybe, or tucked beside her seat. The video of a huge blaze between structures was so brilliant I had to squint. Difficult to make out where it took place, but I found a hazy memory of an arson spree back when I was doing my best to *not* attend high school. Right when I bailed on the last foster family I'd ever need. No wonder I wasn't paying attention.

A silhouette crouched on a rooftop in the left corner of the video turned toward the camera, then disappeared into the wreckage.

"Bits and bones," Javon said. "That's all Procyon found. The whole place was an inferno. So, the twins got written off as dead and the staves got retrieved for the next operative."

"Retrieved?" I stared at the video. "From that?"

"Get why I wasn't worried about the plane blowing up?" Javon smirked. "They were barely scorched."

"I spent years in seclusion," Edie said. "Busy taking care of Mom. She was put into a wheelchair, with no hope of walking again. Given a nice pension and shipped off to a quiet corner of Nevada, so she could live out retirement in peace."

Edie glared at all of us, like we'd been there. "It was a death sentence. Troy and Noah had tried to kill her, and all Procyon could do was pretend she'd never existed. One year to the day before I saw you in my visions, Mercury, she drank a bottle of hemlock."

My insides felt worse than when Troy had pummeled them. What a mess. The twins had left a trail of death and devastation in their wake, and for Edie to find out one of them was still alive …

But there was something else. Something about the way she lay there, her voice catching whenever she talked about them. "You were about their age, right? Were you all friends? That would have—I don't know. Had to be terrible."

Edie avoided looking at any of us, a heck of a switch from her death glare five seconds ago. Even Javon seemed interested in his shoes.

I glanced at Loredana.

"Mercury, I should think it obvious." Loredana's wry smile was the one she reserved for when she thought she was being extraordinarily patience with me.

"And what's that, honey?" I tried leave out the sarcasm but failed.

"She was involved with him. With Troy." Loredana crooked an eyebrow. "Romantically."

"I … Oh. Ah." Heat rushed to my face. No wonder Edie was out of sorts—as in, badly psychologically hurt. Nothing like finding out the person you loved—I assumed, given how everyone else was reacting to the news—was evil, then blowing them to bits, then finding out, psych! Not dead. Alive and well, living just three hours north ten years later.

"I never should have trusted him," Edie murmured. "But I could never see clearly when it came to our future. That blankness didn't bother me. I saved my gift for the Forecast, until it was too late to see what Troy had become. He and Noah … They couldn't be pulled from their path. I begged. And all Troy could say was, 'The power of the Interstice is worth more than anything or any one person.' Imagine those words, directed at you."

For a few seconds, the only sound was the soft whirr of the medical machinery. I finally slapped my hands on my pants legs. "Okay. Now we know. There's a comment in there about half the battle—"

"For heaven's sake." Loredana sighed.

"—But I'll save it for later." I stood up. "Don't, worry Edie—"

"Enough!" she snapped. "Quit *calling* me that, unless you want Doctor Arne's scalpel through your eye."

Geez. What did it matter what I called …? Aw, man. The heat returned to my face like the world's worst sunburn. Edie. Troy called her the same name, the whole time he was palling up to me and Teget. Here I'd been saying the same thing, getting quite the kick out of her irritation. I decided that moment was the perfect one in which to practice restraint.

"Relax, everybody. We got a plan." Javon pointed at the wall.

"Tracking's on it. We wait for new intel."

Intel. Intelligence. Cordelia's flash drive of files. One mysterious, encoded letter. I wondered if Liz had gotten any closer to deciphering it.

"A requisition order is in for a new aircraft, should the need arise." Loredana pursed her lips. "I suppose Mr. Sark will require some cockpit time in which to become acclimated, but I doubt it will be very long a span. In the meantime, if Ms. Pathkiller can give us any details from her time spent with the Reverdins—on a personal level, that is—such data will be vital."

"Ten years is too long a time to not know a man," Edith— yeah, I was trying it out—said. "But when I found him, he acted stunned and heartbroken to see me. I thought, for a few seconds, that the tears were real, until he bested me in a fight." She shook her head. "The same blind spot."

"He was really good at faking his way through a personality," I said. "I'm guessing he was like that before all the private eye training."

"He was. It was his way of coping with the horrors he and Noah faced. I knew it was unhealthy. Argued with him. But he told me he could handle it. Handle the nightmares." Edith scowled. "And there, at the end, he yearned for every nightmare he could get, just so he could hear the Whisperer."

"That don't matter now," Javon said. "We know what he's got, and we know who he's with, so we're gonna find him. The pulsar stave might as well be a GPS. Trackable. Once we find him and this Serena chick, we put a stop to him for good."

"I won't be of any use in that way."

"Hold on. Just. One. More. Second." I stood between them. "We're leaving out the big weird. Namely, when Tenebrae hijacked Edith and she fought me in her office."

Javon looked as stunned as I'd felt this entire conversation. "Since when?"

"Since before I ran after Troy." Edith grimaced. "Tenebrae wasn't trying to hurt you, Mercury, but the instinct of every being he inhabits is to fight, either with itself or with another. He wants your help."

"My help with what?" I blew out a breath. "Is it too much trouble for it to be spelled out?"

"I don't have an answer, I'm sorry," she said. "But if Troy has the pulsar stave, and Serena Cyr walks in the amor Javon described, it's because more than just our world is in jeopardy."

Right then was when everyone's phones started buzzing. A second later, Doc Arne flung open the door into the recovery room. "Loredana! The manager needs you ASAP!"

"Calm yourself, Doctor, and be specific."

"There's a riot at the supermax prison."

Supermax? Great. The place where Winston Yen, architect of most of Procyon's best tech, and traitor to us all, was locked up. Oh, and also, a young woman who Serena had used to try to enslave my fellow superheroes.

I answered my phone. "Ramos? I'm busy with—"

"The prison. I know." Shouts and loud engine noises swamped his voice. "… Getting the task force headed there now. Meet us. Reports are coming back about monsters and zombies tearing the walls apart."

"Well, crap." I pushed past Arne. "Come on, Javon. We've got a teleporter to find."

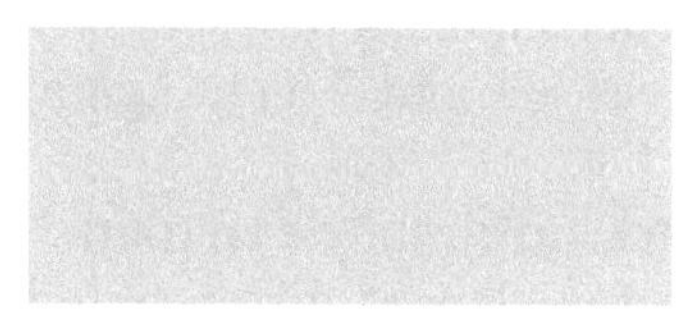# CHAPTER TWENTY-ONE

wanted to rush dramatically from the recovery room, pulsar stave ablaze, ready to fling myself at monstrous adversaries.

What I got was stuck in a policy meeting.

"Hold up, Mercury." Javon crossed his arms. "I'm staying."

"Ah, look, I get it that I'm not the boss of you," I said, "But seeing as how you can—"

"Mercury." Loredana nodded toward Doc Arne.

"—How you can be an asset in a fight, I figured I should issue the invitation. You plus me plus Teget would help even whatever odds we have."

"Yeah, do doubt. But it's best if I stay out of the public eye." He gestured at the wall, in what I assumed was the general direction of the prison. Heck, it could have been a bathroom, for all I know. "This thing? TV cameras are gonna be like locusts. Won't catch me anywhere near it."

"So, wear a mask!" I threw my arms up. "Everybody's doing that these days, anyway. Seriously, guys? Just give me the firepower I need!"

"You'll have it." Edith was already stripping the leads to her medical equipment from her skin. She swung her legs over the side of the bed.

"Absolutely not." Loredana planted her hand dead center on

Edith's chest. She glared at us three guys in turn, then let her stone-cold irritation settle on Edith. "I am *not* authorizing the deployment of our Forecaster into the field, especially when it is into a situation of variable threat in an unknown environment. And Mr. Kimball is correct: Whatever his assets, splashing his likeness across the news would harm Procyon, mask or no mask."

"Great," I muttered. "Which leaves me and Teget. Again. Maybe Wilhelmina's over her cold."

"Lieutenant Ramos and his task force are doubtless en route." Loredana checked her phone. "Given the elapsed distance and their aerial transport, I would estimate their arrival in less than fifteen minutes. I suggest you and Gemini make the most of that window."

"No offense, Loredana." Edith shoved her restraining hand aside and stood. Her legs wobbled, but only for a second. "But my body is ready. The mind—the mind will have to adjust. And technically, I outrank everyone in this room except for Javon."

"Now, wait a second!" Doc Arne snapped. "If you think for one moment that your physician is going to roll over and—"

"Shut it, Doc." Javon pushed him out the door he'd entered, then closed it in his face. Javon grinned at Edith. "Better?"

"Much. Thanks for that." Edith clasped hands with him.

"Blast it all," Loredana muttered. "I do not need a mutiny."

I patted her shoulder. "Sorry, babe. She's probably right. Do me a favor?"

"Gyros will have to wait, Mercury." She rose from her bedside sheet and gave me a peck on the cheek. "Now, please, get moving before I throw my own tantrum into the mix."

She left the room, speaking softly into her phone. Javon was right behind her.

I clapped my hands together and grinned at Edith. "All right! Let's get your bow and teleport out of here."

"Garvey had Security bring my belongings back to Procyon. It should be in the armory." Edith smirked. "But first, I'll secure pants."

I looked down at her legs, bare from knees to toes, and the hospital gown covering the rest. "Oh. Right."

Six minutes later, my crack commando unit appeared from a swirl of light inside the security fences surrounding Bulwark State Prison, forty miles up the coast. Me and Teget at the front, stave and ax ready. Edith between us and behind, wearing her standard cutoff flannel shirt with blue jeans. She bore a recurve bow covered with bizarre carvings, an arrow with a wicked four-bladed head nocked and fifteen more in the quiver strapped to her back. The red gaiter for concealment purposes completed the ensemble.

Garvey brought up the rear, with three others from Procyon security—two men and a woman. They were clad head to foot in black, from the helmets to the boots and all the body armor you could imagine in between. Their faces were masked, too, so the only patches of skin I saw were the strips around their eyes. Each one had double gray stripes on their shoulders and wielded a Heckler & Koch MP5 submachine gun, with suppressors and flashlights and every other nifty gun gadget you could imagine.

We were too late. Which we knew. The attack had already been in play when we rounded up our team. But I hadn't expected the devastation. As in, crumbled concrete walls and collapsed razor wire fencing. Inmates must have tried to scatter, but guards were busy rounding them up into a makeshift corral of three prison buses.

Dominic grimaced as three inmates tackled a guard, only to be swamped by two more guards. "I take it we're not here for this kind of crowd control."

A flash of golden light illuminated a jagged hole torn in one side of the prison.

"Nope." I pointed. "Okay, gang, let's move in. Heads on a swivel. That's a thing, right?"

"If you say so, sir." Garvey's voice was muffled through his mask. He flashed a couple hand gestures. His security crew fanned out ahead of us, duck walking into the yard.

"Okay. You know the deal." I tapped Dominic on the chest. "Beam home but stay on the phone. I'll let you know when we need to bail."

"Are you sure you don't need the backup?" Dominic flashed the Echo Watches on his wrist. "You've seen what they can do."

"The decision isn't his to make." Loredana's voice filtered through my earbud via the link we had with Tracking, and through the earbuds we all wore. Even Teget, who was at that moment leaning to the side with a quizzical expression. He looked like a dog trying to decipher his owner's commands. "We're taking steps to minimize our risk. It is bad enough being overridden into having Edith accompany your team. I will not have another operative—and his powerful relics—put in danger of capture."

"Roger that." I knew what she meant. Tried not to take offense. But considering we were there because I'd lost half the pulsar stave, the growing sense of irritation only, well, irritated me. "We're headed in."

"Do be careful."

"Always am."

Loredana snorted but left the verbal rejoinder unspoken.

"Godspeed." Dominic fired up the Echo Watches and vanished in a burst of light.

"Let's move." I jogged across the yard, Teget and Edith behind me, the latter lagging by a few striders. She might not be running at 100 percent but she sure was gonna try and prove otherwise. Garvey and his people bracketed the blast hole, weapons trained on the interior. A breeze caught the stench of burnt fabric and plastic, overlaid with a whole lot of body odor. There was another smell—the sour aroma of astral fiend slime.

And the particular singeing aftermath of the pulsar stave's use.

Garvey flicked two fingers left. A pair of his people—Sandoval and Reese, judging by their nametags—stepped inside, covering the right angle of the battered hallway with their weapons. The woman, Asato, flanked Garvey as he went left.

I eased inside, trying to watch all approaches, but staying low in case anyone came around a corner blasting. Flashlight beams caught cascades of dust, turning their glow into slashing streams of illumination. We were at a T-shaped intersection, a long corridor lined with doors ahead of us.

"No bodies," I murmured. "Good sign."

A shriek rattled the air from far off. Human cries answered it, cut off in mid-shout.

"*Ch'irak'i.*" Teget's whisper was harsh, sharp-edged like the blades of his ax. His body was tense, ready for a fight or a race, like those lions you see on the Nature Channel right before they pounce on a gazelle.

"Ahead from this junction is access to the maximum-security wing in which Winston Yen is held," Loredana said. "I have your locations. Prison security has mostly abandoned the building, and the bulk of inmates have been accounted for, either on the premises or in the woods nearby. Twenty-seven are at large."

"I'm betting a couple less than that," I hissed. "Move!"

Garvey's team hustled ahead of us, flashlight beams sweeping every door and every open passageway. Nothing jumped out at us, so that was good.

I let the pulsar stave's energy build, so that my supersuit glowed just as well as those flashlights, but it flickered. Twice.

Teget glanced at me. "What is wrong?"

"Nothing. It's fine." I held the stave closer. Maybe it was a proximity thing. I hadn't used the suit for a while. And the stave hadn't been back to Meda for the recharge that my dear brother insisted it needed. Of course, it could also be that I'd never once fought using only half of the stave. My entire tenure with Procyon? One big weapon that split in two. I knew what it felt like. Knew how it fought. Sure, I had lent it temporarily in battle.

But it was gone.

And it was being used to destroy the place where we'd locked up one of our worst enemies.

Garvey held up a fist. Everyone froze. Even Edith paused mid-step, her bow aimed at the dark end of the corridor. "Motion," he muttered.

I looked at Teget. "Draw straws?"

He scowled and stormed the next intersection.

There was a yelp, followed by the sound of metal striking flesh. A man flopped onto the floor, sliding up against a mound of collapsed ceiling tiles. He wore an orange jumpsuit, with a guard's bloodied shirt on over top. He wasn't gonna pass for a corrections officer any time soon. Even with the baton in hand.

"Imposter." Teget snatched the baton from his grasp and snapped it half like a dry twig.

The man's eyes widened. "Okay, okay! Don't kill me! I was tryin' to—I had to get outta there! The monster killed the guards! They were like a pair of mummies!"

"Get this knucklehead out of here, Garvey." I stepped over his quivering form and glanced around the hall. Darkness to the right. Faint purple glow and bloodcurdling screeches to the left. Well, I knew which way we had to go.

"Reese. Take him outside the wall. Move." Garvey didn't look up from his weapon as the security officer half-escorted, half-dragged the whimpering prisoner out. That was when I recognized him—he'd been locked up for planting a bomb outside an IRS office a few years back. The explosion killed forty people. Guess life-sucking monsters made even a terrorist question his bravado.

Another shout. Three people ran out from the next intersection, up to our left. They saw our party and made a beeline for us.

"Heads up!" I crouched, ready to launch into a run. Teget did likewise.

"Stand by." Loredana's interruption made me jump. "Elizabeth informs me there is a tachyon surge which her computer has flagged as unique but repeated."

I grimaced. "What does Cyril mean by that?"

"Hey, Mercury! It's the same signature as what we saw last year when we watched the fiend-hound hop-skip around San Camillo and the surrounding area using that kind of rip-based teleportation and the more I think about it the more I realize it's almost like what Serena Cyr employed to escape from that warehouse fight you—"

"Okay, thanks, gotta go!" No need to let Liz ramble on when imminent death might be lurking around the corner.

"Go on." Edith stood between us, bow raised. Her right arm trembled, only for a second, then locked solid as she drew in a breath. "I have the shot."

"Cool." I took off.

But my speed wasn't what I expected. Here I thought Teget and I would have sprinted the length of the corridor together, one on either side, skirting the two panicked prisoners and lone guard trying to get everyone out. Instead, I wound up ten feet behind him. Doesn't sound like much.

When the fiend-hound loomed around the corner, though, it might as well have been ten miles.

My brain locked up at the sight of it. I hadn't seen one since Arkwright killed his own creation to amp up his powers in Syndax's lab in downtown Rampart, Colorado. This one was way bigger than its predecessor—the size of a grizzly bear, only leaner, with two gnarled front legs and powerful rear ones, and a face that hinted at someone's attempt to make a dog, a mountain lion, and a bear share lineage. Adding glistening spikes along its spine and overlapping scales down its rib cage and haunches didn't help the nightmare image.

The eyes were the worst. Dogs should have two. Not eight. And they shouldn't be soulless, midnight black, shimmering with a purple afterglow.

The fiend-hound slammed into Teget, knocking him *through* a wall—thankfully, not one made of concrete. Then the creature pivoted toward me and screamed, its mouth a long, jagged maw that sprayed glowing blue spittle as three-foot long tentacles lashed the air.

All of that happened in slow motion, which was awesome, because I got the chance to twist past the fleeing bystanders, spin myself midair, and slash through the stabby mouth tentacles.

That burst of energy siphoned away from my superspeed, and everything got back to normality way too fast.

I hit the floor just in front of the fiend-hound—forget it, bear-fiend was more accurate—and slid underneath its legs across slime-spattered polished concrete. Which worked out great because the beast was on its way down from a leap.

That advantage got lost when the stupid thing *inverted* like an astral fiend. I'm not talking turning on a dime. I mean, flat out was pointing one direction, then turned itself inside out like it was made of putty, before winding up the opposite orientation. So, instead of slicing through its armored backside, I was staring into its face from six feet away. A powerful, four-clawed paw swiped for my face.

I intercepted the blow with the pulsar stave, sending off a spray of golden white spikes that brought daylight into the dark hallway. Even over the beast's roar, I could hear the piercing—I don't know, a *thwish?* But it was way too loud, almost like an eagle's cry.

A brilliant gold light, not dissimilar from the stave's, exploded on the side of the bear-fiend's head, sending it reeling. I glimpsed an arrow shaft protruding from between the glistening gray and purple hide. The bear-fiend howled, batting at the weapon in hopes of dislodging it.

Another shout. Teget leapt through the hole he'd made in the wall, blood streaming down his face, his teeth gleaming like he was a maniac vampire. He landed atop the bear-fiend, right between the twin rows of spikes, and drove the ax into its hide.

The sizzling that resulted melded with the monster's renewed screams, which was great, because my stomach revolted at both the sound and smell. I rolled out of the way and swiped through a leg with the stave, severing the bear-fiend's left paw, leaving behind a stump that oozed blue-gray while sparks fell from a glowing line of cauterization.

"Weapons hot!" Garvey's bark nearly made me leap up, loud

as it was through the earpiece, and that would have been a very bad idea.

Three automatic weapons opened fire, their hammering discharge echoing off the confined space of the hallway. I wanted to hold my ears—because tinnitus is no joke, people, and I'm too young for hearing aids—but instead I got myself out of the intersection.

Teget backflipped, landing behind the bear-fiend, as round after round from the three MP5s punctured the monster's hide.

It writhed and howled, its voice scratchy and hoarse. Its thrashing tail, spikeless but still a powerful, scaled weapon, one that took chunks out of cinderblock walls and ripped apart drywall like it was tissue. That's when I realized it was twisting its hind end in giant, macabre imitation of a kitty readying to pounce.

With three unarmed people hunkering under the protective fire of three—make that four, with Reese returned—Procyon guards and Edith, who shot another arrow into the beast's face.

"Down, boy!" I lunged for the tail and pulled.

There we were, engaged in an insane tug of war. The dumb critter kept trying to thrash me off, but I held firm. "Teget!" I shouted. "Little help!"

With another battle cry, he swung the ax over his head and brought it down so hard it cleaved the tail in two. I staggered against the wall, holding four feet of twitching bear-fiend.

Blue mush oozed from the wound. The beast stumbled, rose again, and galloped toward the gathered team.

Their fire slackened as they switched out magazines on their weapons and backed away into the corridor. But Edith strode ahead, her eyes purple lanterns in the dim atmosphere of the hall. Her bow's runes shown with the same glow as the pulsar stave. "Pin it down!"

Yeah, yeah. I was already climbing atop it, with Teget right behind me. He drove the ax into its spine, halfway up its back, while I channeled as much power through the stave as I could. A stream of golden sparks shot from both ends, forming energy blades, and I stabbed down right behind the bear-fiend's skull.

At the same moment, Edith launched a third arrow into its eye cluster from four feet away, as tentacles reached out for her.

The bear-fiend let out a final, piteous cry, then collapsed. Air gushed from its lungs. Worst death belch ever. I gagged.

Its body began an immediate decay, so fast that by the time Teget and I dismounted, and Garvey's team approached, there was nothing left but a foot-tall lump in the rough outline of a bear-fiend, the pulsating blue sludge steaming as it dissipated.

"Okay." I swiped goo from my face. "Nice work, kids."

"Is everyone unhurt?" Loredana's voice came across the earpiece as clearly as if she were standing among us. "Elizabeth informs me the creature disappeared from cameras and our drone-based sensors."

"Yeah, we're good. And it's dead." I grinned at Teget who held his ax aloft until it scraped the ceiling. "Kinda celebrating."

"Then by all means, don't let us spoil the revels."

Uh-oh. Wrong English accent.

Winston Yen walked around the corner, hands clasped behind his back, as if he'd come inside from a lunchtime stroll.

"Hello, Mercury." He smiled. "Jolly good to see you again."

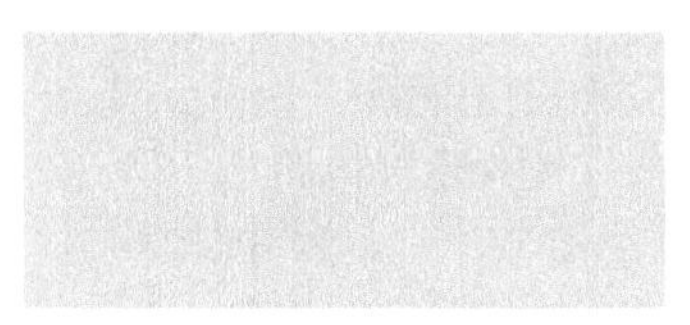

CHAPTER TWENTY-TWO

O h, great.

Don't ask me why I froze. Winston wasn't a fighter, or a monster. Short, thin, wearing a loose-fitting jumpsuit, with newly bleach-blond spiked hair. The goatee with moustache wasn't a bad look, but he'd grown a little neckbeard with the black bristles. My brain dutifully reminded me of all the times I'd been invited to his and Marigold's apartment for dinner, or the movie nights we'd spent at a handful of theaters.

But it also alerted me to fear—fear at remembering him backing up his wife as she used the night's blade in concert with Teget's ax and the pulsar stave to rip apart the barrier between Earth and the Interstice. I'd never have stopped them alone.

Of course, if he hadn't betrayed Procyon and all the Foundation held dear, none of that would have happened anyway.

"Imagine my surprise when I saw you here." Winston held a book aloft. Nope, not the Bible. Not even a copy of *Law Degrees for Dummies*.

Teget, ready to leap at his next target, brushed blood from his forehead with the back of his hand. "Has he painted your likeness on that tome?"

Seriously? The novel? Now?

"It's pretty good," Garvey muttered. "Sir."

"Nobody asked anybody." I sneered at Winston. "Gotta say, re-submitting yourself to custody is a gutsy move. Even if you did try to kill us with your friend the bear-fiend."

"Bear-fiend." Winston chuckled. "You always did have a knack for cracking good nicknames. This beast is a gift from my associate, Alexander Arkwright, who Marigold informs me is not as dead as you once hoped. Sadly, he couldn't be here with us today in person, but I do understand he's here in spirit."

"Stand down," Garvey said, "And you won't be harmed."

"Oh, I shan't be doing that. The standing down, that is. I have an escort."

Troy stepped into view, the other half of my pulsar stave dripping sparks like a Fourth of July sparkler hooked up to a nuclear reactor. He carried it easy, that same relaxed but ready stance I used when I was tense for a fight. Troy had foregone his casual civilian garb for gray fatigue pants, a black vest worn over a red T-shirt, and fingerless gloves with rubber knuckle pads. "You really did go all out, did you? And in more ways than one. Hello again, Edie. I see Mercury was able to upgrade your accommodations."

I fantasized about an arrow piercing Troy's forehead, ending this nightmare once and for all, but nothing doing. That was because Edie was trembling, her eyes wide, breathing slow and shallow. Her bow was aimed for the floor. I'd never seen her face so twisted with anger, not even when Tenebrae had possessed her so she could attack me.

"Mercury." Loredana whispered my name, though in an urgent and decidedly un-hot way. "I have them on camera. Garvey's vest. We must take Winston alive. The information he could tell us about our enemies—"

"Got it." I tried to keep my reply muted and muttered. Too bad I'd never taken up ventriloquism.

But when the third person joined the trio of bad guys, I swore aloud.

Serena had called her Xia when, almost eighteen months

ago, she'd entrusted the late twentysomething woman with the black blade formerly wielded by my cousin Crux. Crux had been Kutsatuta, an outcast from Meda the city, and had signed up in Arkwright's crazy army until he'd failed one too many times to kill me. That had earned him the death penalty at Arkwright's hand. And had put the sword into play.

It had been a powerful enough weapon when I'd clashed with it one-on-one, and then in split into two swords. But Xia had used it to command the symmachites, taking control of not just Teget but Dominic, Ramos, and even Brandon Tusk in his guise as the Drake City superhero Airfoil. Only the timely intervention by some of Brandon's erstwhile allies—as in, his teenage son and surly old mentor—and the pulsar stave's surprising ability to burn symmachites out of a possessed body had ended the brawl in our favor.

Xia a one-way-ticket to federal prison.

Yet, there she was, all broken out of her cell and wearing the same prison garb as Winston. Her eyes were a dark emerald, catching some of the fleeting light from emergency bulbs. I couldn't tell if she was constipated or plotting my murder.

"Since nobody's making a move, and doesn't seem inclined too, I recommend we call truce. Time for us to slip out, and you to withdraw," Troy said.

"No way. Come on. You're supposed to be a stealthy operative. How'd you figure making this much noise was gonna go?" I shook my head. "SCPD's task force should be here by now. They'll have surrounded the place. And if you think the feds are gonna sit this one out—when you blew holes in their max security prison—I've got a grumpy Homeland Security agent from Montana who'd beg to disagree. So, new deal: Drop the pulsar stave and we'll stun you into compliance nice and easy."

"You're a terrible negotiator." Troy spun the stave once, catching it with a *slap* against his palm.

"He is, quite," Winston said. "Poor lad never could see his way out of a situation without resorting to physical violence."

"Gee I wonder why?" I glared at him. "That is how I was trained from Day One."

"Steady," Loredana's voice murmured. "Liz has another tachyon build-up, behind the wall to your right. It could be another beast preparing to skip into your corridor."

"We're leaving." Troy took a step toward us. "You should too."

Garvey and his team shifted, weapons ready. "Give the word, sir."

I held up a hand. "Nobody's blowing holes in anyone. I'm not eager to explain them as human Swiss cheese if Bowe asks."

"It's really too bad," Winston said. "You should have taken the chance to withdraw."

Edie's gaze, focused on the far corridor and some unseen point above everyone's heads, snapped to the right. She spun 90 degrees, snapping up her bow. "Down!"

Garvey was well-trained. So were his people. They ducked, shielding their faces …

As the wall to the right blew out along a twenty-foot stretch.

The corridor filled with drywall dust, as chunks of both hard and soft consistency pummeled us. I coughed away the haze as a huge shape loomed in the space where the wall and ceiling had been. Sunlight filtered through a jagged rift.

"—Drones are down!" Loredana cried. "We've lost access to the security feeds! I can't see anything!"

"Oh, don't worry, I can." I held the stave to block the incoming fist.

Might as well have been holding up a paper towel to stop an arrow. In a split second, I recognized the scaly armor of Serena's latest toy—the shell, Teget had called it. Except, the fist was triple what it should be. Like hand-shaped bowling ball.

The blow knocked me through the wall to my left.

Correction. I went through the wall with Serena plowing another huge gash. Must have been easy for her, since she was twelve feet tall, wide as a bulldozer, and bristling with clanking, overlapping scales. A single purple eye slit gazed at me with a dispassion that didn't match the glee in her voice. "How about some fresh air?"

Yeah, it was a cheesy line, but you know what? Since she had expanded her killer armor and thrown me clear out of the prison into a triangular exercise courtyard, I wasn't about to critique.

Even with my head ringing, the gunfire from Garvey's team was easy to hear. Teget, instead of being his usual bellowing self, used the cacophony as his cover to fling himself and the ax at Serena's backside.

Which would have made for a great sneak attack—and possible amputation—if Troy hadn't intercepted with a strike that sent Teget crashing into a basketball hoop. His impact bent the pole.

Serena's arm morphed into a blade four feet long and slashed down right at my face.

I forced the suit to go camouflaged and flipped sideways over a toppled picnic table.

Her cutting edge crushed the table like tinfoil. Me? I blended against the third of the three walls, the suit's adaptive mimicry making me just another slab of cinderblocks.

"For heaven's sake, use the dust to reveal his position!" Winston yelled from somewhere behind.

Thanks, traitor. I didn't bother with subtlety and ran for Teget, blasting at Troy with the pulsar stave and zigzagging as I went. One of the four shots I let off got lucky, clipping Troy's shoulder. He spun, head rebounding off the bent basketball pole. He dropped the pulsar stave.

I ducked under a sweep of Serena's huge, metallic arm, as she fired searing bursts of purple-tinged energy at Garvey's team. And where the heck was Edith? She should never have come! What had she been thinking, besides looking to get another shot at troy? Gee, that had worked out well.

The stave was right there. Six feet away. My fingertips brushed it.

Xia snatched it from my reach.

She stared at it, mouth agape, as it sprang back to life from the inert metal it had become when Troy let it slip. She spun it in her fingers.

"That isn't yours." I gestured with the remaining half I had.

"It could be." Her voice was striking—a soft but cutting tone, with a hint of musicality, like she could break out into song and entertain an entire barroom. "It should."

"Yeah, no." I caught her in a chokehold, and, before she could come up with a strategy for her newly acquired and recently stolen weapon, I pressed one end of the stave toward her neck so I could stun her to sleep.

Except she interposed her pulsar stave between her skin and my stave.

A percussion of air tossed us ten feet from each other. I blinked spots from my vision. Since when did the stave fight against itself?

Behind her, Teget had the ax handle across Troy's neck, as the latter pounded on him with blows. Serena swept aside another swath of cinderblocks, raining debris on Garvey and Sandoval. Where was Reese? A black helmet protruded from a collapsed steel beam. Amato hunkered inside the corridor, her right arm bent at an angle human bones shouldn't attempt.

It would have been nice to get a bird's eye view of the whole place, but our comms had gone down. Nothing but static on the earbud.

Xia was back on her feet. I faced her in a similar stance. This wasn't gonna get less messy, that was for sure.

"All occupants! Lay down your weapons and surrender!"

That bullhorn-enhanced voice sounded suspiciously like Ramos'. And it really was him, plus a dozen of his closest armored pals with the Extraordinary Crimes Task Force swarmed the battered courtyard from both sides. They were armed with automatic rifles, plus four guys had heavy grenade launchers. Didn't really want them firing those in a confined space, but hey, not much else was denting Serena's armor.

A roar grew overhead, until a Blackhawk helicopter blotted the sun, its giant, bug-shaped shadow covering the ground.

"Stand down or we will open fire." Yep, definitely Ramos' voice echoing around us.

Troy broke free of Teget, slashing through Teget's vest with a hidden combat knife, and kicked him against the wall. "Move, move!"

SCPD fired on Serena, their bullets tearing what was left of the courtyard apart. Someone—Ramos, I think—shouted for them to quit shooting, but it didn't stop two guys from popping grenades at Serena. They exploded on her chest and side, enveloping her from the waist up with flames.

Which she laughed off.

Her energy cannon tore through the ranks of the task force, scattering men like discarded action figures. Cries of pain split the air.

I took advantage of the confusion to engage the suit's camouflage. I tackled Xia, blocking her blows with my pulsar stave and trying to get ahold of hers, but she just. Wouldn't. Quit!

BAM!

The bullet ripped across the top of my right shoulder and knocked me off my feet. I gasped for air.

Xia sprinted over rubble, heading for the source of the gunshot—

Winston. Holding one of the MP5s Garvey's team had brought in.

More grenades launched. Serena was on the move, her armor shrinking, yet as she ran, she swept her sword arm around, deflecting one of the explosives. It blew up, catching the other incoming grenades and detonating them in turn.

She fired her cannon again, cutting down two more cops. I didn't see blood or gore, but they weren't getting back up anytime soon. That left her facing Ramos, as he pushed a chunk of concrete the size of a trash can lid off his leg. The cannon's crackling maw was thirty feet from his face but there was no way she could miss.

I groaned and dragged myself up the wall. If I could nail her with a shot from the pulsar stave—

Light flashed. Brilliant light. And wind whipped up a storm of grit, powder, and shards of, well, everything that broke.

Dominic vaulted out, landing in a crouch, in his signature black high-collared shirt, fatigue pants, and black mask. He blasted Troy with both Echo Watches. The shrieking devices caught him in the chest, reducing Troy's taut, muscled form into a quivering mass of uncooperative muscles. Apparently, he'd been going for Teget's ax, because it clinked against crumpled asphalt soon after.

A cheerful *whoop* followed Dominic out of the portal—Wilhelmina, wearing a black shirt plus exercise pants with a red line down either leg. She, too, had her nose, mouth, and chin obscured with a mask.

She landed on Serena's back. "Y'all mind your elders now!" she snapped, driving the slender Medan dagger deep into Serena's shoulder blade.

Serena howled and swatted at her opponent. The shell surrounding her morphed her hands into elongated claws that removed Wilhelmina with a single swipe. Then she whirled and aimed her sword at the chopper. I thought for a moment she was going to blast it out of the sky, but the blade itself fired into the air, dragging a long, slender chain that rippled with purple energies and bristled with tiny black spikes. It impaled the chopper, punching out the roof, where it tripped the propellor blades to pieces, Metal shards sprayed across the prison roof.

There was a bang, a puff of smoke, and the chopper plummeted for us.

Forget that. Drained as I felt, with the suit losing its power, watching Xia and Winston pull Troy to his wobbly feet, I knew there was a reservoir of energy left.

In my prosthetic leg.

I used it to leap in an arc, catching Wilhelmina in midair. Well, colliding with her, really. But we both landed on the opposite end of the courtyard, away from where the chopper dove into the last remaining wall.

It plowed through the blocks, metal crunching, smoke billowing throughout the semi-enclosed space. The prison roof buckled, collapsing onto the wreckage.

The chaos gave enough cover for Serena to pull aside a portal, same as she'd used to escape from me at the warehouse. She disappeared through, as Xia and Winston dragged their disabled leader.

Leaving us with a crashed helicopter that was rapidly spilling fuel all over what used to be the prison workout yard, and who knew how many sparks around.

"Nice catch." Wilhelmina held the side of her head and moaned. "Sakes, child. I might be—"

"Getting too old for this?" I helped Teget to his feet.

She smacked my lower backside with the flat of the dagger's blade. "No! I might be needin' more exercise. Plus I figure I'm still woozy from my cold. Too old, my foot."

"I'll see about getting you some sparring time." I held Teget's shoulders. "You okay? Steady?"

"Steady enough to help." Teget stowed his ax and shoved aside rubble covering the fallen SCPD task force officers. "We must get them to safety."

Drip. Drip. Drip. Jet fuel. Safety was right. "You two, link up with Garvey—"

Light flashed again. Garvey and the three Procyon team members were gone. So was Dominic. "Okay, well, I guess that works."

Teget and I pulled the pilot and co-pilot from the chopper. Both were alive but in rough shape. Of course, there was no time for stretchers.

Edith had already helped Ramos get some of his officers clear, and was pulling an injured cop free of debris when Wilhelmina caught up with her. I joined them, the wounded pilot slung over my shoulder like a sack of flour. "Welcome to the party."

"Mercury …" Edith took the officer's arm and assisted him in a quick march through the prison corridors. "When I saw Troy—"

"Save it," I growled, "So we don't all blow up."

CHAPTER TWENTY-THREE

Apparently, my worries about an exploding helicopter were off. It didn't turn into a fireball. But that didn't help me feel better.

Reese was dead. So were two SCPD officers. Not Stan Bradley. He'd been one of the guys with a grenade launcher. Edith and Wilhelmina had dug him out last. And he was kind enough to swear at me the entire ten minutes it took to load him into an ambulance.

Five prison guards had also died in the assault, along with eight inmates. Nobody talked about whether the latter were just as innocent as everyone else. Bad guys, sure, but did they deserve to get murdered in Serena's rampage?

Bottom line was, sixteen people weren't going to see their friends and families, two of our most dangerous enemies were freed from prison, and half the pulsar stave was still out of reach.

I sat on the couch in our condo, the next afternoon, glaring at the other half. It sat on the kitchen counter, a dull metal paperweight.

"Does glowering help heal your wound?" Loredana brought me a cup of mint tea.

"Thanks. And no." Inhaling the aroma did get me to stop thinking about the pain for two seconds. Advanced as my healing was, a hole remained through my shoulder muscle. The right arm wasn't moving much better than a zombie's desiccated limb. And I was about as chatty as a newly minted member of the undead.

Minted. Mint tea. I snorted. Almost a chuckle.

"I see." Loredana sipped from her mug, a blue one emblazoned with a white image of a Dalek and the words "CAFFEINATE! CAFFEINATE!" underneath. "You've barely said a word since the prison."

"Didn't think there was a need for me to repeat, 'We screwed up,' over and over again."

She rolled her eyes. I'd brought that gesture to the marriage, proud to say. "Really, Mercury, there is no sense to this endless self-flagellation. Troy and Serena bested all of us. This is simply a matter of changing tactics. We are faced with a different kind of enemy—a woman familiar with Homeland Security and the ways of federal investigations, alongside a man who was one of our operatives for more than a decade. It makes perfect sense they gained the upper hand."

I had a response for that, a real zinger, but my brain put the brakes on that runaway car. No way I was gonna point out the deaths to Loredana. She knew better than anyone the risks normal people took when they got mixed up in our crazy, superpowered, monster-filled world. "I get that. It's hard to not beat myself up about it when I'm the one Procyon keeps leaning on to run the show out in the field. Not gonna lie—I miss the old days of just me, solo slaying monsters."

"You've lost that independence."

I shook my head. "It's not that. I can handle less independence."

Loredana smiled and took my hand. "I should hope so."

I grinned and pulled her closer. She curled up against me and I wrapped my arm around her shoulders. Gave her a kiss on the neck. "No complaints there. What I meant was, the responsibility of having to watch out for everyone else. Having to make sure they don't die while I'm trying to take down the bad guys. Teget, Ramos, Edith, Wilhelmina, Garvey …"

"All of whom don't need or ask for your protection. They know the dangers. They go willingly into the fight." Loredana pressed the back of her hand to her mouth. Her face looked pale and drawn. "Apologies."

"No problem. The tea help?"

"Yes. Doctor Becker says it could be a simple matter of stress, but he wants me to see him again tomorrow."

"Probably a good idea. You've been run down for a while, and being Javon's chaperone—"

"Has been less onerous than both of us make it out to be." She poked my ribs. Thankfully, not where they were bruised.

The door intercom went off. Loredana handed my tea and crossed to the foyer. "Have you brought it?"

"Of course." Teget's clipped tones sounded staticky. "There was no trouble."

"Very good." Loredana unlocked the front door. She winked at me.

"Please tell me Liz has a new secret weapon." I set the mugs down on an end table and clasped my hands in mock piety. I mean, not that I was mocking piety. Not with everything Ramos had modeled. And I'd tried praying. Wouldn't knock it. Defensive? Me? Never mind. "Because I wouldn't mind a modified stasis gun or a giant freeze ray again."

"Nothing so exotic."

Metal clanked on our door. Loredana opened it.

Teget took a knee. He held aloft a bag from Katsaros Deli, my favorite sandwich joint over on 25th and DeLeon. Which I should have detected a mile away, because the heavenly scent of gyro meat had preceded my brother through our condo entrance like a seventy-piece marching band. "My lady."

Loredana laughed. "Please, join us."

"'Bout time to eat, that's for certain." Wilhelmina stepped between Teget and the door frame. She elbowed his head on her way through. "Get on up and open those bags before I have to knock you down and take 'em myself."

Teget chuckled but did as instructed. He'd foregone his typical Medan garb for a T-shirt and jeans, items he'd probably snagged from the guest rooms at Procyon. But he still had the leather sling for his ax, which didn't look weird at all, hanging from his back.

Ramos was the last in. He was on his phone, carrying on a hushed conversation, and was the only one dressed like he was going to be late for a committee meeting. Granted, that meant a crisp blue polo shirt and pressed khakis, with the SCPD badge shining prominent on his belt, opposite a holstered pistol. "Understood. Thanks for the update."

I watched them warily as Teget and Wilhelmina unwrapped the five sandwiches. Loredana rejoined me on the couch. "So, ah, is this a staff meeting? Because I didn't have time to scribble an agenda on a napkin."

"The best word for it is an intervention." Ramos sat across from me, his mirrored sunglasses dangling from his collar. "A reminder for you to get moving again."

"Okay, yeah." I gestured at Teget. "Throw me a sandwich, then. I'll need something in my mouth, so I don't say anything condescending."

He glowered. The sandwich stayed untouched. Instead, he tossed the pulsar stave. Might have thrown it at my head. I chose to believe it was a friendly passing of my weapon. Either way, I caught it.

"You would do well to keep that with you at all times," Teget said. "We cannot afford a lax attitude regarding our adversaries any longer."

"Wouldn't say anyone's been lax." Wilhelmina had already taken a hefty bite from her sandwich. She wiped her chin with a napkin. "These circumstances are trying for many a soul. We've got enemies cooperating on a scale not seen in a long time."

"Precisely what I was explaining," Loredana said. "Thank you."

"And these enemies wouldn't have a fun new player if it weren't for more of Procyon's foul secrets," Wilhelmina continued, her tone sharpening. "Bad enough kicking an operative to the curb, but killing one? Killing his brother? And leavin' a mess behind? No one solved anything back then. It was kicked down the road for us to handle now. I'd've marched right on up to Jack Jackson's office and slapped him myself if I'd known what the truth was."

Loredana's posture stiffened, like she was in fact in a committee meeting. "It was a regrettable mistake. One I'm sure Procyon has no intention of repeating. But dwelling on that does not help us end the present calamity."

"Which is bad, if I understand it all." Ramos steepled his fingers. No sandwich for him. Not yet, I guessed. "Xia—she was the one who used that dark sword to control us. Control me. And now she's out. Do we really need to speculate at length as to why that is?"

I shook my head. I'd figured it out as soon as we'd gotten the call about the prison break. "They're gonna come for the sword next. Makes sense. I mean, I don't know how they're planning on finding more symmachites, seeing as how we destroyed that one batch Serena had gotten her hands on. Teget? Any word on them from back in good old Meda?"

He had his mouth full, so replied with a simple shake of his own head until he'd finished chewing. "I have no stories from the temple, nor can the elders give me advice, as all they know of those creatures has faded into myth and legend. There is little to tell of the sword, either, as it had passed into the possession of the Kutsatuta."

"Which is how cousin Crux got it." I massaged my temples. "Sandwich me."

That got the much-needed gyro spiraled in my direction. Should ask Teget if he was up for tossing a football. "So, the Kutsatuta—all the nasty Medans who for good or bad reasons got themselves kicked out of the home city—wound up with both the armor shell and the black sword. Anybody else think they ordered them off Amazon?"

"Sounds a whole lot like the Whisperer's been passing out treats." Wilhelmina discarded her wrapper into our trash can. Wait a minute. Had she finished the *whole thing*? "Got something for a parched old woman?"

"Beer and other life-sustaining liquids in the fridge." I savored the first bite of the gyro.

"Is there anybody who knows what else that sword can be used for, besides controlling symmachites?" Ramos asked. "Because if they wanted it badly enough to kill two of my people, then they're not going to let a small inconvenience like not being able to find those miniature robots stop them. It has to have another purpose."

"I agree, sentinel of the law." Teget thumped his fist on the counter. "Whatever that purpose may be, and for whatever destiny it was created, the sword must not fall into the hands of our enemies, for they would pervert it to evil ends."

I thought about applauding because it was a bold enough statement it warranted a ringing soundtrack. But my hands were full of sandwich. "Okay. That's one plan of action—make sure the sword is secure. How about it, oh darling of mine?"

Loredana wrinkled her nose, a smile quirking her lips. "The sword was stored in the deepest levels of our silo compound, north of the city. Most of the more sensitive items and records, especially those salvaged from the ruins of the original Historic Vaults, were there, however, with the completion of our new facility, the process of relocating them has proceeded apace."

"Is there anything left there?"

"Only the most sensitive of the items." She drained the rest of her tea. "Excuse me. I shall make a call."

Loredana stepped away from the couch, phone in hand, and walked down the corridor toward our bedroom. I could hear her phone's touchpad beep as she dialed.

"Is that it then?" Ramos frowned. "We make sure this sword is secure and leave it at that? Because given the way these people have operated, Mercury, it'd be the height of our own arrogance to sit around waiting for them to strike a third time. They're going to come for the sword."

"No doubt." I picked up the pulsar stave and pointed at Ramos. "Here's the thing: the new HQ has more bells and whistles than the last one. And by bells and whistles, I mean armed drones and hidden laser emplacements, among other fun toys. Nobody using tachyon-based weaponry—like this bad boy, for instance, is gonna get within a half mile of HQ without us seeing that person like a lit-up Christmas tree in the middle of a city-wide blackout."

"Good afternoon," Loredana said from the hallway. "This is Mrs. Lark-Hale. I should like to inquire the disposition of a vehicle in our motor pool. Yes, Unit Number Thirteen. I'd be happy to hold."

"Thirteen." Wilhelmina made a face. I hoped it wasn't from the cider she'd tasted, because it was my favorite brand and she'd better not waste a drop. "I ain't much for superstition but still, child …"

"It is merely part of the code." Loredana's cheeks gained pink.

"Thirteen doctors," I whispered. "On *Doctor Who*."

A throw pillow hit the back of my head with a *whump*. Great aim aside, why did we have throw pillows in the hall?

"Yes, thank you. I am still here." In the silence that followed, I turned toward her. Loredana had one hand on her hip. She tapped a bare foot. Her eyes narrowed. I felt bad for whoever was on the other end. "I see. Very good. I shall require an appointment to verify its condition, in half an hour. No, no delays. You may ask the manager if you wish but I will keep the appointment, nonetheless. No, this is *not* a request. Good-bye."

She gave me a look that made me *really* glad we were on the same team. Not that I was afraid. Just … Impressed. "We have an appointment in twenty-nine minutes to make certain the sword is secure."

"Nice." I headed for the fridge. Wilhelmina passed me a cider bottle. "Am I winning the lottery on this one? Do we finally get into the Historic Vaults?"

"That is the idea."

"Awesome. Sucks to be Alvarez."

Loredana arched an eyebrow. "Actually, I think between the two of us we can exercise a considerable advantage over him and eliminate his reluctance to allow us access."

"How's that?" I pointed, my face as dead-earnest serious as I could manage. "I am *not* complimenting him."

Ramos snorted. "That would be a stretch for you."

Loredana sighed. "Nothing so bold. We must simply leverage our acquaintanceship with Mr. Kimball, a person whom I've spent many an hour over the past week and with whom you have faced enemies in combat. Such things would help him to see our side of an argument, wouldn't you agree?"

"Well, I'll be," Wilhelmina murmured.

Teget burst out laughing.

I pressed my hands and the bottle of cider to my chest. "I love it when she gets diabolical."

Whatever else her plans, Loredana's gathering of our core crew at our home did the trick—it lifted me from my funk.

Other than a brief mention, Ramos didn't say anything else about his officers who were killed, and I didn't, either. We both knew what the score was. And those people had signed on to the task force fully cognizant of the risks.

But I hitched a ride in his Dodge Charger over to Procyon rather than going with Loredana, all the same.

"Thanks for having our backs, at the prison," I said.

"You're welcome. It's what we do, you and I." Ramos' eyes were shielded by his sunglasses. He waited, blinker clicking, for traffic to pass so we could enter the Procyon driveway.

Hadn't I just said I wasn't gonna talk about it? "It should have ended up differently."

"Their sacrifices, Mercury. Their choices." He blew out a breath. "But I'm tired of attending the funerals of my people. All this death and sickness and anger … It was bad enough, knowing about the things in the dark before the last year."

"I hear you."

"That doesn't mean I won't continue the fight. It's what I'm called to do."

"You really believe that, don't you?"

There was a gap in traffic. Ramos took it, pulling us up outside the new concrete and steel gate, with its burly security guard behind bulletproof glass. "I can't believe God would put me in the path of this evil if He didn't want me to take action against it. It's not *right*."

I thought of Winston and me laughing our way through a terrible movie, and Marigold hugging me as they invited a lonely operative into their home for a night of friends and food. Then I remembered stabbing her.

"No," I said. "No, it isn't."

We cleared security thanks to my ID and to Ramos being on the short list of people trusted with Procyon's secrets. Loredana met us at the front door—which was propped open. Cold air washed out, beating back the summer heat.

Garvey was there, too, armed. As were two more of his guys a few feet inside.

"What's the deal?" I gestured. "That thing should be sliding open."

"It appears to have suffered a malfunction. Though I'm assured it's not mechanical. It's tied to some of our less sensitive security systems." She raised an eyebrow at Garvey. "Such as door locks."

Garvey looked like he'd been called to the front of the class for watching YouTube instead of the lecture. "Liz says they're working on it, ma'am. She's got some of my techs trying to keep him out, but it doesn't seem to matter that we've got all new passwords."

"Him?" I groaned. "Winston."

"Indeed. Mr. Yen's knowledge of our security and information systems does not seem to have been hampered by his incarceration."

Ramos scowled at all of us. I was sure his teenage boys and twin daughters had seen the same sour expression loads of times before. "Are you telling me you didn't overhaul your security when the feds locked that man in their supermax prison? In case of this eventuality?"

"Duh. We did." I waved my hand as we walked, because Loredana had already left us in the figurative dust. "But it must be like Garvey said—he's got another way in. Winston improved every system we had in the old building, and even with all the hardware destroyed—"

"Considerable resources were saved on our offsite servers. And in hardware that was rescued." She held the door to the basement stairwell, which was an unmarked slab of gray metal. "Such as Cyril."

Oh, crap. If Cyril had left a virus or a chip or who knows what in Liz's pet computer—the *best* electronic brain on our side ...

The stairwell led to a section of basement not listed on any building chart or map. A thin, blonde woman with retro Fifties style eyeglasses sat at the desk near a floor-to-ceiling armored hatch that looked like we'd need a bunker buster missile to breach. "Hello, Mrs. Lark-Hale."

"Good afternoon, Allison. We have our appointment."

I caught her hesitance, just a fraction of a second, before she smiled. "You bet." She reached under her desk.

Massive *clicks* echoed from the hatch. After the seventh, it split down its center and rumbled open on tracks embedded in the wall—a wall I realized was about three feet thick.

I stepped through the threshold first, into total darkness. The vault was cool and dry. A faint whisper came from vents above my head.

Lights blinked on. One row at a time, twenty deep and four across. A pale-blue glow illuminated shelf after shelf, hundreds of them, black metal with silver mesh.

Every single one was empty.

Loredana's hands shook. She dropped her phone on the polished concrete.

"*Ay mi.*" Ramos made the sign of the cross. "We're too late."

"No way." I shook my head slowly. "No way they could have got in and out with no one noticing. Cameras—right there. In the corners. Right? They were working, weren't they? We've gotta get Garvey on this!"

"Hold up, man."

Javon?

He and Alvarez waited by the secretary's desk. She was tapping away on her keyboard like there wasn't a major calamity unfolding. And where had those guys come from? Had Garvey called up and told them we were here?

"I'm not holding anything up, *man.*" I stormed up to Javon's face, hands ready to reach for his collar—but if I did, I wondered if he would slip out of my grasp. "Somebody emptied the entire Historic Vault!"

"No kidding." Javon crossed his arms. "It was me."

CHAPTER TWENTY-FOUR

I had to give Loredana credit. She waited until we were in the privacy of Alvarez's office before verbally shanking our bosses.

"Of all the addle-brained decisions this organization has made over the years, in the name of secrecy and safety, this has to be the most incompetent, spineless, idiotic of the lot!" she snapped.

Alvarez sat behind his desk, chair pushed back against the coffee cabinets. He rubbed at his chin with one hand and pressed his other against his arm, watching Loredana as she paced the middle of the office. Javon was at his usual post by the door, his posture giving the impression he was unconcerned, but he rubbed his left hand's fingers together. I swore I saw them dissolve and reform.

"I should have been informed." Loredana spun toward Alvarez, her finger extended like a rifle. "The disposition of the relics and files contained in the Historic Vault directly impacts Operations. How am I supposed to guarantee the safety of Procyon—of this world!—if the means to do so are kept from me?"

"Hey." Javon took a step away from the door. "You think you're the only one who knows what's best? This is exactly why we couldn't tell you what we were doing."

Loredana looked like she'd been physically struck—which jacked up my blood pressure, believe me. "You—Why you couldn't tell me? I have given everything to Procyon. I have given my life! I have given *everything*! And you would skulk around behind me—"

"Everybody skulks!" Javon growled. "This whole organization is about skulking! Hiding things in shadows, keeping the darkness away from the world, and meanwhile all of us? We all pay the price. But we go on keeping the secrets—from humanity, and from ourselves. So, you want to keep ranting? Have fun. Go until you run out of breath. Won't change what we did."

Loredana clenched her fists. I thought she was gonna take a swing at the guy. But she just glared at them, a slow sweep around the room. Any idiot could see she was struggling to regain control. She wasn't the kind of person to let a debate devolve into personal attacks. Tact was her best weapon.

Alvarez glanced at me. "Mr. Hale? You've been quiet. That's unlike you."

I was kicked back in the chair, leaning it against the far wall. I grinned. "Didn't sound like she needed my input. Anything I was gonna say, Loredana said thirty times better. But since you asked my opinion—"

"That isn't what I mean."

"—You're morons." I shrugged. "Professional analysis, free of charge."

"You got no right to sit there critiquing us for making decisions neither of you two are qualified to make," Javon said.

"Oh, I'm pretty sure that since we've saved the city and the world at least ..." I made a show of ticking off numbers on one hand. "... Four times, we get an extra special say. It's not like you were out there trickling between monsters like sand in a timer, Mr. Board Person. And Alvarez's superpower seems to be pissing people off. So, I get why Loredana's upset. By the way, her getting upset makes me irritable."

"You don't understand—"

"Blah, blah." I cut through Alvarez's protest. "Here's the thing: I don't care *why* you guys faked moving everything into the Historic Vaults. Your reasons for doing that were either good or bad. I'm used to people in charge making dumb decisions. What I what to know is, where did you move everything?"

Alvarez lapsed into a brooding silence. He was a pro at anything involving the word "brood." Javon pushed off from the door frame and skirted around Loredana and I.

"Oh, for heaven's sake!" Loredana snapped. "You'd bloody well better tell us because we'll find out ourselves in a matter of hours! Please do us the courtesy of wasting less time."

Alvarez shook his head. "This is uncalled for. Whatever decisions are made at this level—"

"The contents are getting moved to Patchwork," Javon said.

Alvarez gestured at the ceiling and muttered in Spanish.

"You can argue the breach of protocol later, Hector, but I'm making this call." Javon scowled at me. "Not that I think you two are right. It's just easier to tell you what the score is now so you shut up and we can move on."

Loredana folded her arms. I scratched the back of my neck with the pulsar stave.

"So, are we good?" Javon asked.

"We are not in any sense of the word," Loredana said coolly, "But do continue."

"Start with the whole, 'What the heck is Patchwork?'" I added. "Don't tell me Procyon has a base under an old quilt store."

Javon snorted. "Nah. It's a facility used by the Foundation since at least the eighties. Anything we find of either major threat or tremendous value gets locked in. It's one of the most secure facilities we've got. Makes Fort Knox look like a cardboard lemonade stand."

"And you wanted the sword buried in there, along with everything from the Historic Vaults." I frowned. "Let me guess. The board's trying to avoid a repeat of Arkwright trashing the original vaults we had here."

"Not knocking your security folks, or how you handled things." Javon held out his hands. "But you gotta see it from our end. Procyon in San Camillo got compromised. Arkwright, with the Hedron of Orbits as his weapon, was a bigger threat level than anything we'd faced since the earliest days of the organization. The Kimballs had run Patchwork on the side for decades. It made the most sense for me to get my butt out here and start the move."

"Ah." Loredana arched her eyebrow. "Hence the true reason for endless hours and days spent touring headquarters and the silo. You were keeping me distracted."

Javon grinned. "The company wasn't all bad, was it? But yeah, you're right on. Alvarez told me you wanted in the Vaults. How was he supposed to keep getting things boxed up if you poked your nose in?"

"Seriously? How asleep at the wheel were we, to not notice piles of stuff getting shipped out?" I asked.

Javon wiggled his fingers like they were a pair of legs walking. "Because the tube system underneath the new HQ has been shunting vault contents without *anybody*—except a few security people—noticing."

I stared at him, then slowly rose from my chair. "Hey, ah, Loredana? This would be a good time to tell me you know about this secret tunnel. Because that's something the head of operations should have been told."

"I knew it was on the new schematics. And I knew it was to have its terminus in an old storage structure on the northeast corner of the city, utilizing existing tunnels connected to the previous emergency evacuation line for the vault." Loredana made a face as if she'd found a bug in her tea. "What I had not been told, however, was that the operational date had been moved up."

"Surprises all around." Alvarez sighed. "Listen, please. The vault items are safe. That's all that matters. The last batches are being moved out tomorrow. We've kept this as secret as possible."

His computer flickered, died, then hummed as it restarted.

"Not again," Alvarez moaned. He picked up his office phone.

"Dead. I know the techs are doing their best, but these incursions are becoming a true nuisance."

"Winston strikes again," I said. "Good plan. Keep moving that stuff while he infiltrates Procyon's information systems."

"The tubes are off of those systems," Alvarez said. "Running on an independent power source. All communications on this project are being done in person or via paper notes. There's nothing for him to track. We even required the notes be handwritten."

Oh. Well, that *was* pretty clever. I would have thought of it, too, but probably after they did. Still, I was in no mood to let them celebrate. "Okay, so you've got all this stuff shipped out to your top-secret hidey-hole. I want on the next truck to your Patchwork so I can see the sword for myself."

"No way," Javon muttered.

Alvarez was just as firm about it. "Absolutely not."

"May I remind you all," Loredana said, "That the sword does not belong to Procyon, or even this world. It is the property of Medan citizens."

"So is every other relic we've got stashed away, or used by operatives," Javon said. "That don't mean we're going to go repatriating all of them."

"That wasn't what I was suggesting. Since Mercury is of that world, he—and by rights, Teget—should be allowed to inspect the safe holding place for something crafted on their world. Need I also point out that, thanks to Teget, Procyon was given access to see the very temple from which our relics were derived?"

"That's a thin legal thread," Alvarez murmured.

"One which I'm prepared stretch, when I submit a formal request to the board to be allowed access to Patchwork."

Javon rolled his eyes. "Man. Are they always like this?"

"Yes." Alvarez rubbed his face. "But as you said, the sooner we acquiesce, the sooner they stop bothering us."

"That's the spirit!" I patted Javon on the back.

"Don't touch me again," he said.

"No problem." I clapped my hands together. "So, where is

this super-secret base?"

"Northeastern Colorado. Under a whole bunch of dusty hills and scattered aspens. Home to a lot of nothing."

"Okay then. We can get ourselves a ride on your next truck."

"Nope." Javon shook his head. "You want in? You take the teleporter. I'll escort the three of you. No extra vehicle traffic. And we're keeping everybody in the dark about our transportation of the vault contents—which means you two, too."

"Super. Glad to see you guys are so trusting."

"I won't give my spiel about secrets again, Mercury, but if you want in on this place, you're gonna have to play by our rules," Javon said. "Get ahold of Gemini, and we'll read him in on the situation. The three of you can go. That's it. No more of your tagalongs or your 'team,' as you keep calling them."

"Don't trash talk my people." I poked Javon's chest. That time, he did disintegrate himself, so my finger went right through and back out again. Felt like I'd punched my hand through thick fog. At least it didn't come back out damp.

"Why not? You're sloppy. We've seen enough of that lately. You want to do us all a big favor?" Javon opened the office door. "Go home, wait by the phone for the next astral fiend call-out, and try not to lose the rest of the pulsar stave."

He breezed from the office, leaving Alvarez, Loredana, and I kind of staring awkwardly at each other.

"I'm afraid he's right." Alvarez cleared his throat. "Until we hear word from Tracking and Forecasting on the whereabouts of our enemies, there isn't much you need to concern yourselves with. Homeland assures me they're watching every airport and road for Syndax activity."

My turn to snort. "Yeah, that's great. I bet they'll do an awesome job, like they did catching up with Syndax in Oregon."

"I had better check in with Garvey to determine if we've had any security breaches." She scowled at Alvarez. "Beyond the obvious, of course, sir."

As soon as she was out the door, I tossed Alvarez a salute.

"See you around."

"I hope not soon." He resumed tapping away at his keyboard.

Yeah, I thought. *Me too.*

Next stop: Tracking.

What were the chances I was gonna go lounge around the house when my team needed me, especially after Javon's jerk comments?

Between slim and none.

Ramos was waiting for me outside. He nodded toward the elevator. "That didn't go well, did it?"

"Oh, I don't know, I thought it was really sweet of Alvarez to offer us all ice cream and massages. Too bad he doesn't serve whisky like Jack used to."

"This is serious, Mercury."

"No kidding. Short version? All our historic stuff and/or powerful relics got moved to another secret base, and you're not invited."

"Guess that means I'm stuck with regular paperwork and protests." Ramos shined his sunglasses on his shirt sleeve. "I'm headed back to the precinct. Do you need a lift?"

"Nah. Come by for dinner?"

He shook his head. "I do have a family, you know. They enjoy my presence. Even the teens. You and Loredana should dine with us, though. I'll text Olivia and ask."

"Thanks. We could use it. I'll check in with the boss."

Ramos *tsked* with his fingers. "*Cuidarse*. She's not going to like too many of those jokes. Stop by around 7:30."

Dinner would be nice. A family meal. And Ramos was being extra generous with his time, which I attributed to him being awesome. Nice not having to assume he had an ulterior motive—unlike other people I was supposed to trust.

I followed the curve of the hallway to my next destination. Turned out Tracking was empty, except for Edith.

Yeah, not Liz. I didn't see a single soul in the room. Edith sat in the center of the floor, between Liz's console and the stations closer to the giant wall screen. Twenty red splotches were scattered across a big, glowing map of San Camillo and the surrounding counties, out to a 100-mile radius.

"Is this a promotion or a demotion?" I pulled up Liz's chair, flopped my butt down, and kicked my shoes up onto a console. Wow. If I stretched my back out any farther, I'd fall asleep. The thing was the most comfortable chair I'd ever encountered.

"Neither. I'm searching and assisting." Edith's eyes were closed, but I swore a faint purple hue seeped from under her eyelashes. "Liz is having computer issues. She has all her techs downstairs messing with a mainframe."

"And the great Liz herself?"

"Next door, sobbing over Cyril." Edith opened one eye. Yep, definitely a purple glow, albeit one that faded. "Sobbing's not the right word. But you know how much she adores that pile of circuits."

I shushed her. "Hey, don't let her hear you say that. What have you seen? Something helpful about our buddy with the stolen pulsar stave, I hope."

Edith's upright posture sagged—just a bit, at the shoulders. "The visions are unclear. They overlap, like multiple strips of film held one in front of the other with a spotlight shining behind them. Focusing is difficult. I'm too close to this hunt. It's not just looking for another potential operative. I've already found this one and … I suppose there's a part of me that doesn't want to find him."

"I get that, I guess." I tapped my feet together. No place like him, am I right? "So. About the prison … I know why you froze, and I wanted to tell you, it's not your fault. Even the best freeze."

"Thanks, but that's a stupid thing to say." Edith stood and stretched. She could have taught a Pilates class that would have done wonders for my back—and my aching shoulder gunshot wound. "I did fail. People died because I didn't react. That won't happen again, no matter what caused it in the first place."

I considered that, as I took inventory of the still-visible array of scrapes and bruises on her arms, neck, and face. "Okay. But I need your promise that you're good to go the next time we need you out there."

She gave me one of her sly smiles, the kind that reminded me of a mountain lion finding a slow jogger on a deserted trail. "I'll remember."

The glass door off to the left side of Tracking slid open. The whirr of ventilation and the hum of closely packed machinery followed Liz as she hurried out. Her red Chucks looked neon in the dim lighting. "Mercury! Cyril's been infected and I don't know how I'm going to fix him because everything I've tried has only made matters worse but the manager says if I can't we're going to have to wipe his hard drive—!"

"Hey, hey, take it easy." I scooted out of her chair, which was a good move, because she tackled me with a hug. Put a lot of fun extra pressure on my wound. I grimaced and said through gritted teeth, "He'll be fine, right? You can fix him. I bet you've got six more ideas about how to go about it."

"Maybe." She sniffed and rubbed tears from her eyes. "Eighteen ideas, actually. I can't believe Winston did something like that! The programming was dormant for years! That whole time he was mentoring us and teaching the newbies how to get Tracking in the best shape it could be ... How could he lie to us like that the whole time?"

I thought of the secrets held by the higher ups at Procyon— and heck, even the secrets they'd kept from me about my origins before things had blown up in their faces when Teget successfully exited a rip for the first time. "Sometimes, people keep the truth hidden because they're afraid they'll hurt others. But the Yens ... Liz, they gave up to evil. Marigold sure did. She was twisted by the power she wanted. And Winston loved his wife, so much so that he'd do anything for her. I think that kind of power warped him, too. He could justify anything in pursuit of it."

Edith nodded. "Wise words."

"Don't act so shocked. I pay attention." Especially to guys like Ramos.

Liz sniffed again and glanced back at the room. A giant metal frame surrounded banks of black computers, like someone had crammed twenty hard drive towers into one container. Lights blinked on their fronts, mostly red, with scattered green and a handful of yellow. Would it do any good to pray for a computer to stop breaking down? I hadn't ever asked about the specificity of supplication. Whew.

"Don't worry about it. Find your way around one problem. Then pick up the next." I patted Liz on the shoulder. I hoped she was going to be better—I was running short of pep talk material.

"Oh! Problems." She handed me a printout. "Here you go. Cyril did crack this before he went on the fritz. I would have gotten it to you sooner but I wanted to make sure I had classified files migrated onto other drives separate from the network so Winston can't track them down. I guessed it would be better to get you a hard copy and lock up the rest. You should probably delete all that stuff off your phone."

Geez, she was right. But I was too busy gazing at line after line of black letters on the sheets of paper. "How about that," I murmured.

"What is it?" Edith leaned over my shoulder.

"A coded letter between the Kimballs from 1903," I murmured. "When they were hunting some kind of symmachite in Florida's swamps. And Liz just broke the code."

"Yeah, great, isn't it?" Liz's smile vanished. She seemed dead serious about whatever was on her mind. "But I wanted to ask you something else. You don't have to answer if you don't want. Before you read the letter."

I sighed. "What is it?"

She held up her phone. It displayed a book cover—the e-book copy of *Mercury on Guard*. "How come this guy didn't put me in the book?"

I groaned.

Edith squinted. "That's not supposed to be you on the front, is it?"

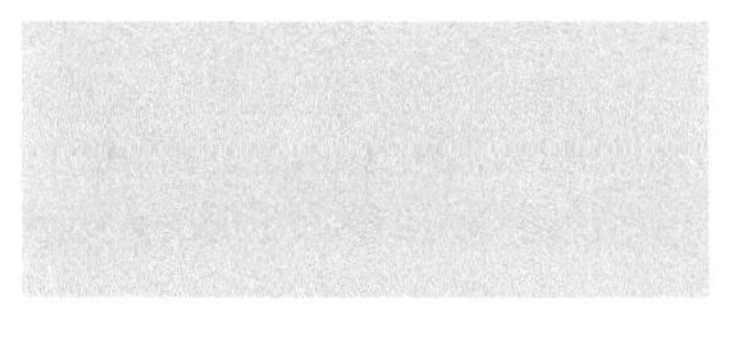

CHAPTER TWENTY-FIVE

Fourth of November 1903

  My dear Owen,

  It is by no means an easy task I lay upon your shoulders. If you'd have met me when I was your age and told me all the things God would have in store for the next sixty years of my life upon His good earth, I'd have laughed in your face and called you a fool.

Here we are, though, on the edge of the next dawn on our cause's horizon. You know as well as I do the vital role Procyon plays in the defense of all that is good and holy from the dark forces marshalling far beyond these mortal shores. It isn't for the Kimballs to wield the pulsar stave. It isn't our destiny. That burden falls to others.

What we can do, then, is be the shadow.

Let the light of the pulsar stave shine bright against the monsters that crawl forth from the deepest void. We will stay out of its glare, never drawing attention, never making ourselves known to the enemy. That's what our ally requests.

I don't know who he is, or what he truly wants. We have the proof of our own eyes and of the old records we've uncovered that he is willing and able to stand with us against the vile minions of the Interstice. That is why it is so important we take good care *of his soldiers. We can give them comfort, aid, and allegiance in this fight.*

I'm too worn out by time to take up this new burden. Your father doesn't have the fight—not saying he's not a good man, mind you, but his gifts lie in the political arena. He's the one to keep Procyon organized and growing, so that it can shore up our temporal defenses.

You, my boy, have the will and the fire to do what we can't.

I won't tell you what decision to make. You're a young man with your own mind to make up. I know you'll pray upon it. You'd be dull as dishwater not to. So, let your granddad leave you with this bit of advice...

There's a lot more to this world than you.

A man can't go through his life mindful of nothing but his own well-being. There are times that require him to set down what he wants and take up the needs of others. I'm not talking about a short tick on the clock, either. It could be years. It could be the rest of your natural days.

But you'd be able to rest your head at the end of a long life, comforted in the knowledge you've done what's right, even if only a handful of others know it, too.

Don't be mistaken—once we make this deal with Tenebrae, there's no going back. The Kimballs and his soldiers will be one army.

And don't fret about proving anything to anyone. You've already done that a hundred times over.

Your proudest granddad,

Lucas

I leaned back in the chair, sunlight turning the letter golden. My mouth was dry, not just from reading the words, but from the fact that I knew what they meant.

Ramos had his elbows on his knees, leaning forward in rapt attention. "Unbelievable."

"It is that." Loredana sat beside me. She held out a glass of lemonade, the ice still crackling. "May I propose a trade?"

I nodded. We switched contents of our hands. I slugged back the liquid. Talk about a brain freeze. Then again, maybe a brain freeze would shock me into thinking straight again. "Ramos said it. What I can't believe is why Javon's kept this secret the whole time we've been trying to figure out who Tenebrae is and what he wants. Scratch that—he just made it clear he loves his secrets."

"And if I were a Procyon board member, I wouldn't want to spill any information about how our most influential family was in league with a being from another dimension." Ramos leaned back in the chair. It rocked gently.

I shook my head and gazed out at his neighborhood. The Ramos house was a cozy bungalow in a quiet residential neighborhood, sporting a wraparound porch and enough bedrooms for himself, his wife Olivia, and their four kids. The heavenly scent of beans, rice, beef, onions, and a dozen spices I couldn't identify drifted through the front screen door and open windows. A few kids were out playing in their driveway four houses down the street. A dad was barbecuing on the front lawn even farther. Sure, the occasional siren split the constant rush of traffic in the background, but it was easy to imagine everything was okay with the world that evening.

Except the stupid letter was there.

"Have you shown this to anyone else?" Loredana held the paper up to the light, squinting at the cursive handwriting as she did.

Couldn't blame her. I'd done the same thing when I'd stepped out of Tracking to read it. Then I'd found Loredana out in the parking lot. I think we'd both read it five times. "No. Just you guys. Liz probably read it, but she was way preoccupied with making sure Cyril wasn't gonna crash or get his hard drive erased."

"Well, then." She pursed her lips. "There are two possibilities, along the line of what you two have mentioned. One: Javon Kimball is keeping this secret from everyone. He has already admitted to you his abilities are derived from symmachite variants living in union with his body."

"Which I'm still having a hard time believing," Ramos murmured.

"Really?" I snickered. "Being tossed through an interdimensional portal, shooting monsters, and meeting my pen pals from a land of magic were easier to stomach?"

"That isn't what I meant." Ramos took a sip of his glass of red wine. "This Javon's powers—they're different from anything else I've seen, on the side of the good guys, that is. I'd be cautious around him. It makes me wonder what else your foundation is hiding from you."

"Story of my life." I held up a hand. "Hold up. Sorry, Loredana."

She sat drumming her fingers on her knee, her legs crossed. "Interruptions aside … The second possibility is Javon Kimball has made the board aware of his condition, and as Lieutenant Ramos has alluded to, Procyon could be keeping this yet another secret."

"Which would suck."

"Indeed." Loredana handed me the letter—and swiped back the glass of lemonade.

"What, not a permanent trade?"

"You shall have to procure your own beverage."

I reached behind my chair for the bottle of Corona. Empty. I sighed. "Any more possibilities? Got something behind number three?"

Loredana took a slow sip. Never let it be said she couldn't be dramatic. "Mr. Kimball is aware of his abilities and what makes them work but is unaware from whom they were gifted."

My turn to raise an eyebrow. "You think he doesn't know about Tenebrae? Or at least, doesn't know the symmachites in the Kimballs come from him?"

"As I said, it is one of three possibilities."

"*Loco*," Ramos murmured.

"Yeah, you said it." I made a face. "He's the guy with all the answers—Tenebrae, I mean. At this rate I'd be better off praying to him."

"Mercury!" Ramos backhanded my shoulder. The injured one.

"Hey!" I gritted my teeth. "And also, ow! What's the big idea?"

"Deny God all you want, but you won't flirt with heresy on the doorstep of my house." Ramos pointed a finger. "You might not believe in Him or His plans, but I do. I won't stand for your lip when it comes to prayer. Understood?"

"Yeah, okay, I got it. It was a joke."

He scowled. No more verbal chastisement necessary. There I was, guest for dinner at the house of a guy whose life I'd saved—and who'd saved mine. "I'm sorry about that. You know me. When I don't have the answers, I get snarky."

"Which is also your response when you're tired, or hungry, or bored." Loredana sipped her lemonade, looking pretty innocent for someone who'd just dropped a sick burn on her husband.

Ramos coughed. He might have been choking with sudden laughter on his wine.

"Ha ha, you guys are hysterical." I couldn't hide a grin, though. "Man. Okay, so the question is, when do we confront Javon about this?"

"Or do you confront him?" Loredana asked. "He is a valuable ally."

"If he really is your ally." Ah, Ramos. The perpetual ray of sunshine.

"You're not wrong to ask that," I said. "He sounds like he might have split allegiances. But we'll have a chance to pin him down when Dominic beams us to the secret base."

"I take it I'm not invited."

"Sorry, Ramos. Only got tickets for three."

"Don't worry. I have enough on my plate without taking a field trip to heaven knows where, since by the way you two have been talking, it's not like it's around the corner."

"Good. You can keep us posted on when the trucks leave and

where they're going."

"The what?"

I leaned forward, dropping my voice another octave—though I don't know why I felt the need to be super quiet. We'd been blabbing about interdimensional monsters and other threats for the past half hour. "Javon and Alvarez. They're moving more historic vault stuff out tomorrow. Should be a steady stream of trucks on the northeast side of town."

Ramos scratched at his chin. "I'll get Bradley on it. If there's been any odd activity, Narcotics might have it on their radar, too, if they think it's smuggling. I'll text you if I turn up anything."

"Thanks. Though to be honest, I'm not even sure what set of wheels they use for transport."

Thumping music echoed down the block. A squat, sporty Honda Civic painted blistering orange jerked to a stop in front of the house. Had to be a mid-1990s model, but the owner had tricked it out with a spoiler, and flashy rims, none of which matched in color. The orange was a couple different shades, once I got a better look. "Uh-oh, Ramos," I said. "Do you get to ticket drivers when you're off duty?"

He set the glass down and stood, hands on his hips.

Loredana giggled.

"What?" I asked. "Let me in on the joke."

Two teen boys got out of the car, carrying bags of groceries— the tall, skinny, broad-shouldered Hector, and the stout, burly Alejandro. They had matching haircuts, spiky and black with one side swept over. They were chattering in Spanish, laughing and swiping at each other, until they saw Disapproving Dad watching them.

"Oh, I get it." I cupped my hand to my mouth and hollered, "Busted!"

"Mercury!" Loredana whacked me.

"Gabriel!" Olivia's voice sang through the open window. "Are the boys back? I thought I heard their obnoxious music."

"You did hear it." Ramos flicked his hand toward the door

in a gesture that said *Get inside now and we'll deal with your trouble later.*

"Good! Tell them I need those avocados *pronto*! You can yell at them when they finish."

I didn't get a chance to see the looks on the boys' faces as they scurried inside because I had my head back as I about died from laughter.

Loredana was curled up on the couch. I stuck the Tupperware of leftover chimichanga in the fridge. She hadn't eaten much. The stress of the last week must have really gotten to her. I hoped Doc Arne could prescribe something to get her through until this was all over.

I sat at the counter and pulled up Cordelia's secret files on a tablet. Not a Procyon one. And I made sure the Wi-Fi and data were shut off. Wasn't gonna take any chances with Winston trying to spy through any electronic peephole he could find. Loredana had bought that particular tablet after his imprisonment.

A couple searches in, and I had some more detail on the Kimball clan. The photo of three guys in Florida was who I suspected—Lucas Kimball, the granddad and co-founder of Procyon, at age 86, with his 54-year-old son Logan and *his* 24-year-old son, Owen. Which would make Owen ... I squinted. He'd be Javon's great-great-grandfather.

"Passed symmachites down four more generations," I muttered. "But what was the point? Why would Tenebrae need it? Unless he was at war with the Whisperer and wanted some extra insurance."

My phone buzzed. Wilhelmina? "Hey. How's it going?"

"Oh, just enjoyin' a quiet night that's about to get a whole lot livelier. How's about you come on up to Rosa Roja? I got some friends who need to have a word with you."

Great. Pain lanced through my temples. "Please tell me it's muggers. Or drug dealers. Or drug dealers who mug people."

"Child, these folks are the kind who would hug you instead of punch you."

I sighed. "Okey-doke. Give me fifteen. Because I'm walking."

"I knew you'd be happy to oblige." She hung up.

Wow. Nothing like spending the rest of the evening chastising wannabe superheroes, instead of lounging around with my wife. Hooray for the Mercurians.

I snagged the supersuit. No way I was actually walking.

Time to run.

Rosa Roja wasn't completely deserted of people. With evening having fallen, the streetlamps lit the pathways winding between trees and moss-covered ruins of old San Camillo. A lone policewoman passed on horseback, her mount snorting and tossing his mane as his hoofs clacked along the asphalt.

Probably he hadn't noticed when I leaped across Thirteenth Street, landing among the crumbling walls of an ancient hacienda.

Finding the Mercurians didn't take much brainpower, either, because the big band of dummies were huddled in shadows, dressed in their yellow-sleeved uniforms. Okay, so they weren't uniform uniforms, because only the colors matched. Some had T-shirts. Some had sweatshirts. Others went sleeveless but had tied bandannas around their biceps.

Wilhelmina sat at their periphery, fingers flying through a bold green sock. It was tiny, though. I wanted to ask her if she had great-nephews or nieces, but decided it wasn't the right time, not for someone who'd only recently gotten over the deaths of her husband and daughter at the hands—or tentacles—of astral fiends. That was why she'd left Procyon.

I kept the suit's camouflage engaged and whispered, "Wooooooo!" in my best creepy ghost voice.

"You're goin' the right way for a stabbed eyeball," Wilhelmina murmured, without looking up from her knitting. "How's Loredana?"

"Sleepy. Not very hungry. She's been stressed out. Rough stomach, trouble resting, that kind of thing."

"Mm-hmm." She pointed a needle at the gathering of eight Mercurians. "You recognize this group?"

They had their masks pulled down, faces illuminated by their cell phones. One was the Latina I'd met a while back when Wilhelmina had gone bonkers. Then there was the skinny Black kid I'd rescued along with his female companion when they'd tracked me to the warehouse fight with Serena. And a third was a burly guy with a beard, dark-rimmed glasses, and brown hair cut short.

"Josh!" The woman slapped his arm. "I think he's *here*!"

That would be obvious because I let the camouflage fade away slowly. What can I say? The moment needed some drama, especially if I was gonna get them to listen to me. "Hey, gang."

"Wow! I didn't think he would actually show up, Tina!" Josh, the guy with glasses, grinned great big and laughed. "Hey! Everybody!"

The Black teen spun around. He had a baton in hand, like a police-issue one used for, um, encouraging obedience. "I knew it! I knew you'd come! Hey, I'm Vic." He left the other seven gawking at me, phones aimed for my masked face, and offered his hand to shake.

"Good to see you again. Thanks for not following me into any more dark and scary spaces."

He shuffled his shoes. "Oh, uh, yeah, that was a bad idea."

"How's your friend?"

"Clare? She's good. Better. Scared off the streets, though." Vic's expression lost some of its boyhood. "It got us thinking, you know? About how this isn't a game. It's for keeps. More than the keeps we think of when we're busting heads."

I nodded. "Good deal. That means you're learning." I gestured at Wilhelmina. "My friend here says you wanted to talk with me."

"They need direction, child." Wilhelmina stood beside me. "They got their hearts in the right place, but they're skirting between the law and what's right. Don't always mean two things overlap."

"Well, I'm sure not here to lecture on the moral ambiguity of vigilantism." I lifted the bottom half of my mask so they could see me grin.

Hushed laughter went around the circle. "So, you'll do it then?" Tina asked. "Thank God! We were hoping you'd agree. I know you must be busy with your, um, monster-slaying ..."

"I ... agree to what, exactly? Just so I make sure I get it right. You know, in my phone reminders." I glared at Wilhelmina through the opaque eye slits of the mask.

"To train them." She smiled sweetly and hooked her arm through mine. "Why, Mercury Hale is gonna be the one to show you folks how to wage the war against darkness, without getting yourselves in too much trouble, and how to keep a watch around your neighborhoods for not just the things police will handle when you call 'em, but for signs of the creatures that plague us."

"Yes!" Vic clapped his hands.

"This is so cool," Josh said.

"Yeah, it sure is something." I tugged on Wilhelmina's arm. "Give us a minute, okay?"

I found a spot where a collapsed adobe wall made a shadowed, sheltered overhang. "Are you insane? Is this what dementia starts out as? I'm not training a bunch of nutjobs in dollar store costumes! We've got a major crisis on our hands!"

"If it were as big a crisis as you're whinin' about, you'd be in Tracking, not out here," Wilhelmina snapped. "Face facts, child— whether you intended it or not, you created these folks. They saw the good you did and when you stopped, they took up the slack."

"I never meant to be a superhero to the neighborhoods!" I threw my arms wide. And bashed my knuckles on the wall. Because of course I did. "That was to earn money when I was out of job!"

"And you never thought about the consequences of walking away when you were done." Wilhelmina poked my chest with her knitting needles. "Whether you meant it or not, Mercury, you gave them hope. When you didn't come back to the streets, they went out and made their own hope. So, the least you can do is take responsibility to make sure they don't get theyselves killed."

Argh. Headache again. But she was right. I hated that. "Fine," I said through gritted teeth. "Fine. Sure. What's a few more nights of lost sleep? Okay, I guess if it helps them not get eaten or shot, it'll be worth it."

"All right. Did you hear that, kids?" Wilhelmina stepped out from the shadows and beamed at everyone like I'd just agreed to run for president. "Mercury is gonna show you how to be heroes."

Whispered cheers and high-fives went around the group.

"This'll be fun," I muttered.

She patted my cheek. "That's my boy. Now get to work."

"Wait." I literally dug in my heels as she pushed me out toward them. "Aren't you gonna help out?"

"'Course I will." Wilhelmina winked. "But you get 'em started, so I don't make you look bad when it's my turn."

CHAPTER TWENTY-SIX

An hour later, nobody was cheering. Except Wilhelmina.

"Good job!" She hugged Josh, as he leaned against a rotting cubicle partition. He had a bruise on his jaw. At least his glasses weren't broken. He'd lost them, sure, but one thing at a time.

"Thanks." He winced, then hobbled back out into the open space at the center of the shuttered office building.

I'd picked the call center for that very reason—no one had used it for a long time, probably because all the calls had been shifted over to robots or people who called themselves "Tom" but whose time zone placed them on the other side of the planet. There were three dozen cubicles arranged in three lopsided rows along the far end of the sprawling space, and office furniture scattered in between. Which was great because obstacles made for good practice.

I stood in the center of the tile floor, spinning the pulsar stave idly in my right hand. No lights, except for rows of windows admitted amber rectangles. The stave, though, made for a pretty visible target. "Okay. Let's try two at once, because—wait for it— not all bad guys will be courteous and attack you one at a time."

Tina and Vic glanced at each other, totally telegraphing their move, then rushed me. Tina had an aluminum baseball bat and

Vic, his baton. Had to give them credit—Tina went low, for my knees, while Vic swung at my face, and they coordinated their attack from opposite directions. But I was the guy who spent years battling actual monsters, plus whatever mercenaries Syndax could throw at me. This was amateur league.

I dropped my head and neck back, watching curiously as the logo of the San Camillo Peregrines went past my nose, that stupid cartoon bird of prey snarling at me. Meanwhile I slashed out with the stave, parrying Vic's baton, and kept moving to the left until my foot connected with Tina's ribcage.

I was in slow-mo mode, which was cheating, I know, but I wasn't about to take it easy on these guys, because if they could handle *me*, they could handle a drug dealer with a broken bottle.

End result? Tina on her side, clutching her *other side,* tears leaking from the corners of her eyes while she glared at me. Vic staggered past me, staring at his empty fingers, but spun around when he realized he was unarmed, and I still had my weapon. I slapped him to the floor with another very restrained blow.

"Man," Vic panted. "You suck."

"No." I pointed the stave at him. "*You* suck, relatively speaking. I'm showing you how fast your opponent can be. You've been picking fights with guys who are drunk or stoned or hopped up on meth. I haven't seen you take on anybody who's at full strength."

"But we're not up to fighting supervillains or monsters like you do," Tina protested. "We're trying to protect our neighborhoods."

"If you're gonna do that, you have to be faster than anybody else who thinks they can take over where you live." I turned, slowly, so I could take in all eight of them with the stave. "Think you can take me out? I bet you can—if I were wounded or distracted. Keep working with me, training against me, and you can take down anyone who poses a threat."

"Be easier if we could shoot them," another girl muttered.

"No way. Not an option." I held up my phone. "Not unless you want this to all fall apart. Kill someone, and you become just another violent menace on the street. People already think that kind of thing about you, but death … You're not ready for it. It's better if you're never ready for it."

Nobody had any arguments against that one. I offered Tina my hand. She took it, let me pull her shakily to her feet …

Then swept a fist at my nose.

I blocked her wrist with mine, the one holding the stave, and let the weapon glow between us. Sparks skittered down my arm. Made for great special effects as the suit soaked up energy. I grinned at her. "Better. Good stuff. Okay, you guys pair off for a while in cubicles so you can practice fighting in tight spaces—and take a break from the worst of the bruises and give each other baby slaps instead."

They laughed and set off among the ruined office remnants, finding confined quarters. Wilhelmina clucked her tongue from where she sat thirty feet away on an old desk. "Lord, I never thought I'd see the day when you were teachin' instead of learnin'."

I leaned against the other end of the desk. "Not bad for the student becoming the master, right?"

"Didn't say that. Let's call it, the student becoming less of a thick-headed dummy who can share somethin' good from his experiences."

"Great pep talk." I held my hands to my face. "I can feel my self-esteem soaring!"

She chuckled, but the levity died off so fast I thought she'd stabbed herself with knitting needles. "It's good to have people like this out there, no matter what the law says. Cops can't be all places at once. At least they can give the hoodlums something to think twice about."

"Yeah, well, let's not mention any of this to Ramos. Last thing he needs to worry about is me training vigilantes, and really inexperienced ones at that."

"He's under a mountain of strain, that one."

"Tell me about it." I looked at her. The lines on her face seemed deeper, more crowded. Of course, that could have been the lousy lighting. "What's on your mind? More than bringing me out here to play Mr. Miyagi."

"Ain't just the lieutenant I'm worried about. The newcomers—Kimball and Pathkiller."

"Ah." Muffled grunts and clatters of weapons against cubicle walls trickled down to us from elsewhere in the building. Sounded like practice was going well. "The heirs to the throne. What about them? Edith took bad hits from Troy but—"

"They both got themselves compromised." Wilhelmina's knitting slowed, but her movements became sharper, more precise. No way I wanted a finger in the way of those needles. "Edith, bless her, she's been granted a great gift, her and a whole line of her family. But Troy got to her in a way an astral fiend can't. Didn't try to leach her life out of her. He went straight for the heart."

I nodded. "That's a heck of a wound."

"Mm-hmm. Makes a person do all sorts of things she wouldn't." She glanced up at me, her eyes catching the dim light from the street. "Leads them to mistakes, turns them down the wrong path, even haunts them until they walk away from everything. Spoken by someone who knows what that kind of hurt brings, child."

"I know you do." I touched her shoulder. "So, I need to make sure Edith is on her game. We talked about the prison, so I'm not too worried about a repeat freeze, but you're right, we've got to watch out for her. And what about Javon?"

"Him." Wilhelmina wrinkled her nose. "And to think I call *you* child. He's got all that power crawling under his skin, according to you, but you're saying he's got a link to Tenebrae he might not even know about. That's bad enough, but for what Troy makes him."

"Troy hasn't even—"

"Reckless." She wagged a needle in my face. "Reckless and sloppy. He's got a lot to prove, that young one, and with Troy runnin' around out there with the famed pulsar stave in hand—"

"Half of it."

"—He's got the perfect way to prove himself to the rest of Procyon. Prove he's more than just a pretty face who grins, shakes hands, and signs paychecks. He gets too outta hand, someone's got to slap him back into line."

I sighed. "I'm pretty sure if I slapped him, my hand would go right through."

"Don't mope none. I ain't mean you have to do it alone. We're all here with you—Loredana and me, Ramos, Teget, even Liz and Garvey. Dominic, too. I saw how you were at the end of the prison brawl, Mercury. You're doing more than fighting. You're leading." She pointed into the distance, where the shadows of the Mercurians in training flickered against illumination from their phones and the broken windows. "That's what I wanted them to see. You're a symbol, sure, but you're also a man they need to see take charge and bring them hope."

"There you go again." I frowned. "A lot of talk about me giving hope to people who don't even know me. They've got to find it in themselves—or maybe in Ramos' God, if they're of that particular flavor."

"Like I said already, you started it." She chuckled. "Lord knows it wasn't anybody's ideal presentation. But this is what we got. Stick with it."

"Or else there goes the neighborhood, right?"

"Child, the more the darkness pushes free of its bounds and people see it for what it is, they're gonna look for light. The tangible kind." She touched the pulsar stave. Its glow brightened until we were both basking in it like a lantern in a forest encampment. "And you got to be the one showing them the way to stop the evil, like it or not."

Wow.

No pressure.

By the next day, I was sore from being smacked around by eight strangers, even if they didn't get that many hits on me. They had staggered home with a whole lot more injuries than I did. Wilhelmina had smiled and spent the whole evening unscathed, which didn't seem fair, until I considered that maybe she didn't want those kids to know just how good a fighter she really was.

"Shall I retrieve an icepack from the infirmary?" Loredana asked as we walked into Tracking.

"Nah, I'm good." I made a show of flexing in my T-shirt—and gotta say, I looked pretty good. "Have to keep up this serious regimen if I'm gonna be just as cut as the guy on the cover."

Loredana rolled her eyes. "Yes, goodness knows you've completely let yourself go. Why, you must be a single beer away from what is deemed a dad bod, I daresay."

I snorted at that. "If anyone we know has a dad bod, it's Ramos. Isn't he the real hero?"

"Ah, I see my words return to haunt me."

"Hey, you made the original crack, so—"

"Shhh!" Liz's warning was about as loud as a broken steam pipe. Not that I'd ever seen one, I don't think, but that's how I imagined it. "He's thinking!"

"He" in question had to be Cyril because Liz was hunkered among a new row of monitors in a half circle around her tablet-desk. Way too many lines of text, code, and numbers for me to look at. It made the green gibberish of the Matrix as easy to read as a kindergartener's ABCs. Graphs flickered across the right screen. Maps flashed on the left.

Edith stood behind her, holding the back of Liz's chair. I leaned in. "This, ah, means Cyril's doing okay, right?"

"I don't understand all of it. Something about a temporary partition." Edith shrugged. "But she's crunching the numbers, and her computer hasn't broken. Yet."

"Of what numbers are we speaking?" Loredana asked.

"Neutrino counts and tachyon spikes." Liz sucked on the straw in her cup of soda. "I've had Tracking monitoring both ever since we figured out that's what Tenebrae used to make his way into this world or at least hitch a ride with anything coming out of the Interstice, but it took Cyril *forever* before he could get the right algorithm running so I'm really hoping he can crack this before whatever Winston put into him breaches the partition on his hard drive."

A lot of info, but at least she cut herself off. I didn't have the heart to right then. "We're betting this will help us nail down where he's next gonna show up?"

"And where Troy is heading," Edith said. "Because he's using Serena's ability to teleport around."

"I think it's tied to the armor, but I can't prove it yet." Liz tapped a trio of commands. A rectangular window appeared in the center screen. Purple dots ringed in red blinked to life around San Camillo, then further north, at Bulwark State Prison and even Shotgun, Oregon. "That's everywhere we know she's been, plus some."

"Fascinating." Loredana tapped her shoe, probably because her mind was running the implications of this new and very awesome means of tracking. "Using this as a predictor will help us mobilize a response with greater accuracy, I take it. I shall alert Mr. Garvey."

"Mercury." Edith left her spot behind Liz. "I need to borrow you."

I glanced at Loredana. "You gals good?"

"Hmm?" Loredana's gaze was locked on the screens. "Yes, quite."

Guess that meant I had permission. I followed Edith over to the server room door, where there was relative privacy in the corner of Tracking. "What's up?"

"Before you go … I have to show you something." Her eyes had the faintest tinge of violet to them. She'd gone all somber, her stance solid, like I'd seen her do in Forecasting.

"Not a big fan of these visions but, I'm guessing, I'm gonna want to see this." I grimaced. Last time, I'd seen a target island in a rainstorm long before I'd physically arrived—and way before it was raining. Your guess is as good as mine as to whether I imagined it, or she really did show me the future. I held out my hands, palms up. "Let's do it."

She grabbed both, her fingers curling, nails digging into my knuckles. Her eyes shone light flashlights, and her voice was a deep, sonorous command: "*See.*"

I swooped through the walls of Tracking, out over San Camillo Bay. The blue morning sky tore in half, like a ripped piece of paper, and piercing gold light pulled me through.

Shallow seas. I stood ankle deep. It stretched forever. I couldn't find a single landmark on any horizon.

The golden sunbeams blinded me, pulled on my body until I stumbled into a hazy room ... The living space of a Medan house. No mistaking the architecture or the cooking ware.

There was a man kneeling, hair black and cropped, his sharp cheekbones broadened by a proud grin. A woman, with long, brown curls and Asian features, held out her hands to a tiny toddler. The cute little kid staggered away from a chair, hands free, giggling.

When he made it, they cheered, the mother drowning his face in kisses. And the loudest huzzah came from a girl, maybe five-years-old, in a dress the color of purple lilacs. She hugged her little brother and whispered something in his ear.

The door banged open. A shadow cast onto the family.

The little girl began to cry ...

I gasped. My heart raced. Sweat covered my face and chest, so much so my T-shirt clung to me.

Edith released my hands. "You saw it? What does it mean?"

"How the heck should I know?" I rasped. "Man. You filled my head with crazy images—"

"They're coming. She's going to be taken away." The light faded from her eyes. "Or they have already done it. It's a blur. But the sorrow ... That's real. What I know is, you have a chance to fix it, at the right moment."

"Just once, I'd like better clues."

Edith leaned closer, her chin brushing mine. I caught a whiff of mint as she whispered, "You help Tenebrae, and he helps you."

"Mercury?"

I jolted away from her. Not weird looking, nope, not at all—me all sweaty in a corner with Edith. Didn't help Loredana wasn't wearing office gear. Didn't mention that did I? She had on her gray shirt and fatigues, with her favorite MP5 slung over one shoulder. The Browning semi-automatic pistol she'd gotten from her dad was holstered on her hip. I bet she had her silver revolver hidden somewhere less conspicuous.

"If you're quite through, Gemini has messaged me. He's here and prepared." Loredana pursed her lips. "Provided I'm not interrupting."

"I've shown him all he needs," Edith said.

"I'm sure." Loredana looped her arm through mine and led me from Tracking. "Elizabeth, kindly keep me updated. Now excuse me whilst I make sure my husband takes his clothes off."

So I could get into my supersuit.

That was the part Loredana left out. But hey, good exit line, right? She must have learned it from me.

I was pulling the last tight spots out of the suit—it gets a bit, um, clingy—when Dominic entered in his signature blacks. Javon was with him, wearing the same sleek outfit he'd donned in the raid on Troy's house. "All right." Javon grinned at us. "Gang's all here."

"Here" was the empty Historic Vault, still empty. But that was the point—it was time for a field trip to make sure all the important stuff was safe.

Teget joined us, too. He'd been bunking in one of the extra operative rooms that I'd sometimes used when I needed to spend the night, get cleaned up, and otherwise recover in peace after a harrowing fight with astral fiends. He was dressed in a muscle shirt and athletic shorts, a sheen of sweat over every muscles. "I would much rather embark with you, than waste my hours in sparring with that ridiculous contraption upstairs."

I clapped his shoulder. "Thank for the sentiment, but we couldn't get you a boarding pass. Hang here and be ready in case any fiends pop up. You'll be the first line of defense."

Dominic spun up his Echo Watches and bingo, we had a rippling portal in the room. Wind lashed at our clothes. "Hey!" I shouted. "Have you even been to this secret base? I thought you had to see it first!"

"I did!" Dominic made a face. "Loredana texted me a picture and gave me coordinates. So, it's good enough to take us there."

"Way safer than jumpin' out of a plane like a moron!" Javon shoved me through.

"Safe travels!" Teget's farewell warped into mash of discordant sounds.

Going through the portal wasn't fun. I may have mentioned that. The average human brain has issues with feeling like it's been two places at once. But I was used to it enough I didn't dissolve into a blubbering mess.

Didn't barf that time, either, which was a nice bonus.

But Loredana did.

Our surroundings solidified into a rock tunnel with metal grating for a floor. More rock was underneath. Water trickled between those stones.

Loredana braced herself against a wall and wiped at her mouth with the back of her hand. "Egad."

Javon chuckled. He pulled a tiny box from his pocket. "Mint?"

"Thank you." Loredana emptied four into her hand and shoved all into her mouth.

"Wow, okay." I patted her on the back. "This is what we get for cutting our vacation short. Next week, back to the beach."

Dominic bumped into me. He stared at the ceiling, the tunnel, and the pitted, water-streaked steel door in front of us. "She was right," he murmured. "I've been here—or a place like it."

There was a tan, bullet-shaped robot standing on wheels by the door. It was one of those types like I'd seen private security companies around San Camillo use, a regular modern-day droid. I sauntered up like I owned the place. "Hey, R2, we're here to see Obi-wan."

Procyon's version of everyone's favorite cinematic robot rotated silently on three wheels and aimed a machine gun at my belly button.

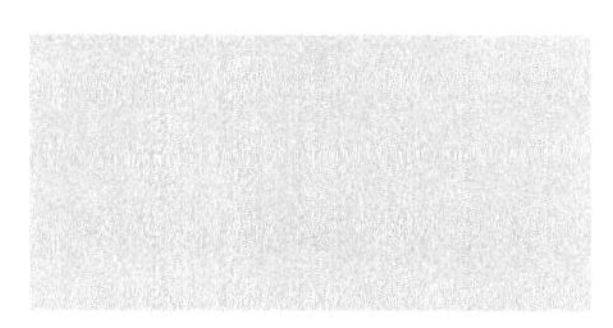

CHAPTER
TWENTY-SEVEN

Believe it or not, I showed restraint. The killer robot did not become a pile of molten plastic and metal on the floor.

That gave Javon time to flash a Procyon ID badge in front of a bubble-shaped camera lens that must have been the robot's eye. "'Sup, Twiki."

The red light rimming the eye flickered, then turned green. Without putting its gun away, Twiki spun back around and rolled toward a flat black panel to the right of the door. Huge metal locks, which sounded the same as the ones for the Historic Vaults, clanged.

"You name your robots here?" I slowly drew the pulsar stave, keeping it inert but ready to lop the bullet-dome's head off if need be.

"It's either that or a nine-digit serial number. Besides, Mom loved *Buck Rogers*. She had the hots for Gil Gerard."

Dominic chuckled. "So did my mother."

"Right on." Javon held up a hand. Dominic slapped him a high five.

"Gentlemen." Loredana stepped past us. "Though it brings be great joy to see our operatives forming a rapport based on childhood experiences, our escort is leaving us."

I breezed around the new fan bros and caught up with her.

The tunnel beyond the door had rock walls with steel panels. The floor was metal grating suspended a few inches over rock. There were more hatches every twenty feet or so, alternating on either side of the hallway. All were marked with numbers, slipped inside clear plastic plates mounted at eye level. "Gotta say, I'm getting a real *Raiders of the Lost Ark* vibe from this whole place. That, and,having some serious flashbacks to the Medan temple."

"I assure you its layout is purely practical."

"But the location isn't." Dominic and Javon were with us. "I know where we are. Well, perhaps it's better to say I know in what building."

"Really hoping this isn't a 'I could tell you, but I'd have to kill you' kind of secret he's figured out, because he is our ride home," I whispered to Loredana.

She snorted and covered her mouth so she could stifle the rest of the laugh.

Dominic sighed. "I meant this is the same facility as Procyon Home Guard's forward base outside of Rampart on the other Earth. Not precisely the same, but these halls, and the rock itself—I recognize the geology and the structural influences."

Loredana let her fingers graze the damp rock surfaces as we walked, tracing a vein of what I figured was quartz. Because it was sparkly. Hey, I am *not* a rockhound. "That seems accurate. I shall have to inquire of my counterpart as to when their facility was built versus this one."

"The doubles." Javon shook his head. "I got briefed on that, back in the day—"

The day? I rolled my eyes. He was like *twelve*. Okay, to be fair, he was probably only four years younger than me.

"—But I don't have the urge to go meet my evil twin."

"They're not all evil," Dominic said. "Just some of them."

"The ones you roll up, right?"

"They are wanted for crimes on the other Earth and if we find they've infiltrated this one—"

"Quite enough discussion of classified information, thank

you," Loredana said curtly.

I peeked into the tiny window of one door as we passed. There was a steel shelving unit with black containers lined in gold, three of them, one on each shelf. The edges generated a soft light, which was helpful since the room lacked illumination otherwise.

The corridor came to a T-shaped intersection. We followed Javon to the right. A second robot was waiting, which was kind of cool and kind of not. Facing another machine gun sentry didn't freak me out as bad the second time, but had to say, my pulse dipped down as soon as Javon's ID turned the robot's red circle to green.

"Do you guys have anyone alive running this place?" I asked. "Because the Terminators sure are out in force."

"That's quite enough, Mercury. They're clearly *not* Terminators." Loredana winked at me. "It's obvious to anyone with a modicum of sense that Procyon has employed Daleks to guard its secret facility."

Dominic and I snorted in stereo.

"Skeleton crew." Javon did sound amused. Must not be a *Dr. Who* fan. "And if they're not hanging out at the exterior entrance, they're in some of the storage pods doing research. Whole place has security cameras and motion detectors. Staff are ID tagged, too, just like us."

"Like us ..." I patted my pocket. "Ah. Our badges."

"Yep. Double duty."

The windows along the left side of the corridor were at face height and narrow, the glass reinforced with crisscrossing wire. I glanced at a light that flickered through one—and froze so fast Dominic slammed into me.

"A little warning next time." He pinched his nose, eyes watering.

I pointed. "You ... Guys. Is that ...?"

Javon looked through the window. "Oh. Yeah, that's the E.T. Not on the tour. C'mon."

Even Loredana lost capacity for speech. She stood beside me, eyes wide, hand over her mouth.

The room beyond was a huge hangar, with about the same volume as those ones you see at big international airports. Probably could squeeze a 737 inside. Which meant that the vehicle I was gawking at was a bit smaller than a passenger jet, but not by much. It was a big gray triangle, covered with a hexagonal pattern that seemed to ripple occasionally under the blazing lights set on the walls and on tripods. Blue and orange lights lined its edges. I couldn't see any windows. There were funky bulges at each point of the triangle.

And the whole thing was floating.

"You've—" I grabbed the sides of my head as we followed Javon. "When were you gonna tell us that Procyon has a UFO?"

"Never, if I'd had my way," Javon muttered. "But since you're keepin' everything else you see in here a secret, I figured, what's one more? Besides, it was worth it taking you this route just to get you to shut up for a while."

Well, he wasn't wrong. I didn't have anything insightful to add for at least the next minute and a half. Might as well have been an eternity.

We took another right and wound up in a short hall, maybe 20 feet long, with five doors coming off it. The second door on the right was labeled, "BBS011219." My brain was still reeling from what I'd seen in the hangar, and trust me, it took a lot to make my brain reel after everything we'd been through.

Javon held his ID to another of those black panels.

<Identification—Kimball, Javon Duke Lucas. Confirm.> The voice from the panel was female, and bored. If a programmed voice could be bored.

Javon leaned forward. A red light blinked, illuminating his left eye.

<Retinal scan match. Identification confirmed.>

The door unlocked.

"Open sesame," Dominic murmured.

"Hey." He beat me by two seconds, not even kidding.

Javon admitted us to a room that was built of light. Glowing rectangular panels covered the ceiling and walls, separated by aluminum panels a foot wide. Made it feel like we were the ones stuck inside a cage, under a researcher's spotlights. I could see my reflection perfectly in the stone floor, which could have been polished obsidian.

The black sword rested on a Plexiglass stand, suspended at chest height. I'd told everyone it was like that nanotube stuff you read about—an absolute black, staring into space without any stars. Like the center of a black hole. The space stuff probably came to mind because, well, I'd just seen a UFO parked in the garage. The sword itself was a cross between a katana or ninjato, only bigger and broader. The hilt was black, too, without a hint of any other color. It could have been carved out of the same obsidian as the floor.

"Okay." Javon leaned against a light panel. "There you go, kids. One sword, safe and sound. I told you."

"Yes. We appreciate you humoring us over our concerns." Loredana could have been correcting a mistake on a student's paper. "But I will feel more relieved once I have a full tour of your security checkpoints, given that we bypassed the main access via the Echo Watches' mode of transit."

"Hey, even if I hadn't phoned ahead and given the crew up there some notice that we were gonna show up in the main hall, they would have pinpointed us in a second." Javon ticked off with his fingers. "Already said it—cameras, motion detectors, thermal sensing, and the robots. The whole works. They can pin down a guy, and in twenty seconds, you'd have six more armed guards for backup."

"Then I am especially glad nothing malfunctioned. Still, the tour will be forthcoming."

"This isn't San Camillo HQ, and I ain't one of your coffee runners."

I leaned toward Dominic. "As much fun as it is watching Loredana tear this guy a new one, I'm just glad the sword is in one piece."

"Yes. I can see why it's buried way down here." He walked around to the hilt and crouched, so he was looking at the handle end on. "Did you see this?"

"See what?" I stood over his shoulder.

"It's hollow." He frowned. "There's writing etched around the pommel. Tiny, though. I can't make it out."

I nudged him over. "Lemme take a look."

"By all means, expert of ancient things."

"Hey." Javon pointed at me. "Hands off, man."

"Relax. I've already gotten to hold it. You know, when I burned the symmachites out of my body with the pulsar stave." I grinned. "You might want to remember that if we ever get to brawling."

Dominic wasn't kidding, though. The letters were tiny. Actually, I didn't know if they were letters, because they didn't make any sense to me, but I'd seen them—

Hang on a second.

I held up the pulsar stave. Yeah, the markings weren't identical, but they were close enough for government work—or private monster-slaying foundation work. And given the size of the hollow cavity. "Hey, Javon. With all the security in this place, is the sword itself alarmed up?"

"Only if you try to take it out of the doors or off its pedestal."

"Cool." I put the pulsar stave inside the pommel.

"What on Earth are you doing?" Loredana had her hands on her hips.

"Relax," I said. "See? It fits. Nothing to worry about."

The pulsar stave ignited, *inside* the sword. And purple sparks rippled along both edges of the blade. The stave's glow seeped up the pommel, illuminating the carvings as well as a patchwork of tracings on the flat surface of the blade.

"Wow," Dominic murmured. "I've never seen it do that before."

"No kidding." My headache came back, with a sudden

vengeance. The more I stared at the carvings, and the symbols, the more my temples throbbed. Looking away was probably a good idea.

Except that I couldn't.

This is the key. He is the gate.

Those weren't the Whisperer's words. I recognized Tenebrae's insistent tone, bouncing around my skull. I could feel the words as solid as stones. I shook my head.

"Hey. Are you all right?" Dominic touched my shoulder.

Part of me recognized the friendly gesture. Another part of me—a part that I didn't recognize, that felt like it had just moved in—caught him by the arm and flung him over the sword's pedestal.

Dominic smashed into a light panel on the opposite wall. Cracks radiated outward as he crumpled to the floor.

Loredana's hand was on her belt, but her face was the absolute portrait of worry. "Mercury!"

"Okay, I don't know what he's playin' at, but I know how to stop it." Javon stepped in front of Loredana, fists clenched, the purple lines of his suit aglow.

I wanted to tell them I was sorry because I was—or part of me was. A small, screaming part that slid down a ravine into the darkest, quietest corner of my mind. Whatever or whoever was running the show wouldn't let me speak, wouldn't let me make eye contact. I couldn't do anything except fulfill what had become the most powerful, overwhelming urge I'd ever had.

The key. Edgeweld. Take it.

So, I did.

The instant I picked up the sword, the last scraps of me wound up boxed inside that dark place, my awareness of everything else going on in that room hazy as a California dusk in the worst summer fires. But I could tell enough to hear the far distant sirens, see the room bathed in red light from those panels that had all changed their shade, and feel the vibrations in the floor as Loredana drew her silver revolver.

Mercury.

"Mercury!" Loredana shouted. "Put the sword down! Please, this isn't you!"

You have Edgeweld. This is the key. This is the one. He is the gate. Help.

"Drop it, Hale!" Javon snapped. "You know what I can do!"

The gate.

Of course.

It made a whole bunch of sense, so my arms drew back the stave-enhanced sword, ready for a swing.

"No!" Loredana's aim never wavered. I loved that about her, even if I was staring down the muzzle of her gun and she was doing her best to not shoot her husband in the face.

"Stand back!" Javon's fists disassembled, then his arms, and I knew he'd sweep around me or through me before striking from out of nowhere.

Good thing—for somebody, anyway—was that all movement froze. Even Loredana's finger perched on the trigger.

The key.

Even when my mind and body were being hijacked, I was still pissed off at being lectured. Okay, fine! Time to use the key on the gate.

So, I stabbed Javon with the Edgeweld sword.

Or tried to. As soon as the tip of the blade made contact with his chest, white sparks skittered across his suit, down his arms, up his face, though his legs. It was like seeing through his body to his blood vessels, until I realized I really was seeing through him—because Edgeweld forced him apart.

Javon screamed.

It only lasted a second, though, before his entire body became a swirl of golden particles, churning in an airborne whirlpool. I could have been looking down into the eye of a miniature hurricane. Those gale-force winds pulled me in …

And through.

I splashed face first into water. Sputtered a lot. Got up, or tried to, but my legs were so wobbly, I wound up on my rear end. Soaking wet.

The stale, dry air of Patchwork base was gone. A soft, cool breeze came from the west. Or the east. Zero clouds in the sky—pale violet.

Wait a second.

Where was the sun?

I stood up and made a half-hearted attempt to dry off my butt. Nope. I was as soaked as if I'd wet myself. Great thought, I know. But the headache was gone, and so was the mental pressure that had reduced me to a semi-violent puppet.

The landscape around me was breathtaking. It was a shallow sea, shin-deep, of crystalline waters over white sands. Stubby trees no more than eight or ten feet tall were clumped together, winding roots covered in smooth, tan bark. The leaves were a shimmering opal, catching light from whatever source was brightening everything and casting rippling rainbows along the water. In the rare place ground poked above and remained dry, it was eggshell colored sand sparkling with powder blue crystals and streaks of orange pebbles.

A trio of gulls wheeled overhead, their calls a song that would rival any orchestras—except they weren't gulls. Weren't even birds. I stared at three silvery flying lizards, each sporting two pairs of diaphanous wings.

"That's—huh." I let the sword dip into the water.

A shockwave, small but insistent, rippled outward in concentric circles until I lifted the blade again.

Footsteps sloshed through the water behind me.

Really didn't want to turn around. But if something horrific was gonna kill me, I guess having it happen in a literal paradise wasn't too bad.

The figure approaching me was nine feet tall, lean, built of solid muscle—and solid light. I shielded my eyes, wincing, until the being grew a white tunic with tall collar and white trousers. The face dimmed, until I could make out purple eyes that lacked pupils and an impassive expression, carved as real as if he'd been built of granite.

Two creatures rose from the water. I held the sword aloft, ready to fight, because I was facing two giant versions of symmachites, each one easily twelve feet and bristling with spines. But I couldn't help gape in awe at the bronze patterns, the gold traceries bled, the coruscating flesh …

Because they were big brothers to the tiny new symmachites that had formed the fake astral fiends I'd fought. Even the one who'd interrupted my vacation.

All of the sudden, even in the middle of the trippiness, I had an insane craving for pineapple ice cream.

"Hello." The voice was mellow, yet firm. "Do not fear. These are my children. I am Tenebrae."

I held out a hand. I mean, how else do you greet an interdimensional being? He had hands, for crying out loud. "Hey. Mercury Hale. I'm—"

"You," the ancient entity who'd been part of the great Medan civil war and had drawn me into another, unknown dimension, interrupted, "Are an idiot."

CHAPTER TWENTY-EIGHT

Okay then.

I folded my arms, taking care to not slice the aforementioned appendage off. "That's, ah, quite the judgment, Tenebrae, considering we've never formally met. You don't see me comment on your choice of wardrobe."

"Covering is necessary for your comprehension."

I sighed. So, it was gonna be one of *those* conversations. "Look, as amazing as this place is, I've got stuff to do. I don't think Javon's super happy with me for activating his superpower and turning him into a human portal and—hey, how does that even work? Never mind that my wife was readying to shoot me!"

"There is no time."

"Kinda what I mean."

"No, listen." The word hit me with concussive force. I staggered a few steps back. "Here we exist. There, they wait. When we have finished, you will return to then, not later, not before."

"I'm ... What?" I shook my head. "Hang on a second."

I turned the sword over, so I could get a better grip on the small portion of the pulsar stave protruding from the pommel. If I was gonna be stuck in a new realm for a while, I wanted my familiar weapon ready to rock.

My hand stopped an inch from the stave. It was glowing, from the wrist right to the fingertips, and refused every command.

"The pulsar stave must remain with Edgeweld," Tenebrae said. "Thus, you are tethered here."

"Great." I gritted my teeth. As soon as I withdrew my hand, the phantom pressure subsided. "Let's back up. How about you tell me why you've been harassing me for 'help,' only to trick me into your dimension and then call me an idiot?"

"I don't have a choice. This is how it will play out." Tenebrae cocked his head to one side, like a dog waiting for his master to speak. "Communication has always been difficult to manage. I tried multiple avenues, but all were problematic."

Swirling pieces of craziness crashed together in my head. "Like building your own astral fiend out of the teeny-tiny brothers of your bodyguards," I said, indicating the two eerily silent giant symmachites looming over him. "And when I didn't pick up what you were putting down, you reached out to Wilhelmina, and then Edith."

"I did not realize their provenance. They were not of Meda. I had not made the connection until I witnessed your birth."

I raised an eyebrow so high Loredana should have given me a medal. "I'm pretty sure there were no family photos, man."

"I saw. I was there."

"But … you hadn't."

"I have. I was. I see it now."

I rolled my eyes. "If this is the way it's gonna go, I'm gonna need for you to dumb it down so I—" My face heated up. Yeesh. Better not give more ammo to the being who thought I was stupid. "Forget it. Help. You said you needed help."

"Yes. Against the Whisperer."

"Well, who doesn't!" I flung my arms wide, Edgeweld slashing through the air. "What do you think I've been doing? What do you think Procyon's been trying to keep from happening? They've fought back every incursion the Whisperer's made for a century and a half!"

"I know. I've seen them."

"Then why do you need my help?"

"Because I have already failed. I will always fail." Tenebrae gestured to the sandy beach of the nearest mangrove cluster. "Listen."

I took a seat, not because he ran me like a puppet again, but because I figured if I was gonna be stuck there a while, I might as well be comfortable. "Why can't you stop him? Your power—"

"He and I are kin. Formed from the same spark. Two parts of one whole." Tenebrae made a looping motion with his left hand, and the giant symmachites melted into the shallow sea, disappearing as they—I assumed—split apart into thousands and thousands of their miniature selves. "We were given charge over our realms. The Interstice, and Sadeh."

He pronounced it *Saw-deh*. "Nice place. Way better than the Interstice."

"One was not always separate from the other. Mine was an expanse of water; his was of land. It had a glory and a beauty that surpassed even here. But when the walls arose, all was split between good and evil. The Whisperer chose lust over service, pursuit of power over satisfaction of care. Nothing would satiate him."

I didn't like the sounds of that. Hearing that the Whisperer had turned a gorgeous paradise into the grating wasteland I'd seen was somehow worse than discovering the Interstice had always been messed up. "How does Meda fit in? And Edgeweld?"

"Let me show you." He held out his hand.

I hesitated, unsure I should part with my last half of the pulsar stave, but really, if the guy had meant to steal it, he'd missed all the best chances. I gave him the sword.

Tenebrae grasped the handle. Golden white energies flared along its length. My eyes stung. I'd never seen—or heard—that much power pour out of the pulsar stave. It rang with a majestic tone that reverberated inside my mind and throughout every cell of my body.

The sword split into two blades. I'd seen it before, but instead of Tenebrae pulling them apart to make separate weapons, he stood and swept it before him. Purple sparks leaped from the flat surface of one blade to the other, tearing the air in front of us apart until we gazed through a rift twelve feet across.

I was staring onto a battlefield.

The people were of varied ethnicities, wearing ancient garb like robes and leathers with studded armor and bone-laced helmets. Their weapons were swords, spears, and shields, like anything you'd see on a National Geographic special about the ancient Middle East.

But not all the weapons.

I recognized the broad sweep of the night's blade, the shining edges of Teget's ax, and even the blistering light of the pulsar stave. There were dozens of other weapons, of myriad design and function. One man flickered across the battlefield, vanishing and reappearing in the same psychedelic windstorm the Echo Watches produced—and killed three fighters with searing blasts to their faces.

"This—that's Meda," I stammered. "The civil war. The one that sent losers into exile and the winners established the temple so they could safeguard whatever relic remained."

"It could have split the realms apart," Tenebrae said. "Had I not intervened."

And there he was in the vision, a being of pure light, landing among the warriors with enough force to bowl dozens over. He had Edgeweld as his weapon—one sword in each hand.

"Teget was right," I murmured. "You *were* there. You killed thousands on both sides to end the fight."

"That was not my goal. I wanted to take them away and give them time to consider their folly. I had enough time. They could have shared in it."

Another being crept through the battling ranks, this one a shadow of a person, trailing misty darkness, clad in a suit of scaly armor that made it grow to twice its size. The shell. The armor gifted to Serena. Except the Whisperer was the one wearing it.

"He was not supposed to be there." Tenebrae sounded as if he were attending a funeral. "He was not supposed to take form. But the rebels had crafted the shell, prepared it to hold him together, so he could face their enemies. I should have considered another path. Instead, I plowed forward in my single-mindedness."

Which apparently meant colliding with the Whisperer in a titanic clash. My eyes widened as the miniature images of them grappled in the middle of the battle, forcing both sides to separate, and the air around them warped—became twisted. Hot air over asphalt, times a thousand. It split into dozens of shards, a broken mirror showing just as many slivers of other worlds, some recognizable by their terrain and plants, others way too alien to be anywhere in our solar system. Or even our dimension.

The mini-Tenebrae tried to expand one sunny realm with Edgeweld, but the Whisperer clawed at his side. A shockwave of energy poured out, grasping at as many people as it could touch, and when the resulting thunderclap abated, the bulk of the fighters on both sides were just … Gone.

Not even ashes left.

"Where'd … they go?" I couldn't help whispering.

The image faded. Tenebrae plunged Edgeweld into the sand. I swore he was supporting himself like an old man with a cane. "I wanted to bring them here. To show them peace. But the Whisperer—he dragged most to his realm, where he promised them life forever. Who would not be seduced? Will you see?"

I really didn't want to. My stomach couldn't have felt sicker if I'd just gotten over two stomach bugs back-to-back. "Do it."

He ripped the air apart again, and there was the Interstice, just as bleak and foreboding as I remembered, except there was more burned vegetation. Like it hadn't had time to rot away into dust yet.

And the people—thousands of warriors—

They were changing.

Moans and screams filled the air as their bodies blackened, and purple growths erupted from their skin. Clothing steamed away. Metals melted into their flesh. Their eyes bulged, distended, and bubbled up. The irises and whites faded to a blood red.

Tentacles sprouted from their backs as their limbs shriveled into nothingness.

"Oh, no." I got to my feet. The sick feeling spread until my whole body was shaking. My breathe came fast and shallow. "No, no, no. They're … They can't be people. They shouldn't be!"

But me wishing it wasn't gonna change anything. Tenebrae was showing me the ancient past, after all. There was no denying the fate of those warriors from Medan's bloodied field.

They'd all been twisted into astral fiends.

"No!" I knocked aside the sword. The image vanished. No way I was ever gonna be able to rinse it from my brain, though. "Do you know how many of those things Procyon's eliminated? Do you have any idea how many *I've killed*? And now you're telling me they were all people? I could have helped them! I could have tried to save them."

"Mercury," Tenebrae said. "Your heart does you credit. But they were no longer human. Their souls found their resting places, for good or ill. The Whisperer warped the frames of meat left behind. Whatever you killed, do not be distressed over their fates."

I grasped the sides of my head. It was way too much to process. I backed away, my shoes splashing into the water. Sand swirled around them—sand, or swarms of symmachites.

A terrible though hit me. I glared at Tenebrae. "Let me guess: These microscopic soldiers of yours were your experiment."

"Never!" Tenebrae's outrage hurled me a dozen feet. I left a trough along the short beach as I crash landed. Really wished I hadn't let him take the sword, which contained my only weapon. There wasn't enough energy stashed in my prosthetic leg to be of much use. "I wanted to bring them refuge. Instead I could only rescue a portion from the Whisperer, as they were butchered into his unnatural forms. Bringing them here halted the process, making them arbiters of good instead of agents of evil."

"Okay," I wheezed. "Guess … That's in your favor. But I still don't get what you need from me. What am I gonna do that something—someone like you can't? You two are on a level of strength I can't ever get near."

"In our realms. Outside of our realms, our power wanes, until defeat is inevitable."

"Yeah, well, good luck getting …" I stared at him, propped up on my elbows. "Hold up. The Whisperer's thing all along has been breaking down the walls between dimensions. He wants to go to Earth, to dump the Interstice into our world and combine the two."

"But if he is drawn out before his time, if offered the ultimate prize, then he may attempt a crossing in his current form, instead of taking a body." Tenebrae offered me a glowing hand.

"And Troy has the pulsar stave." I let him help me stand. "Heck of a prize for the new boss."

"This you must prevent."

I brushed sand off my pants. "Sounds like a tall order for an idiot."

"Forgive me. I spoke in haste. Your kind is—taxing to deal with."

Couldn't help bleak chuckle at that one. "You're not wrong. Okay, well, unless you got any better pointers on how to stop the bad guys, you'd better send me back."

"Only this—the three are united."

"Three. You mean, the Medan weapons?" I frowned. "The night's blade is back in Meda and Teget has the ax."

"They are not. The three have never been one. But they will. When the time is right, you have already come back to me."

Argh. "You've gotta stop talking like that. I get the whole Time is Weird Here thing, but man …"

Tenebrae handed me Edgeweld. "Return."

I'd barely gotten the stave removed from the hilt when the world around me shattered into a billion fragments. Felt like my body did the same thing, and even though all I felt relaxed physically, my brain freaked out. I screamed.

Which is what I was still doing when I found myself on my hands and knees in the vault where Edgeweld had been stored, everything bathed in red light.

I scrambled onto my knees. I'd reappeared behind Javon. He was frantically patting his stomach and spine, I guess making sure his body had been reassembled correctly. Loredana still aimed her weapon, toward the stand, except I wasn't in front of them. Dominic groaned over by the wall, where he flailed a bit as he got himself upright.

"What was that? What happened to me?" Javon's voice had gone high-pitched.

"My bad," I muttered.

Loredana spun around, pivoting her aim, but then tucked the pistol away. She was on her knees in an instant. "Mercury! Good heavens. What's happened to you?"

"Forget him." Javon grabbed the sword from where I'd dropped it on the floor. "He tried to stab me with that thing! And I came apart without—!"

"Relax. You're a gateway." I hugged Loredana and gave her a kiss. "I'm okay. Wow. I really wasn't gone long, was I?"

"Long enough for me to want to hit you." Dominic pulled himself up the wall. He rubbed the back of his head and winced. "I'm fine, really, in case anyone else is interested."

"Sorry about the body slam." I tucked the pulsar stave into my belt and grabbed Javon by the shoulder. Poor guy was staring at the sword, his other hand pressed against his stomach. "Look, I met Tenebrae. Pretty sure he made a deal with Lucas Kimball so your bloodline would have a gateway person available if he ever needed one. Bonus—you still get superpowers."

"You sayin' you saw Tenebrae—through me?" he asked.

"Yep. Like going through a rip, only smoother." I grimaced at the memory of being pulled to bits. "Except the return was kinda messy."

"Remarkable. And when you were inside, what did you learn?" Loredana asked.

"A whole bunch about the Interstice and astral fiends and what the Whisperer's got planned next, but now Edgeweld is secure, we've got to keep it away from Syndax no matter what."

Javon's phone buzzed. He answered, still staring at me. "Yeah?"

"What's an Edgeweld?" Dominic pressed between us.

"The sword. That's its name." I grinned. "It makes the rest of our fun Medan weapons look like overpriced toothpicks."

"Be right there." Javon pushed past us for the door. "Last convoy's comin' in. I need to supervise the unloading."

"We shall remain behind to secure the sword." Loredana reached for Edgeweld.

"Nope." Javon swept it from her grasp. "I'm hangin' onto this for a moment until I figure out how we're gonna lock Mercury up."

Lock me up? That's when I realized, the alarms were still sounding distant in the hall.

And four Procyon security guys in body armor were waiting outside the hatch, SCAR rifles aimed at us.

Loredana matched Javon's pace, with Dominic right behind, as our newly expanded group marched back down the corridors we'd used to enter and kept going toward another hatch.

"This outrageous!" Loredana strode right past the guard robot waiting on the other side of that hatch without bothering to flash her ID. It took one of my new best armed buddies to calm down the robot as it turned its machine gun toward her. "Mercury has uncovered vast new intelligence and you are letting wounded pride prevent you from seeing that fact."

"What I'm doing, Operations Director, is handling the situation before anyone else uses my gifts against me," Javon snapped. "You'd better stay calm yourself, or these guys are gonna lock you up right alongside your boy toy."

We'd entered a broad chamber of concrete and steel, with catwalks spanning the width of the new cavern. It was lined with Mercedes vans, pickup trucks, and sedans, a dozen by my count. Metal rumbled at the far end and daylight spilled in. I squinted against the sudden sun as the silhouettes of black trucks grew.

My phone buzzed. Really? Now? I gestured at my pocket. "Mind if I get that, guys?"

Javon frowned, but he was preoccupied enough by the arrival of the trucks that Loredana cut between me and the guards. "Allow this man to answer his phone or you'll all be out of jobs," she said.

"Fine, go ahead," Javon muttered.

Good thing. It was Ramos, who wasn't a big fan of voicemail. "Hey. Nice timing."

"You're the one who wanted to know about the convoy that left here the other day. Stan Bradley pulled CCTV footage from that building you mentioned, but no luck on the plates yet. I get the feeling our searches are deliberately blocked, no matter how much of a glitch the tech people tell me it is. We're still trying to get all four vans IDed."

I glanced up at the black vehicles with tinted windows that rolled up alongside a long, concrete loading dock. We were all gathered at the end nearest the chamber's hatch. Four vans and an SUV with security backup?

"Sir!" One of the security guards who was supposed to be watching me pressed a hand against his earpiece. "Nobody in the booth's been able to raise the team leader!"

Javon tensed. "Get everyone back. Now!"

Dominic leapt between us and Javon, the Echo Watches igniting, and I braced myself for the portal that would yank us to safety—

The lead van blew up.

Wind and dust hammered me. Flames washed the ceiling and walls. I grabbed for Loredana, covering her as best I could as one of the security guards fell on top of me. Another blast—this one bright purple—shrieked around us and more debris rained down.

I saw Serena step from the van's wreckage, her scaled armor coruscating with violet energies, as concrete dust blotted out my sight.

CHAPTER TWENTY-NINE

Don't let anybody tell you otherwise—tinnitus is a big deal. I was seriously gonna have Doc Arne take a closer look at my eardrums when we got back.

Assuming we got back.

I thought the debris raining down had blinded me. Turned out, the ceiling had collapsed, along with half the steel girders strung across it. Where there'd been a twenty-foot reach to the roof, there was now a gap just a couple feet tall at the top of a huge pile of rubble.

I heaved the guard off me and promptly swore, because, yeah, that gunshot to the shoulder? Might have healed to a scar but it still ached like it was fresh.

The guard moaned. Guy still had a pulse, but his face was covered with blood. Another of his buddies was smashed beneath a collapsed catwalk. No pulse for him. I wanted to throw up, but Loredana squirmed beneath me.

"You okay?" I pulled her up.

"I—yes. I believe so." She rubbed blood off her lip. Her red hair was doused in gray. The MP5 had been torn from its strap and was crushed under a rock. "Where are Mr. Kimball and Gemini?"

Well, crap. I didn't see their limbs poking out from beneath what used to be the chamber walls and ceiling. The other two security guys were helping their wounded buddy by bandaging up his head. "Hang on, I'll try to climb up. Our Syndax friends are probably on the other side."

"Be careful. I daresay we're currently outmatched."

No kidding. I tried my phone, to see if we could call for help. The signal was dead. I couldn't connect onto data either to send a message. I glanced at one of the security guys. "Comms?" I asked, tapping my ear.

He shook his head. "They're toast. Nothing but static."

"Then you'd better hustle back to wherever your office is to get the word."

He nodded and took off, scrambling over the broken boulders and looming chunks of concrete that hadn't been obstacles before.

Meanwhile, I scurried up our brand-new artificial cliff. I only slipped twice. Could've been worse—six feet from the top, another chunk of steel broke free from the ceiling and slammed down beside me before tumbling back down the way I'd came. Loredana and the two security officers made it out of the way.

I peered up over a jagged rim of steel. Two of the vehicles—a van and the SUV at the back—were intact. They'd emptied out ten Syndax soldiers, plus Xia and Troy in addition to Serena. The latter picked up Edgeweld, a smile blossoming as she examined the midnight blade. "Now there's a friendly face."

"It looks good on you, but you're not the one who needs it." Troy knelt by Dominic, who was quiet and still. For a second, I thought he was dead, which seized my guts worse than I'd have thought possible. But Troy waved over Syndax brutes. "Get him up. Make sure those devices aren't damaged."

Like they had blueprints for the Echo Watches. Another pair dragged Javon upright. Our fearless Procyon board member mumbled under his breath, but still seemed out of it.

Xia, meanwhile …

Serena handed her the sword. "Time for you to take the leads."

Leads? Didn't she mean lead? But Troy popped the top of a

plastic vial under Dominic's nose. Xia's eyes glowed purple and she lifted Edgeweld, the tip of the blade just inches beneath the vial. A spiral, like someone had swirled pepper in the air, whipped up into Dominic's face. Ruddy streaks with maroon tinges.

His breath caught. His eyes rolled up until just the whites were visible.

"That's it. The last piece." Serena sighed, like she'd come in after a long jog. She sagged against Troy, who held up her arm. "I'm all right. Alex—he's made sure the Whisperer knows we're ready."

"Nice to hear you all are keeping in such tight communication." Troy whistled and made a circling motion with his hand. "Group up! We're leaving."

Seriously? I squirmed closer to the gap. If had more time, I could break through the gap and get down there to—I don't know. Do something heroic? Me against a whole bunch of them, three of whom had superpowered weaponry. No doubt I could purge the symmachites from Dominic with the pulsar stave. I'd done it before. Heck, I'd done it on *me*, too.

But there was too much debris. Even as I put my shoulder against the bigger chunks and shoved at it, it knew it would take too long. Plus, Loredana was below, so anything I blasted out of the way could cause a rockslide back down onto her and the surviving Procyon security guys.

Serena pushed away from Troy and spread her arms wide. Purple lightning leapt out from the wall nearest the ruined trucks, forming a rip right there in the garage.

I stretched out, aiming with the pulsar stave. I could blast Xia right there. Maybe if I channeled enough energy into it, I could obliterate Edgeweld, too.

But I couldn't. Something inside made me hold off. Maybe it was the thought that Xia had been drawn into this mess without clear knowledge of what was going on. That she might be as much a pawn as Dominic, controlled—if not by symmachites, then by blackmail or threats of violence or whatever. As far I as I knew, he was a victim of trafficking who'd been randomly given Edgeweld at a black-market auction last winter. Or maybe it was wondering how Ramos would handle the situation. Would he assassinate someone like I was contemplating?

Didn't matter either way because I waited three seconds too long. The entire team blinked out, with Javon and Dominic under their control.

I swore and punched the nearest target—which, turned out, was a jagged chunk of concrete. Hooray for bloody knuckles.

"Mercury? What's happened?" Loredana was helping the wounded guard to his feet.

"Troy and company. They took Dominic and Javon."

"Bloody hell." Loredana scowled. "Come down from there. We have to see about clearing the entrance."

"This thing have a back entrance?" I craned my neck, giving the gap at the top of the debris pile a second look. "Because if you guys back up, I could try blasting our way out. And right now, blasting would do me a world of good."

Hang on. What was that? Sounded like a mouse chirping. And I swore the rip had left an afterimage blinking on a windshield.

"I shall have to consult the base schematics." She glanced at one the guards. "What of it?"

"There is an emergency hatch at the far end, ma'am," he said. "But I don't think there's any vehicles parked out there right now."

"Very good." Loredana picked up her phone. "Security? This is Loredana Lark-Hale. Yes … We have casualties. Send emergency medics as soon as possible."

I squinted down through the gap. Not my imagination. There was a blinking light, except it was inside the truck's windshield, not reflected off the outside or leftover from the rip.

It was red. And it was numbers.

"Call them off!" I scrambled down the pile so fast I twisted my ankle, but good news, it was the prosthetic one. I slammed onto the floor, reached down, and bent it 90 degrees back into the correct angle. "We've gotta move! Their leftover truck's rigged to blow."

"Blast!" Loredana snapped. "Security, belay that! There's another explosion imminent."

We helped the guards toward the garage hatch as quickly as we could. It rumbled open. Twiki and one of his robo-pals were there, with a stretcher mounted between them.

"Could've used those machine guns," I muttered.

"Yes," Loredana said, panting. "I daresay Anton Chekhov would have been most disappointed."

We set the wounded man on. Those robots could *move,* let me tell you, because we had to run into the corridor after them just to keep up. A guard slapped the panel to close the hatch.

The explosion sent us to our knees, a flash of light and burst of dust squeezing through the gap between doors right as the hatch slammed shut. The whole corridor rumbled, and I hung onto Loredana as dirt and shards of rock rained down. Whatever else, Patchwork's builders had reinforced it well.

"Wow." The guard—Nimick was on his nametag—brushed dirt from his face and stared at us. "Does this happen a lot to you guys?"

"The bombs, not so much. But it gets pretty exciting." I helped Loredana up. "Let's take a look out there."

It was bad.

The second explosion had only exacerbated the cave-in. A pair of tiny orange emergency bulbs offered little illumination for the short section of the garage we could get to. I coughed and waved dust out of my face. "Don't suppose we can dig our way out the top?"

"Negatory, sir," Nimick said. "Garage is a hundred feet down."

"Perfect." I pinched the bridge of my nose. "Hey, Loredana, now would be a good time to tell me there's a hotrod personal jet stashed at that back entrance, one that nobody knows about. Or that somewhere in this place is an artifact that generates a portal."

"Sorry, love, neither of those things are on the inventory, at least as far as I'm aware." Loredana sighed. "Getting us to San Camillo is of the utmost importance."

The other hatch opened. The other guard was already on the move with his wounded companion, in the care of the robots.

"Oh, man." Nimick sagged against the open hatch. "Dan's dead. What am I gonna tell his aunt? She thinks we guard government paperwork."

"Procyon will make the appropriate contact. Rest assured, he will be given a proper funeral and burial, and his kin will be treated with the greatest respect." Loredana touched his shoulder. I'd never seen her have to take on this role before. But I figured, with all the chaos of the last year and a half, she'd had to do it a lot. "They will be told as close to the truth as we can manage."

"Yes, ma'am. I understand." Nimick rubbed at his eyes. "I just wish—I wish people could deal with it, so we didn't have to hide what's really going on, you know? The truth's a scary thing but sometimes I feel like we should get it out there, like a doctor delivering the bad news."

"Welcome to the club," I murmured.

Loredana scowled at me, but when she spoke, it was in a soft tone directed at Nimick. "That is a valid consideration, but unfortunately, there are things for which the world is not ready …"

I was still waiting for the rest of her inspiring comment as I checked my phone. Had signal. Time to let Liz and the rest know what had happened.

But Loredana was staring past Nimick, at the stack of rubble. Then she turned slowly, until she was gazing back down the corridor. "Loredana Gertrude Lark-Hale," she muttered. "You are an absolute *twit.*"

"You okay?" I asked her. And yes, I knew her middle name was Gertrude. It's on the marriage license at home, obviously.

She ran.

I blew out a breath. "Really gonna get that cardio in today, Nimick," I said. "Keep up."

We were almost caught up to Loredana when my phone buzzed. I motioned for Nimick to keep hustling. I slowed to a jog, so my speech would be understandable. "Liz?"

"Mercury! Hey! I didn't know if you could get cell phone reception in Patchwork which I totally don't know where it is, but Mr. Alvarez got a secure link to boost the signal that's a neat thing to think about when you get into how it works—"

"Liz! News, please."

"Yeah! Okay. Neutrino counts and tachyon spikes." Liz sucked on the straw in her cup of soda. "I've had Tracking monitoring both ever since we figured out that's what Tenebrae used to make his way into this world or at least hitch a ride with anything coming out of the Interstice, but it took Cyril *forever* before he could get the right algorithm running so I'm really hoping he can crack this before whatever Winston put into him breaches the partition on his hard drive."

"You and me both. Don't leave me hanging."

"Remember Serena's armor? We got a hit. There was a spike on the south edge of the city, at the old Echelon Plaza mall."

"That dump?" I pictured weed-infested parking lots and crumbling concrete. "Please don't tell me they're spawning astral fiends in the middle of a shopping spree."

"No, it's—"

"Wait. Hold up. Let me guess. It's abandoned."

"Um, yeah. It is. Creditors foreclosed on it four years ago. How'd you know?"

"One of these days I'm gonna write a study for Procyon about how we should just plant cameras in every single empty building around San Camillo."

"Anyway, they're there. I mean, Serena and the rest of her people. Definitely enough change in the ambient background radiation to account for the pulsar stave's presence."

I grit my teeth. Troy was gonna have to pay for that, sooner or later. "Good deal. We're without a teleporter right now."

"I know! Mr. Alvarez is shouting at everybody. I think

Garvey's getting a team ready, but we're waiting on our aircraft to show up from maneuvers. Oh, do you guys need transport?"

"Nah. We're … Loredana's got a plan. I'll let you know when we're getting close."

"Hey, Mercury? Is Dominic going to be okay? I heard they took him and Mr. Kimball."

"Relax. We'll get them back." I hoped. At least it wasn't my first experience with symmachite-possessed teammates. "Let me know if anything else changes."

"Be careful!" She hung up.

"Hardly ever am," I said.

Wherever the local security office was, I never found out, because Loredana's crazy, wordless run ended up at the doors to the hangar.

"Director Lark-Hale?" A short woman with white hair was waiting for us. She wore a light-green turtleneck shirt and forest green slacks. She had the appearance of a person who enjoyed being out in the sun, brown eyes gleaming as she smiled. Maybe early sixties? I wasn't gonna ask. Kind of reminded me of Helen Mirren, with her hair cut in a bob just like the actress. No English accent, though. When she spoke, I heard New Jersey.

"Yes." Loredana regained her poise instantly, the second she transitioned from a full-on sprint to a purposeful stride. "Good afternoon."

"Let's skip the polite talk." She said it almost like *too-awk*. "Melissa Mazzoli, director of Patchwork. You got any idea how long I've run this place? Twenty years. Next week is the anniversary of my appointment."

"Careful," I said. "You know what happens in movies to the guys who mention they're due for retirement in a couple days."

Nimick snorted. But Mazzoli pinned him down like a butterfly with a, well, a pin when she stared at him. Hey, give me a break, my ears were still ringing along with the rest of my head. "Good thing I'm not a guy. You must be Mercury Hale. The one with the mouth."

I grinned and produced the pulsar stave. "Don't forget this."

"Sure." *Shore.* Mazzoli ignored me in favor of Loredana. "So besides blowing up my base and getting my guard killed, is there something else you want? Because we're sealed in down here and until security's happy no more terrorists are going to beam in, you're both stuck."

"This is rather presumptuous of me, I understand," Loredana said as smoothly as if she were requesting cream in her coffee, "But I shall need to borrow your alien spacecraft."

CHAPTER THIRTY

M azzoli shook her head. "Just ask for the keys to the kingdom, why don't you?"

"Hang on. Let's recap for the slow person in the bunch." I held up my hands. "The ship—flies?"

"It's been on a couple test flights. You're not supposed to know that. No one is. Except you, Nimick, and you're paid *not* to know."

"Yes, ma'am."

"Go check in with the chief and see how we can clean up this mess. Then see the doc."

Nimick trotted off. Mazzoli blew out a breath. "He's a good kid. I can't believe we lost Dan over this. It's not the first time someone's died here, but it's rare, and it usually involves something Procyon brings in. Now I've got to fake a story to sell to his family, which sucks worse than telling them the truth, not to mention the bad guys got away with a stolen mystical sword, a Procyon board member, and one of your operatives."

"Hence why I require your project." Loredana gestured through the windows. "If I am not mistaken, there is nothing that can get us back to San Camillo faster."

"How do you know how fast the ship can fly?"

"I have no idea of its velocity. I can only assume, within a reasonable margin of error, that it is far faster than anything of this world."

"Good guess." Mazzoli crooked her mouth in a smile. "This is nuts. But I guess if I didn't want nuts, I should have stuck with cosmetology school. Follow me."

She used her ID badge to swipe us through the double airlock hatches. The spacecraft loomed overhead as we walked in, our footsteps echoing in the canyon-sized room. I wasn't a fan of how the skin of the ship moved anywhere light shone on it, like a stiff breeze over grass, and held still where it was dark.

"Absorption panels," Mazzoli said. "That's our best guess. Imagine our photovoltaics on steroids. They soak up any light source, storing the converted energy. There's a readout in the cockpit that would register an uptick if you shined your phone's flashlight on the fuselage for a few minutes."

A pair of women were busy at a long, L-shaped table, poring over computer screens and sheets of paper. The taller one, blonde hair tied up in a ponytail, gaped at us. "Um, ma'am?"

"Don't worry about it, Harriet. They're borrowing our ride."

Harriet, the blonde, shared a look with the shorter black woman working beside her. "Face it, not the strangest order she's ever given us," the Black woman said.

"Diedre is right. And it is an order." Mazzoli jerked a thumb over her shoulder.

Diedre put her hands on her hips. "Anyone want to tell me why we're not flying this for them? Because I'm the qualified pilot."

"This is Loredana Lark, of Procyon in San Camillo," Mazzoli said.

"Oh." Diedre grinned, scratching at the back of her neck in an awkward fashion. "Sorry. C'mon, then, we'll get you situated."

"Absolutely!" Harriet blushed as she met Loredana's eyes. "Sorry is right, ma'am. I didn't realize who you were. I'm guessing your assistant's coming too?"

"I—hey!" Loredana pecked me on the cheek as she and

Mazzoli followed the two researchers up a ramp extending a dozen feet from the underside of the ship. I hustled after them.

I stumbled on my way up but couldn't see anything that would have tripped me. The ramp was smooth. I squinted against the bright white lights. The walls had a dark, scaly surface to them, pitted with markings. Orange lights as slender as spiderwebs were laced overhead.

It wasn't until I caught up with everyone in the corridor that I realized why it felt like I was walking through an invisible swamp. "The gravity's messed up in here. Stronger than Earth's, right?"

Harriet beamed. "Yes! Most people don't recognize the shift. Did the director brief you about the gravitational variances of the species' technology?"

"No, but I have Airfoil on speed dial."

"The flying guy from Drake City?" Diedre slapped Harriet's arm. "I told you it had to be gravity manipulation!"

"Ladies." Mazzoli slid her ID through a card reader that had been mounted outside the hatch ahead of us. The portal slid silently into the walls, *Star Trek* style. "Save it for the cockpit briefing."

Yikes. The space hadn't been meant for man or woman, that was for sure. Four seats—stools, really, were arrayed in a shallow arc. The two stools up front, their backs spindly and arched, were within reach of eight handles or levers each. Fortunately, someone—I guessed Harriet and Diedre—had rigged a human-designed aircraft console, albeit small, to what had to be the pilot's seat.

Loredana sat there, scanning the human console and the bizarre, crooked alien screens around her as Harriet and Diedre buzzed around her with their tutorial. I sat next to her, then almost jumped up as four straps leapt over my shoulders and spun around my waist. Snug as a bug, as the saying goes. But given the lights on the ceiling, I couldn't help thinking that stupid bug was stuck as lunch in a web.

"You should be able to get there in about fifteen minutes, once you're airborne and up to speed." Mazzoli crouched in front of me. "Keep your eyes open. Syndax doesn't have anything that can match this for speed but that doesn't mean they won't lob a missile your way if they get the chance."

"Super. I didn't know they had missiles—wait, fifteen minutes?" I blinked. "How fast does this thing get?"

"She held Mach 8.5 for a while. Deidre thinks she can push nine."

"That's—a lot of thousands of miles per hour."

"Math genius." Mazzoli slapped my knee. The one above the prosthetic leg, of course. "Good luck out there. And try to bring the ride back in one piece."

Before I had the chance to ask any more intelligent and/or dumb questions, Loredana touched the nearest panel to her left hand. A display of light two feet high and about six feet across curled around the front of her seat, like a huge visor of transparent … Well, heck, it was a big holographic screen. Smaller panels showed schematics of the ship. Another screen of human design had the same schematics outlined in green, with markings in English for things like "Propulsion 1" and "Weapons."

"My word," Loredana whispered. "It's come alive, hasn't it?"

The subtle vibrations under my shoes built until the whole ship felt like it was trembling. I hoped that was because it was anxious to get up and fly, and not because it was gonna explode. I'd had enough explosions for one day.

Diedre gave me and Loredana new earpieces. "These are hooked into the communications system, which should work. Harriet and I can guide you if you have any problems."

"You two aren't coming?" I asked. "Seems like having the two experts along would be really handy."

Mazzoli shook her head. "I'm not about to risk my top engineers for this project with the San Camillo crowd."

"Wait," Harriet protested. "We can help if—"

But their boss had already ushered them from the cockpit, and the sealed hatch cut off extraneous noise. Loredana's hands rested on the human controls, as easily as if we were in her personal Cirrus jet, but I knew her silence meant she was concentrating. And possibly scared.

"Hey." I gripped her hand. "You've got this."

"Thank you." Loredana touched her earpiece. "We're quite ready."

"*Roger that.*" The voice buzzed in my head. "*All systems looking good. Max One is ready for takeoff. Opening hangar doors.*"

A huge *clang* echoed throughout the space, audible even through the skin of the spaceship. Light spilled down in a straight line, bisecting the hangar, as the roof split in two and rumbled apart. Streams of dirt trickled down. I didn't want to know how much soil covered the room. Really hoped a poor jackrabbit didn't decide to investigate.

"*Max One, this is Control. Power to hover nodes.*" That was Harriet's instruction.

Loredana punched a couple panels. The ship lurched, then rose slowly, as if it were on an elevator, except one of those handy 3-D readouts showed it floating on its own. "Roger, Control. Nodes powered. Ascending."

And boy, did we. The rate of climb increased until we popped out of the hangar like a cork, shooting up into the air. At least, that's what it felt like, until Loredana tapped another panel.

A broad arc of the metal wall in front of us dissolved, revealing a panoramic view for miles around of dusty plains and rolling hills.

"Remarkable," Loredana murmured.

"*Copy that. It's a projected viewscreen that looks about as real as you can get.*" Diedre's tone sounded wistful. "*You're at five hundred feet and rising. Engage the drives whenever you're ready.*"

Loredana glanced at me. "I am open to better solutions if you have any."

Despite the anxiety churning my innards, I grinned at her.

"You kidding? Let's see what this puppy can do."

"Very well. Main drives—now." She eased the control handle forward, like you'd see an airline pilot do.

The Max One shot forward like a jet fighter off an aircraft carrier's catapult.

I grabbed onto those weird handlebars. Apparently, it wasn't a problem for the spacecraft's builders, needing something to hold, because there were no arms on the stupid stools. My chest ached and my breath caught in my throat. I couldn't see the numbers for how fast we were going, but they were tiny yellow digits on Loredana's display that spun up *fast*.

Loredana laughed, and said something, which I couldn't hear over the roar of the spacecraft around us or the occasional BOOM from us breaking one sound barrier after another. I gestured to my ears, and she tapped a switch. "I said, pity I forgot my sunglasses!"

Then she sent the alien spaceship into a barrel roll.

I shouted, an equal mix of panic and exhilaration. Loredana laughed even more and let out a whoop at the end that made mine sound like a kid's imitation. I concentrated on the horizon, watching the terrain disappear beneath clouds as we approached— was that Denver?

Next thing I knew we were at twenty thousand feet with Rocky Mountains' peaks behind us.

"How are you kids enjoying the flight?" Mazzoli sounded like a parent who'd just watched her offspring master riding a bicycle without training wheels.

"Glorious!" Loredana reached for the light displays in front of her. "This transparent screen—"

"A holographic interface. Way beyond anything we have. You can interact with it."

Could we ever. I beat Loredana's fingers to the hologram and swiped through a range of displays so fast that I wound up down in the menu that must have been reserved for the previous owners. I recoiled at the sight of a creature with a face like a cross between a Klingon, a wolf, and pony. Punching it in the nose in real life would have broken my fingers on bony armor. It had four arms, which would have made it an unfair fight. "So, uh, anybody tell these guys you have their spaceship?"

"The quartet of occupants died on impact. We have their remains on ice. Sorry, there wasn't time for that part of the tour." The hologram danced back to its original display of maps, ranges, and numbers. *"We should have locked you out of that prior to departure."*

"Pity," Loredana said. "I should like to meet them."

"Seriously?" I snickered. "You'd need both of us to shake hands."

"Nothing that would faze a true follower of the Doctor." Loredana held the back of her hand to her mouth. "Oh."

"If you're gonna ralph, I don't see any barf bags aboard."

"No, I'm fine. I rather think I indulged myself with that barrel roll." She brushed aside a map of the United States marked with strange glyphs and enlarged the small numbers I'd seen earlier. "Very good. We're approaching Mach Seven."

Yikes. Forty-nine hundred miles per hour. I didn't want to think about what would happen if something smacked into us at this speed. But our altitude had topped out at 45,000 feet, so at least we were high enough we didn't have to worry about bugs on the windshield—or other airplanes.

"All right. We'll keep you on the radar."

"Hey, how's Patchwork holding up? No signs of other Syndax activity?" I asked.

"Not yet. We've got crews on the scene clearing rubble from both sides. Procyon in Rampart has a team on the way to provide extra security. We're keeping it off the news so far, but I'm coordinating with the board on a good cover story."

"Okay, just don't mention a gas leak. It's been done to death."

Mazzoli chuckled. *"Copy that."*

I shook my head. Sounded like things were getting better on the ground, for them anyway, but Edgeweld the sword was still in Xia's hands and Troy had the pulsar stave. The combination of the two was what had let me contact Tenebrae in his realm.

"What worries you?" Loredana asked. "Besides the obvious."

I motioned with my hand across my throat. Loredana touched a panel. "There," she said. "They are no longer listening in."

"Plugging the pulsar stave into the black sword—Edgeweld, in Tenebrae's words—it kept me anchored in his dimension. In Sadeh. He kept telling me I would help and could help but was rambling about three into one." I scowled. "Really wish he'd been more black and white."

"This being—given your momentary disappearance to us lasted quite a while for you—is it fair to say his presence is variable with regard to time?"

"Yeah. I don't know. Could be like the delays we've had before, when we've gone through the Interstice, or like you told me Dominic experienced when he took the Transect to the alternate Earth. Anyway, Tenebrae didn't make a ton of sense but I'm willing to bet this is all why Troy wanted the stave and the sword. It's his key into Sadeh, and if he can get there—"

"It gives the Whisperer a means to enter that dimension," Loredana said. "Oh my."

"Right? Gets better. I'm supposed to draw the Whisperer *out* of the Interstice so we can defeat him."

"That does not sound likely, unless ..." Loredana touched a panel. "Hmm."

"What?"

"A blip on radar. Not a missile. It's gone now."

"You sure it's not a missile?"

She arched an eyebrow at me, as if I'd just asked if her hair was still red. "I would know, darling."

I winked at her. "Never doubted you, babe."

"As I was saying, perhaps allowing the Whisperer and his cronies to come near their possible goal of infesting this new dimension, Sadeh as you call it, would leave him vulnerable enough for us to strike."

"Not a terrible plan," I said. "Because I know I'm ready to

strike."

Loredana's console beeped at her. "Ah. We're approaching the California border. Ready for descent."

I wound up flexing my jaw a bunch so I could pop my ears as the cockpit pressure changed on our way down. We broke through clouds, and sure enough, there were the browner parts of the state—okay, mostly Nevada. I spotted a tiny blue blotch far off. I poked my finger at the holographic map and the computer or whatever brains were running the ship gave me the helpful label of "Pyramid Lake."

"One moment." Loredana indicated her earpiece. "Incoming call."

"Who's the lucky contestant?"

Liz's voice broke through a stream of static. "Hey! Everyone's headed out. Into the field, or to the mall. Umm, tactically, I mean. So, that's good."

"Great, Liz. Speaking of the mall, do you have eyes on Dominic or Javon?"

"Not yet. But there's maybe five dozen Syndax mercenaries, all armed."

"Oof." I glanced at Loredana. "You're getting a lecture ready about proceeding with caution, right?"

"Don't be silly." Loredana dropped the spacecraft into a steeper dive, one that made my feet rise up off the deck for a moment. "I do believe rash action is the order of the day."

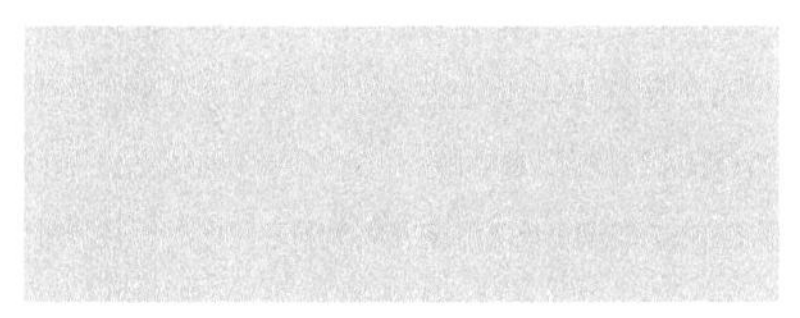

CHAPTER THIRTY-ONE

Last time I'd been to Echelon Plaza was when I'd run away from one of my foster families at age fifteen. It had been on the decline then, with about every fourth store empty. Flash forward a decade plus, and, well, you know the phrase about time not being kind? Time had been a total jerk to Echelon.

It sat back off the main drag through the Palmera suburb, surrounded by rundown subdivisions and crumbling apartment blocks. Its U-shaped outline made a great hiding place for Syndax, especially since the open part of the U faced the hills sloping down to the San Camillo flatlands. The building was three stories of white concrete and glass, though most of the latter had been long ago shattered or removed. Clumps of weeds and clusters of saplings poked through the pavement, making driving around to the back side of the mall tricky if you had a tiny car like mine, but it meant the Syndax vehicles scattered about the property had great chokepoints to halt approaching traffic.

The driving rain made everything dark, even in Max One's augmented cameras—or whatever alien sensors translated outside input to images on our huge display. I pointed at floodlamps gleaming inside the U. "Check it out—eight trucks back there. And a bunch of blotches that could be people."

"Give me a proper count, please." The muscles on Loredana's

forearms stood out as she piloted the ship down through the rocky atmosphere. We bounced against our straps like we were taking mountain bikes over a trail of loose gravel.

"Ah, give me a sec." There wasn't a handy dandy user's manual, but as soon as I poked my finger at one of the tiny silhouettes, the figure glowed with a red outline. "Cool. Maybe—select all?" I encircled them all. The readout counted forty-six.

A new indicator appeared on Loredana's human-installed console. <Forty-Six Targets Acquired.>

"Ack!" I slapped the outlines away. The number dialed down to zero. "Belay that or whatever!"

"Perhaps targeting their vehicles would be of better use."

"Yeah, you think?" I wiped sweaty palms on my supersuit's pants. "So, one of these has to be … Ha!"

I'd found infrared, I assumed. All those black silhouettes glowed yellow and red. Even ones I hadn't spotted before that popped out like lightbulbs in the gathered vehicles. "Looks like the trucks at the big party are empty. There's two or three in each vehicle they have around the parking lot. I count … eight of those sentries."

"Very good." Loredana banked the ship into a tight right turn. "Let's see as to whether those unmanned vehicles carry any important ordnance, shall we?"

I was glued to the displays as we spiraled in through the rainy sky. Drops streamed across the cockpit, but they were blurred behind the holographic image. I thought for a moment we might get the drop on the Syndax shindig below us—until specks of light appeared across the group. Clinking noises resounded outside the ship. "I'm guessing we're getting shot at."

"Yes, incoming fire. Nothing to fret about."

"Yeah, whatever this thing's made of bullets don't seem to bother it much." I glanced at Loredana. "Please tell me we get to shoot back."

She touched a panel. "Control, this is Max One. We are sustaining ground fire. Weapons free if you please."

"I knew you were going to ask for that." Mazzoli sighed. *"You heard her, ladies. Plasma strikers online."*

I swore I heard someone *squee*. Could have been Harriet. Diedre's response was way more professional. *"Roger that. Plasma strikers unlocked. Check your panel labeled PW-Oh-One, Max."*

"Checked and confirmed. Thank you." Loredana reached for a joystick with a red trigger. She input more commands. "Mercury? Targets, please."

I grinned and poked through the cluster of six trucks forming a phalanx at the head of the U. They blinked with red outlines. "Done and done."

"Delightful." She squeezed the trigger.

The ship's front end bucked with the rapid discharges, *whump, whump, whump,* one each second. A muffled shriek followed each one, like an astral fiend's outraged cry. Must've been even worse in the open air. The searing whitish-blue and green bursts raked the trucks from end to end, exploding interiors, lighting fuel tanks, and tearing doors off. One pass, and those trucks were molten scrap spread over a heck of a debris field.

The Syndax gang scattered but kept up their shooting. A couple of puffs of smoke appeared, and explosions tossed the ship about. "Grenade launchers!" I warned.

"A tad late," Loredana said. "Hold on."

She wrenched the controls and we pulled out of our righthand tight turn into a left-hand bank, regaining altitude as we passed.

"No sign of Procyon yet," I said, "Which sucks because I bet Garvey would get a kick out of all this and because I really wish someone was filming this from below!"

"I sincerely doubt Manager Alvarez would be pleased by your posting our borrowed extraterrestrial spacecraft in strafing run."

The ship lurched in the middle of our climb, like we'd hit a massive speed bump. I grabbed for a console. "Turbulence?"

"Some. Though I'm not monitoring any on local channels—"

The ship dropped again, this time tipping to the left. Our airspeed plummeted.

"What in the world?" Loredana grappled with the controls. "She's not responding!"

"No kidding!" I stared at the console.

We slowed, slowed, slowed, until we were barely moving—even though the engines rumbled at what had to be full throttle.

"I have a radar contact," Loredana snapped. "Bearing—"

"Uh." I poked her and pointed at the screen.

A man in a gray cloak and gray jumpsuit floated in front of us, a dark figure against the afternoon gloom, hands outstretched.

The Ashen. Enemies of the Garrison, which was Airfoil's team. Basically, a bad guy with the same gravity manipulating powers.

"Oh, bollocks," Loredana muttered.

"Yeah, okay, new target!" I swept my hand for his image on the screen—

But we flipped upside down.

Loredana fired anyway, her bursts cutting up into the clouds. The Ashen hurtled away, toward the roof of the mall, and Max One was free again, allowing Loredana to bring us back around toward him.

Fancy flying wasn't gonna hold him off forever, not if he could get a gravity grip on us a second time. I unstrapped from the stool. "Get me close. The pulsar stave can shut down his medallion, just like I did on the Bermuda wreck."

"I don't think it's wise to skydive in the rain so as to test that out!" Loredana snapped.

"Not high on my bucket list either but it's better than getting squashed!"

Max One's nose dipped toward the roof of the mall, where the Ashen had made a crouched landing. Loredana bracketed him in the center of the cockpit screen and fired again. The blasts tore chunks of whatever they put on mall roofs, shattering rusted air conditioning units. Huge holes opened up as the blasts dug trenches toward the Ashen.

He disappeared behind a curtain of debris.

"Nice shooting!" I grabbed Loredana's shoulders and kissed

her on the cheek. "Now set us down so we can—"

We stopped so suddenly I would have bounced off the inside wall of the cockpit if I hadn't hooked my hands through Loredana's seat straps. As it was, I twisted both my wrists.

Loredana snapped forward hard enough to bounce her forehead off the console. She let out a cry of surprises that cut off into a moan. Blood streamed from a gash on her forehead, and her arms went limp.

I glanced up at the screen and winced, not just because I'd put a massive crick in my neck, either.

The Ashen floated in the middle of a huge crater in the mall roof, with apparently enough power to not fall to his death and stop a big spaceship in midair.

I ignited the pulsar stave and slashed through Loredana's straps. "And this, kids, is where bail!"

The stave's energy was a welcome jolt, like caffeine in the bloodstream on a drowsy, gloomy morning. As soon as I had a good grip on Loredana, I siphoned everything I could into a run through the cockpit door.

And I did mean *through*. At the speed I was moving, it took a quick blast from the stave to rip the door to tatters. My bad. Really hoped Mazzoli didn't have her heart set on getting the ship back in one piece.

Because judging by the groans pervading the hull, and the way the walls and ceiling buckled toward me, Mr. Ashen was doing his best to smash us up like a ball of paper.

The ramp cracked open as I ran, letting damp air and driving rain slash inside—a good thing, because I had no idea where the "Let Me Out" switch was. I lifted Loredana across my chest and let myself fall onto my back, so I could slide down the ramp and through the narrow gap.

And out into open air.

We flew through the rain, toward a square of what used to be a garden surrounding a fishpond, except the grass had mostly died off and the pond was only half full of scummy water. I let loose with a blast from the stave, which slowed our descent enough I could spin on my back before we hit the water.

Don't get me wrong. Taking a swim on a hot summer's day is about as refreshing a feeling as you could get. But landing in tepid water coated with algae in the midst of a lukewarm rain? It was as gross as it sounded.

I let go of Loredana, so she could float, and rebound off me, as my back and shoulders rebounded off the bottom of the pond. Nothing cracked, and I didn't paralyze myself, so, win.

Sounds were muffled, but I could see shadows all around us, shadows that got sharper when the floodlamps blazed down into the pond. Arms pulled Loredana out. Another set grabbed me. I figured it must be what coming to the surface after being baptized felt like: breaking the surface, gasping for air, getting that rush that, hey, I wasn't dead!

Right up until the rifle stock smashed across my cheekbones.

I rolled onto my back, still gasping, only from the pain instead of the return of oxygen. Surprise Number One: The spaceship wasn't destroyed. Surprise Number Two: The Ashen guy flew over the edge of the roof, I guess to try again with his powers from a different angle, but he must have let his reach slip because Max One blasted away. The engine surge left the entire mall and everything around it shaking. Even the rain looked like it came down in a curve for a moment.

Okay. Focus, Mercury. Ship gone. You and Loredana on the ground. Ashen above.

Syndax handily in reach.

I smashed the pulsar stave into the goggles and helmet of the guy who'd pulled me out, leaving spattered blood, crushed cartilage, and cracked plastic in my wake. What can I say? It was my favorite move. I let the stave fuel my anger and vice versa as I swept it across the chest of a second guy, turning his rifle to molten metal and setting his body armor sizzling. I grabbed the collar of the third guy to get too close and pulled him to the ground so fast his helmet splashed into the muddy garden, his legs flipping up and over.

Had to hold out until Procyon could get there. Had to keep Loredana safe.

Which was going great in those few seconds until a golden-white blast hit me full in the chest. I flew backward, feet leaving the ground—

And stopped in midair, again, that time without a spaceship around me.

The Ashen guy descended, and even with his powers crushing the air from my lungs, I got satisfaction from the way his outfit was singed. The cloak fell away, rain turning to smoke where it put out the smoldering embers.

"You guys … No capes, am I right?" I choked.

Silence, except for the rain that was slowing to a drizzle and the rumble of running boots. Six Syndax mercenaries surrounded me, rifles ready to perforate whatever was left of my body when the Ashen was done with me, or if I got free. Their buddies were busy using extinguishers on the fires the rain hadn't already doused among the wrecked trucks. There were two more Humvees and a cargo van up against the east wall.

But most of the activity was inside the mall's main vestibule, a huge space as broad as a football field, hexagonal, and open from floor to ceiling with the two upper stories surrounding the edges. A silver steel platform had been set up in front of the double escalators. Javon was trapped there, arms lashed by cables to the stanchions rising on either side from the platform's base, ankles locked in thick manacles. He wasn't going anywhere unless he activated his wacky disintegration powers.

Unfortunately for me, he looked like was out cold.

"Mercury." Serena walked up, with Xia at her side. Both were clad in black jackets and maroon pants, with Dominic trailing behind. Xia had Edgeweld, the blade pointing out from her side almost lazily. Dominic followed it like there was a physical leash tied from the blade to his neck. "I knew you'd show up. You're good like that."

"Thanks … I think." Geez. Talk about constricting. "Hey, can you … Have your super friend back off a smidge? If you're wanting to gloat … I can't breathe well enough … for snarky comebacks."

"He's not going to kill you. Don't—" Serena's voice broke. She stumbled, nearly hitting her knees, but Xia caught her.

"Your armor," Xia said. Her voice was soft but musical. "Put on the shell. You can't heal without it."

"I know that!" Serena snapped. She shook off the support, staggered, and then spread her arms wide. The scales rippled out from her body, seeming to grow clean from her flesh and clothing, until she was covered from neck to toes. Her face seemed less pale.

"Heck of a trade-off … for a gunshot wound." I sneered, even as the Ashen's pressure on my ribcage increased.

"He's not making it easy for us to keep him alive, is he?" Xia watched me, her gaze searching for … what? There was a flash of something when our eyes met, like a mutual recognition, and she looked back, I figured to check on Dominic.

"I could flatten him." The Ashen's voice was cold and flat. "No worse than stepping on bug."

"You might get a chance later, if you hadn't screwed up taking down that—whatever it was," Serena said. "Decrease the pressure on him and bring him down."

I peered through the clouds—the rain had stopped by then with only a few drops remaining for the party. A distant glow of blue and orange was growing fainter by the second. Man. I knew the ship could motor but it could really *motor.*

The Ashen's fingers flexed. I settled until my shoes touched the pavement, as gun muzzles followed me the whole way. But the force against my ribs, against my whole body, got worse. "Not … better," I croaked.

Serena's energy cannon crackled to life as she leveled it at the Ashen. "What did I just say, Vanchev? Drop him!"

The Ashen slammed onto the ground next to me, sending up a shockwave of rain. Half the Syndax guns swiveled his way—and

I realized there were another dozen mercenaries emerging from where they'd taken shelter around the ruined mall.

The Ashen ripped his hood off. He couldn't be older than me, with buzzcut blond hair and freckles, his eyes a stormy gray. "I'm here on my own, lady, but don't think for a second I won't mash you all flat if I don't get what I want. I should have taken the initiative when you both humiliated me at sea."

I rolled my eyes. "A kid? You've got to be kidding me. This punk was the one who tried to nab symmachites for science experiments?"

"How do you think the Ashen reacted when that Garrison scum dumped me on their figurative doorstep?" He shook his head. "This is my chance to earn my way back—"

Another gold blast struck his chest. He crumpled, panting, and the invisible grip holding me vanished. I sagged, sucking in lungs full of air, as the Syndax guys swoop in and relieved me of the pulsar stave.

"That's not what the Whisperer wants, Will." Troy stepped up, the pulsar stave's wayward half—*my* stave—still glowing from the expert shot he'd taken that had temporarily disabled the Vanchev guy's medallion. He pressed the stave against Loredana's head like a gun. Troy hadn't bothered with a ballcap, letting his hair and face get soaked, but grinned all the same. "When our master makes his comeback, Mercury Hale's going to have the front row seat for the show before he becomes the first of many sacrificed for a better world."

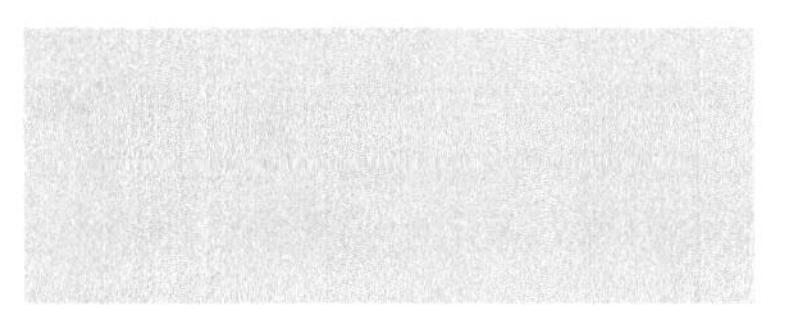

CHAPTER THIRTY-TWO

I didn't feel a whole lot better about Vanchev getting Tasered by the pulsar stave, because Troy was the one doing the Tasering, and he had both halves of the weapon. He handed Loredana over to a couple of mercs, who had to grapple with her for control because she'd woken up after the blow to the head she'd taken aboard the Max One.

"There's no need to be so rough." Her wrists were bound together, but she pulled her arm away from a mercenary's grasp.

The guy must have been mollified by her soft tone and the accent. "Sorry, I—"

She whipped her elbow up into his throat. The poor dude gagged and dropped his weapon.

"Hey!" The other soldier swept Loredana's legs out from under her, so she landed on her knees. "Give me a hand with this one."

Another mercenary showed up, helping him truss her up. He lifted his gun's stock overhead.

"Knock it off!" Troy snapped. "Bad enough you let her get the drop on you, without having to beat her up more than she's already been. Make sure she's secure and bring her to the platform with the rest."

"You should totally try loosening her restraints," I said.

"Works great."

More mercs prodded me along. My aerial count had been pretty close—there were more than fifty. Some must have been obscured when we made the attack run. Man, I knew the economy was tight and all, but how many people could you sign up at once? Guess the promise of money plus super-powered steroids was tempting, especially if it beat arguing with people at the front doors of Wal-Mart about whether or not they should wear a mask.

"Feel free to gag that one if he gets too mouthy." Troy joined the pulsar stave, then gave the combined weapon a good twirl. Raindrops sizzled where they met with sparks. "Now that's a good sign, having these two together again. Thanks for that."

"Don't put your eye out." Seriously, I was digging deep for any way to deflect from the rising panic. It was just the two of us, without our biggest weapon—you know, the UFO—and even with Procyon on its way, probably still outgunned. But the buzz of tachyon energies stored up in my prosthetic leg was a nice ace up the sleeve. Or up the supersuit, which retained some of that energy, too.

Winston ripped that thread of hope away as soon as Troy and the mercs marched us into the empty atrium. He was dressed way nicer, in a neon green button shirt and khakis, his hair freshly re-blonded. Whatever was on the tablet he held kept him mouthing words to himself, a constant mutter that I really hoped wasn't to Marigold, seeing as how his dead wife was merged with the Whisperer in an evil dimension. He looked up at our footsteps and let out a tremendous sigh. "You lot are utterly inept, have I mentioned that? Remove his leg. And strip him."

Troy made a face. "He's captive. There's no need to humiliate the man."

"It's a reservoir for the same extradimensional energies that fuel the pulsar stave and every other bloody relic that comes out of the Interstice!" Winston snapped. "Which I have no doubt lets him pull off a surprise kick even when he's been relieved of weaponry. And that suit—it's one of my very own projects, stolen property, if you will."

Troy glanced at my guards and nodded.

"Wow. Talk about a new low." I clenched my fists but stood by the nearest lopsided mall bench. My guards tugged the supersuit off and detached the leg, leaving me sitting on that bench in a pair of red boxers. "You guys got a spare? Maybe some pants no one's gonna miss?"

"It won't matter a deuce how many legs you have once this is all said and done, Mercury." Winston gestured at Javon as if he was showing off the Thanksgiving turkey. "Once we open this fellow up, the power of the Interstice will become unstoppable—"

"Right, yeah, and there'll be a cleansing of Earth, all its griminess washed away, astral fiends will frolic, blah, blah." I shook my head. "The pitch still sucks, okay? And you already tried opening a stable rip to do that. Spoiler: It failed when I stabbed your wife."

"Okay, now you can hit him again," Troy said.

The blow to my shoulders knocked me off the bench and sent a lance of pain through my partially healed gunshot wound. Managed not to throw up, which was a plus. Landing with half of one of your legs gone isn't easy. Pretty sure I was bleeding from the intact knee.

"Ta and thank you for that," Winston said.

"So glad you've found new friends," I growled through clenched teeth. But I was most worried about Javon strung up on that platform, and the way Serena kept eyeing both him and the Edgeweld sword. "What's your new evil plan, then?"

"Terribly sorry, Mercury, but I'm well aware just how fond of a good monologue you are." Winston chuckled, which is an awful sound coming from the guy who's trying to destroy the world. "Suffice it to say, I have former-Special Agent Cyr to thank for ferreting out the details—or rather, giving me enough clues from Procyon's Historic Vaults to piece together the true nature of your dear board member. Serena?"

"We're ready." The shell of armor formed a helmet and

faceplate, obscuring her equally creepy smile.

"I need the stave." Xia's voice was a solemn whisper.

"Right." Troy grimaced as he powered up the weapon, then struggled to separate it.

"Been a few years?" I asked. "Need a tutorial? I didn't have time to put something up on YouTube."

That time Troy smacked me one, by planting the pulsar stave in my gut. I doubled-over, focused on the irony of blacking out from lack of air when the world was about to get flooded with hideous, life-sucking tentacled monsters.

"For goodness' sake, stay quiet," Loredana hissed.

I winked at her, which was tricky with bleary eyes. "Just keeping them focused."

Troy grunted. The pulsar stave separated. "Got it. Here." He handled one half over to Xia.

She inserted it into Edgeweld's pommel.

Well, crap. There I was, hoping Winston had bluffed about figuring out stuff. But if they knew how those two pieces of the puzzle went together …

Xia strode to the platform, raised the sword, and thrust it at Javon's abdomen.

He must have been sedated, to be out that long with no ill effects, because as soon as the sword triggered his disassociation, he awoke yelling. The cry morphed into an electronic buzz, which then got lost in the whirlwind of the portal his body opened into Sadeh with that familiar blur of golden particles. I glimpsed the endless sea dotted with alien mangroves.

But before the portal could drag Xia in, she reached back for Serena, who grabbed her hand. Serena leapt onto the platform, standing *inside* the gateway to another world.

And she triggered a rip.

Javon's mutated cry became a monstrous moan, one that shook the mall and its foundations. Dirt vibrated and floated a couple inches off the floor. The rip, black and violet-edged, writhed inside the portal to Sadeh, with lighting tendrils slicing through the golden ring.

"It's working!" Winston shouted. He held his tablet at face height, so he could read whatever was on it while getting a clear view of the—thing they were creating. "Maintain that position. The tachyon pulses are forcing the neutrino stream into alignment. It shan't be long now!"

"I'm holding it!" Serena snapped. "But this armor had better stay together!"

"It will! Mari assures me it can't fail!" Winston closed his eyes. "My darling, yes, I shall see you again soon."

A distorted shriek whistled through the bizarre portal, then another, until a nail-scaping choir of astral fiend calls filled the air. The rip undulated, its dark surface clearing, as the bleak landscape of the Interstice faded into view, *inside* Sadeh.

"My word," Loredana murmured. "They're invading another dimension."

"Close." Troy tapped the pulsar stave against his leg. Who did that guy think he was, taking my moves? "Absorbing it. The Whisperer's been holding a grudge for, oh, a few millennia. This is payback, and an upgrade of his powers. Best way for him to bring Earth into the fold is if he can walk out of the Interstice free and clear."

I tensed, every muscle on fire. Free and clear? Then what Tenebrae said about me needing to destroy the Whisperer had a razor's edge chance of coming true. "Gotta be nice, having a prize to hand over to the big boss."

Troy grinned. "Prizes. Why do you think we brought along your pal Gemini?"

I stared at Dominic, who was off to one side, stolid as a statue. The flashes from the competing portals made the Echo Watches glow. Okay, kinda forgot about those. The Whisperer getting his semi-corporeal mitts on the pulsar stave was bad enough, but if he had access to two devices that could be used to form more portals? Didn't the guy have a corner on that market?

Serena shouted. The purple lighting that crackled from her

armor had swung into a vertical loop, as streaks of light from Sadeh refracted into rainbows. For a moment, the atrium and even the parking lot outside glowed like the midday sun had broken through the clouds.

"She's losing it!" Troy hurried to the platform. "What's the deal, Yen? Does Xia need the other stave?"

"No! A single half is enough to get through to the other dimension." Winston's eyes were wild. He seized a handful of his hair. "It's—What? Yes. I hear—Of course! The gravitational constant is all over the proverbial map. We need to stabilize the entire space around the platform, or the rip runs the risk of collapsing."

Troy spun, found Vanchev curled up against a distant wall. "Get him on his feet and over here!"

The young Ashen started when mercenaries hauled him upright and dragged him, half walking, half stumbling, toward the center of the party. "You have no right to—"

Troy punched him across the jaw.

"That seems unwise," Loredana muttered to me.

"No kidding. Let's aggravate the dude with poor impulse control who can turn us all into human pancakes," I said. "Can't believe Syndax thought it was a great idea to pull him into their mix."

"The only thing worse than assuming Vanchev is here independent of the Ashen is the presumption he is operating under their orders."

Yikes. I didn't want to dwell on that possibility.

The radio on one of our guard's belts crackled. "Go ahead."

"Procyon is at the perimeter. We've got them locked down for now. What's the boss say?"

"He's a little busy," the merc said. "It's more of that weird stuff. Take the juice and kill all of them—except the Indian chick and the ax man. Boss wants them alive."

"Roger. Out."

I frowned. Did all goons everywhere sound the same? Because

I'd sworn I'd heard the voice on the radio before. Not at Procyon, and it definitely wasn't Teget ...

"Here! Stand right. Here." Winston pulled Vanchev's arm until they were directly behind Serena and Xia, about twenty feet back from the platform. "I need a field of compressed gravity around the platform and its environs."

"Heavy? Light?" Vanchev held up his hands. "I could crush them or float them if we're not careful."

"It bloody well better not do either!" Winston snapped. "I just need the gravity *constant*."

Vanchev's face took on a dreamy expression. His outstretched fingers twitched.

It was hard to tell the effect, until the rip stopped wavering and the Interstice became a solid picture instead of a mirage. The gold particles faltered. Purple lightning leapt out, hitting the atrium walls, and glazing stretches of the floor.

The mercenaries had their guns ready, the whole bunch dazzled by the dramatic, otherworldly light show, which was great because they weren't paying attention to me. My leg was propped against the opposite end of the bench from where I sat. I scooted over an inch. No reaction from the mercs. I tried six more inches. Nothing.

My foot squealed on the tile floor.

One of the mercs turned around, his weapon aimed at my chest from six feet away. Not ideal. "What's going on?"

"I was attempting to get a better view of the situation." Loredana squirmed against her restraints and curled her lips into a smile that turned up the dial on my body temperature. "Would you be so kind as to lend a hand?"

"No way. Not after you bashed Carl's larynx," the guy said. "He's gonna need surgery for that. How else is he supposed to win the next karaoke contest?"

I scooted some more since the guy had veered toward Loredana. My prosthetic was only a couple feet away. And since these dummies had bound my hands in front of me instead of behind …

"My heavens. That does sound terrible. I am truly sorry, you know, but what could one expect of a woman in my position?" Loredana frowned, as if searching for the answer to a deep question. "Why karaoke, if I may ask?"

"Carl's the best. I won fifty bucks last time he took to the mike." The merc sighed. "If we don't get to hear 'Pretty Woman' again, Fridays will never be the same, you know?"

Geez. If I start laughing, I'm never gonna get this done. I'd made it to the end of the bench. The leg was right there.

Loredana stood, less than a foot away from the guard. "It would have been nice for Carl to be here with us."

"It's steady! Hold the field!" Winston's shout drew everybody's attention toward the portals. A barely visible shimmer surrounded the intermingled portals, like the soap bubble effect Dominic's Echo Watches could produce. I stared as astral fiend tentacles lashed the air around Serena and Xia, reaching hungrily but ignoring those two as targets. "Serena, withdraw!"

She pulled Xia down off the platform. They stumbled, but Troy was there to catch them. Even with Serena's shell of armor outside the portals and Edgeweld withdrawn, they stayed open— and expanded, the mingled gold and purple light spilling beyond the soap bubble.

"Keep that core stable!" Winston snapped. "Release it too soon and space-time could collapse in on itself."

Even as he said it, colors bled into the dingy mall, dripping down the platform and mingling on the floor. Patches of blue sea and alien mangrove sprouted, mixed with ash-colored boulders. Sunny skies appeared above the Sadeh sections, while dark storm clouds rippling with thunder grew over the Interstice portions, all confined to the inside of a three-story atrium that should have been home to mall vendors selling expensive crap nobody needed.

I grabbed the leg and slammed it back into place. The sting of the pulsar stave's absorbed energy was immediate. I let it surge through my body, drenching every cell, until I felt like I'd drank an entire Starbucks café. How buzzed?

I broke my manacles, tore the seat off the bench, and flung it like a Frisbee at the guard nearest Loredana.

The crunch and shout were audible across the room. Loredana seized his gun as soon as he collapsed, letting his body fall against her as a shield. "Shoot and he dies!" she snapped.

"Who cares?" Troy shouted. "Kill them both!"

The roar of vehicle engines interrupted, putting a pause on the impending bloodshed. Out in the U-shape of the mall, where the burnt-out Syndax trucks were located, three Humvees rolled up. I groaned.

"Isn't that lovely?" Winston chuckled. "Reinforcements."

He was still laughing when another roar grew overhead and a spindly, raven-colored version of an Osprey tiltrotor burst through the thick cloud cover, propellers like buzzsaws, red and green lights blinking from the wingtips. It parked itself in midair, turned ninety degrees, and opened fire.

Not on the Syndax trucks, but on the other Humvees, the ones already parked against the side of the mall.

The mercenaries who happened to be outside scrambled for cover, firing automatic rifles skyward as they sought escape. One of them dropped, sprawled in a puddle, as blood sprayed around him. Others shouted and adjusted their aim.

The new Humvees on the scene? They skidded up around the wreckage, doors flying open. More people jumped out—not Syndax soldiers, but men and women in the black fatigues with gray stripes signature to Procyon security.

And my brother hurled himself hollering into the midst of the enemy, his ax blades slashing. Wilhelmina was right behind him, leaping over his shoulder as her dagger found targets.

"Hang on, Mercury!" The driver of one Humvee? Tina, the Mercurian, clad in those yellows and blacks I found really annoying but right then wished I owned a pair.

Awesome.

I used the last of my powers to speed run for Xia, slamming

into her with the force of a dump truck. She slapped twenty feet into a clothing store's wall, leaving a crumpled ring where she shattered drywall.

I ripped the pulsar stave half from Edgeweld, and faced Troy with both, fully aware I'd waded into battle in my underpants. Look, it wasn't the way I preferred wading into battle, but a guy's gotta go with what he's got. Time to make the best of the situation.

"My turn," I snarled.

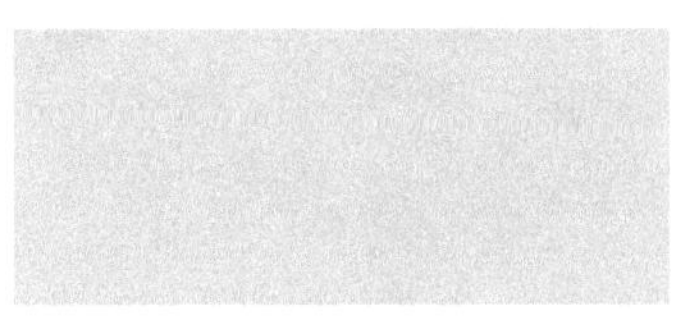

CHAPTER THIRTY-THREE

First thing first: figuring out how to disarm and defeat Troy before getting back into my supersuit, because there we were, in the midst of a brawl featuring almost a hundred people, and I was stuck in my shorts.

It was like those nightmares where you show up to school undressed, except nobody was laughing at me, because they were too busy shooting and getting shot at.

"Keep the portals stable!" Troy snapped. "I've got this one."

"Yeah." I grinned. "You wish."

Troy and I collided in a shockwave that threw of sparks and sent dirt rippling across the floor. Syndax mercs went rolling away, along with Serena and Winston.

Dude was good. He blocked every blow I could manage, even though I had one more weapon than he did.

Meanwhile, Loredana had fallen back toward the open parking lot, firing bursts into soldiers while she avoided stepping in the growing patches of Sadeh and the Interstice still spilling forth from the massive portal. Her opponents staggered the opposite direction, dragging Winston with them even as he fought against their grasp in a vain attempt to manage his freaky pseudo-science experiment.

A section of mall wall behind Loredana ripped apart, courtesy of Wilhelmina. She blew through drywall like it was tissue paper, knocked two soldiers down, and slammed into Troy's backside. He hurtled into a pillar and rebounded with a sickening *crack* and a meaty *whump*.

"Sakes, Mercury!" She stumbled into me. I caught her arm, but she shook off my grip and prodded my exposed ribcage with the pointy end of her modified Medan dagger. "Get your pants on while I distract these fools!"

"Best idea anyone's had all week!" I sprinted for the bench, dropping into a slide as bullets ripped through the air overhead. Loredana had crouched there, ducking her head as she ejected the spent magazine of the rifle and slapped a new one in. "Hey, babe."

"I stand corrected." She looped an arm around my neck and pulled me close, so she could whisper in my ear. "You do have abs."

I burst out laughing and kissed her.

Took me a record twenty seconds to get into the suit, which include the last couple in which I flung myself up and over the bench, upside down. Halfway through the flip, I sighted on two mercenaries closing from opposite angles on the bench where Loredana took shelter. Two quick blasts from the pulsar stave put them down, arms and legs sprawled at awkward angles.

By then the battle was moving out into the parking lot as the boundaries twisted. Wilhelmina had jumped upon the dazed Troy, who managed to intercept her swipe with the dagger, so it didn't remove the top of his scalp. Her raspy cry was as harsh as any banshee's, but Troy didn't falter under her onslaught.

Serena, recovered from her stumble, had Xia back on her feet, too, as she shouted commands that had something to do with consolidating forces and clearing the field. All around her Syndax soldiers formed up in pairs as they took cover on the far side of the U-shaped center lot of the mall, which made complete sense. I would have done the same thing, what with Procyon Security forces storming around the opposite end. They used their hijacked Humvees for barricades and found out pretty fast those rigs weren't entirely bulletproof as they began to resemble cheese graters. Tires exploded in bursts of air and showers of rubber shards.

Things were sort of under control. So, I set my sights on Vanchev—you know, the young Ashen using his gravity powers to stabilize the terrible flood of two dimensions into the world I was kinda partial to. But I hadn't taken a couple steps into a speed run when a heavy object hit me so fast, I found myself fifty feet away, tangled in a pile of empty DVD racks.

Turned out I'd been hit with a human missile, called Xia. She recovered first from the surprise attack, seeing as how it wasn't a surprise for her, and kicked me across the face. I rolled with the strike, so I didn't spend the rest of the epic fight with a broken jaw but doing so gave her a chance to wrest Edgeweld from my other hand.

Super-duper.

Even less awesome? Serena charging my way, like a metal-clad rhinoceros. Which I was pretty sure was something I'd seen in a movie once, without getting a chance to find out how the scene ended.

I leapt straight for her, spinning as Xia slashed with Edgeweld through the air I'd vacated. Another twist, and my acrobatics paid off when I stuck the landing on Serena's shoulders, added a second backflip, and cut at the armor on her spine with the blazing energies of the pulsar stave.

She howled with pain and dropped like a cut tree.

Okay, so the first part happened. Not the second. Nope. Instead, the jagged ridges running up and down her back exploded outward, slivers slicing through my supersuit in a couple places. Talk about the world's worst papercuts, magnified by a hundred. I fell across the store's threshold, my hand slick with blood as it came up from one of the larger cuts.

"Glad I got a sneak peek at you before the end." Serena raised the arm cannon, two feet from my face, which was not meant to repel Interstice-powered beams of evil, just so you know.

I swore someone drew a line of lightning across my vision. Whatever it was, Serena screamed, because her cannon erupted in a firestorm of violent flames, their centers white hot, engulfing the rest of her arm.

Edith Pathkiller, clad in a form-fitting gray jumpsuit with black panels, lowered her bow. She nodded at me, from far across the mall's atrium, then sent another arrow at Troy's face. Because why not?

He was already out of its way, headed for me, with Wilhelmina left in the middle of six Syndax guys, none of whom looked happy to see her if their guns were any indication. But that didn't deter her from scowling at them, her dagger held back and ready. "C'mon now!" she hollered.

The enraged cry from overhead was enough to change their minds.

Teget plummeted from the third story, crushing one merc under his landing. A swipe of his ax felled two more, and he plowed into the remaining three as they opened fire. Might as well have been shooting clouds, for all the good their stray bullets did.

I caught Troy's incoming charge just as Xia swung for me from behind. Okay, that meant Troy was *way* more impressive than I thought, because it really was hard fighting two weapons with one—and I had one more opponent than he did. "Teget! The portal guy!"

"I have him!" Teget led Wilhelmina as they rushed Vanchev, but the kid managed to wrench one hand toward them, two fingers pointed.

My brother and my mentor floated up to the second story, legs pinwheeling as they tried to continue their run. Then they stopped, clamping together, as did their arms, and I sweated through my one-man swordfight with Troy and Xia as I tried to figure out a way to save them from being mashed into paste.

Winston had the solution.

"No! Let them down, you twit!" he screamed from behind whatever barricade his Syndax bodyguards had set up. "You're letting the portals destabilize!"

He wasn't kidding. The growing infiltration slowed, and the rip faltered, its edges contracting. But the Sadeh element of the portal regained some of its luminosity, even with Edgeweld in Xia's hands, busy with trying to disembowel me.

The whole thing would have been a bigger mess if Procyon hadn't been keeping the bulk of the Syndax goons busy outside. The VTOL aircraft wheeled overhead, letting off streams of tracer fire from whatever massive machine gun was mounted under its chin. More sounds joined the fight—bigger engines, and sirens. Four big Bearcat armored trucks rumbled into the fray, red and blue lights flashing off SCPD insignia emblazoned on their sides.

Ramos.

He was in the lead, because where else would the man be? Body armor and all, M4 rifle at the ready, he shouted orders that Detective Stan Bradley, his burly colleague, was only too happy to repeat and punctuate with profanity. They lent their weapons to the shootout, while Ramos dragged the now-hapless Mercurians from the line of fire.

It wasn't easy to keep track of where everybody was and what they were doing, but as soon as Vanchev released Teget and Wilhelmina, I spotted an advantage. The dual dueling with Xia and Troy was wearing on me, as evidenced by the burning in my muscles and the ripe BO emanating from my suit. Hey, I'd be the first to admit, I needed a shower.

I ducked the pulsar stave Troy swung at me, right as Xia brought Edgeweld down toward my head. The weapons intersected in another blast of energy that threw pieces of metal shelving into the air, momentarily blinding my opponents.

Which gave me a chance to deliver a punch to Troy's midsection that folded him over my fist like a soaked dishrag.

Vanchev had refocused his gravity powers, and the rip spun back to life. As it did, the Interstice sections growing all around us glowed. The shrieks took on sudden clarity.

Astral fiends emerged from everywhere.

Five, six, seven … Nine of them.

"Bloody hell!" Loredana's cry of surprise cut across nearly everything, because the gunfire—even that of the Syndax goons—had slacked off at the sudden appearance of real, live monsters. "Fall back! Defensive positions!"

Ramos was there, at the entrance to the mall, covering Loredana with three-round bursts from his M4 as Procyon security surrounded her. They moved as a group of one, six people and twelve legs, until they had joined back up with the police task force and the rest of Procyon.

"Light 'em up!" Bradley hefted his weapon of choice—a stubby grenade launcher, a gray tub with a trigger and a huge drum magazine of rounds. It spat out grenades with a flash of fire and a *whoomp*. The first explosion caught an astral fiend clean in the face, reducing its toothy maw to an oozing, pale-blue mess, as concentrated gunfire cut through the rest of it.

Great. I jumped over a trio of flailing tentacles and landed square on a fiend's eyes, digging the pulsar stave into its hide so I could sandworm ride the sucker with the best of them. "Because I didn't have enough to keep track of already!" I yelled, as it stabbed deeper into its core.

The fiend screamed and I screamed right back, head spinning with exhaustion that had finally caught up with me through the constant stream of adrenaline. Worse was the nagging sensation that I was forgetting something …

Make that someone.

"Mercury!" Teget was hurrying for the portal, slashing his way through one of the newly arrived astral fiends. "Dominic needs us!"

Dominic? Still controlled by symmachites—and Xia had gotten that stupid sword back.

Sure enough, Dominic was marching like the brainwashed dude he was, with Xia behind him, Edgeweld poised over his right shoulder. I swore I could see the faint mist produced by a concentrated swarm of symmachites as they kept him docile.

The rip ahead of them pulsed with purple lightning, oddly silent even as storm clouds oozed into the mall atrium. A shadow filled the eye of the storm, shrinking from a colossal wraith to human size—an obsidian statue, with eyes like amethysts and silver veins pulsing through its form.

The Whisperer.

A terrible fear leached through me, worse than an astral fiend latching on to draw my life out. I hadn't seen the Whisperer that clearly since the Battle of North Beach when Marigold had died in the attempt to merge Earth and the Interstice. She'd been absorbed into his shadow, taking on a feminine statuesque form, but this … This must be what happened when the Hedron of Orbits was obliterated, and Alexander Arkwright along with it. The Whisperer's physical form was androgynous, like Tenebrae.

It was evil. It was reaching for Dominic. And the big dope was reaching right back.

Best case scenario? He'd ask politely for Dominic to hand over the Echo Watches and who knew what that would mean in terms of increased power for everybody's favorite nefarious being. "Teget!" I shouted. "Bum's rush!"

He twisted his torso and let the astral fiend deliver a hefty slap, sending him hurtling like a home run. I redirected pulsar stave energy through the suit, into my leg, and pushed off with a blast of light that shredded my former mount.

We intersected with Xia's march just an arm's reach from the portal.

Teget landed low, shoulders catching her in the knees. I went high, grabbing onto her right arm and latching my fingers around Edgeweld's hilt.

But another set of arms seized me—Dominic's. I felt the sizzling heat from the primed Echo Watches, ready to sear my face off. I sneered into his angry, but blank, face. "Take a nap, man."

I planted the pulsar stave on his forehead.

The scream that issued from his mouth was an electronic symphony, badly tuned, as the stave worked its mojo on the symmachite-infected operative—namely, burning the little suckers out. Dominic toppled backwards, away from the portal. The Whisperer's phantom arms stopped short, fading as they tried to claw at him through the rip's perimeter.

Didn't want to continue the fight there, but the portals were dragging us in. Which left me with one option.

"Hold on!" I yelled to Teget. "Road trip!"

I jammed the pulsar stave into Edgeweld's base.

Blazing sun rolled over us. Earth—as in California, San Camilo, the abandoned mall, and the manic battle around us— faded in a hiss like ocean surf.

I braced myself for a landing on a sandy beach shaded with weird crystals, or even a faceplant into warm, gentle waves of that shallow Sadeh ocean. Instead, I wound up in a heap of arms with Xia and Teget against a floor—or rather, we skidded on one of the rugs layered over that floor. Except the rugs didn't move.

I blinked at the white blocks and the glowing light globes. The ivy. The plants rustling in a gentle breeze through bronze-fitted windows. The room was hexagonal.

"Home," Teget murmured. He held Xia down by the shoulders, his ax pressed to the top of her spine in case she tried any fast moves. "How is it possible?"

A woman's laughter interrupted whatever calm, collected reply I had. There was something off about the room—a hazy quality to every I looked at, like the furnishings and even the stone blocks themselves refused to stay still. Either that or I was having trouble focusing. On everything.

Except her.

"Get off of me!" Xia snarled. "Where are we?"

"I've seen it," I murmured. "Edith showed me."

"How, Mercury?" Teget asked. "This is our home in Meda."

I pointed.

There was a man kneeling, hair black and cropped, his sharp cheekbones broadened by a proud grin. A woman, with long, brown curls and Asian features, held out her hands to a tiny toddler. The cute little kid staggered away from a chair, hands free, giggling.

When he made it, they cheered, the mother drowning his face in kisses. And the loudest huzzah came from a girl, maybe five-years-old, in a dress the color of purple lilacs. She hugged her little brother and whispered something in his ear.

Teget cried out and fell off Xia. He was on his hands and knees, arms shaking, the ax forgotten on the rug beside him.

"It's them." Tears filled my eyes. My chest ached like all the astral fiends in the Interstice were sitting on it. "Isn't it? Mom and Dad. Cyllene and Sabik."

"Yes." Teget's voice was choked with an emotion I could only guess was equal parts sorrow and longing because that's what had incapacitated me, too. "Yes. And you, Mercury. But the girl …"

Xia was on her knees. Weeping.

Even as I wondered at my anonymous enemy showing either joy or sadness at this past tableau of my happy home life, I took a closer look at Cyllene sitting on that C-shaped divan—the child's chair, my grandfather Naos remembered it. The heritage was a no-brainer.

"Purple lilacs," Xia said, her head shaking. "I loved that dress."

CHAPTER THIRTY-FOUR

When Tenebrae arrived, I had no idea. I was too entranced by the glimpse at what my life had been before my parents had gone to Earth, me in tow, and died battling astral fiends on the streets of what I thought was my hometown.

"The three are one," he said. "As they have never been. What the Whisperer never knew will be his end. From the beginning."

"Really wish you could speak, I don't know, something that makes more sense." I had to grab the tops of my thighs to quit shaking. "Doesn't have to be English."

"Are—is this real?" Teget stood, his legs trembling. "Are they—?"

"This is then, seen now. Two moments touch, across planes." Tenebrae's form kinda fizzled, like a TV losing signal for a second while you fiddle with the antenna to get rid of static. I know, old reference, but it was the best I had. "It was necessary."

"You're kidding, right?" I pointed at Xia, who had forgotten all about Edgeweld and was especially transfixed by the five-year-old version of herself. "We had time before! You could have told me we have a sister!"

"Time before." Tenebrae solidified with a rumble like approaching thunder. "Dealing with your kind strains me."

"Yeah, if you think that was a strain ..." I slung back my mask and ran a hand through my hair. Okay, easy, Mercury. Don't freak out. As nice as the blast from the past was, I had to get back to the battle. To the future. Or present. Whatever. "When is this?"

"The time before. After this world completes its next journey around its sun, Sabik and Cyllene will leave for Earth, with you. Teget will remain in his grandfather's care."

I frowned. "And where is the little tyke? Not using Dad's ax as a pacifier, I hope."

"I was not born yet." Teget cocked his head like a dog pondering a troubling scene. "The beads on the wall—they mark a year and more prior to my birth."

Beads? There was an array of them lined up in a vertical abacus, reds, oranges, and yellows separated by bronze clasps. The display was two feet tall, tucked in a corner, half-hidden by a diaphanous curtain emblazoned with stylized clouds. "So, I was itty bitty, and Xia was—"

"Dione."

She said the named *Dee-own*. I looked at her. The hard-edged, vacant expression she'd carried since I first saw her in a Gdansk nightclub as part of Serena's clandestine auction of Edgeweld, was gone. She actually smiled. "It's—my name. Dione."

"Our sister," Teget breathed. "Why did we not know?"

I shook my head. "The only one left to tell us would be Naos, if he had survived."

My stomach lurched as the rest of Edith's vision caught up to me. In the next few seconds …

The door banged open. A shadow cast onto the family.

And the little girl began to cry.

"Father." Sabik was on his feet, phasing through us like we weren't there. Which I guess we weren't. Or was he the incorporeal one? The exhaustion wouldn't let me think straight. "I don't think this is wise."

"Then it is good for all of us that wisdom comes with age." The man in the open doorway was taller than everyone else in the room, us visitors included, with swooping black hair that was going gray at the temples. His presence was commanding, kind of like what Ramos could pull off in a tense situation, but so much more intimidating I sucked in whatever gut I had. There was no mistaking the blue coat and leggings of his temple outfit. "Dione must come with me, or this family remains in peril."

"She will only be in peril because you would have us run from danger." Cyllene stood behind the younger version of Dione, clasping her like a precious locket. "Have we not the weapons of our ancestors? Bring us near the threat and we will end it."

"You would endanger Mercury? And the unborn child you carry?"

Teget sucked in a breath.

"Do not be an emotional fool, Cyllene."

Sabik poked a finger right in the center of that blue coat. "Have care! You will not speak of my wife with such disregard."

"And you, *son*, will remember your place."

"I won't let you take our daughter, Naos!" Cyllene cried. "Our family will not be torn apart.

I felt like I'd been beaten up by Troy Reverdin, all over again. My good old grandfather Naos, towering like a monster at the head of the room, his son and daughter-and-law ready to rumble.

"He did," Xia—Dione, I mean—whispered. "He did take me away."

I touched her shoulder. Wasn't sure why. She had been trying to behead and/or dismember me about ten minutes ago.

"It will not be safe any other way." Naos seemed to the deflate, as if his bluster had been an act. "The Whisperer cannot have her—and if your three children are known to him, he will concentrate his efforts on Meda. The relics will never be safe. She must be removed from the field of battle before he can claim her, as he will."

"But you cannot know this is the only way!" Sabik said.

"I do. It is what Tenebrae has seen."

Sabik recoiled from his father, stepping back into the room, until he almost looked like he was guarding his family. "That—

No. Impossible. It is forbidden."

Naos folded his arms. "So it is. So I have done all the same. It was the only way to have foreknowledge, and if I am to be forgiven, I must confess. The power he wields—"

"You of anyone know the strictures." Cyllene's angry tones had faded to sorrow. Or disappointment. "Why no one should conduct audience with the Whisperer or Tenebrae. Those beings are not our allies."

"But Tenebrae is not our enemy. He offers us a path. One to success, if not now, then tens of years beyond this moment."

I shivered at the words. Tenebrae was beside me, unmoving, unspeaking. Had Naos seen this moment? Lived with it for more than twenty-five years before I'd shown up in the same living room after Teget led me and my friends through a frantic escape from the Interstice?

Naos walked into the room. He knelt before our sister. "My precious Dione, are you scared?"

She nodded, her chest heaving. "I don't want to leave Mama and Papa."

"You must, my girl. It is the way we must walk to protect all we have—our very life." He smiled. "Come, take my hands."

Dione clung to Cyllene. "No! I am scared."

Naos' face went rigid. "We all are scared. But I will not let fear rule us."

He swept Dione from Mother's arms. Their synchronized cries cut through me. Teget was a wreck, his teeth clenched, tears soaking his beard. Dione couldn't stop shaking her head. I held her arms.

Sabik did the same to Cyllene, restraining her from following as Naos plunged out the open door. "Stay here! Cyllene, my angel—"

"He is taking her from us!" She turned and hit him, blow after blow, on that broad chest concealed under a leather vest. "How can you let him? Your own kin!"

"Because he is right." He grabbed her wrists. "If Tenebrae has shown this path, we cannot diverge. This is true. We know it."

"But I—" Her voice caught. "I cannot see her again."

"We may still. Someday."

I hoped they had, before they died.

Throughout all that, the littler version of me had sat on the floor, brow scrunched in that dour way babies do, as I gnawed on the edge of my fist. I babbled incoherent sort-of-words and tried to get on my feet but flopped down. Infant me started crawling for the door.

"No, Mercury." Sabik knelt. He held me face to face. And his sad eyes—the half-smile—the brush of stubble against my cheek—it exploded out of my memories, from some place locked away deep in the back of my mind. "It is not time. You will know, when it is, when you take your place with the stave and the ax and the blade. Then our destinies will be complete, all of ours, in you."

Cyllene was at the door. "I cannot stand by and not see her leave. I will not pretend she is not our daughter."

Sabik nodded. "I will only ask that we remain steadfast when the time comes."

She didn't answer. She leaned her head against the door jamb, staring into the distance, as a child's cries faded …

Just like the scene around us did.

"No!" Teget lunged, but his stomping bootsteps morphed into splashes. He tripped on a mangrove root and crashed into a spread of branches.

Yep, back in Sadeh. Endless gorgeous natural beauty. Except I was so sick to my stomach I had to bend over and splash water on my face. "Are you serious? What did Naos do, lock her away in a tower until her hair grew forty feet long? And how'd she wind up in Europe?"

"Dione lived with the Kutsatuta for five years." Tenebrae gestured to her. "Until the Whisperer learned of her presence with them."

"Those guys were exiles from Meda!" I snapped. "You sent my five-year-old sister to hang out with dangerous rebels?"

"Not all who were exiled were a danger, but those that were attempted to seize Dione from her caretakers. She escaped from them within the Interstice, and I was able to safeguard her in Sadeh, but at the cost of years. Once I was certain the Whisperer had all but forgotten her presence, I sent her to Earth."

"That—I don't remember any of it. I barely remember my parents. What did you do to my mind?" Dione asked.

"I kept it from breaking. It was … an error. I had not realized the toll living in my realm would take on a linear being. When you arrived on Earth, your memory was muddled, though portions slowly reasserted themselves. As they are doing now. You will regain more and more."

Dione clutched the sides of her head. "It's impossible. I was on the streets of Baltimore, working odd jobs for the past few years. I had to build my life from scratch. Doctors couldn't make sense of it. Until I was kidnapped."

"For the auction in Gdansk." I glared at Tenebrae. "Which, I'm guessing, wasn't an accident. The Whisperer must have known—"

"*Raca.*" Tenebrae's formless face spat the word with a gust of power that shoved at my chest. "The fool. He thinks his agents found a drone to carry out his will, someone to steal Edgeweld and twist it for evil. No. I saw her as a child with potential for good, and I was there when the three of you were here. Are here, in front of me. Those times, you would call them, were one nexus. She received Edgeweld because it had happened, so I fulfilled it."

"This is madness." Teget pointed a shaking finger at Tenebrae. "You have meddled with time itself and pulled apart the threads binding our family."

"Only to weave it now and prevent the Whisperer from having torn it apart years ago. For that, you should be grateful."

Teget and Dione retrieved their weapons, brandishing them before Tenebrae, and I didn't know much about dude's fighting prowess, but considering he was semi-incorporeal, I wasn't ready for a test. So, I stuck myself in between my angry siblings and our cryptic time tour guide. "Okay, I get it. We're all pissed. We can sort it out later. Right now, we need to get back to the fight and finish it. And yeah, Tenebrae, I really hope you're gonna give us the chance to disembark right after we left, like I did when I jumped back out of the Javon portal the first time." I winced. Right, Javon. "He's not ... dead, is he?"

"No. He is in pain but lives. His gift was not meant to be distorted as this.

A sharp hissing cut through the air. Patches of dark roiling clouds bulged throughout the sky, purple lightning tearing at what I assumed was the very fabric of Sadeh. "The Interstice?" Dione squinted. "It's trying to come here."

"The Whisperer would consume all this if he could. But you saw him. His form is ready. You can take him when he emerges."

I sighed. "Sure. Because why not? Let's get going, already."

I grabbed the pulsar stave, still inserted in the sword, but Teget stopped me from withdrawing it and sending us back home. "It would behoove us to seek guidance from on high."

"Go for it." I twisted the stave. "While we're on the move."

I removed and separated it from the sword. As we plunged through a wall of solid light, I didn't tell Teget I'd already tried three wordless, silent pleas.

Fingers crossed that the Big Man was listening.

We emerged out the other side of the Javon portal in time to see shadowy forms dive in from the front. Three of them. Our outline was way too familiar. No time to think about any potential paradoxes if we'd hit ourselves, because we didn't, so it was all good, right?

"Xia!" Serena bounded onto the platform, her armor scorched but still fearsome. "You have to use the sword!"

"Don't worry," Dione snarled. "I will."

She plunged it at Serena, but that lady hadn't gotten to be a Homeland Security agent by being slow on the uptake. Serena rolled with the blow, as the blade scraped along the right side of the armor shell. They went down grappling for the weapon, Dione screaming rage that I'd bet had been pent up for way longer than anyone realized.

"Okay, no worries there." I aimed the pulsar stave at Vanchev, who was still pouring his gravity manipulation straight at the portal. "Let's get that guy."

"After we marshal our forces." Teget knelt to check on the body at our feet.

Body? Just Dominic, very much alive and kind of whiny. You'd think he'd never been purged of mind-controlling microscopic robots from another dimension before. "You've got to find," Dominic panted as he rose shakily, "A better way to do that, Mercury."

"You're fine, you big baby. I'm not about to leave you as the enemy's newest pet zombie, not if you've to stick around to make sure I take this mess more seriously, right?"

"Perhaps." He smiled and rubbed his forehead, right where I'd made contact with the pulsar stave. "Is there a mark?"

"Three inches across and glowing purple." I rolled my eyes. "There's nothing. So … the situation."

All things considered, it wasn't too grim. The combined might of Procyon security and SCPD's task force was holding back the astral fiends, keeping them corralled in the U-shaped parking lot-slash-garden of the mall. Loredana was easy to spot, red hair like a campfire, as she and Ramos led shifting teams of armed men and woman to punch holes in the fiends. Wilhelmina did her part by slicing tentacles that got too close, while Edith slung arrows into their eyes.

The Syndax mercenaries were hunkered behind the astral fiends, shielding Winston and … Wait, where was Troy?

Oh. He flung Serena and Dione apart, his face contorted with anger, the pulsar stave aglow. When he spotted me, he got even madder, if you can believe it. "What did you do? How have you screwed everything up?"

I sneered at him, but said to Teget and Dominic, "He really doesn't know me, does he?"

"Clearly not," Teget said.

"He wouldn't be asking the question if he did," Dominic added.

"Show's over, Troy!" I realized my taunting might be premature, what with Vanchev still holding a portal to two worlds open, but hey, I couldn't help enraging the ex-operative who should be dead. Call it a gift. "You wanna try that one-v-one again? Because I'm—"

"Kill them all!" he roared.

I had no idea how he thought he was gonna pull that off, with his forces divided, as Teget, Dominic, and I surged toward him—until an invisible force smashed us to the ground.

Us, and all our forces. Everyone was incapacitated. All we had left was the VTOL craft overhead, its motors whirring as it emptied its mounted machine gun into the astral fiend.

"I can't—do both, you know!" Vanchev's voice rasped. He had one hand aimed at the portal, and the other at us. "It's—too much!"

"You don't have to hold it for long." Troy sprinted for me. "Just long enough for me to squish this pest."

I could barely move, barely breathe, but all it took was a couple inches to get my eyes in line with Dominic's. "Spin … Us … Up."

Dominic ground his teeth, even as blood seeped from under the Echo Watches. They must have been scouring his wrists as they activated. The high-pitched whine was more tortured than I'd ever heard it, but it worked.

We blinked out.

I thought we'd reappear in pieces in his loft back in Rampart, but we were intact. I had a second or less in which to suck in air, and gasped, "Vanchev!" before Dominic sent us teleporting again. I struggled to bring the stave to bear.

Just. One. Inch. More.

The world coalesced around us. I was staring at the back of Vanchev's blond hair.

He choked, a brief, quiet sound, like a surprised cough. The pulsar stave stuck out of his back. Sizzling golden light erupted from his chest.

The gravity fields collapsed, and not just the ones squishing everyone, but the ones formed around the portal. Golden particles wound down, piecing Javon back together bit by bit. He collapsed onto the platform and slumped onto his side, the rise and fall of his chest barely visible through the shredded remains of his clothes.

I yanked the stave free. Vanchev toppled, eyes vacant. The stave was slick with blood. Fatigue and anguish drowned. So tired of all this. I understood why people used the expression, sick to death. "Nobody else has to die," I murmured.

Mercury …

It was the terrifyingly familiar singsong call of the Whisperer, in Marigold's old voice.

But it was so strong it knocked me to my knees, like someone had made me wear a helmet studded on the inside with needles.

Everyone else had collapsed screaming, too—Procyon, police, Syndax. Even the astral fiends.

When I could look up, through tear-filled eyes—talk about pain!—all I could see was the rip, alive and well, still spewing both the Interstice and Sadeh into our world.

And the towering, black stone body of the Whisperer himself striding out into Earth, with nothing stopping him.

CHAPTER THIRTY-FIVE

The Whisperer walked a zigzag toward us, footsteps falling only on the patches of Interstice that had oozed from the portal. There were a bunch more, I realized, encroaching on the entire atrium, and spilling into the parking lot. The garden was coated.

Astral fiends recovered first. They went into standby, tentacles waving in time with one another, like they were all lined up for a rock concert.

That would have been hysterical if gibbering fear hadn't crushed all logical thought from my head.

I joined Teget in a straight-up run to friendly lines. Loredana wrapped her arms around me. Ramos dropped his gun. All around us, Procyon security and San Camillo police were in varying stages of despair.

Dominic flashed into our midst, cradling Javon against him.

"We should—" I shut up, until I could say words again without sounding like I was scared of the dark. "We could take him out."

"Are you kidding?" That was Stan Bradley, his eyes so wide I thought they'd pop out. "He'll kill us all!"

"I don't want to die," Dione said. "Not here. Not this way."

"Calm down, okay?" I didn't believe any of that. I glanced

at Loredana. She was chewing her lip. "We've—we can do this, right?"

She shook her head.

"Loredana?"

Back and forth back and forth, until she sank to her knees. She choked on deep gasps. I couldn't tell if she was sobbing or about to throw up.

Teget fell to his knees and let the ax crash beside him. "I cannot stand against him!"

Their terror made perfect sense. Even the tiny, bold piece of my brain that kept shouting *Get up there and cut his head off!* got overwhelmed by the unyielding desire to run far away. Let the astral fiends take the city. It was the Whisperer's anyway.

No. Not on my watch.

I grabbed Teget and yanked him upright. He tried to shove me away. "Come on! All of you guys! We've got fight—!"

"*Stand down.*"

The words slapped me so hard I froze in place. So did everybody else. Breathing, blinking, sure, but nobody was going anywhere. Just like the Ashen using his gravity powers, except we weren't dying.

But I would have picked that to stop being afraid.

"Look at this." The Whisperer stopped his approach twenty feet from our lines. Man, he was huge—bigger than I ever remembered the shadow. Ten feet, easy, with silver ridges protruding from his arms, legs, and the muscles all over. The mouth and nose were carved of the same obsidian as the body, but moved, like liquid. Enough to let him smile. "I told you a long time ago, Mercury. This is how it begins. The walls have come down—and at last, I can step beyond them. See how I have already ended the bloodshed? Pathetic. You toy with great power and call yourselves heroes, when you can't begin to imagine the sheer magnitude of the majesty that can be achieved."

He beckoned to Troy, and Serena—and Winston. "These faithful servants, though, are more than cognizant."

They didn't seem scared—in fact, they hurried right up to the Whisperer, like dogs promised treats. I half expected panting tongues.

"This *is* delightful," Winston murmured. "Can you see them, Mari? Can you see how far they've fallen?"

Something in the Whisperer's expression shifted, softened. His—its?—voice took on that sing-song cadence again. "It's not as satisfying as running him through with my own blade, but it will have to do."

"I think I'm the one who gets that honor." Troy sneered as he surveyed us. "Him first, then Edie. She's been begging for it."

Even odds as to whether Edith was scared senseless or bent into a rage. She had an arrow nocked in her bow but couldn't raise it, heck, couldn't even move her arms. Fingers twitched against the bowstring.

"I want them to see." The Whisperer's voice took on a charming lilt, easily recognizable to a few of us as Alexander Arkwright's. "The Hedron of Orbits killed me, but when it did, I was joined to the Interstice in ways you can't fathom. The Whisperer has shown me wonders, which we can now bring to Earth."

"Thanks to Tenebrae," the Whisperer said in his familiar, mind-rattling phrases. "The fool capitulated and abandoned you all to death."

I managed to glimpse movement in the sky, without shifting my head. The Procyon tiltrotor wasn't overhead—it had landed out in the vast parking lot, beyond our huddle of good guys and bad guys. A small figure was on his hands and knees, motionless. Cope?

So, the Whisperer's reach was far. Probably brought on by the Hedron's gravity-whamming powers. I bet a good old-fashioned tachyon weapon could glitch him, though. Which I'd be glad to deliver to his nose. If I wasn't about to wet myself.

A new sound reached my ears—murmuring. That was Ramos, kneeling next to me. Eyes upraised, lips moving, in Spanish. *Gloria al Padre, al Hijo y al Espíritu Santo …*

The Whisperer swung toward him. "Stop it! Be quiet!"

Either he couldn't make Ramos zip his lips, or … Wait a second. Now *there* was a thought.

"*Como era en el principio, ahora y siempre …*" Ramos glared at the Whisperer. His face turned an inch.

"No." The Whisperer loomed over us. "Stop! Stop speaking!"

"Let me kill him!" Troy held the crackling pulsar stave six feet away from us, like a bolt of lightning in his outstretched hand. His body shuddered under the exertion of the gathered energy, and his eyeballs did their best to imitate headlights.

"Do not touch him!" The Whisperer reached with his claws. "Give me the stave and let me claim the weapon from him!"

"… *Por los siglos de los siglos.*" Ramos shuddered. His arms jerked. His fingers fumbled for the crucifix behind his collar. "I'm—not afraid of you. I won't be. Not anymore."

Something snapped in the air, like a window breaking and air gushing in. I could feel the pulsar stave's strength coursing through me, pooling in the suit, compressing in my leg. Whatever crippling terror I'd been cowering under lifted in an instant.

"It can't be." For once, it was the Whisperer was the guy with the confused look on his face.

I sneered up at him. "This is gonna be fun."

My leg propelled me up like a cannonball and I punched him across the face with a fist enclosed around the pulsar stave.

Winston's surprised shout gave way to the familiar screech of energy discharging from the pulsar stave. An explosion of light scattered Procyon—my people!—but before Troy could let off another burst a bolt zinged through the air. His neck snapped back at an angle I knew couldn't be fixed by any chiropractor; the crack accompanying it made sure.

Troy lay dead on the ground, an arrow's shaft protruding from just above the bridge of his nose. The pulsar stave rolled across the asphalt.

Serena was the one with guts enough to go for it—but so was

Ramos. They each caught an end of it.

Loredana, her face streaked with tears, but her expression otherwise crowded with frustration, let Serena have all six shots from her revolver as she fired over Ramos' shoulder.

The Whisperer's roar of anguish was a mad mix of Marigold screaming, Arkwright howling, and the Hedron bellowing like a foghorn. He swung for our people like he was hitting a home run but didn't actually connect with anyone—yet the force of blow bowled a dozen people over, Loredana and Ramos included.

Dione broke free of the mass, though, as she vaulted over the crumpled remnants of a truck door. She slammed feet first into Serena, their combined impact tearing a gouge in the asphalt of the parking lot

I landed behind the Whisperer and slashed at him with the stave.

He deflected my strike with his right arm, sparks showering us both where the jagged metal protruding from his veins reacted to the stave's energy.

"Mercury!" Teget plunged the ax into the Whisperer's side.

The Whisperer shouted in what I guessed was more surprise than pain, and backhanded Teget—but the attack had been a distraction, because my brother's tactical like that. I jumped up as the other half of the pulsar stave spun over the Whisperer's head, and I snagged it mid-air.

Stuck both pieces together.

Held a living lightning bolt in my hands.

I don't know if the stave was celebrating being back with its rightful owner—and decent roommate for the past four or more years—but it lit up the gloomy afternoon again, so much so I thought it would shred the clouds.

Best thing I could think of was to bring it down on the Whisperer's head.

What I wanted was a crushed stone skull. What I got was a miniscule *clink* and splitting pain in my wrists.

"I bring order to this chaotic world, and you hit me?" he

howled. "I won't be insulted!"

He lifted his arms and the remaining astral fiends surged to life again, as even more slithered out of the ground. In a few seconds, we were all fighting against them—Teget and I battering tentacles aside, Wilhelmina slicing them away from Procyon security as they shot for the eyes, Edith plinking arrows into their faces as Ramos and Bradley directed SCPD's grenade launchers into their targets, Loredana accepting a SCAR-L from Garvey so the two of them could step back, on their knees, to shoot steady bursts into the monsters' midst.

Dione grappled with Serena, pressing Edgeweld against her as Serena struggled for an advantage with the sharp edges of her armor.

A whistle cut through the air, faint by comparison but with enough of a different tune for us to take notice. Cope waved from back inside the black VTOL craft—and its multi-barrel machine gun whined to life underneath the cockpit nose.

"Cover! Up or down!" I somersaulted over a fiend as I ripped its backside open with the pulsar stave.

Hundreds of rounds, the tracers blazing among them, cut through astral fiends. Sodden chunks of hide careened like those bouncy balls you buy for a quarter from a vending machine. Thick, blue ichor sprayed everywhere and spattered everyone.

The bullets just caromed off the Whisperer. He stormed toward my landing site, flicking two fingers, which was enough to obliterate an entire astral fiend into shredded goo.

So why hadn't he done that to me?

I swung at him again, but he dodged and then an icy cold stone hand clamped around my neck. He lifted me three feet off the ground. "I wanted to you to see this, the end of your adopted world," he hissed. "As I take the people from you one by one."

"*Devil!*" Ramos seized a grenade launcher from an officer stunned into inaction and fired a round our way—which, I didn't have time to tell him, would vaporize me, too, until I could break free.

The Whisperer stopped the shell midair. "No more interference from—"

The portals howled.

I mean, like all the wolves in the world pissed off at once. Even the Whisperer shuddered, so much so that the grenade vaporized from his invisible grasp, and his fingers dropped me.

One of Tenebrae's giant symmachite guards stomped into our world. And no, I had no idea how a thing that looks like a massive pearly alien starfish stomped when its legs were—spiny appendages, I guessed. But it looked bigger, maybe fourteen feet instead of ten.

The Syndax mercenaries had finally gotten their acts back together and shifted aim, peppering the symmachite giant with bullets. It swiped at the atrium entrance, ripping entire walls away like it was no more a problem than yanking curtains off a wall.

By the time it broke free, the upper spine cracked the bottom of the third floor.

Holy cow.

It was *thirty* feet tall, and judging by the shadow, getting taller.

"Destroy it!" The Whisperer stepped over me, headed for the new obstacle. "He's coming for us!"

Yeah, Tenebrae? He appeared among the few patches of Sadeh that had spread throughout the parking lot, and then it really was like sunny summer, making me wish I'd brought sunglasses—or could borrow Ramos' pair.

"You," the Whisperer snarled.

"I've seen your defeat." Tenebrae sounded unbothered by the chaos, as his monstrous guardian symmachite smashed three astral fiends when it plodded toward him. "I see it now."

I stabbed the pulsar stave through the Whisperer's left leg.

Winds roared outward, flattening me to the ground and obscuring everything around me in dust and asphalt chunks and purple lighting. Golden sparks cut my skin. I held on as the Whisperer battered me with blows, but if I came unanchored, I was screwed.

The obsidian and the gold clashed above me, with more forms appearing around them—transparent beings, streaks like wings stretching at all angles, joined in combat like an angry halo of war. I couldn't hear or see anyone else, but I wasn't scared. I wasn't even worried. Shouldn't I be? There'd been a lot of times I thought I was gonna be a dead man.

I couldn't leave my friends behind. I couldn't leave Loredana behind.

So.

Get.

Up.

I yanked the stave free of the Whisperer's leg as the wind tore greedily at us, dragging me and him and Tenebrae along. The Whisperer's dark shape loomed over Tenebrae's, the golden light flickering, as the writhing violet maw of the rip tugged at us. Tentacles popped out of the ground, wrapping around Tenebrae—and me.

The cold felt like it was crystallizing every cell in my body. I clung to the energy from the pulsar stave, begging for more—just a little bit more, okay?

Then the monster symmachite's spine or arm or whatever swept through our midst, shearing tentacles off as the individual symmachites separated into buzzing streams. They swiped the Whisperer off balance, and Tenebrae …

He pushed me away.

Obsidian and gold spiraled through the portal, as who knew how many millions of the miniscule symmachites spun in a fury that brough the winds to a standstill, then shot out over the entire parking lot in a brutal, blazing wave of light. Patches of the Interstice and Sadeh vanished. Everything I could see that wasn't of this world got drawn back through the portals right before they collapsed.

Then I slammed face first down on the tile floor of the atrium. I yelped at the pain in my nose. Got a puddle of blood in my mouth, for all of that.

And yes, the gunshot wound on my shoulder still hurt, on top of everything else. Thanks for asking.

"Mercury!"

Loredana knelt over me, Ramos on the other side. His hand turned me over. Hers cradled my head against her lap.

"It's—ow." I winced, because it felt like I was laying on a bed of rusty nails sharpened with steel wool. "Over. I think. It'd better be."

"The portal is sealed." That was Dione, limping along as she and Teget supported each other, mutual human crutches. "They're both gone."

"Hey, um, I'm all for celebrating—" I made a *whoop-dee-doo* gesture with my index finger. "—But anybody want to go capture our least favorite person in borrowed Interstice armor?"

"She has fled," Teget grumbled. "With your traitor."

Great. Winston, the mad scientist, loose. I slumped against Teget's lap.

"Sir?" Garvey and one of his people, Sandoval, were hunkered over Javon's limp form. Poor kid. His shirt had been shorn away, giving us all a perfect view of his well-sculpted body, which was riddled with cuts and bruises. "He's breathing but unresponsive."

"Medics," Loredana snapped. "Now."

Wilhelmina wiped soot from her face with the back of the hand that held her dagger. "Anybody else going to tell an old lady why we don't have this one in shackles?"

"At least take the sword back." Edith had an arrowhead inches from Dione's nose. "Unless you're that lazy."

"Take it easy," I said. "I'd better explain, but let's get everyone fixed up first, before we all get to meet my sister."

"You can't be serious," Loredana said.

"Like a regular old Jerry Springer special," I muttered.

CHAPTER THIRTY-SIX

Our people suffered a ton of injuries, but no deaths. Silver lining? Sure. But five of Garvey's security team were restricted to the infirmary as they got stitched up. Three were transferred to San Camillo General Hospital under the strictest secrecy—with escort from our pals at Homeland.

Yeah, Agent Hudson Bowe showed up. At the mall, actually. It was his feds, black face coverings in place, who rounded up the leftovers of Syndax's mercenary army. Bradley had radioed back and brought a small fleet of ambulances. Between the two of them, the battle site was cordoned off in no time.

Didn't want to think about who was gonna get stuck with the bill for the yawning gash the giant symmachite had torn in the front of the abandoned building, or all the rest of the damage done.

Cope gave us a ride back to HQ on his new toy, a Bell A-280 Valor. He seemed exhausted but grinned the entire way, happy as the proverbial clam at the controls of an Osprey's sleeker, speedier brother.

But like I said: infirmary.

Bowe was decent enough to wait elsewhere, probably up in Alvarez's office. I'd already gotten my bandages, but I hung around Javon's bedside. The guy hadn't said much, which, as you can probably guess, was a bad thing.

"I'm keeping him heavily sedated." Doc Arne muttered the explanation through a surgical mask. "When he first came to after the EMTs brought him up, he did that."

Arne indicated a chair embedded in the wall.

"Ah." I scratched the back of my neck. "His powers are working."

"Not well. And out of his control." Edith sat at Javon's right side, holding his hand in hers. "He'd been forced into that form for so long, I don't know what it did to him."

"Have you seen anything?" Loredana asked. "In your visions, I should say."

Edith shook her head. "Nothing. The visions aren't coming right now. I tried to calm myself, to see, but all I get is noise."

"Given how disrupted two dimensions were, as they collided with our own, I should say I am not surprised." Loredana touched my arm. "We should go. Manager Alvarez is waiting."

"When isn't he," I said. "Keep us up to date, will you, Doc? When Javon can talk, we'll need him back."

"You'd be better off praying for him like your friend Ramos," Arne muttered. "Because med school didn't cover bodily disassociation. We'll be lucky if he can ever regain normal brain function again. Do me a favor and get out."

Guess it was nice something hadn't changed.

We met up with Ramos, who was on his phone outside the infirmary. "Yes. I understand. No, no, I don't think—I understand. Thank you."

I grimaced as he smacked his phone against his palm. "Too bad you can't slam it down like in the old days."

Ramos glowered at us. "The media are all over this event. There was no way to keep a lid on it, not with a massive police response, gunfire, and an unregistered aircraft all in play."

"I take it I shall have my hands full denying what truly happened," Loredana said. "Once again."

"It will take a great deal more than that." Ramos swiped

across his phone, then held it up for us to see. A YouTube video played, no volume, but let's just say it was a major national news organization juxtaposing images of the destruction—plus scenes from the North Beach Battle, Cavill Cemetery, and every major fight I'd fought in the past year. All with a shiny Procyon logo slapped alongside.

"Whoops," I murmured.

"Hale!" Cue Alvarez, storming up to us with Bowe right behind him. Like Laurel and Hardy, those two, except both were trim and fit. "Get to Tracking before that brother of yours does something monumentally stupid."

I didn't bother with a snappy comeback, because Teget could be like me—rash action, table for two. We hurried down the corridor, and the five of us squeezed through the door to Tracking. Yep, there was Teget, in hushed conversation with Dione. Dominic was leaned over Liz's computer as she gestured wildly.

"Ah! Mercury!" Teget clasped my hands. "I am glad you have come to see us off. You fought well, brother, and I shall tell all our peoples of your continued bravery when I return to Meda."

"Return?" Bowe shook his head, the stars and stripes on his face covering shining under Tracking's lights. "Not a chance. Since everybody else up and forgot, I'll remind you: That young lady broke out of a federal penitentiary."

"Yeah, and then she got her brainwashing broken and joined the good guys." I shrugged. "Sorry, Bowe, she's not sticking around to get locked up again."

"I'll answer whatever charges you have, sir." Dione had her hands on her hips. "But I've lost a huge chunk of my life. It's time to regain it, starting with going home."

Bowe rested the heel of his hand on his holstered gun. "Ma'am, it's within my authority to take you back into custody. Lieutenant Ramos can back me up on this one."

"Lieutenant Ramos has enough paperwork to deal with and injured officers to watch over." Ramos clapped my shoulder. "I have to run. Call me later."

"Sure. And, hey ..." I lowered my voice. "What happened back there? With the Whisperer? You broke through when nothing else would work."

"You've seen it before, Mercury. At Cavill Cemetery." Ramos shook his head, a smirk on his lips but with a sense of amazement about his expression. Like he didn't know whether to believe it, either. "We think it's answered prayers when we get the job we wanted, or our candidate elected. This was a reminder there's far greater results possible."

He left me staring after him, wondering when I would ever get him all the way figured out—or the faith that turned him into probably the most fearless person I knew. And my brother was the guy who ran screaming into hordes of monsters with an ax.

"I'm serious." Bowe's complaint verged on whiny. Not a good look for the guy. "Serena and that Winston geek are on the lam. We're playing whack-a-mole with all the tiny subsidiaries and shell corporations that popped up when Syndax Multinational dissolved since last year, but now that they've got a certified genius on their hands, we need every break we can get! My jurisdiction—"

"Doesn't extend off the planet." I gave Dione a hug. "See you soon?"

Her face flushed. "Yeah, soon, I hope. I've got to spend time with both my brothers, now that I can."

"We'd be delighted to get to know you more," Loredana said. "Upon your return. Gemini?"

"First stop, coming right up." Dominic had Edgeweld in a scabbard slung across his back. "Then Patchwork."

"Now, wait a minute!" Alvarez snapped. "No one is taking those two—"

"Do give Ms. Mazzoli my apologies for any damage done to her facility and to the borrowed aircraft." Loredana speared Alvarez with a look as sharp as Teget's ax. "Oh and do give her this for safekeeping."

She handed Dominic a clear plastic box, sealed with tape. A brass-colored medallion, still hanging from a chain, was nestled inside.

"Hold up." My eyes widened. "Isn't that—?"

"I retrieved this from the body of the Ashen agent named Vanchev. Doubtless the name carries familiarity for you, Agent Bowe. Until such time as the Garrison can be consulted, it will remain in Procyon custody." Bowe was next on Loredana's target list, as she stared him down. "And we shall inform Homeland of its final transfer, of course."

Bowe sighed, the sound like a bear settling down for hibernation. But at least he wasn't ready to draw his gun. "Fine. It's not like they've been communicative since we botched that retrieval out in the Caribbean. But as for this young lady—"

Dominic winked at us and charged up the Echo Watches. He, Teget, and Dione disappeared in a whirlwind of light and sound. Papers throughout Tracking rustled like falling leaves, but I didn't see any hit the floor.

"Yes!" Liz stood up, her arms spread in victory. "Hooray for old-fashioned paperweights!"

I glanced at her table. The paperweight was a copy of *Mercury on Guard*.

"You gotta be kidding me," Bowe muttered.

Our least favorite Homeland agent was gone, with Alvarez assuring him we'd be good to our word and operational security blah blah. I was way too tired to care. So, I snagged a rolling chair and put my feet up on Liz's desk. "So, how's it going?"

She frowned. "I've got way too much data to crunch, Mercury, and Cyril's still not a hundred percent so he's taking longer with everything but the good news is all those sensors I loaded on the Valor that Cope flew—"

"Elizabeth believes we are soon to experience a destabilization," Loredana said.

"Destabilization?" I made a face. "Of what?"

"Of rips. I mean, of the barriers between our dimension and

the Interstice. Here." She tapped a couple spots on her tablet, muttering to herself as she clearly didn't like what she saw, then manipulated more panels.

"Hey." I pulled Loredana in close. She brushed the back of my neck with her hand. "How secure is Patchwork anymore? I mean, with Syndax having driven right up to the front door and blown it open."

"That's not a terrible issue." Alvarez was the one who answered. He stood in the doorway, trying to straighten his tie. The knot wouldn't budge. "I've already spoken with Director Mazzoli. There's a contingency in place."

I grinned. "Not like an Edith contingency, I hope."

"Too soon, Mercury." Loredana rolled her eyes.

"The relics will be safe. She'll see to it. The bigger question is how we handle this media storm brewing. I have board members screaming at me and with Mr. Kimball unable to clear anything up, I have a feeling our attempts to obfuscate aren't going to be much use."

"We'll do our best, sir, though we may have to become creative rather than rely on the standby of mass hallucination and gas leaks."

"Terrorist activity it is." Alvarez finally unraveled the tie and shoved it into his pocket. "Come on, then. We have reporters waiting downstairs. I doubt Agent Bowe's enjoying himself."

"Not until after the show." I bumped Liz's monitor with my foot. "Got something?"

"Hmm? Oh! Yes." Liz sent information to the large monitor. The normal peaks and troughs of tachyon spikes over four years, contrasted with the past hours since we'd faced off with the Whisperer and Tenebrae. "The normal fluctuations are more random, and there's a lot more of them. Cyril's having a hard time adapting his algorithm to predict them. And if Ms. Pathkiller's out of commission …"

"Yeah. I don't like it either." I rubbed my face. Suddenly got a whole lot more tired. "So, when's the next rip?"

"Probably next week. And there might be more than one. The frequency and duration ..." Liz chewed her lip. "It could be bad."

The four of us waited in silence. Not good news. I, for one, didn't want to hear that my day—or night—job was about to get harder. "Any chance we can stop it?"

Liz shrugged. "I think it has to do with the way two dimensions clashed with each other while leaking into ours, but until I get through all the data Cope brought back on the plane, this is my best guess, you know?"

"When can you give us a more definite answer?" Loredana asked.

"Weeks. Maybe months." Liz folded her arms and sat back in her chair. "Sorry, guys."

"Not your fault." I glanced at Alvarez. "But I guess this means Procyon's operatives get put on high alert for the next while."

He nodded slowly. "Not that I'm keen to agree with you—ever—but yes, that should be our next step." Alvarez indicated the door. "After the press, Mrs. Lark-Hale."

"Rather it was astral fiends," she murmured. Then she gave me a kiss. "Start dinner for us once you're home?"

I stretched my arms as they left the room. "Only if I can sneak out the back door."

"Mercury?" Liz stared at the screen. "I'm worried about Winston."

"Me too. I'm assuming you mean his ability to break into Procyon's systems."

"Yeah. I've got everyone working overtime to set up new firewalls, and to move more files onto devices not linked to the servers." She sighed. "But, I mean, what you told me about the battle—he doesn't sound okay."

"He hasn't been okay since Marigold went nuts. And I think a long time before that. Probably he was a good actor." Which hurt like a stab wound to say. Didn't make it less accurate. "We'll find him, and we'll lock him right back up. Don't worry."

"I'm only worried," Liz whispered, "If he keeps getting away.

More people could get hurt. You guys could *die*. Maybe … Maybe he should first."

After thirty seconds of watching her work in deep concentration, I eased out of the chair and left Tracking before she could see how worried that comment made me. Because if Liz was onboard with us killing Winston—or *me* killing him—then we had bigger problems than destabilizing dimensions.

Morale was swirling down the drain. And it was up to me to make sure everyone stuck together, because there was no way we were gonna come out on top if we let dark thoughts seep into our brains.

Mercury …

And speaking of whisper …

You tried to end me and failed. Don't think I've forgotten.

"We cut you," I muttered. "And next time? We're gonna leave you in pieces."

I plugged in an earbud and cranked up Metallica's as I headed for home.

I wasn't kidding about the back door. Snuck out right alongside the company Dumpster.

Except then I remembered my car had gotten dropped on its roof when Cope strafed all the Syndax rides outside Troy's cabin. "Okay," I said to the squirrel perched on the Dumpster's edge. "What's next?"

A car horn honked. I half-expected Ramos to holler at me for loitering from the comfort of his Dodge Charger. Instead, a maroon, 1990s LeSabre rattled around the back with Wilhelmina behind the wheel. "Well, hey, there. You look like a boy who could use a lift."

I slid into the passenger seat. "Only if you can be quiet-like."

She grinned. "'Course I can."

The Buick roared up the service path, around the side of Tower Three, and out into Procyon's parking lot. I caught a glimpse of security SUVs, news vans, and a gaggle of people spaced out around the door. We blew past, out the gate, and peeled onto Bay Avenue.

"Don't want to, though." She chuckled.

"Wow." I shook my head. "You're pretty chipper for having been sick and coming through that battle."

"Weren't nothing but a thing, child. I seen you moping around the headquarters, taking the blame for all this on yourself."

"Yeah? Is what I was doing?" I snorted. "We barely won. And I didn't get the job done."

"Sure, you did. You showed we can hurt the Whisperer. Cunning moves. And you've discovered an ally that weren't nothing but a myth." Wilhelmina nodded. "I think you're doin' just fine by us all."

"Thanks. Bad enough our team got beat up. Now I have to add another Christmas card to the list."

"Sakes." Wilhelmina squinted over the steering wheel. "That young lady's gonna need your help and your care to get herself caught up."

"Yeah. And we're gonna need her if things get as bad as Liz thinks they will."

Wilhelmina hummed a tune instead of replying. I ignored how much faster than the speed limit she was driving.

"Let me ask you this, though," I said. "Having Tenebrae track me down—he knows more about what's going to happen. But I can't see it. What happens if I make the wrong choices? There's no do-overs. Everything I've done, everything we've fought through, it's all permanent."

"Mm-hmm. What's your point?"

I blew out a breath. "Why doesn't he just tell us?"

"Who, he?"

I pointed up at the car's ceiling. "Him."

Wilhelmina laughed. "Ain't his style. You've got to lean on faith, child."

"Easy to say when you've got it."

"Give it time. He'll find you if it's his will. Then it will happen. Do an old lady and former operative a favor, though."

"What's that?"

She winked. "Don't forget to make room for the little surprises in life."

I checked the news while I made a huge plate of beef and nachos, with a salad to boot. Loredana looked like a queen addressing her court when I caught sight of her spinning the latest Procyon story. A text from her buzzed a minute later. <Eat without me, please. I shall be late. Sorry. All my love.>

<K. Love you too.> I cleared the message. I'd set a photo as the background wallpaper—me, Teget, and Dione. The whole family, as far as I knew. Better keep it as a reminder of all I had to hold on to.

Loredana's message left me with a quiet night on the couch, a plate cleaned empty on the end table, and my sketch pad spread on my lap. The pulsar stave leaned against the cushion, between me and a pillow. Wasn't about to let that out of my sight any time soon.

I penciled in the mall, with deep shadows around its crumpled façade. And I drew the broad, shallow seas of Sadeh.

By the time she got home at quarter past nine, I'd abandoned drawing in favor of more eating. Dessert, that is.

"You okay?" I dug into the pineapple ice cream. Finally. Talk about a reward.

"Indeed. It seems." She sat beside me on the couch and traced her fingers around the top of the empty glass. Her glass of iced tea.

"Found this in the couch. From the other night." I produced the pizza token with a flourish. "We forgot about it."

"I could never forget about it."She kissed me and then smirked. "Only momentarily fail to recollect its placement"

"Love you, too." I grinned and squinted into the half empty wine tumbler in my hand, leftover from dinner an hour ago. "You want a sip?"

"No, Mercury, I had best not. It's … not the healthiest option."

"Yeah?" I chuckled. I patted my belly. "Worried about calories? Because we both know my radius exceeds yours. Even with the abs."

She poked my ribcage, right above the pulsar stave. And laughed. Which meant I wasn't a dead man, for the moment. "It's not that."

"But you're not sick, right?" I took another bite of ice cream. "I mean, you were gonna check in with Doc Arne so he better not have been a—"

"He was fine. Professional. And discreet. He gave me the answer to a question I had."

"Okay. So, sick?"

"Only in the mornings."

I sputtered ice cream.

"I'm pregnant." She smiled. "Surprise."

"Wait." I choked for breath. "What?"

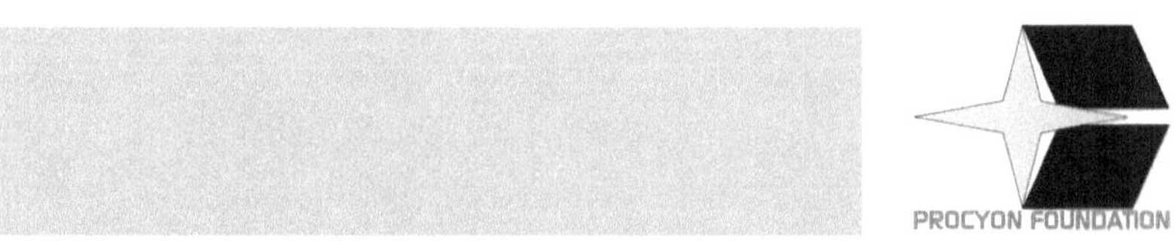

Mercury's adventures continue...

Stay tuned

www.steverzasa.com

www.ingramcontent.com/pod-product-compliance
Lightning Source LLC
Chambersburg PA
CBHW051207190726
48288CB00006B/1843